WARREN ROCHELLE

HARVEST OF CHANGELINGS

GOLDEN GRYPHON PRESS • 2008

This is a work of fiction. All the characters and events portrayed in this novel are either fictitious or are used fictitiously.

The prologue was first published, in a somewhat different version, as "Different Rooms," in *Romance and Beyond* 2.3 (Fall 1999).

LIBRARY OF CONGRESS CATALOGING–IN–PUBLICATION DATA
Rochelle, Warren, 1954–
    Harvest of changelings / Warren Rochelle — 1st ed.
        p.   cm.
    ISBN-13: 978-1-930846-52-4 (alk. paper)
    ISBN-10: 1-930846-52-5 (alk. paper)
    1. Fairies—Fiction.   I. Title.
PS3618.O34H37 2007
813'.6—dc22
                                            2006038678

First Softcover Edition 2008.

In memory of my mother,
Louise Glosson Rochelle, 1929–2006,
and for my father,
Charles E. Rochelle

In my Father's house there are many mansions: if it were not so, I would have told you. I go to prepare a place for you.
— John 14: 2, *King James* translation

To be what we are and to become what we are capable of becoming, is the only end of life.
— Robert Louis Stevenson

Fairies, away!
A *Midsummer's Night Dream*, II, i

Acknowledgments

Thanks to my family and friends; especially Mark Fleming, a careful, considerate, and tough reader and good friend; my brother, Barry, who answered (and still does) endless questions so I could get all kinds of details right; my brother, Greg, who kept asking me when the next book was coming out—here it is—; my brother, David; Ellen McQueen, the dearest of friends, for her good heart and good ear, as I read aloud many different versions; my colleagues at the University of Mary Washington, especially Chris Foss, for his helpful advice; Gary Nelson, for everything; for my great and good friend, Christine Sanderson who made sure the Catholic passages were done right; to the children at Powell and Bugg Elementary Schools, Raleigh, NC, 1982–89, who were the inspiration for the main characters, especially for Russell and Jeff; my editor, Gary Turner, at Golden Gryphon Press, who continues to make this process great fun, and Marty Halpern, GGP's other editor, who keeps Gary in line.

HARVEST OF CHANGELINGS

Prologue
The Tale of Ben and Valeria
1980-81

*O*NCE UPON A TIME THERE WAS A MAN WHO FELL *in love with a fairy and took her for his wife.*

That's how fairy tales are supposed to start and the story I am going to tell really is a fairy tale—although it is really a tale about fairies. I'm not a fairy, but I married one. My son is half-fairy and his friends are fairies in smaller fractions.

But they all come much later in this tale. I want to start at the very beginning, the root of the matter. I need to trace all that happened that brought me to *here*, this place with this open book and its broad, blank pages, and this bottle of ink. I have kept a journal since I was in high school; my art teacher required it. He wanted us to make the connection between seeing and thinking. But I was never consistent with it until after Malachi was born, so when I try to remember all that happened between Valeria and me, I find myself uncertain and wondering if I am really remembering or conjuring up the gaps between memories. I did jot down bits and pieces, images, but not enough. I never even took her picture. Now I want to remember and I can't—not all that I want to remember.

Some things I remember all too well.

My son has asked me to tell him this story of his mother and his father countless times—so much so that I feel I know all of it, every detail. I don't. But any story is an interpretation of a memory of an experience. This story I tell my son is just that. Sometimes it is a revision, sometimes I remember something I have forgotten, or I forget what I thought I knew. He is only ten. I do not tell him the things a man and a woman can fight about. I do not tell him that his mother loved other humans before me, that she was a "human lover," a scandalous thing in some fairy families. I do not tell him she could be patronizing of less-educated humans. After all, she was a fairy, not an angel. I do not tell him—or anyone—everything. There are parts I will not tell; there are parts I cannot tell. Instead, I would rather skim the waters of our lives for only some of the bright leaves of memory. I did not even begin telling him this story until he was ten.

So, let me begin again as I begin each night that I tell this story to Malachi: the story of a man and a woman, his father and his mother. It's a love story, I tell him: husband and wife, father and son, friend for friend, just love. I think there may not be any other kind of story.

Once upon a time there was a man who fell in love with a fairy and took her for his wife. The man, Ben, did not know Valeria was a fairy, a Daoine Sidhe from the Irish stories, the first time he saw her. He only knew her name by accident. The mail carrier had delivered 1411 Beichler Road's mail to his house, 1413. He had called to her from his porch the third afternoon after her arrival—in a taxi, laden with suitcases: Lana Carter? No, Valeria she had called back. Valeria what, he had wanted to ask her, Carter? But he hadn't. Her voice was beautiful, fair and sweet, and she was beautiful. Her hair was the color of light, a finely spun light of gold and white, a light that seemed to glow, as if her head was bathed in a living, non-burning fire. At first whenever Ben saw her, he thought of his dead first wife, Emma. Emma's hair was red and long and frothy and he would wrap it around his arms in bed. He felt guilty about Valeria at first: it had only been two years since Emma had died. It had been a hot June afternoon and he had been in the kitchen, his head in the refrigerator, rummaging for a beer. Emma had gone to get the mail. He heard her call out—but it was only a sound, not his name. Something fell. Ben ran, dropping the beer, and found Emma, crumpled on the flagstone walk, an odd dent in the side of her head. The doctors later told him it was a freak accident, she had fallen just so, cracked her skull, broken her neck. She had tripped on a loose flagstone. There was nothing he could have done.

The doctor, Ben knew, was wrong. He could have fixed that flagstone. Emma had asked and asked and he had put it off. His laziness had killed Emma.

Ben had sat there by her, waiting for the ambulance, fanning her; June gets so hot in North Carolina. While his guilt still lingered, now he could remember it all, and not cry, and his heart no longer ached as it had and the woman next door was so very beautiful and her hair glowed and when she looked at him, he could see her eyes were an intense deep green, viridian, emerald, jade, spring light in the forest after a sudden storm. And his body had ached when it remembered.

So Ben watched her, casually at first—he didn't want her to think he was stalking her. Besides, he saw very little of her, as she was rarely up or out when he went to work at the library in Garner, North Carolina, the little town where he lived, just south of a bigger city, Raleigh. He began to think he would never do more than that, until one afternoon three weeks after the golden-haired woman had become his neighbor. Ben had left the library, hurrying to miss the rain. The sky was dark and heavy with clouds. As he walked home, across the field, across the parking lot, past the shopping center, lightning crackled across the sky and the wind began to rise, the leaves turning over, as the trees' whispering grew louder and louder. The rain got him as he crossed the road between the shopping center and his street: hard, quick rain. He ran to his house, and as he fumbled for his key on his front porch, he glanced over at the house of the golden-haired woman. And he saw her: not in the yard, or getting in or out of her car, but in the sky, flying on the winds of the thunderstorm.

Ben stared. He slapped his cheek, rubbed his eyes, felt his forehead, glad of the porch and its box of dryness. He kept looking: yes, it was she, the golden-haired woman, flying in the storm.

By the next morning, Ben had, however, managed to convince himself he had been imagining things. What he had seen was not possible. People did not fly. They didn't disappear, either, he told himself after breakfast as he started his walk to work. There she was, in her backyard, her hair shining in the early morning sun, and then, a sudden flicker of light and she wasn't there.

The next afternoon, late, at twilight, Ben was in his own backyard, ostensibly to pick up branches knocked off by the storm from his willow oaks and pines. He made sure he picked up each branch one at a time, and he kept watching her house. A half-hour after Ben started his cleanup, there was another flicker of light, and she was there, standing where no one had been standing before.

Ben knew he wasn't crazy. He remembered, from years ago, when he read The Lion, the Witch, and the Wardrobe, what the professor had told Susan and Peter when they asked him if Lucy was crazy for telling them she had gone through the wardrobe into Narnia and insisting her story true. Either Lucy was mad or lying or telling the truth, the professor said. One only has to look at her and see she is not mad and they knew she was not a liar, so she had to be telling the truth. I am not mad, Ben told himself, nor am I sick, with some sort of fever and delirium. Someone at work would have told me. So what he had seen had to be real. The golden-haired woman was magic—a magical being, a witch, or a fairy.

Ben didn't know what to do, so he did what he knew how to do. He collected books from all over the library: Celtic and Irish mythology and folklore, Irish fairy tales of the Daoine Sidhe, Scottish tales, The Blue Fairy Book, and the red, the yellow, the green. Anthropology, psychology. He scribbled notes on a yellow legal pad, tucked leftover catalog cards in book after book, and again he felt guilty because of Emma and he kept telling himself: she is two years dead. But, if Valeria is a real fairy—well, they were dangerous, weren't they?

Ben read and read.

He might have read for a lot longer if Jack hadn't caught him at it.

Jack Ruggles was a writer and an English professor at NC State University and Ben's friend. His dark brown hair seemed to have never known a comb and stuck up in odd tufts all over Jack's head. He then lived across the street from the Garner Public Library and he haunted the place, taking home stacks of novels, browsing through the magazines, and asking Ben endless reference questions. For his novel, he told Ben; he had to get the facts straight. Fiction had to make sense; real life didn't.

Jack's real life sure didn't.

Jack's wife had, one morning early in the spring, gotten up, dressed, eaten, drank, and gotten in her car and drove away, with Jack's son, Thomas. She had never come back. Jack was in his first year of a custody fight.

Ben was at the reference desk one late May morning, surrounded by his fairy books when someone's question had taken him into the stacks. When he came back, Jack was standing there, reading his yellow legal pad. Jack looked up when Ben cleared his throat.

"Who's Valeria, Ben? Can she really fly?"

At first, Ben didn't know what to say to Jack. To say anything would be to give up this special and beautiful secret, this golden pleasure he had had and no one else. Yet, he needed to talk and Jack was his best friend.

"She's my neighbor, the blond I told you about. I think she's a fairy."

"A dyke?"

"No, you idiot: a fairy. You know, like in The Blue Fairy Book," he said and held up the book. "You know, with wings and fairy gold and—"

"She has wings?" Jack asked, as he flipped through Ben's legal pad.

"You know what I mean. I've been watching her—and I think she may be watching me, too." The last part he wasn't sure about—maybe he had imagined her glances over the fence, her quick head turns at the door. Imagining it? Maybe he was imagining everything: the fairy flights, the disappearances, and this was just one more thing, surely he was going crazy—

Jack waved his hand to cut Ben off. "Well, my reference question for you today is what is Ben Tyson going to do about his fairy babe? Don't stew over all that stuff, find out."

So, if it hadn't been for Jack, Ben might have never met Valeria. He would have never found the courage; he would have talked himself out of it; he would have convinced himself it was hopeless—he was hopeless. Ben argued; Jack insisted. And one hot, early June night, Ben knocked on Valeria's door, carrying a Food Lion bag with an Angel Food cake and a bottle of white wine. (And five ten-penny nails in his pants pocket—just to be on the safe side, Jack had said. Iron's poisonous to fairies.)

Valeria, laughing, let Ben into what looked first like an ordinary living room, like any other living room he had ever been in: couch, chairs, lamps, pictures on the walls, bric-a-brac on the shelves. Then he looked around again. The TV was on without sound and he couldn't remember ever seeing any program like the one on. The lamps weren't electric. They were lit candles inside glass globes, yellow flames flickering and cutting away the darkness with yellow shadows. He looked back at the TV: it wasn't. It was a terrarium with a very strange-looking lizard perched on a rock in the middle. Smoke trailed out of its nostrils. And one of the pictures: a deep black pool, surrounded by white trees with silver and golden leaves. He stared, stepped closer: yes, the trees were swaying to an invisible wind. He looked back at Valeria, who sat in the armchair, her hands in her lap.

"I shouldn't have looked back at you," she said. "But I think I wanted you to catch me."

The next night they went out to dinner in Raleigh, to Swain's, a steak house. She walked around the car three times, muttering under her breath, as Ben stared. Safe-travel charms, she explained, and protective wards—like an alarm and a force field—just in case the Fomorii tried something while they were in the restaurant.

The Fomorii, she explained, as they drove, were dark elves, black elves, evil fairies. The shadow lords. Princes of darkness. The bad guys her people were fighting back home. (Thesaurus, she added, was one of her favorite games. She had memorized whole sections of Roget's.)

"They shouldn't be able to get to this universe, not anymore, but we can't take the chance."

"The princes of darkness?" Ben grumbled, shaking his head. He reminded himself he had asked for this, he had to believe her, no matter how fantastic any of it sounded. He had really seen her flying in a thunderstorm, and there was the picture and the little dragon and she had been looking at him. He looked over at her as he drove: for the first time, he could see points on her ears. She looked back and laughed and shook that bright hair and her ears were round.

"I let the glamour slip," she said. "Wouldn't do to not have it in the restaurant, now, would it?"

"Glamour?"

"An illusion I cast to hide things . . ."

I did not learn this entire story in one smooth, continuous flow. Rather it came in chunks and odd pieces, as Valeria and I came to know each other. But what I will tell you is the story assembled, the chunks connected. Valeria's people, who really are the Daoine Sidhe, and the Fomorii, have been at war for all of Valeria's life, and for years before that. Compromise and negotiation had been tried and failed. Truces had been made and broken too many times to count. Now, there was only war. The Fomorii came from another room. Creation, she told me, is like a huge, old rambling Victorian house, with different wings everywhere, rooms, towers, stairs, and causeways. The universe of humanity, the Earth, the Sun, the solar system, the galaxy—everything—was in one room. Faerie, the home of the Daoine Sidhe, was in another, next door. And next door to theirs was the universe of the Fomorii. The Daoine Sidhe believe the Fomorii fouled theirs and had come seeking another. How? Through the doors between rooms, between universes. That was how she had come to ours. Remember, she said, all those Irish stories about doors into the hills, warnings about stepping into fairy rings, that time ran in different ways here and there? I remembered. On certain days—Halloween or Samhain—the doors can be opened. May 1 or Beltaine is another day. And so she had come here.

※   ※   ※

Fairies, Ben learned at their first dinner, had particular diets. No salt, no spices, and no meat.

"But, Valeria, this is a steak house. Why didn't you tell me?" Ben hissed across the table, trying to ignore the waiter who, fortunately, seemed mesmerized by the light, which had been blinking ever since they had sat down.

"You didn't ask, Ben. There are Talking Beasts in Faerie and out of respect to them, no one ever eats meat. No salt and no spices, either—bad for our digestion. Do you have any wooden knives, forks, and spoons?" she asked the waiter, who quickly looked down. "And could you light our candles, please?"

"Wood? I can find some plastic," the waiter said, as he lit the candles, as if beautiful women asked him for wooden cutlery every day.

"How did you manage to ride in my steel car?" Ben asked, feeling guilty about the ten-penny nails now in his jacket pocket. They had been jabbing his leg.

"Skingloves," she told him and slowly pulled off one. The glove was transparent and soft, yet tough. "Leggings, too. Besides, I like humans, always have." Much later, Ben would learn just what she meant by that, of the human lovers she had had in the past and in another land. Loving humans had caused no end of grief with her parents. And he would learn her past was a lot farther away than his.

They learned from each other, at that dinner, in a coffeehouse after a movie another night, on walks around the neighborhood, sitting on each other' porches . . . Ben learned the Daoine Sidhe had few machines and a longstanding misunderstanding with the Catholic Church over what was a good and a bad fairy. The Daoine Sidhe had visited the human universe often—before the war. They had come to teach. What? Oh, all sorts of things. They were the First-born in their world; dwarves, swimmers, and the wood-folk were the Second- and Third-born . . .

Ben, when pressed by Jack years later, could not say exactly when he fell in love with her or when he knew she was in love with him. He tried to remember when he fell in love with Emma and he couldn't. Love came slowly for Ben—no magic glances across the room, no bolts of lightning—but rather like a glass beneath a dripping faucet, filling one drop at a time. There was no one movie or dinner or late-night swim, but at some time during that summer the drop fell that over-flowed the glass and they were in love. Everyone else knew before Ben did: Jack, Mrs. Carmichael, the head librarian, even the volunteers who came in to shelf books.

* * *

Jack wanted to know what it was like to sleep with a woman who could do a little magic—not that she ever did much; the wards, lights, teleporting hither and yon, small stuff. All that I told him and all that I am going to tell here is that it happened inside a white flame that rippled around, between, and through us. The flame changed colors, becoming a living kaleidoscope. And that when I woke, later, the lights still lingered in her, rippling across her back like moonlight through a venetian blind someone was opening and closing. I walked around her house, in its warm and close dark, just to touch her things, straighten the magazines she had brought back from her jaunts around the Earth. I walked in her kitchen, a somewhat bare room, as she tended to short out small appliances and when we ate at home, I cooked, in my kitchen. I walked back to her bedroom and straightened the things on her dresser: a brush, a comb, a tiny bottle of perfume. I looked at the perfume for the longest time, trying to read the fine, italic words on the label, but they were in a language and an alphabet I didn't recognize. Then I lay back down in her warmth and went to sleep.

I told Jack nothing else. I have told Malachi nothing at all of that night. And this is all I will tell you of it.

Ben and Valeria went to Ocracoke the first of August, for two weeks. There they stayed in the Crews Inn, tucked away on Back Road, and every day they rented bicycles and rode up NC 12 to the beach. The sea reminded Valeria of home and as they walked on the white sand she told him about the sea that had been in front of the house in which she had grown up, a multi-colored sea: gold, silver, green, white, blue, and grey. Dolphins and whales, along with the merfolk, the swimmers, lived in her ocean, and, yes, of course, dolphins and whales were intelligent and could speak—or rather were telepathic. Ben remembered thinking then that all the fairy tales he had ever read or ever heard: good fairies and bad fairies, talking animals, and mermaids, and all the rest, were true. All the stories were true.

Two nights before they were to go back home, as they had lain in bed together, Ben braiding her long, golden hair through his fingers, Valeria told him she was expecting, gravid, in the family way—

"Pregnant?" he had said and she had said yes, and told him other things he needed to know.

She was fifteen days pregnant and a Daoine Sidhe pregnancy was eight months long. In two-and-a-half months Valeria wouldn't be able to teleport anywhere, as the baby might be left behind. In three-and-a-half months Valeria wouldn't be able to leave the house. She would be glowing and exuding light from practically every orifice in her body and would no longer be able to control it as she usually could.

And after the baby was born—a boy—she would have to go back to Faerie, without the baby, without Ben.

Ben could not understand why. Why hadn't she told him this from the very beginning? Because she had decided not to go back, ever—furlough or no furlough, she was going to go AWOL, desert, go walkabout. Then she had seen him and met him and fallen in love. Then she had decided to take him back with her, war or no war—she wasn't going to leave her human lover behind, not this time. But the baby had changed everything. Why? A half-human baby would be very vulnerable to the Fomorii for too long a time, not until he is trained into his powers, powers a fairy child would learn to use the way he learns to walk and talk. The baby needed to be human first, then a fairy. And Ben would have to stay and raise the boy until the war was over and she could come for them both.

Besides, she said, as they argued and walked the beach and argued and packed and drove to the ferry and argued and rode the ferry over Pamlico Sound to Cedar Island, the gulls diving for bits of bread, she was needed in Faerie. There was one more thing she hadn't yet told him: she was on the Dodecagon, the ruling council, one of the twelve most important people in Faerie. Valeria was the Prime Mover, the head of the council. She had been foolish to think she could escape her responsibilities, that she could abandon the cause of the Light beyond the Light, which would go out on both worlds if the Daoine Sidhe lost.

She showed me my light once, the light that is part of the Light beyond the Light.

"I have a light, too?"

"Yes, but it's really hard for humans to see their light, their aura—at least it used to be."

We stood naked in front of a mirror and slowly the light in the room dimmed and the light around me became visible. A pale blue-grey light outlined my flesh. Another layer, rainbow-colored, enclosed the blue-grey. On the top of my head, at my throat, my heart, my solar plexus, my stomach, and my groin, there seemed to be inner fires of different colors. Just beyond the rainbow layer, beginning at my head and spreading down was yet another layer, bright yellow.

"A halo," I murmured. "Does everybody have a halo and all these layers of light?"

"Yes."

I lifted my hand and the layers of light moved with me, sparking and shooting off tiny falling stars.

The trip home to Garner was in silence. For a week we stumbled around each other, muttering and grumbling. Mrs. Carmichael asked me if I was sick; she told me she hadn't seen me so despondent since Emma died. I wanted to talk to Jack, but he was out of town, so, to my surprise, I drove into Raleigh to St. Anthony's, to Father Mark, the same priest who had come to see me when Emma died, the same priest I told to go to hell, punctuating my command with a slammed door. I was afraid he would do the same; instead he listened. At the end of my haphazard story, a mélange of generalities and specifics (I just couldn't tell him Valeria was a Daoine Sidhe), we were well in late summer twilight and the light in his office was changing and moving, as it burnished his white hair, outlined the gold of his glasses. He looked hard at me and told me I had left parts of the story out, and so he didn't quite understand it all. But, he said, leaning into his desk, to love another is to accept them as they are, and not to try and make them into what we would want them to be. My love for Valeria couldn't be based on her promising not to die like Emma, on her promising to be what she wasn't, to do what would make her what she wasn't. Did I understand? Yes, but what do I do? Go home and love her, he told me. Believe that she loves you. Believe in your love for each other. Go home, Ben.

So I did.

There were times that fall when Ben almost forgot Valeria had to leave. He almost forgot at Halloween—Samhain—when his house— their house, now—was the closest to being haunted as it had ever been. Green witch-lights glowed in pumpkins all over the yard and, no matter how hard the neighborhood kids tried, they couldn't get near one. What looked like ghosts drifted and moaned in the trees. Banshees wailed in the darkness, sending kids screaming down the street.

In Faerie, Valeria told him, Samhain was not disguises or loud noises or scary stories. Samhain was a festival of lights. Great bonfires lit the mountaintops. Valeria remembered seeing the flames from her home by the sea. At midnight there were prayers, songs, poems, or simply conversations with the Good God and Goddess wherever one was: on the beach, in a forest glade, or the Great Temple in the White City. To remember the dead, to say good-bye to the old year, to welcome the new. It was a night when you could see another's soul, plain and visible.

She made Christmas a festival of lights as well. The tree was filled with multi-colored, shimmering lights drifting in and out of the branches. Outside she sent more lights to roam the eaves, porch railings, weaving a shining net over the house. By then she was showing and she was luminous—the light grew as the baby grew, she said. Her mother had told her it was to light the way for the baby's soul. Daoine Sidhe mothers couldn't stop the glowing at five months—all their energy was spent in the baby. Ben had been able to deflect the neighbors' questions about Valeria's absence: bed rest, doctor's orders, at her mother's, where he went every weekend. He had to park his car at the library on weekends and sneak in his house to make that story work. To answer questions about the decorations: experimental special effects, like the movies—a friend worked for Industrial Light and Magic, really, no, trade secret, but be on the lookout at the theatre. One of his neighbors, months later, swore he saw the same lights in a film. Ben had just nodded and said, "See, I told you so."

There would have been still more questions about the fey crèche Valeria sat beneath the tree. Fortunately no one, except for Jack, ever saw it. The crèche had three babies inside, the Three Sons sent by the Good God and Goddess: Oberon, Pan, and Triton. Then, she set four candles in the window, for the Four Teachers, one of Earth, one of Air, one of Water, one of Fire.

And Ben started going back to mass. He stuffed dollars in the votive offering box each time and carefully lit the tiny candles in the blue and green glass jars with one of the long sticks stuck in a sand pot. He argued with himself as he lit each candle: this was a superstition, this was a prayer to keep her, this was the Catholic magic he laughed at, this was all he could do to keep her here.

In the first week of March the baby was born.

"The baby's coming. Ben, wake up, wake up. My water broke; I'm in labor."

Ben turned over groggily and looked up into Valeria's face. He had never seen her radiating so much light before. He could barely look at her. The room was filled with light.

"The baby? Now?"

"Yes. Do you remember the things I need for you to do? Are you awake?"

"Wide awake."

"Remember, this isn't an ordinary human birth. Close all the

curtains and blinds—otherwise the neighbors will think the house is on fire . . ." Valeria went on, giving Ben a detailed list of things to gather, what temperature the room should be, how far apart her contractions were, how much time that meant, and so on. He didn't tell her she had given him almost the same list two months ago, and a month ago, and a slightly revised version last week. He just nodded at each item as he twisted the bed sheets with his hands, telling himself to be calm, just be calm, take slow, deep breaths, count to ten, be calm . . .

"Well, Ben? Get busy!"

He got busy.

Our son, Malachi Lucius Tyson, was born four hours later, just before dawn. When he came out, head first, there was a tremendous explosion of light. He slid into my hands all wet and slippery and hot. I had never felt (and have yet to) a healthy baby so hot before. I cut the cord and wrapped him in a wet towel, steam rising into my face.

He was the most beautiful baby I have ever seen.

Ben thought it was Malachi's crying the next night that woke him. He sat up quickly and rolled out of bed. The baby was fast sleep. Ben stood, one hand on the crib, listening. He could hear Malachi breathing, and then softer, yet in the same rhythm, Valeria. He heard the faint tick of the clock on the dresser. And a thump in the living room that shouldn't be there, followed quickly by another, dull and heavy on the floor. A bird—a bat against the window—could he have possibly left the window open?

I still remember what I was thinking, trying to make sense out of an impossible noise. I still remember wishing I had a baseball bat or a tennis racquet as I went down the hall to check, feeling foolish.

They stood by a picture of Faerie Valeria had hung in Ben's living room, right above the table where she had set the terrarium with the little dragon. There were two of them, shadows blacker and darker than anything Ben had ever seen. Their shadows swallowed light. Ben watched as the moonlight was sucked up into their darknesses. The nearer one sniffed and turned, and looked directly at Ben, its eyes dark red fires. It took one step forward, its claws scratching on the wood. Ben stepped backward. The Fomorii had come; they had gotten through after all. And it was in the middle of the night and Ben was stark naked.

The nearest Fomorii took another step toward Ben and spat on the floor. The spit hissed like water tossed into a frying pan. Then it cracked a whip. Sparks flew and Ben felt the air in the room suddenly grow hotter and closer. A few more steps closer and he knew the whip would have left a burn on his chest. The monster cracked its whip again and this time caught Ben on his leg. He screamed and the two Fomorii started walking slowly toward him, one behind the other, backing him down the hall. Why should they be afraid of one naked human when they were winning battles against the lords of Faerie?

Faerie. Nails, iron, the blood metal. He knew they were from yet another universe, but maybe, just maybe. The ten-penny nails were still in his jacket pocket, right where he had left them months ago. Behind Ben, about six feet away, was the bedroom door, a white rectangle, the light contained inside the doorframe, as if someone had caged the light. Had Valeria set the wards? But he had been able to go out—did the wards know him, let him come and go? Could they keep out the darkness? The jacket—where was it?—his closet.

The Fomorii were less than five feet away. He saw them clearly: crests erect, black scales, yellow fangs, yellow claws, those red eyes. He took another step backward; the Fomorii matched it. The bedroom was less than three feet away. Ben could hear Malachi screaming. He took another step backward, felt something give, and he was inside. The Fomorii stood at the door, stopped by the light. He glanced to be sure Valeria had the baby and he bolted for the closet and the jacket and the nails.

"I forgot to set all the wards. I was too tired; I forgot; I thought we were safe. I can't hold them much longer—I just don't have the strength . . ."

He didn't even look at her as he frantically searched for the nails. When Ben found them in his jacket pocket, he yanked them out and turned as the Fomorii snarled, in one fluid motion. The air and the light in the door shimmered and for a very brief moment he saw what looked like a very fine spider web crack in a windshield. Both Fomorii cracked their whips and hissing fireballs the size of basketballs flew through the shimmering air that now seemed to fill the room. Valeria matched the fireballs with her own lightning bolts, exploding them like fireworks. The air in the door shook again, vibrating, and broken, bits of shattered light cascading to the floor. The first Fomorii stepped into the room, the darkness coming with him, a living, silent, foul-smelling storm cloud. It ate the light, breaking it into firefly-sized pieces. With the nails tight in his hand, wishing they were longer, Ben ran straight for the monster and stabbed at him, slashing open one scaly, black arm.

The darkness froze. The second Fomorii froze. The wounded one screamed and moaned and then it began to melt, its crest drooping and oozing, the scales blurring, everything blurring into a dark, vile, smelly mess on the floor. The second Fomorii ran and Ben could hear another shattering of the air. The darkness vanished at the shattering and there was only the grey-blue dawn light. Ben could see the sky and a few stars out the window. The only other lights in the room were the baby and Valeria. She looked at him and he looked at her, the nails still in his hand. At Ben's feet were tiny bits of darkness, like black soot on the floor.

We never really talked about what happened. I wish we had. Jack tried to make me talk to her, but I couldn't.

"You haven't talked about it at all? Ben, you fought off the Forces of Evil and saved your woman and your child and you can't talk to her about it? Ben!"

"You don't understand. I had nails, iron nails, in my jacket pocket in our bedroom, the room our son was born in. Yes, those nails saved her and Malachi, but I got them to protect myself against her. Remember?"

"She must have said something," Jack muttered, as he carefully mixed the gravy and mashed potatoes on his plate together. We were in the Kuntry Kitchen for our regular Friday lunch.

"She told me why the Fomorii came. They were assassins." And I told him the rest: that she was not just one of the Twelve on the Dodecagon. She was the Prime Mover, the head, the focal point. If they got her, the tide of the war would change. That they even got through was a sign she was desperately needed back home.

"Tell her I told you to get those nails. Geez, Ben, she's leaving. You gotta talk to her."

I shook my head and asked Danielle, our waitress, for more sweet iced tea. I didn't want to talk about it anymore.

Valeria and I never mentioned the nails.

Valeria left April 30, Beltaine Eve.

"*Are you just going to draw a pentagram on the floor at midnight and step through it?*" *Ben asked a few days before. He wasn't angry; he was just sad; they both were. They were in the bedroom and Valeria had just put Malachi to bed. They stood by the crib and watched as he dreamed, his breathing slow, easy, the sheet rising, falling, his fists by his face. The floor was still speckled with the black soot. Ben had tried every cleanser he could think of—Murphy's Oil*

*Soap, Pinesol, Formula 409—nothing had worked. Valeria had fi-
nally made him stop: the soot had bonded with the wood. He would
have to replace the entire floor, she had told him, and destroy the
wood. She had given him instructions how. Floors made of oak, holly,
elder, thorn, ash, hawthorn, and apple wood were going to take some
doing.*

*"No, I have to go to the nearest gate," Valeria said and made some
imperceptible adjustment to Malachi's covers. "I'll take a taxi. Let's go
in the living room or we will wake him up."*

*"Take a taxi? You can fly, or teleport, can't you?" Ben asked, fol-
lowing her down the hall. He would have to replace the floor in the
hall, too, and the living room. The embedded black spots were everywhere. Valeria had told him the longer they remained in the wood, the
weaker it would be until the floors just collapsed. And that sometimes
the black spots could make anyone that walked on them for too long
sick of heart, and eventually, of the body. They sat down on the couch,
and Valeria leaned into Ben, her head on his shoulder.*

*"I don't have the strength for it, not so soon after delivery. Ben, I
really don't want to go. You know, if the Fomorii hadn't found me,
tried to kill me—I would have stayed, Dodecagon or no. But there is
just too much at stake, and I need you both to be safe. Without me,
you're safe. With me, you're not."*

"Can't I go with you to the gate?"

*No, she told him, it wouldn't be safe. She didn't even want him to
know where it was. Besides, it would make leaving all the harder.*

I needed to hear that: she would have stayed. She had forgiven me
the nails.

I said I told my son almost nothing about his mother until he was
ten. I think now I was wrong to do that. He needed to know who and
what she was, if for no other reason, to know who and what he was
and was becoming. If I had, I think it would have made the first part
of his puberty, when his fairyness started to manifest, so much more
bearable for the both of us—much less scary for him. But I would
have denied him that, if I could. That was wrong, too, I know. But I
was so afraid of losing him as I lost her.

Now, I know there are worst things to be scared of than losing
someone you love.

I have told him this story now I don't know how many times.
Malachi knows it by heart. And no matter how many times I tell it,
the ending is always the hardest: I have to tell him how his mother

died and that there was nothing I could have done to save her and that she died so that he and I would not die, that she loved us that much. I do not tell him that there seems to be no limit on how many times a heart can break, or that when I grieved for his mother, I grieved again for Emma, for loose flagstones, for human weakness, for not being enough, for feeling that I had failed again. I do not tell him I was angry with both women, with myself.

It hurt to watch the taxi turn into the driveway, Val gather her things, kiss and hug Malachi. When she turned to kiss Ben, they were both crying. Neither of them could say anything. Valeria touched Ben one more time, lightly, just the tip of her glowing fingers on his cheek, and turned to go down the front steps onto the flagstone path to the waiting red taxi.

Valeria was halfway between the steps and the car when the air shimmered, broke, falling in a rain of broken light, freeing the other Fomorii. It snapped its fire whip when its foot touched the earth, a snap so hard the whip broke, releasing a huge fireball, a miniature comet, with a tail of flames. The fireball was aimed at Ben. He could see it coming, smell and feel the approaching heat, and he knew there was no time and nowhere to go. Then Valeria threw herself in front of the fireball. Ben screamed: Noooo, don't, don't, nooo. The fireball exploded on impact.

Or did she explode? Ben was never sure. The resulting white fire burned away the night, the dark, the stars, the Fomorii, and the fire whip, Valeria, and part of the yard, the flagstones, the shrubbery. The shock wave, a sudden rippling, an airborne tide, hit Ben in the chest, throwing him back, into the flowerbeds, into the pansies and daffodils. The living room windows all shattered, the taxi flipped over, once, twice, three times, slamming into the fence. Ben never knew what happened to the driver; he was gone when Ben, some time later, remembered to check. The flagstones melted, as did a good part of the asphalt driveway. And there was nothing left, except the melted glassy earth, the burnt grass, and a fine ash, of either Valeria or the Fomorii. The police and fire department arrived to find Ben still lying in the flowerbed, the grass still on fire, the gravel and asphalt molten. At least, Ben thought, they had something to do. A paramedic helped him up into a barrage of questions. All he could think to say, since the taxi hadn't been considerate enough to explode, was ball lightning. The police, at least, kept the neighbors at bay.

"There's not a cloud in the sky. Ball lightning?" a sergeant asked, one eyebrow raised.

Ben nodded, and repeated his story and told them again and again he had no idea where the taxi driver had gone. Finally they left, and Ben repeated his story to the handful of neighbors still up, and then, shaking his head, no more, enough, went back into the house, and sat down on the couch. He couldn't do anything else. He couldn't think, talk; he could barely breath. When Malachi started crying, he was finally able to move. The clock on the dresser said three-thirty. He didn't turn on a light; he didn't need to. The baby glowed. Something new hung from the crib mobile Jack had given them, a slender, silver-grey necklace with one dangling charm. Putting Malachi on his shoulder, Ben held the charm in his hand. It was also silver-grey, heavy, and shaped like a star, a small star with twelve points.

By then Malachi was yelling so loud, Ben could have used him to guide in airplanes at RDU. Leaving the charm to dangle on the mobile and rubbing the boy's back, Ben went into the kitchen. There, on the table, inside what looked like a nest of light, was a bottle. Ben carefully put his hand through the light-nest and it faded away, as if someone had blown it out, as he picked up the still-warm bottle. He knew it was Valeria's own milk—one from the precious few bottles she had left. He went back into the bedroom to the rocking chair and sat down, yawning, with Malachi in the crook of his arm. He looked up at Ben as he sucked noisily, with golden eyes, from her mother's family, Valeria had said.

"I think you have my nose," Ben whispered.

Ben knew that eventually he would have to cry. He knew it wasn't going to be easy to raise an infant alone. For the first time he was glad Emma had left him money. Mrs. Carmichael was going to be shocked when he asked for paternity leave.

Father Mark would help; so would Jack.

Malachi was asleep. Ben gently slid the nipple out of his mouth and wiped the milk off his chin. He stood up very slowly and carried the baby back to the crib. He put him down and, after covering him, stepped back, and in the early morning shadows of the room, Ben watched his son sleep. As Malachi breathed, the light around him vibrated, contracting and expanding. Ben moved closer and put his hand on the baby's head and curled his golden hair around his fingers: warm ribbons of light. In a month or so, Valeria had told him, Malachi would stop glowing. He would be like any human baby then, at least until puberty. Ben wished then that he had thought to have a family picture made, to put on his desk, where Emma's had sat. With his free hand, he flipped his fingers at the charm and started it swinging back and forth over his son's head.

Ben did weep, eventually.

And Ben raised his son as best he knew how, with the help of those friends who loved him, and Malachi, who was always small, was a good boy, and he and his father lived happily together for ten years.

Then everything changed.

I
Tuesday, May Eve, 30 April - Wednesday, Beltaine 1 May 1991

Malachi Lucius Tyson

MALACHI CLOSED HIS EYES. MISS WINDLEMERE read the poem, surely the most boring poem in the English language, in her clear and precise and completely flat voice, draining any and all feeling out of the words, if there had been any in the first place, until only the moral was left. Malachi was convinced Miss Windlemere believed the only good stories or poems had to be little homilies, tiny sermons. It wasn't that Miss Windlemere was opposed to fun in school—after all, Malachi thought, she had put up a May Pole just outside the classroom. Tomorrow they were all supposed to do some sort of dorky dance with crepe paper streamers around the pole and the boy and girl with the highest grades in spelling would be crowned May King and Queen. Just like the little statue of Mary at church, with her floral coronet that Mrs. Nowalski made every week out of the flowers in her garden: pansies, petunias, tiny yellow buttercups, daffodils, paperwhite narcissi. Malachi had asked if the girl had to be like the Virgin but Miss Windlemere didn't think it was funny.

Would she ever finish? Malachi opened his eyes to look at the clock and its too slow second hand over the blackboard: 2:05. Another entire hour, sixty more minutes, three thousand six hundred seconds, before school was out for the day. And after that: four more weeks, four more weeks of Miss Windlemere and her flat voice and this classroom and Vandora Springs Elementary. Twenty days. Never mind the number of hours; it was too many. On the last day of school Malachi would walk out, never to come back. Fifth grade was going to be in a new school: Nottingham Heights Elementary. Malachi wondered if his next teacher would have the same posters placed neatly above each window: *Truth is Beauty, Knowledge is Power, The Early Bird Gets The Worm, Variety is The Spice of Life.* Posters, Malachi was sure, that had been up on the wall since the school was built, as *Knowledge is Power* and *Truth is Beauty* were getting frayed around the edges. Someone had left a spitball on the worm.

"Now, class, take out a piece of paper—don't rip it out, Ellen, how many times do I have to tell you that?–name and date in the upper right hand corner. Danny, stop staring out the window. Thank you. Now, class, I want you to write your own May poem using your spelling words . . ."

Geez, another spelling word poem. Danny had the right idea—if Malachi could just get outside. He sniffed the breeze that had found its way into the classroom: warm, light, laced with the faint, faint fragrance of nameless flowers. And was that a cardinal—that flash of red taking flight? If he could just follow that bird—go whenever, wherever—Malachi sighed and got out a piece of paper and watched as the minute hand moved to 2:09. Could he? His wrist on his desk, Malachi raised his hand. His pencil slowly rolled out of its groove and up against his wrist. He had never tried a trick like this before, though. It had only been in the past month, since Malachi's tenth birthday in March, that he had found out he could do these tricks on a regular basis. Pencils, though, were one thing, clocks were another. But still, if he could *move* the clock hands to 3:05 and trip the bell in the office, he'd be out of here. The very first trick, back in October, had been an accident. Malachi had dropped the kaleidoscope Uncle Jack had given him under his bed and it had rolled out of reach. Even lying flat on his stomach and stretching his arm as far as he could, Malachi had not been able to reach the metal tube, and there just wasn't enough space between bed and floor for him to crawl under. Moving the bed wasn't an option, as it folded out of the wall—the previous owners liked boats, his dad had explained once. He had closed his eyes and imagined the kaleidoscope rolling to him, and it did. Just a few inches, but the kaleidoscope had moved.

He pinched himself: yes, he was awake. Just because he was on the floor, dust bunnies around his ears, with his eyes closed, didn't mean he was asleep. Maybe the floor was curved, or maybe the house was really a boat and had hit a big wave. Maybe there had been an earthquake. The second time Malachi tried, the kaleidoscope skittered across the floor into his hand, leaving a very faint, blue trail behind it. It had happened again, a few days later, on Halloween. Miss Windlemere, to everyone's surprise, had worn a black witch's dress and hat to school. She had even cackled a few times. Wasn't she supposed to keep her true identity secret? She had just about been ready to sit down at reading group when Malachi *pushed* the chair back. Miss Windlemere had dropped straight to the floor, collapsing just like the Wicked Witch of the West.

But only in the past few weeks, since his birthday, had Malachi been able to count on the tricks. Kaleidoscopes, toy cars and trucks, stuffed animals, balled-up paper, pencils, books—all of them had flown about his bedroom, leaving fading smoke-blue trails in the air. And if he could *move* all those things, how hard could the clock hands and the office bell be? *I can do this.* Malachi bent low over his desk, so Miss Windlemere couldn't see he was only pretending to write. He clenched his fist and tightened his chest. *Focus, see the bell, the clock . . . There.* The afternoon bell rang, shattering the class's sleepy silence into a rush of voices and moving bodies. Miss Windlemere jumped up from her desk, looking first at the clock and then at the class as it surged up and out, moving around her like she was more furniture.

"Wait, that can't be right, it's not 3:05, wait, good-bye, good-bye . . ."

I did it, I did it, I did it. Okay, careful, don't push them out of the way, but I bet I could; it wouldn't take much. Blow them away, like the Big Bad Wolf. Just huff and puff, and blow them all down. Serve 'em right. Not now. Walk, run, shove, like everybody else. Maybe I ought to give Miss Windlemere another surprise—yeah, move her chair out, there, until it is right behind her and when she steps back— Yeessss. Malachi stopped at the door and looked back. He had never seen anybody so surprised in their life. He *blew.* Miss Windlemere took a quick step back, her hair suddenly loose about her head, and dropped heavily into her chair. When the chair started spinning in circles around the room, she froze, her hands in the air, her mouth open.

"Good-bye," Malachi yelled and left, as the chair began to slow down. He didn't want to hurt her, just shake the old lady up a little. If Miss Windlemere even suspected Malachi had anything to do with the moving chair and the early dismissal, she'd kill him. Then the principal would kill him. And after that, his dad.

Sailing paper airplanes around the classroom had been the last time they had called his dad. "You had everybody making planes?" his dad had asked, shaking his head. They were walking home from school after meeting with the principal. "Everybody? Why do you do this stuff? How do you think I feel when I get these calls from your teacher and the principal? Malachi? Are you listening to me? Look at me, Malachi." His dad stopped walking and squatted down to face Malachi. They were a block from home on Vandora Springs Road, right in front of the Easy Eye Optometrist. A big eye stared down at them from the roof of the low, brick building. For a long moment his father said nothing, until Malachi finally looked away. He hated it when his dad did this. Go ahead and yell, get mad, not this. "I want you to be happy, son, and you have just gotten more and more miserable this entire year, doing more and more stupid stuff like this. Maybe asking you to tough out the teasing was a bad idea. Maybe that new school we talked about is the answer. I met the principal; she's a really nice lady. What do you think? Can you hang on until school is out?"

That had surprised Malachi: he had been sure his dad wasn't seeing him anymore, wasn't seeing what was happening, didn't want to see.

Once outside the classroom, he scooted, keeping close to the wall, and just beneath a row of crayon drawings of spring flowers hanging from a cork strip. The drawings brushed his head as he ran, heading for the exit as fast as he could. He didn't want the principal to catch on that something wasn't right—which wouldn't take long, since there weren't any buses outside, none being due for another hour.

The front door of Vandora Springs Elementary burst open, throwing out a crowd of ten or twelve boys and Malachi, all hooting and hollering. *Keep going, just keep going, once I make those pine trees on the other side of the parking lot, I'm home free. Heck, there's the principal. Go, go, go.* The other boys ran out into the bus parking lot into a bigger crowd of kids, all looking for buses and parents' cars that weren't there. Malachi ran with them and then kept on running, even though a few other kids called after him. For a moment he thought he heard an adult voice calling him as well, but he kept running. He ran until he was inside the trees' shadows and didn't stop until all the voices faded and grew faint. It wasn't much of a woods, just sort of a cul de sac between the school and a subdivision, mostly pines and cedars, some scraggly maples and sweetgums, a handful of big old oaks, honeysuckle and blackberry thickets. Too overgrown really, but it was sanctuary and Malachi was sure nobody would follow him. He rubbed his back against a thick pine and slowly slumped down to the pine needle-covered ground. There were bits of spider webs stuck to his face and his chest. Malachi kicked a few pinecones out of his way.

He shook his head. Dad was going to be furious. One of those kids would tell on him to the principal; they always did. The phone was probably already ringing at the public library. He could hear his father's slow, careful, at-work voice: "Reference?" Then there would be the shift and his father would start talking faster, his words tumbling together. That was when his father changed from Benjamin P. Tyson, Head of Reference and Assistant Branch Librarian at the Southeast Regional Branch of the Wake County Public Library System to Malachi's dad, Ben Tyson.

"I wish I had *blown* down everybody in the hall," Malachi said as he tossed pinecones. He could have pretended he was a hurricane, with howling winds. Or a tornado that would pick them all up to be dropped into mud. Or maybe just move them, the way he had Miss Windlemere's chair: pick them up and drop them in a dumpster.

There weren't too many kids at school that Malachi liked. Or wanted to like. Ever since kindergarten he had tried and tried to fit in and make the others like and accept him, but no matter how hard he tried—bringing brownies to school, getting into trouble on a regular basis—nothing had quite worked. Some kids were okay, but no one was really his friend. Starting school had been something of a shock in the first place. Malachi hadn't known how different he was until then. His world had been the kinder, gentler adult one of his father, the folks at the library, Uncle Jack, his father's best friend, Father Mark. There had been Thomas, Jack's son, but he had been so much older Malachi had never thought of the awkward teenager and now brooding young man as a friend. Besides, until he was sixteen, Thomas had lived with his mother most of the year, and only visited his dad a few weeks in the summer and some holidays. None of them had told him he was going to be the shortest, have the blondest hair, or that golden eyes were anything out of the ordinary. Most of the camouflage Malachi had tried hadn't worked. He had blacked his hair with shoe polish in third grade. His father hadn't punished him for that—going to school the next day with a shaved head had been punishment enough. All that had helped was not being smart. No end of earnest and long conversations with his teachers and his father and Uncle Jack made him waver from getting a succession of B's and C's.

"But you could get straight A's, son. Remember those games

Jack's friend played with you? They were intelligence tests and—"
"B's and C's are safer, Dad."

He knew his dad was convinced Malachi would give up the low grades at Nottingham Heights. Maybe.

Having Father Mark around had helped. The old priest had reassured Malachi again and again it was okay to be different, that it didn't matter, and things would be better when Malachi was older, just wait and see. Malachi had been Father Mark's unofficial helper since first grade: dumping the offering baskets, straightening the missalettes in the pews, collecting the old bulletins. When the old priest died the summer after second grade Malachi felt the world had become a more dangerous place and third grade proved him right. Some big fifth grade boys zeroed in on a tiny, towheaded kid with funny-colored golden-brown almost yellow eyes. Dog-eyes. Dog-boy, Old Yeller, Pee Wee, Shrimp, and Chihuahua Boy had followed him ever since. No amount of explaining his eyes were golden-brown and not yellow did any good.

Nor did asking his father for contacts.

"Contacts? You have perfect—better than perfect vision, son. You don't need glasses, not like me, and you probably never will," his father had said, not even looking up from the book he had been reading. The pair of cheap sunglasses Malachi bought at Kerr Drugs only lasted for a day. The music teacher wanted to know how he could see with them on inside. The other kids laughed, the glasses were put in the teacher's June box, and she called his father.

Malachi hated it when his father got mad. And since the beginning of this school year it seemed like he made his father mad every other day. He could even name the day it started back in the fall, when he had *pushed* that chair out from under Miss Windlemere in her witch costume.

He hadn't been able to wait to tell his dad about it. Malachi had run all the way from the school to the library. He hadn't stopped running until he burst into his dad's office, dodging three or four shelving carts, grumbling blue-haired library volunteers, and shouting hello at the desk clerk on the way.

"Dad, Dad, you'll never guess what happened at school today. I can do—" Malachi said, as he brushed past the fake giant cobwebs strung across his dad's office door. His father, who had been peering intently into a computer screen, held up one hand.

"Just a minute, son, let me finish this last paragraph of this report—have to send it in to the main branch tomorrow—just a little bit more."

Malachi picked up a heavy, acrylic paperweight from his dad's desk, and started tossing it back and forth, from one hand to the other. He wondered how they had gotten the butterflies inside. Maybe the butterflies—a red Monarch, a yellow one, a white one—weren't real. Maybe the butterflies had been happily flying along, no, maybe it was magic—

"Okay, there, finished, and save, and print," his father said and then wheeled his chair around to face Malachi. "Son, put that paperweight down before you drop it. Thanks. Something happened at school today?"

Malachi told his father what had happened, talking as fast as he could, his hands moving like excited birds. ". . . and then she just dropped to the floor. It's magic, Dad; I can do magic, that has to be it. I *moved* her chair right out from under her just like this—"

"What? You did what? You moved your teacher's chair and she fell. Magic? You can't do magic. Your imagination has gotten way, way out of hand."

"Dad! It has to be magic! You should have seen her face when she hit the floor, and that witch hat fell and—"

"Never ever do that again. Never. Do you understand me? Don't. Malachi, are you listening to me?"

"Dad, I didn't mean to, not really. Why are you getting mad at me? That old witch—sorry, Miss Windlemere, wasn't really hurt. I'm talking about magic, Dad. It's real. It's true, I don't know how it happened to me, but—"

"You heard me: Don't. Ever. Do. That. Again. Pulling out your teacher's chair—you could get expelled. Are you listening to me? And to make matters worse, you are making up a story about how you did it."

"I'm not making it up and I didn't pull out the chair—not with my hands. Are you listening to me? I made it happen—I *pushed* the air and—"

"I said: never again."

His father was yelling. Malachi stepped back. He had never seen his father so mad or heard him so loud. People outside his office were trying not to listen or look.

"Do you hear—what am I doing?" His father, his face fast turning red, quickly sat down in his chair. "Malachi, I'm sorry. Go home. Just go home; we'll talk later."

It happened again at supper. Both Malachi and his father were out of sorts after what happened at the library, and mealtime conversation was mostly pass that, please, thanks, and not much else. When Malachi decided he wanted more bread he decided not to even bother asking. Let's see if being magic was more than the chair and the kaleidoscope. For a moment nothing happened. Then, wobbling and dipping, rolls falling onto the table, the bread bowl drifted over the carrots and string beans and salad to drop with a bang in front of Malachi. His father stared at the floating bowl, transfixed, his hand and water glass frozen in midair.

"Dad? I know you saw that. See, I am magic; it's real. I made the bread bowl float across the table. What's happening to me?"

"I didn't see anything. Nothing is happening to you, nothing at all. Next time you want some bread, just ask me and I will pass it to you, okay?" his father said, his face even harder and colder than he had been at the library.

"Dad, you were looking right at it. I made the bowl *float*. It's magic, you saw it. What is wrong with you? All right—watch this."

For a very long moment, nothing happened. Then, with a rush of air propelling them, the salt- and peppershakers launched into the air. Following them, but less steadily, were the mashed potatoes and the green beans. The potatoes fell first, potato-side up, the bowl splitting in two as it smacked the floor. The saltshaker made a soft landing in the potatoes, and the beans just drifted back to the table. The peppershaker exploding, showering the table, all the food, Malachi, and his dad. *Moving* things was harder than Malachi thought, especially so many things at one time. It made his head hurt. His father, who had sat very still during the entire display, finally moved when he started sneezing and brushing the pepper off.

"Magic is just for fairies, not for people. Stories. If you can't behave, maybe you should go to your room," his father finally gasped out, when he stopped sneezing.

"Dad, are you crazy—you saw, I know you saw—"

"Go to your room."

"All right, I will," Malachi had yelled. He slammed his bedroom door as hard as he could and threw himself on his bed, crying. *What was wrong with Dad? Why was he so mad? Why was he pretending he couldn't see what had happened? What's wrong with me? I didn't do anything bad . . .*

That had been in October. Neither Malachi nor his father had mentioned Miss Windlemere's chair or the bread bowl since. It was as if the magic was happening in another room, a place different and secret from their everyday lives. Malachi was sure his father knew—

there were times he would look up from doing his homework or reading a book or watching TV to see his dad staring at him. "What is it, Dad? What's the matter?" Malachi had asked a few times. "Nothing," his father had said. "Nothing's the matter." The secret had to stay secret, an invisible and offstage presence that haunted 1413 Beichler Road. Malachi wished, over and over again, that he knew why. He hated not being able to talk to his dad about it. Not talking about the magic didn't make it any less real. Magic? Was that what it really was? In a lot of the stories and books he had read since he had *moved* Miss Windlemere's chair the magic had something to do with spells and making strange things in huge bubbling cauldrons. Witches and wizards did magic like that. Fairies, on the other hand, were different. They *were* magic. When Malachi figured that out, he was almost satisfied. What about the other meaning of fairy? The one he wasn't sure about, the one he had heard some older boys whispering and laughing about? Malachi wanted to ask his father if he thought that was right: witches did magic, fairies were magic, what the older boys meant. But he asked nothing.

But despite the silence, everything else was pretty much the same, which made the weird silence tolerable. Uncle Jack still came to dinner once or twice a week, although now he sometimes brought his new girl friend, Hilda. Malachi and his father still went to movies in Raleigh every now and then, and some Sundays they would make it to mass down the street at St. Mary's. School, homework, the library, and the ghost safely in another room.

Malachi, of course, did not stop doing what he called little magics: *sliding* the chalk just ahead of Miss Windlemere's fingers, *pulling* book markers out of all the books on her desk. Or, as he had done yesterday, *nudging* a softball in mid-air to pop the head of one of his tormentors. The boy had deserved it. He had been picking on Malachi on the bus, calling him Old Yeller and baby, and what was a little bitty baby doing in school, huh, cat got your tongue, little bitty feller? No, Malachi had thought when the ball smacked the boy's head, but I just got you. And a week ago, he had found out he could raise the wind, be the Big Bad Wolf.

Malachi got up from the tree and brushed off leaves and pine needles. He had also practiced in his room at home, after his father thought he was asleep, or out in the woods, in places like this. He started walking deeper into the little grove. There was a clearing that he remembered from the last time he had gone exploring in these woods. Besides, he didn't want the principal to find him; at least not right away.

"Dad's going to be really mad when he finds out," Malachi muttered to himself as he followed a winding dog-path. He was sure by now his father had been called and was probably on his way to the school. And no matter how hard his father was pretending, Malachi was sure his dad would figure out how the school bell had gone off so early.

This is a Good Place. He had come to the clearing, which was almost a perfect circle cut out of the trees, as if someone had lifted up everything with a huge cookie cutter. Weeds, tall grasses, leaves, and branches covered the ground. Tiny pine and cedar saplings, spindly oak and maple saplings. Small blue and white star-shaped flowers were scattered inside the circle like sprinkles tossed on a cake. Malachi's feet crunched on acorns. He stood in the middle and looked up into a smaller circle of sky, its irregular rim made by tree branches.

He had been dreaming of this trick for as long as he could remember, and now, after the softball, the bowl, the chalk and the chair, and today, after the clock and the bell—well, could he do it—could he be like the wind?

Okay, here goes. One, two, three, up where the air is clear, up in the stratosphere, let's send it soaring, let's go fly a kite . . .

At first, like with the dishes at the table, nothing happened. Then, Malachi *pushed* against the ground and shot straight up, one, two, three, four feet, then stopped, faltered, and dropped like a stone into the leaves. *I can do this. Just like the clock. The dinner bowls. I can do this.* Malachi lifted more slowly the second time and stopped a yard up. It was as if something shifted in his brain, something clicked, and there, now he could see what to do. He dove up and out and into the breeze.

Malachi flew.

He swooped up to the top of the nearest tree and then down and up again, turning his body over and over as he did, making spirals in the air. He dove in the warm air and did somersaults all the way down, and then a sudden flip, and he was skimming the tops of the saplings, like a rock skipping on water. He plucked leaves from a big oak and then dodged them as they drifted to the ground. He floated on his back, on his stomach, on his side.

If he could just stay in the air and never come down. Nobody could come and get him, and any names they would call would just drop on the ground. It no longer mattered that he was smaller than everybody else, with funny eyes and hair, with a dad who was a *librarian* and with no mother at all. Valeria. That was her name, but all Malachi knew about her was that he looked just like her and that to ask his dad about her meant silence and sadness. Could *she* fly? Was *she* magic?

But never mind all *that.* He could fly.

Finally Malachi looked at his watch. 4:30. Better get going. Tuesdays his dad would be home from the library by five. He knew his dad was going to be mad because he had run away from school; that was a given. Making him madder by being late wasn't worth it. Malachi let himself slowly float down to the ground, his feet landing lightly in a bed of moss.

He got home just before five, only minutes ahead of his father. Malachi was in the bedroom, changing out of his school clothes so his dad wouldn't see the leaves and cobwebs, when he heard the front door open, then his father's footsteps, and the thud of his father's briefcase on the coffee table in the living room. Malachi quickly pulled a T-shirt over his head and ran to the bathroom to stuff his school clothes in the hamper.

"Malachi Lucius Tyson. Come here, please."

All three names. He's really mad. Malachi gulped and went down the hall.

"Dad? Dad? I'm sorry—it was an accident—I, uh—" Malachi stopped, staring at his father. Dad didn't look three names-mad. He looked tired and sad; his eyes were red and wet. Dad had been crying. Malachi shuddered; he couldn't believe it, he wouldn't believe it. Was it this magic? No, it couldn't be—anything that let you fly could not be bad—

"Go back to your room. You've scared me to death. I almost called the police. The principal called; he is furious. Miss Windlemere is even more furious. Go to your room. I can't talk to you now. Go."

"But, Dad, I have to tell you, I want to tell you—Dad, I flew today, in the air. Could my mother fly? Dad, please—"

"I said: go to your room."

"Dad!"

"Not another word."

Malachi went to his room.

Much later, after a miserable dinner, surrounded by a thick, sullen silence, Malachi lay on his bed, waiting for his dad to turn in. When he heard his father go into his bedroom across the hall and close the door, Malachi got up. Making as little noise as possible, he went to the back door and gently eased it open and slipped out onto the back porch. Two, three more steps and he was in the backyard.

He glanced next door at Uncle Jack's house—just one light on—Thomas, he guessed, house-sitting. Uncle Jack had gone to some conference or something. Malachi took a deep breath and shot straight up into the cool night air, a shooting star in reverse, blue-white light streaming behind him in a shimmering tail.

By the time Malachi came home the second time it was late, a little after eleven. Malachi knew he was going to be exhausted in school tomorrow, but he didn't care. He could fly. He landed on the front stoop and standing beneath the outside light, fished his key out of his pocket and unlocked the front door. He stepped into a silent house. The lamp on the end table, beside the couch, was on, making a soft yellow circle on the rug.

After cutting off the lamp, he went down the hall. No light edged his father's door. The bathroom night-light made a tiny white sphere, illuminating the linoleum and the bath mat. Malachi looked at himself in the mirror. His eyes weren't just golden-brown anymore. They were becoming the color of the gold crayon in the Crayola box. For a brief moment, his eyes glowed and just as quickly the glow winked out. His hair—was it getting even lighter? And his ears—Malachi turned on the overhead light and turned his head to one side and then the other. Yes, his ears were getting pointed. Dad couldn't ignore these things, could he? Like he ignored the floating bowls? He knew all that was happening wasn't normal. Was he—no, not going crazy?

Dad, you know; I know you know. Why won't you talk to me?

Before leaving the bathroom, Malachi pulled the night-light out of the socket. He had told his dad a hundred times he was too old for a night-light. He very slowly and carefully opened his bedroom door at the end of the hall. The lamps on his night table and his desk were on. His father lay on his back on Malachi's bed, fast asleep and snoring.

April 30, 1991
The Technician
"Campus Magic"

Today is Beltaine or May Eve. Walpurgis Night. Uh? Like, so what? Walpurgis Night, the eve of May 1 or May Day, is, according to legend, the night when witches fly. Beltaine is one of the four most sacred days in the Celtic calendar, and at midnight the way between here and the Otherworld is open. And you are still going uh and so what, right?

*   *   *

A lot of your classmates aren't. According to statistics just released from the Campus Ministries Office, there are at least 250 undergraduates and about 70 graduate students who list their religious affiliation as either Wiccan, Druid, Pagan or Neo-Pagan, or the Old Religion. A coven meets regularly at the McKimmon Center, every third Thursday.

The next time you take a seat in English 111 or Compsci 101, take a good look at the people around you. They probably look pretty normal to you, don't they? Your typical NCSU students. Engineers, foresters, ag majors, pre-vets, teachers, right? Well, one of those civil engineer-wannabes or one of those pre-vets—anyone of your classmates—could be a real, live practicing witch. That's right, you heard me: a witch, or warlock, a wizard. A practitioner of the occult . . .

Russell Avery White

Russell slowly dried himself with a thick, orange towel. He wanted to stretch out the time in his bathroom sanctuary as long as possible. The steam from his shower had clouded the medicine cabinet mirror, the tiles on the wall, even the window. Russell sighed as he rubbed down his legs. He knew he couldn't stay too long, or his step-mother would start complaining how he was monopolizing the room and didn't he realize other people had to take showers and use the john? Didn't the boy ever think of anybody but hisself? Larry? Can't you make your son behave?

Better not push my luck, he thought, and wrapped the towel around his waist and picked up his clothes from the floor. As Russell turned to go, he stopped and looked back into the mirror. For a very brief moment, his eyes had seemed to be greener and brighter than they had ever been. Russell blinked and looked again. The extra-green brightness was gone—had it really been there? A trick of the early light? He rubbed his eyes and took his T-shirt and wiped the fog off the mirror. Nope, his eyes looked like they always did, a grass green, flecks of brown. Must have been seeing things, and feeling things, the fog on the mirror had been warm, Russell thought, and hurried out of the bathroom. He may have been imagining his eyes were turning greener, but he hadn't imagined the noise he had just heard through the thin trailer wall. Somebody was up in his daddy and stepmama's bedroom, and moving around.

Russell listened at the bedroom door for a second: his daddy was awake. He could tell by the heavy footsteps and the sounds of drawers being pulled out. Russell hurried even more quickly down the hall and into his bedroom, pulling the door closed behind him. Meeting his daddy early in the morning, being in between the man and the toilet or the shower, were things Russell avoided. Too many fat lips. Getting in Jeanie's way wasn't much better, although she never hit him. Jeanie just yelled or called his daddy, and then he would get hit anyway. Now that she was pregnant, he barely had to look at her before she started calling his daddy.

His real mama would treat him better, Russell thought. He picked up her picture from his dresser and touched her face with the tips of his fingers. He remembered she had cried a lot before she left; she had cried so much she stayed home from work and wouldn't get out of bed. He had tried to cheer her up, make her laugh, tell her dumb jokes, but nothing had worked. This fall would make two years since he had seen her. She had left when they lived in Lawton County, Oklahoma, near his daddy's folks. Russell had been in the second grade. His little brother, Adam, was starting kindergarten. Adam was having a good year; Russell wasn't. They had been in Tulsa the year before and Russell knew nobody in the rural Lawton County elementary school and he couldn't seem to figure out how to please his teacher. It didn't help that Russell had repeated kindergarten and first grade and was two years older and a head taller than the rest of the class. The second week of school the teacher had told him he didn't know how to be anybody's friend.

"You're like some great big, clumsy dog. Knocking people this way and that and then expect everyone to like you and you're surprised when they don't. It doesn't work that way, Russell. To have friends, you have to be a friend."

Russell had gone up to her desk later to ask her to tell him how to be a friend. He had waited patiently, watching her until she looked up. He wished he could write as pretty as she was doing.

"About how to have friends, I just wanted to ask you to please tell me—"

"Go. Sit. Down."

Three weeks later, the day before Halloween, Russell had come home to an empty house. No mama, no little brother, no daddy. No note on the refrigerator beneath the teapot magnet. No note on the pad by the phone on the kitchen counter. His daddy finally came home, hours later, to find Russell asleep on the couch, in front of the 6 o'clock local news.

"So that's why she kept the baby home today. Took every dime in the place. Bet she cleaned out the bank accounts, too," his daddy had said, after searching the house, Russell trailing behind him, sniffling. "Hell, don't cry, boy. I ain't got time for it. C'mon. Guess I can take that construction job in Texas—get yer things. Going to my daddy's."

"Daddy, where'd Mama go? Why'd she leave? I didn't do nothing; I didn't get in trouble at schoooool—" Russell started crying louder.

"Go on, Russell, get yer stuff. Stop crying 'fore I give you something to really cry about. She just left, that's all."

His granddaddy told Russell he thought it was the medicine she'd been taking. Anti-depressants. Made her act funny.

A card came at Christmas, with a Tucson return address on one side, and a yellow cartoon map of Arizona on the other. Merry Christmas from Mama and Adam scrawled beside the return address. Russell's granddaddy helped him write back, but Russell never got a reply and he never saw his mama or his little brother again. He didn't see his daddy again, except for infrequent visits, until the next summer. Larry White showed up one hot July afternoon with a new wife, Lizzie, and a new pickup, and took Russell to Kansas. They only went back to Oklahoma, once, to bury Russell's granddaddy. Lizzie left, in a flurry of overturned chairs and broken lamps, shortly afterward. Jeanie was next and a move to North Carolina to be near her folks and, as his daddy said, one construction job is as good as another.

"Hurry up and get dressed, Russell. You don't wanna miss the bus. Ain't got the time to give you a ride this morning. You hear me, boy? And don't take such long damn showers—hardly any hot water left." His daddy's voice came through Russell's bedroom door loud and clear.

"Boy?"

"I hear you," Russell said, frozen by his dresser, his mama's picture in his hands. When he heard his daddy walk off to the bathroom, he set her picture down and got dressed as quickly as he could, jamming his feet into his tennis shoes. He could tie them on the bus. Before he ran to the kitchen, Russell took one last look at his eyes in the mirror. It must be the light in the glass, he thought, and ran out the door. For a second his eyes had seemed to be glowing with a green light.

Behind Russell, one thin curl of smoke drifted up and out of the wastebasket by his dresser.

*   *   *

Jeffrey Arthur Gates

Ellen Clark looked at the clock on top of the refrigerator. Ten till eight. Twenty minutes to Jeff's school, then another ten or fifteen more in rush hour traffic on the Beltline to work. Where was the boy? Ellen sighed and set her purse down on the kitchen table. She wished Fred were here so she could ask him to get the boy, but he had had to go to work early and Jeff had promised the night before to get up when his alarm went off, get dressed without dawdling, eat, and be ready to go when she was ready. And the boy had gotten up, washed, dressed, and ate with no dawdling, daydreaming, or malingering. Then half-an-hour ago he had disappeared into his bedroom, saying he was only going to be a minute.

This is silly, Ellen thought, glancing again at her watch. *I know the boy's had a rough time and that he's only been here a few weeks, I know that. And I also know that getting up and going back to school is just what he needs, to start going on, putting what happened in the past. If only he was going to Nottingham Heights now, instead of Brewer.* There was no good way to get to Brewer without the Beltline and Ellen hated the Beltline. She had tried to convince Jeff's social worker and his therapist to let her enroll the boy at Nottingham Heights, but both women had refused.

"Mrs. Clark, you have had how many foster children? Then you know how temporary placements can be. The boy's father hasn't even been tried yet, and we're still trying to find the mother. We like to avoid any more changes in the boy's life than necessary. If Jeff is still with you this fall, then we'll see about putting him in Nottingham," the social worker had said, looking over her glasses and past her paper-strewn desk.

Ellen knew the social worker was right. Still, it was a nuisance, and now the boy was late.

"Jeff! Come on, it's time to go. We have to leave right now. Jeff!"

Jeff sat in the middle of his bed, surrounded by an apatosaurus, a tyrannosaurus, and a pterodactyl. He sighed. He didn't want to make Mrs. Clark mad, but he didn't want to go back to Brewer Elementary, either. He picked up the pterodactyl and started making dinosaur noises as he swooped it down to attack the tyrannosaurus, who was busily trying to chew on the apatosaurus at the same time. What would he say to the other kids? Did they know? Those looks the teacher had given him. And the counselor: he should never have told her. Never. If Jeff hadn't told her, everything would still be the same. He'd be in his own house, in his own bedroom, and all of his dinosaurs would be there, instead of only the half he had managed to take with him when the social worker had come for him. His father would never have looked at him that way and called him a bastard son-of-a-bitch, a traitor—instead his father would—Jeff shook his head, shattering that thought into as many pieces as he could manage.

The bedroom door opened and Mrs. Clark stuck her head in. "It's time to go to school. Come on. It'll be all right, you'll see."

Jeff swooped the pterodactyl down again, to shoo the rex off the apatosaurus. "You all say that. It'll be all right. What am I supposed to say to everybody? About where I was, about what happened."

"Jeff, you don't have to say anything. Remember, I told you the social worker and I both talked to your teachers? It really will be all right. Really. Come on," Mrs. Clark said and walked over to take his hand.

"Okay," Jeff said and let her lead him out of the room. "Oh, wait a sec, I still have the pterodactyl." He threw it over his shoulder and then followed Mrs. Clark. Neither one of them saw the faint blue trail the pterodactyl left in the air, like the fading contrail of a jet.

Hazel Guinevere Richards

Hazel skipped first grade against her kindergarten teacher's wishes.

"Yes, Dr. Richards, Mrs. Richards, your granddaughter is reading on a third-grade level and doing math at a sixth-grade level, but she doesn't play well with the other children. No—she doesn't play much at all with the other children. She isn't socially mature," Miss Kowalski had said, steepling her hands together over her desk.

"But why should Hazel waste her time in first grade?" Mrs. Richards asked. "Once I learn how to make a certain kind of pot, I don't need to relearn it."

"She would be bored in first grade, Miss Kowalski. She might even be bored in second grade," Dr. Richards said.

"There are gifted and talented programs which will compensate, but that's not my point. Hazel will be in GT whatever grade she is in. My point is that Hazel doesn't have any friends. None," Miss Kowalski said, giving up on her carefully selected ed psych terminology.

Dr. Richards and Mrs. Richards looked at each other. "Well," Dr. Richards said, after clearing his throat, "we don't think of that as a great handicap. I'm very involved in my research and my teaching and my wife is involved with her art and her teaching. I have colleagues at NC State and IBM, and my wife has artist colleagues, but we don't see these people socially, not very often anyway. A social life is not something we feel a great need for. When Hazel's parents were alive, they were the same way, busy with their careers and little time for social amenities. We think Hazel should skip first grade, Miss Kowalski. It will be easier for all of us if she does. She will be happier if she is busier in school, and we will be happier."

Miss Kowalski sighed.

Alexander and computers came into Hazel's life not long after Miss Kowalski and the school had given in and agreed to let Hazel skip first grade to second. Her grandfather brought home a computer for Hazel one bright, May afternoon, lugging the boxes up the stairs to her bedroom himself, not trusting the deliverymen not to drop everything. There were already assorted computers, modems, and printers of one kind or another all over the house. Diskettes lay around like old magazines.

Hawthorne Richards talked to Hazel as he slit open the boxes with a Swiss army knife. "If your father was alive, he'd tell you I was never very good with children. Your mother would probably agree. Haze, they'd be right. Your grandmama and I are thinking this computer will make it easier for all of us. And no granddaughter of mine is going to start second grade without a computer. I know you had one in your kindergarten class and there will be one, maybe two or three, in your second grade class, but I want you to have one right here, right on your desk. I want you to be able to use one like you use a pencil. And it will keep you busy. Your father would have told you that neither of us ever had much time for children."

Hazel had just sat in the middle of the bed and nodded while her grandfather talked and opened boxes. Hazel could barely remember her father and mother. They had been killed in a car wreck when she was two, coming home on I-40 from a reception in Chapel Hill. Her father was the designated driver and had been as sober as a stone. The driver who tried to pass them wasn't. Hazel's memories of her parents were nebulous at best: the smell of cigarette smoke for her father and a white blur with a husky voice for her mother. The two people in the photograph on her grandmother's dresser were strangers.

Hazel's grandmother gave her Alexander the day after the computer arrived. Anne Richards called Hazel down to her basement studio, which next to her bedroom, was Hazel's favorite room in the house. There was a kiln in one corner and racks and tables were piled with pots, bowls, pitchers, vases, and curious sculptures of animals and people's heads. Sacks of clay and jars of glaze were neatly arranged on shelves facing the finished pottery. Hazel loved to come down early on weekend mornings and watch her grandmother work. The sun would slowly come in through tiny windows at the top of the walls and brush across the pottery, gilding the earthen hues with yellow and white fire.

Her grandmother looked up from where she was sitting on the floor and shushed Hazel with her finger as she came down the stairs.

"Come look in the box," she whispered and pointed to a small, cardboard box right beside her. Hazel knelt down and peered inside. There was a tiny, grey ball of fur inside, a sleeping grey ball of fur; Hazel could see its back rise and fall.

"The vet said he's a lilac-point—see, he's just a bit darker on his face and his feet and his tail, sort of a blue-grey. Blue eyes. He's just part Siamese, though—see those ghost stripes on his haunches and his tail and how big his paws are? Some alley cat tainted his royal blood. But the vet said a mix would probably have a better personality than a purebred. This is my congratulations-on-skipping-first-grade present and my not-so-good-with-children present. I sometimes wonder how we managed to raise your father," her grandmother said absently. She carefully scooped up the yawning fur ball and put the kitten in Hazel's hands.

"But never mind that. Your grandfather wanted me to get a puppy, but I like cats better. They don't require as much time or attention as a dog. There was a brown kitten that I thought might match your hair, but there was something about this one. I think his eyes will match yours—see how blue they are?"

At five-going-on-six, Hazel didn't quite understand her grandparents' concerns with their parenting skills. They were her parents. At eight-almost-nine, when Hazel was in the fourth grade, and her grandfather brought home a new computer for her and gave the same speech again, Hazel paid no attention. Background noise, just things they seemed to like to say, she thought as her grandfather unpacked the new computer and explained why he wanted her to have it and that he and her grandmother hoped she would be self-sufficient, as her father had been, and not need them so much. Hazel had already learned how to be invisible in the house when either of her grandparents was busy. She could be invisible for days, she thought, as she leafed through the computer manual and the manual for the new software game her grandfather had brought home with the computer, Worldmaker. Alexander drowsed in an open window and a breeze came in from the warm, late April afternoon. She couldn't wait to play the game.

"You're supposed to take them through their history, up to modern times, without losing them to disease, invasion, a natural disaster, whatever," her grandfather said as he pushed in the last plug and flicked on the monitor and the hard drive. "Supposed to be for eighth or ninth grade, but I think you can handle it. Should be a lot of fun, Haze. Let's see what happens when we boot the game up. Okay, here's the first menu. You have to set up the valley the tribe will live in first—see, here are your choices for the valley."

Hazel slid into the chair facing the monitor. *A long wide valley with a slow, meandering old river? Or a short, narrow valley with a quick, young river cutting a gorge down the middle? Or . . .* Hazel looked up. Her grandfather was gone. Alexander had curled up on the edge of the bed, just close enough for her to reach over and pat his head from time to time. The valley needed a name. A blank square blinked on the screen.

"Alexzel, the Valley of Alexzel," Hazel said, liking the sound made when she blurred her and Alex's names. She typed in the letters and pressed enter. When she did there was a sudden sharp pop and a blue light flashed, as if a camera had gone off right behind Hazel's head. For a brief moment the room seemed bathed in the blue light, a light that was so bright and intense that Hazel covered her face and squeezed her eyes shut. Alexander yowled and jumped off the bed to hide beneath it.

Hazel opened her eyes. The blue light was gone. Everything in the room looked to be just the same. The name Alexzel glowed in the middle of the screen. An electrical charge? Lightning? Hazel had never heard of blue lightning and outside the sky was clear and fair.

"Alex—what do you think we should do?" Hazel asked softly. To her surprise, Alexander came out from under the bed, dust clinging to his whiskers. He shook himself and jumped up into Hazel's chair. He sat up and peered into the screen and then gently tapped the keyboard with his right paw. For another brief moment, his eyes glowed an intense blue.

Thomas John Ruggles

Thomas backed out of his father's driveway at exactly 10:45 P.M. They had told him to be punctual and arrive not a minute before or a minute late. He had timed the trip to Clemmons State Forest twice before. He should be at the forest entrance at 11:35. He would sit in the car until 11:42 and then walk down the path to the fire. He glanced over at the Tyson's. Front light on, the living room. Awful late for Ben to be expecting company, he thought as he drove off.

Thomas shook his head. How could he have been so blind all these years? The Ruggles had moved next door to the Tysons when Thomas was fourteen and he had never suspected, never even guessed just who and what Malachi was. Or who and what Valeria was. Or where she had gone. No, he hadn't really spent much time with his father from thirteen to sixteen—just a few weeks during the summer, every other Christmas and Thanksgiving. While his parents had their custody fights, Thomas had been forced to live with his mother. He shook, trying to get rid of those memories. But he had babysat for Malachi more than once when he had moved back after his mother's suicide, and he had never guessed. Sat right beside Valeria once—she had even touched him. But I was just a kid then, he thought. His father knew, and, Ben, of course. But they hadn't seen fit to tell him. No matter. His eyes had been opened; he *knew*.

He had felt the first twinge at Samhain, a brief spark, a rush of energy in the ether. It was his first time with the Glenwood coven and he had thought it was just the excitement of being there with the others, naked before the God and the Goddess. But then he had felt the energy rush a few days later, when he had gone home to retrieve some more of his books and ran into Malachi Tyson. In fact he had surprised Malachi in the backyard and Thomas was sure if he had surprised the boy a few minutes earlier, he would have seen magic in action.

"Hey, Malachi, what are you doing?" Thomas had yelled over the chain-link fence separating his father's and the Tysons' backyards. Malachi had jumped, startled, and then had run over to the fence to shake Thomas's hand. In that touch he had felt the charge again—almost like touching an electric fence. And he remembered: when he was thirteen and home for the summer and Valeria had touched him—the same charge.

There was no doubt now, Thomas knew: here was a tool provided for him, a way to access power, power that he had only dreamed of. That had been the only good thing he had gotten from the three years he had lived with his mother: power was essential.

Thomas pulled into the parking lot at the entrance to Clemmons State Forest at 11:36. Tonight was the Third Challenge. Once passed, Thomas would be a full initiate in the coven. He would be a high priest of the mysteries of the Old Religion, the hidden knowledge of the God and the Goddess, knowledge older than Christ, knowledge those weakling Christians had suppressed and then denied ever existed. Fools. Now, tonight, the power that had been surging in him, simmering like water almost ready to boil, would be finally and fully awake; Thomas was sure of it. And with this power, taking Malachi and the greater power should be easy.

11:42.

Thomas got out of the car and walked across the graveled lot, the blue stones crunching beneath his shoes. He had timed this walk twice before as well. It was exactly 11:50 when he could see the flames flickering through the trees. The air was redolent with incense and smoke. He could smell the heat, as he inhaled, drawing fire into his nostrils. When Thomas could see the others, their bodies white and dark shadows around the fire, he stopped and looked for the shelter someone had told him would be nearby. Thomas undressed carefully, neatly folding his pants and shirt, then his underwear and socks, and everything in a tidy pile at the end of a picnic bench. Then he took the binding cord he had been given and wrapped the braided and knotted red cord around his waist, just as he had been taught, so that he could pull the frayed end through the loop.

There. He was ready.

Now he could feel the heat of the fire all over his naked skin. The fire's shadows bathed the bodies of the others and he could feel them, at the periphery of his aura, which shimmered all around him. The others were waiting for him, waiting for the high priestess to call Thomas for the Third Challenge.

Thomas.

Thomas walked down the last stretch of the path leading to the clearing and the fire and the coven. This time he could feel the sharp gravel on his feet. He took deep breaths as he walked; Thomas had never felt more alive in his life, more aware. The hot, perfumed air, heavy with incense, the insane insect chirping, the sweaty smell of all the bodies, and yes, even the trees, he could feel their awareness, old, profound, slow.

Thomas stopped walking three paces outside the circle. He felt the air shift when the others stepped aside and let him in to face the priestess and the stone altar.

The priestess's face was hidden behind a white mask; all Thomas could see were her dark, dark blue eyes, watching him, her black hair loose and curling with sweat. He focused on her and her alone, her body shining in the firelight and candlelight, a single pale shadow. Everything on the altar between Thomas and the priestess had become different-colored shadows: the pentacle, the bell, and the cups were copper; the athame knife silver-white, and each of the black candles seemed to have disappeared except for their flames. Thomas inhaled and exhaled, filling himself with incense and nothing but incense, and with each breath, it seemed his skin was dissolving, his aura expanding to merge, one glowing filament at a time with all the others. And there were so many others, bits and fragments of their thoughts, feelings darting about and through him—needs, hungers, wants, desires. Behind the priestess the cauldron bubbled and boiled. Thomas heard footsteps behind him, but he didn't turn and look; he remained as still as possible. He felt fingers on his back, his neck, then a blindfold covered his eyes. His hands were pulled behind him and tied together, and then a cord was passed around his neck. His feet were tied together and then whoever was behind him stepped away. Thomas could see through the blindfold the red of the fire.

Then the priestess spoke:

May the Most Powerful,
the great root of existence;
all-pervasive, omnipotent, eternal;
may the Goddess,
the Queen of the Moon;
may the God,
Horned Hunter, Lord of the Night,
may all the unseen Powers:
the stones, the elements,
the stars in the sky, the earth beneath our feet,
bless this place, this time
and I/we/he who are/am/is with Thee.

Thomas answered, words he had practiced over and over and over again:

O Most Powerful,
O Queen of the Night,
O Lord of the Night,
O Most Mysterious, dark, unseen, hidden,
I stand in this place,
open to You.
Open to the changes

in my body, mind, and spirit.
I am Yours,
I am Yours forever, O Mother Goddess, O Father God.

Your energy fills me,
it fills my body, my mind, my spirit,
O Great Goddess, O Great God,
I am one with Your Being.
I am one with Your Being.
I am one with Your Being.

Somewhere a temple singing bowl was stroked and almost simultaneously the others began to drone: "*Aaaaaaaaaoooooooooouuuuuu-uuuiiiiiiiiieeeeeeeee.*" A drum began to beat. Thomas heard, barely, other footsteps in front of him, and then something cold and metallic and sharp pricked his skin between his navel and his groin, his erect penis.

"Thomas, you stand on the boundaries between the known world and the world of the Dark Ones, the Dread Lords, the world of power. Are you ready? Are you prepared? Are you brave?"

"I am ready. I am prepared. I have the courage."

Thomas felt pressure then, first above his heart, then on the opposite side of his chest, then to the right and left of his navel. With each touch the high priestess spoke: "We mark you, then, with Air, with Fire, with Water, with Earth. You are ours."

Behind him Thomas could hear the others moving, their breathing fast and hard. The weaving dance began and someone drew Thomas in and everyone was touching, being touched, everywhere. His blindfold was taken away, and there was no part of his skin that was not touched, caressed, felt by hands and mouths. And Thomas touched and stroked and caressed with his hands and his mouth. The high priestess sang:

O Most Powerful,
O Great Goddess, O Great God,
As you are One,
So, we become one with our brother, Thomas.
O Great Goddess, O Great God,
Let us celebrate the Oneness . . .

Thomas ran, trees all around him, close, dark, green, black. A full moon marked his path as he ran, his feet slapping the earth, cobwebs catching his skin, snagging his hair, branches slapping his chest, cutting his skin. He was bleeding; he could feel his own warm blood on his chest, his arms, his face. The trees moved in a rhythm that matched his heart, the pulsing of his blood. Finally, his chest burning, Thomas came to a bramble of thick, close branches, with thorns that pricked and drew more blood. He cupped one hand over his genitals and pushed his way through the bramble into an open glade. He stood still, panting and bleeding, the warm air tingling his skin. He could still smell the cinnamon of the altar incense, the aroma of the cauldron, the body of the priestess. She stood in the middle of the glade, Aradia, the Goddess, and soon everything, every smell, every echoing touch, was gone: only the Goddess remained. He was Thomas, he was Herne, the Horned God, and he took her there in the tall grass, the earth, the moonlight and the starlight.

The first witch Thomas met was Donald, the roommate with whom Thomas shared a North Raleigh apartment. He had met Donald at the Central Carolina Bank, after reading a note on a bulletin board advertising for a roommate. Donald was from a small mountain hollow deep in the Smokies and he was different from anybody Thomas had ever met. Donald spoke differently, moved differently, and he even smelled differently. A faint touch of spice, of cinnamon, sometimes clove, lingered in any room in the apartment after Donald had been there.

Thomas learned Donald was a witch the second day after he had moved in. He came home after work and walked into an aromatic spicy cloud. The odor led him back to Donald's room where he found his roommate busily arranging things on a small table covered with a midnight-blue cloth. Incense burned on the dresser and the night table. Thomas stood behind Donald, watching as the other man took two white candles out of a leather bag and set one on either side of a curiously carved silver cup. Then he pulled out a silver disk inscribed with a five-pointed star and placed it before the cup.

"What are you doing? What's all this stuff?" Thomas asked as Donald next pulled out two knives from the bag, one black-handled, the other white-handled.

"Setting up the altar," Donald said, sounding surprised. He laid the two knives on the table and turned to face Thomas. "You really don't know?"

"Altar? Know what? Are you in some sort of weird cult?" Thomas asked and sat down on Donald's bed.

Donald pulled out of his bag a slender stick of light-colored wood. "You really don't know? I don't believe it. When we first met, when we shook hands, I could feel you'd been around magic. The stuff is all over you; your aura is so charged with magic that you glow. You're pulling my leg, right? This," Donald said and waved his stick at the table, "is a Wiccan personal altar. This stick is a wand. I'm a Wiccan, a witch. Aren't you?"

Thomas shook his head. "The closest I've ever come to magic was Dungeons and Dragons in high school and college. And I quit playing because it was just a game; it wasn't real. All this is the real stuff? Are you crazy or what?"

Donald said nothing for a long moment. Then he tucked his dark hair behind his ears and took two small, silver bowls out of his bag. "You've been near magic for a very long time; you didn't know it, but you have been near it. And I'm not crazy and this is real. I'll prove it to you. My coven meets tonight. Come with me. Hey, you've got nothing to lose, right? And everybody's naked," Donald added, grinning.

"Everybody?"

"Everybody."

Thomas shrugged. What did he have to lose? Hanging out with naked women couldn't be so bad, now, could it? And if this was real—well. Thomas had liked playing Dungeons and Dragons the most when he was the gamemaster, when he was the one telling the others what to do and when and where to do it. It had been the power Thomas had liked the most. But it wasn't real; it was only a game. Thomas wanted real power, power he could touch, move, taste. He wanted to be filled with power. He wanted never again to be as powerless as he had been when he had lived with his mother. And as for the magic Thomas was supposed to have been near— what was Donald talking about? His aura glowed with magic? And why did all this make him think of Valeria, the long-gone wife of his father's best friend, Ben. Valeria? Power? Maybe going to Donald's coven could help him figure it all out.

Donald's coven met in a large, open room at the NC State McKimmon Center. Thomas was amazed. "You mean the university lets witches meet on campus?" he whispered to Donald as they entered the building.

"Sure. They have to. Freedom of religion, you know. State university, paid for by public funds. Other religious groups meet on campus. C'mon, I want you to meet some people, then I'll show you where to leave your clothes."

Donald introduced Thomas to an engineering professor, her

husband, and their teenaged daughter and son. An English professor who wrote poetry. Two graduate students in crop science, who were working on a joint dissertation on the effects of the moon on the growing season of corn. A couple of undergraduates—one from Durham, the other from Salisbury.

"Everybody here seems so—so normal, Don," Thomas said, still whispering as they undressed in a smaller side room. Donald stepped out of his underwear and laughed.

"What did you expect? Old men and women with warts on their noses?"

"Well, yeah," Thomas said. "I did."

"There are a few of those back home in the hills. Not too many here in Raleigh," Donald said, laughing. "C'mon."

All the ritual Thomas had expected and wanted was there: the incense, the cauldron, flickering candles everywhere, and naked bodies. But something was missing, something he had wanted—yes, there was power, of a sorts, but it, it—it just didn't.

"Do you understand, Don? The coven lacked something I expected. It's all real, just like you said, but, still. I don't know; I don't think I am making sense," Thomas said the next morning as he spooned more sugar into his coffee. He liked it with lots of sugar and lots of milk.

Donald didn't say anything as he stared hard at Thomas. The pause grew even longer as he scraped butter across his pumpernickel bagel. He finally spoke, "I think I know what you are talking about. We're Brethren of the Right-Hand Path, practitioners of theurgy; you're looking for the Brethren of the Left-Hand Path, goetia."

"What?" Thomas said, trying to sound casual, but he understood what Donald was saying. He knew what Donald was going to say. He could feel the next words coming, almost as if they were hovering next to his ear.

"I'm a White Witch. You're looking for Black Witches."

Donald refused to help Thomas find a black coven, insisting there were none in Raleigh or anywhere in Wake County. Thomas knew he was lying. Donald finally moved out and Thomas started looking for himself. First in libraries and bookstores for anything and everything on witchcraft, the occult, astrology, necromancy, Satanism, demonology, ceremonial magic, invocations, conjurations, planetary magic, spell casting and the making of charms, talismans, and amulets, curses, candles, and all forms of divination. He exhausted the Cameron Village branch of the Wake County Library quickly, but Walden's and B. Dalton's seemed to have an endless supply: *The Modern Witch's Spellbook, Wicca: A Guide for the Solitary Practitioner, The Complete Book of Spells, Ceremonies, & Magic.* Gardner, Crowley, Nostradamus.

"Can't keep 'em on the shelves," the manager at the Crabtree Valley B. Dalton's told him. "People can't just get enough of this occult stuff."

Thomas understood. He gave up the North Raleigh Wake Forest Road apartment and found a tiny studio downtown, in Boylan Heights and read and read and read, black candles burning all around him. He was *close*; Thomas knew that, but not close enough.

His father tried to stop him.

"Tom, Tom, what is all this? All these books, these candles, and the place reeks. What are you doing?" Jack Ruggles had said, picking up and putting down the various things on Thomas's altar. "This is witchcraft. Are you crazy? Your apartment feels bad, son—this isn't dabbling in love charms. Son, you've got to stop, before it's too late. Why are you doing this?"

Thomas looked coldly at his father from behind his altar, his books on the occult in disordered stacks behind him. There was little else in the apartment: his bed stuck in one corner beneath a window, the kitchen nook, the bathroom next to that. One couch, a chair, another table, and shelves. Thomas had built two walls of shelves for his books and the herbs and stones and dried flowers he was accumulating. "Do you think my mortal soul is in danger?"

Jack laid down the pentacle and looked at his son. "Yes, I do. I think your soul is in danger. You have absolutely no idea what you are playing with here—"

"I'm not playing; I'm serious."

"You have no idea. This isn't Dungeons and Dragons, Tom. This is real. Magic is real—"

"Oh, and how do you know? What secrets have you been hiding from me? Tell me." He waited, counting off seconds in his head, *one one thousand, two two thousand,* one full minute. "I knew you wouldn't; keep little Thomas in the dark. Well, it's in the dark I'm looking. I need this," he said and gestured to include everything in his apartment. "I need—I want all that this means. I won't be weak or afraid anymore. Nobody will be able to hurt me ever again. You left me, Dad, with Mama when I was thirteen. You let her take me, that crazy woman."

"I lost the custody fight, Thomas. You know that. And you got to come home in the summer—"

"Just for a few weeks out of three long, long years. You didn't try hard enough," Thomas said, enjoying the pain in his father's face.

"By the time she finally offed herself, I had lived with her for three years. Three fucking years. Don't tell me about all the different lawyers you tried. That you got me therapy after Mama's suicide. Don't tell me anything. Get out."

Thomas hadn't spoken to his father since.

It was only a few weeks later, one Saturday morning, that Thomas met a sister of the Left-Hand Path. He was browsing in the New Age Bookstore at Little Five Points. Except for the clerk at the register, the store was empty. Behind the clerk were crystals and gemstones, stones for healing and charms. Trays with amethysts for protection from sickness and danger, iolite to deflect hexes, garnets to increase endurance and vigor. Rose quartz to stimulate love, promote fidelity. Blue topazes to enhance sexual energy. Citrine, peridot, moonstones. Then candles, candles, candles, and more candles. Lemon-scented, rose, jasmine, ginger. Rings, charms, amulets. Runes. Books of spells, divination, Celtic lore and magic, yoga, shamanic magic, but none, to Thomas's sharp disappointment, on black magic. He was leafing through a Tarot guide and didn't look up when the door opened and closed, the door chimes ringing.

"This is the book you need to read now," someone said, and Thomas looked up, startled, at the small, fair woman who stood there and the book she was holding out to him. Her hair was silver-white and her eyes—almost a white-blue. But young, Thomas thought, despite the hair, young, maybe his age. "This is *The Gospel of the Witches*. It's what you're looking for. I came here this morning knowing I would meet someone like you. Your aura is charged with magic; I felt you a mile away. You won't need that Tarot book."

"You felt me, here, and came to give me this book?"

"Yes. Now take it, I promise you won't regret it," she said.

Thomas reached for the book and when he touched it, his body shook, as if he had a sudden, quick fever.

"Read the book and then call the number written on the inside cover."

Thomas nodded, hugging the book to his chest, holding himself to keep from shaking, from crying out. The small woman nodded, touched his arm briefly—a sudden quick shock of current—and left the store.

When Thomas woke up the morning after Beltaine he didn't know where he was or what had happened. Everything around him seemed unfamiliar, brand new and unknown. He closed his eyes, reopened them, and looked again: he was in his own apartment, he was in his own bed. How did he get here? He had been in the forest, around the fire and the cauldron. The others had been there as well, and the priestess, and he and she, and the others—

Thomas got out of bed and stood up. He was still naked except for the binding cord, but his body was different. Scratches, cuts, bruises, dirt, and dried blood were all over his legs, his torso, his arms. There was dried blood and dirt on the sheets in his bed.

Everything had really happened. And not just fucking the priestess in the woods. The others—men and women, fucking, being fucked, mouths, hands—God, it was no wonder his dick and his ass were so sore. Thomas went into the bathroom and stared into the medicine cabinet mirror. His eyes—they were different, weren't they? Yes, darker and redder. And just barely visible, at the edges of his skin, a shimmering, a flicker like a candle flame in wind, his aura? He was hard again and his skin was flushed, warm. He touched himself—a crackling of electricity—and his entire body shuddered in a sudden orgasm. For a long moment, he leaned into the mirror, breathing hard, his hands pressing into the wall. Finally Thomas stepped into the shower, not caring if the cuts and scratches stung from the hot water. He soaped and rinsed, soaped and rinsed, soaped and rinsed, with one thought a litany in his head: *I have tasted real power.*

His mother had been crazy, but still the judge had given her custody over his father. How could the judge do that? Because he had power. He just had to slap that gavel on wood and everybody had to do just what he said. Thomas's father had cried out when the judge read his decision: no, no, no, noooooooooooo. But the judge had ordered Jack Ruggles to be silent and Thomas had watched his father be silent. Thomas's mother had the same power and control over Thomas the judge had. She made all the rules and all the consequences for breaking them and she changed the rules and the consequences whenever she felt like it. Sometimes being late from school meant no TV. Or sweeping a sidewalk with a whiskbroom. Or sitting perfectly still for hours—any movement meant the time had to start all over again. Thomas ran away, once, twice, three times. The mother the police met was someone he only saw in public: sweet, charming, beautiful, oozing sex. Sometimes he had to do that for her, too. There were other games—the ones with sex and death as the prize, with ropes, with chairs, a tree in the backyard, and Thomas touching her, the rope on her neck until the last possible minute—

God, how he hated her. He hated even more being weak, defenseless, afraid.

Thomas watched her die. He was sixteen and finally taller and

*stronger and she played the death-and-sex game one last time, a game
she hadn't played in over a year, and he let her die. He watched her
die hanging from the tree. It was the first time he had ever won the
game—that he had ever had enough power. And it tasted sweet and
sharp and with a bitter tang and it filled him up, making him hard
and strong and powerful.*

Finally Thomas cut off the water and stepped out of the tub and
wrapped himself in a towel. He stared in the mirror again: yes, his
eyes were darker and redder—the iris—not his cornea. His aura still
burned in a faint, cold flame around him. *I am a black witch. I can
do magic, cast spells, incantations.*

He went and dug out *The Gospel of the Witches* from a stack near
his bed. Thomas opened the book to a place he had marked some
time ago and sat down on his bed to reread the passage he had high-
lighted in bright blue. He glanced at the clock on the nightstand:
half-past ten. Thomas shrugged; he would call in sick in a little
while; tell his supervisor he had turned off his alarm. Something.
Ah, yes. It was all so clear. The passage Thomas reread was an alle-
gory of some kind and a prophecy, or so the priestess had told him.
Of what, no one had yet been able to figure out, although sign after
sign was being fulfilled: the return of magic, increased worship of
the horned god and the goddess, the manifestation of power. The
Change was near; its fulcrum had taken human form. If Thomas
could control the fulcrum, well, now . . .

The Chamber of the Dodecagon, The Library Tower, The White City, Faerie

Larissa, the Second arrived at the council chambers first, wanting
to be alone before the others arrived. There was nothing special the
Second wanted to do there; she just wanted to sit in the ancient,
long-unused room and be quiet. She knew that when all the others
came, this sweet, calm aether, free of crackling auric energy,
thoughts, needs, worries, fears, would be gone, and she would be
surrounded by a maelstrom. She rubbed the palm of her hand over
the table. It was as smooth as ever, polished and oiled. How many
years had it been since anyone had sat at this table, sat in this room?
Since before the War, of course. But longer than that, she thought,
before the Great Revolt, and even before that. The air was so empty
of presence—just the indistinct echoes of long-gone ghosts. The
room was small, and there was just enough space for the twelve-
sided table and twelve chairs, the thick, blue carpet covering the

stone floor, and a smaller table by the window. How many times, she wondered, had the magic holding the white stones together been renewed? Or whose hands had made the door out of a blond-colored wood? The door was plain and unadorned and its surface was unbroken by any window. Outside she could see the roofs of the city and the city walls, and just barely, a flicker of sunlight on the sea. But she could smell the sea and the salt, and hear the gulls.

Once, millennia ago, the Council of the Twelve, the Dodecagon, had met in the city that shared its name, the capital. But this was the Third Era and that city and its fair and green continent was long beneath the sea. She supposed the librarians came to this old reading room, to polish the table, oil the wood, sweep the stones, beat the carpet. Did anyone still come here to just read? She had chosen the room because of a dream, of everyone standing at the table. The Second shook her head; it was as good a reason as any. After all, dreams were real, they revealed and explained the second life that everyone lived beneath their waking lives.

May the Good God and the Goddess be with us. The Second had seen the other councilors praying in the Temple of the Three before she had gone into the library. She lifted her right hand in the Sign of the Three, remembering her mother had told her that to make the sign was to say a little prayer with your hands. She then lifted her left hand to make the sign of the Four Teachers, another nonverbal prayer. *Today, someone will suggest I take the chair, the Prime Mover's seat, Valeria is never coming back. It's been too long. You are the Prime Mover in all but name. We are twelve again.* Larissa knew the someone would be right. *But—not yet. I don't want to officially make her dead just yet.*

The door opened then, and another councilor came into the room, smiled at her and sat down at the table. The door opened again and again, and by ones and twos, the rest of the Dodecagon came in and took their seats, until nine chairs were filled. Larissa was not surprised at whom the tenth was; even after much practice, stairs were hard for the four-footed, and the ramps took twice as long. His hooves clip-clopped on the last flight of stairs and then were muffled on the blue carpet. He stood at his place at the table, his arms across his chest, his tail lazily swishing back and forth.

Now the room was bright and the gloom of disuse that had depressed Larissa was gone. Auras shimmered and sparkled, winking in and out of sight. It was as if someone had hung a faceted jewel in a window and the reflected light was splashing the room in pale blues, pinks, greens, yellows, golds, reds. The Second ran her fingers through her grey-streaked hair and her own aura glowed brighter, a rich purple flame. Violet shadows played around her. It was time, she thought, and stood.

"The Dodecagon is in session. Who speaks for the swimmers?" she asked.

The centaur raised his hand.

"For the dolphins?"

The councilor to the centaur's left raised her hand. A leaf dropped to the table. She brushed it aside and raised her hand again. The second leaf was ignored.

"We are all here, then, the Firstborn," the Second said and nodded to the five at her left. "The Secondborn and the Thirdborn." She nodded to the four at her right. "We are in common accord; we have reached consensus. The Straight Road must be reopened; those of our blood must be awakened; they must be called home." She waited as the others nodded and murmured their agreement. All the councilors then joined hands, making a living circle, making the Dodecagon.

"Then, let us begin. In the Names of the Good God and the Goddess. In the Names of the Three, Triton, Pan, and Oberon. The Four Teachers: Earth, Air, Fire, and Water."

For a moment there was nothing, but the sound of people breathing. Then each individual aura grew brighter and brighter, turning the room into the inside of a kaleidoscope, the interior of a rainbow, the colors bouncing off each other, merging, reforming. Blue flame-tongues coursed down the Second's arms and then, with a quick rush, around the circle, consuming each aura, until everyone and everything in the room burned with the blue fire.

Benjamin Paul Tyson's journal, Wednesday morning, 1 May 1991

I don't have to be at the library until noon and I am on my second cup of coffee. There is a stack of books for me to look through and recommend to acquisitions—science fiction, fantasy, mostly. Somebody has to, Mrs. Carmichael had said, so you do it, Ben, dear. I used to wrap them in brown paper books; I mean, it's science fiction—and fantasy. Emma always told me I was rotting my brain . . .

Never mind.

I'm rambling and I need to write this down so I can make sense of it all and remember. Writing, for me, is thinking, a way of giving my thoughts shape and form. And by articulating them I can know them and understand, be conscious of the meanings I am trying to make.

Malachi is still asleep. I didn't wake him up this morning to catch the bus; I waved it on. My boy needs to sleep; school can wait. And somehow it was a comfort this morning to know he was down the hall, as I shaved, showered, ate, read the paper. I could get up and open the door and there he was—and there he is—asleep, on his back, one hand by his head, the other across his chest. My Gorgon son, with snakes of light rippling through his hair. And sparks popping and crackling off his finger tips, a few of them floating like glowing thistle-down in the air.

Valeria slept the same way—with the light-snakes weaving in and out of her fair hair, little bubbles oozing out to float away. I used to lie there and pop the floaters, making a little shower of glowing fairy dust. She said most fairies manifested light when they slept: children all the time, adults the deeper the sleep and the farther they traveled from the conscious mind.

When Malachi woke me last night, he looked just like his mother. And I knew he had been flying, as I always knew she had been. The luminosity was there, plain and visible, layers of light like more layers of skin, sparking, crackling. A cool white, auric fire.

And I remembered when she took me flying with her—

"Dad? Wake up, Dad; I'm home," he said and touched me and I jumped awake, from the shock. "Dad? Why are you mad at me? Dad?"

I rubbed my eyes awake and sat up and hugged him hard. "Mal, I'm not mad at you; I'm scared. I made myself believe this would never happen—and here it is happening. Just look at you."

"But what is happening?" Malachi asked, his voice muffled against my chest. Then he pulled back and waved with his arms, throwing light around the room. "Why can I do this? Why can I fly? Why am I magic? Am I a fairy?"

"Yes, you are a fairy—half-fairy, and that's why you are magic. That's why you can fly."

"But doesn't fairy mean something else? I heard some boys at school making jokes about fairies."

That question. He's just ten. Valeria said he would start puberty at about ten, early for a human, but it would last longer than for a human. As for sexuality, we didn't talk much about that, but she seemed surprised we worried about it so much. People are people, love is love, flesh is flesh. What did it matter? I remember trying to explain why it mattered so much to some people, but I don't think I got her to understand.

I think I got Malachi to understand, but I'm not sure.

"Some people use fairy to mean something else, to mean gay — to mean people who fall in love with people who are the same sex."

"Are fairies like those people? Is being a fairy — a human fairy — a bad thing? The way those boys were talking it was."

"Some are. That doesn't mean you are and it doesn't mean you aren't. And, no, it's not a bad thing, those boys are wrong. There are people like them who do think so, but they are wrong, too." *Please don't ask me any more questions.*

"When will I know?" *Malachi asked, yawning.*

I sighed, and gave him the only answer I could think of. "When you fall in love, you'll know. But don't worry about that. Right now I need to tell you a story," *I said,* "about your mother."

Malachi fell asleep. I will have to finish the story later.

I am going to have to take him to Faerie. I can't teach him how to handle this, use what his genes gave him. God help me. I have no idea how to get him there. Not yet, anyway.

May 1, 1991
The News and Observer
Early Halloween in Raleigh?
If the calendar didn't say yesterday was the last day of April, Raleigh police would have sworn it was the last day of October instead. Police report a rash of minor vandalism, fires without permits, indecent exposure, and drunk driving throughout the city. The Wake County Sheriff's department, and other municipalities, including Cary, Fuquay-Varina, and Wake Forest, all reported similar incidents. According to Raleigh police sergeant Malcolm Stone, the vandalism reported seemed to be on the order of pranks usually perpetrated at Halloween: mailboxes blown up by firecrackers, eggs on doorsteps, and so on.

"Maybe it's spring fever. There just seemed to be something in the air last night. A whole crowd of folks at Bennigan's, over on Six Forks, just took off their clothes. And some of them hadn't even been drinking," the sergeant said.

Stone had no comment on the more serious acts of vandalism reported in Clemmons State Forest and Umstead State Park. Park rangers found evidence of large bonfires . . . Stone did say NCSU campus police prevented a bonfire in the Brick Yard. . . .

II

Lammas-Lughnasad
Thursday and Friday, August 1 - 2
Saturday, August 3 - Monday, August 26, 1991

Thomas

IT WAS THE FESTIVAL OF THE HARVEST, AND THOMAS was to be the harvester.

He stood by the priestess, the cauldron bubbling in front of them, fire licking the black iron, their eyes reflecting the flames, their naked bodies shining with sweat. It was almost as if the priestess had no eyes—only a yellow burning. Between the priestess and Thomas and the cauldron was the altar, a wide, flat cairn of stones, covered with a black cloth. Spread-eagled and blindfolded on the altar was a naked young man. On the young man's chest was a pentagram, with points at his throat, to the left and right of his nipples and to the left and right of his navel. The pentagram had been drawn in thin, red lines. Thomas and the priestess each held an athame, the blades of the white-handled knives even whiter in the firelight. The auras of all present—the priestess, Thomas, the young man, and the coven silently surrounding them—glowed and crackled, a net of multicolored light weaving itself in and out of their bodies.

The hot August night air also crackled and sparked, as the auras shifted, dissolved, reformed. It was as if everyone was inside an electrical storm that was low and close to the ground. Thomas looked up at the sudden light in the night sky: they *were* inside, or rather beneath, an electrical storm. The light in the sky echoed the light on the ground; and every time the auric lights moved, Thomas felt them pass through his flesh. His body vibrated; the hardness in his groin ached. He flicked the fingers of his free hand: lightning sparked.

Thomas had never felt so alive or so strong. And more strength and more power were coming. The priestess nodded at him and the coven, and in answer, the drumming began, accompanied by the oscillating tune of the singing bowl.

"To harvest life, to consume, to drink life," Thomas began and felt the coven, as one organism, take a step closer to him, the priestess, the cauldron, the altar, and the young man.

> *Ancient Ones, Feared Ones,*
> *Princes of Darkness, Shadow Lords,*
> *I am ready.*
> *I am ready to harvest this beating heart,*
> *To feel the unquenchable fire,*
> *To give the living blood to the night.*
> *To you, Great Ones, Dark Ones,*
> *Belong this heart, the fire in this flesh . . .*

Thomas stepped to the altar, the priestess one step behind. The circle took a step closer. Thomas held up his athame, letting the moonlight and firelight bathe the shining blade, as the coven hummed in time with the drums and the singing bowls. The auras now were like great snakes of red light, twisting, turning, passing in and out of all the bodies. The young man's flesh was suffused with the darker red light of his glowing blood. Thomas lowered his arms and then, carefully, carefully, applying only enough pressure to break the skin, re-traced the pentagram on the man's chest. Bright red oozed behind the blade. The man groaned.

> *Make us one flesh in the shadows.*
> *Make us one mind in the darkness.*
> *Make us one spirit in the night.*
> *Let us never forget*
> *The festival of the Horned One, the Goddess,*
> *Let us welcome those who come, who bring the Change.*
> *Open the way, open our eyes.*
> *Set free the endless fire.*
> *I take life to fill my life,*

All our lives.
Fill me, fill us.
Hear us, Dark Lords.
Answer us, in the wind.
Answer us, in the fire.
Answer us, in the darkness.
Answer us, in the warm blood . . .

Thomas looked around him. After this, there would be no return, no going back, no restoration of the Thomas John Ruggles, bank data entry clerk, night NCSU graduate student in computer science and business, son of Jack Ruggles, twenty-four-year-old man whom no one gave a second glance to. To go back would be a long, long journey. *This* would make that journey forever impossible, and seal Thomas into what he was becoming, what he had become: witch, practitioner of the Left-Hand Path, necromancer, servant of the Princes of Darkness. The priestess looked at him, her eyes now two fires burning in black pools. He could feel the multiple eyes of the coven on his skin. Thomas shuddered and then, in one deep stroke, cut through the young man's aura, his flesh, his bone, down to his heart. For a brief moment, Thomas could see the man's heart still beating.

"Now," the priestess said, and cut the man's throat.

Thomas grabbed the heart with both hands, felt the young man's strength, the priestess's strength, the coven's strength pouring into him, and then tore the heart out and lifted it, dripping.

"The harvest!" Thomas cried.

"The harvest," the priestess said, and dipping her own athame into the young man's warm blood as if it were an inkwell, drew pentagrams on Thomas: in the center of his forehead, both cheeks, the hollows of his neck, over his heart, his stomach, his groin, his thighs, and feet. Each time the priestess dipped her knife into the man's chest for more blood, his red aura followed the blade up and out, like long streamers. When she was done, a web of red light enveloped Thomas and the young man.

"All, partake of the harvest," Thomas said, shuddering as the red streamers poured out from the young man and into his own body, oozing through his skin wherever the priestess had marked him.

He tore one bite out of the heart and then gave it to the priestess. She took the next bite and then threw the heart into the coven's grasping hands.

Malachi, Ben, and Jack

"Dad? Dad? I don't feel too good. I'm leaking light."

Ben rolled over and sat up. Squinting from the sudden brightness, he reached out his left hand and turned on the lamp by his bed. According to the clock, it was just past midnight, August 2.

"Malachi?" Ben asked. "What? What did you say? What's the matter, son?"

His son stood just inside Ben's bedroom, leaning on the wall by the light switch. The boy was pale and weak; there were dark circles under his eyes. Malachi held his stomach, light leaking out between his fingers. Blobs of light oozed from his ears and his nose. Thin strings of light leaked from a cut on Malachi's forehead. Glowing, marble-sized tears ran down his face. The light-tears bounced when they hit the floor and rolled away, leaving faintly glowing trails behind them. Tears littered the floor around Malachi's feet. Bigger globs, from the boy's nose and ears fell too, dropping like pebbles and stones on the floor. The light-strings, tiny, tiny snakes.

"Dad. Make it stop. Please make it stop. It hurts. Ohhhh, I'm going to be sick." Malachi ran from the room, scattering the light-balls every which way. The ones he stepped on broke into smaller balls that skidded across the floor, out in the hall, under the bed.

Ben jumped out of bed, jerked on his gym shorts and T-shirt, and ran after Malachi, stopping first to try and scoop up the little balls of light littering the hallway. *Maybe I can push them back inside, get him to swallow them, I mean, aren't they supposed to be inside him?* But the little balls wouldn't stay in his hands. Most he just couldn't hold: they slipped and oozed between his fingers. Others exploded on his touch into even smaller balls, a few more just winked out. Swearing, Ben gave up and ran into the bathroom. The boy was on the floor, hugging the toilet.

"Dad, the vomit's glowing, too."

"Jesus, son, you're burning up," Ben said, as he wiped Malachi's face with a wet washcloth. "Here, rinse your mouth out with some water." Ben handed Malachi a cup and then glanced at the washcloth before wetting it again. Malachi's sweat had left glowing streaks on the cloth.

Malachi threw up again, gagging. Then he fell to the floor, as if hugging the toilet took too much energy. Ben wiped Malachi's face again and then pressed the cloth on the boy's hot, wet forehead.

"Just lie still for a minute; don't move, okay? Don't move," Ben whispered, trying to fight down the fear that was rising up and filling his throat. *What do I do? What in God's name do I do? This isn't some twenty-four-hour stomach flu; he's fairy-sick. What do I do?*

"That cloth feels good, Dad," Malachi said so softly Ben could barely hear him. "But, my stomach—it feels all hot and funny— ohhh—"

Ben held Malachi as the boy threw up a third time. Little came out, but what did glowed. Then, things started to move. The toilet paper roll started spinning as if pushed by impatient, invisible hands. The paper spilled out on the floor, piling up in great droopy loops. The toothpaste tube shot out from the sink and landed in the tub with a thud. A bar of soap started drifting through the air, followed by a towel and a washcloth. A toothbrush shot straight up and broke against the ceiling. Ben realized that the electric lights in the bathroom weren't on, and that all the light was coming from Malachi or the toilet. The room was filled with light, a light that moved as if it were a liquid in the air, bouncing off the ceiling, the wall, the floor, in and around Ben's body, Malachi's body, a body that was transparent, like a human lantern. Ben could see his son's heart beating, the veins and arteries coursing with blood, his lungs, rising, falling.

"Oh, my God, what is going on? What in the hell is happening to my son?" Ben said, still whispering, staring around the room.

Then the wind started, moving as the light moved—no, the wind was the light, the light was the wind. At first, Ben felt a slight breeze, soft, yet insistent on his face, his chest. He could see the light pushing against his skin, dividing and separating around his body. There were little tornadoes, tiny vortexes, scattered about the floor, whirling out into the hall.

"Dad, I can't make it stop; I don't know how. Make it stop, Dad, please make it stop."

Malachi began shaking. Ben picked up his son—would this new transparent body break like glass? No, he felt flesh, even though he couldn't see it. As quickly as he could, Ben got the boy in the tub. Then he turned on the cold water, then the shower. Ben held Malachi's head and kept washing his face as the water beat against both of them, until finally the shaking stopped and the soap and the washcloth had dropped to the floor.

"Mal, how do you feel, buddy? You don't feel quite so hot—a little warm? How's your stomach?" As quickly as it had come, the transparency was gone. But the wind-light kept moving, spinning off the little tornadoes. Ben had to shout.

Malachi just groaned.

"Let's go lie down. Maybe you can sleep it off. Here, let's get these wet things off. Yeah, there. Can you dry yourself? Okay, I'll do it. All right, son." Ben wrapped the towel around the boy, picked him up (*He's so light. When did he lose weight? God, is all this going to kill him?*), and stepped out into the hall, dodging the tornadoes, which danced around his feet like mad tops. As Ben made his way through the tornadoes, they began to slow down, spinning slower and slower.

The light began oozing again after Ben had gotten Malachi more or less dry and into bed. Ben could, with his hand on Malachi's forehead, feel the heat rising again—and he could see it, a faint, red glow just below the surface of his son's skin. Bigger globs of light came out of the boy's ears, eyes, and nose. The globs coalesced into spheres the size of baseballs and started bouncing around the room, hitting the wall, the curtain, the ceiling, Ben, the furniture.

And at the peripheries of his son's body, Ben could see a faint edging of clearness, as if the color of Malachi's flesh had been slightly erased.

The hallway filled with little tornadoes again.

Ben put Malachi back in the tub, turned on the shower, and called Jack.

"Hilda, I know it's the middle of the night, but please wake up Jack. It's an emergency. No, no, no, don't call the rescue squad. I can't explain now, but I need Jack. I know it's three o'clock in the morning. Tell him Malachi's sick. *No, no—don't call the rescue squad*," Ben pleaded. He couldn't see his knuckles gripping the receiver, but he was sure if he could they would be white. He felt if he kept squeezing the receiver would snap in half.

"Ben? Whassmatter Malachi?"

"He's fairy-sick."

"I'll be right over."

Ben hung up the phone and put his head down on the kitchen counter. He wondered what questions Hilda was asking. He had wanted to tell her about Malachi but Jack had said to wait, let her get used to being married and get to know Ben and Malachi better. *He'll have to tell her something now. You don't get phone calls at three in the morning for nothing.*

Realizing he was dripping and soaking wet, Ben peeled off his wet clothes and was putting on a bathrobe when Jack knocked at the front door.

"What's wrong with Mal? What happened?" Jack said as he came in. He was barefoot and had on only a bathrobe. Jack's hair stood up all over his head in his usual little horns.

"He's in the bathroom—he's burning up—I think the water helps. He's throwing up light, bleeding light—his body turned transparent, turned back, there are little tornadoes—never mind, let me just show you."

Light poured out of the bathroom, an intangible flood. Inside, balls of light bounced off walls, the floor, the ceiling. When a ball hit a counter or the shower water, they exploded into tiny stars that dissolved like snowflakes as they hit the floor. Camera-like flashes erupted, bloomed, and died. Snakes of light writhed and twisted in the air, looping themselves around each man's arms and legs, and slithering across their chests. The tornadoes whirled madly in the hall and out into the dining room, the kitchen, the living room, picking up dust, scraps of paper, paper clips, lost coins.

Ben had sat Malachi down in the shower this time, propped up with old pillows. The water was up to the boy's middle. The light leaking from his nose and eyes rolled down Malachi's chest into the water. Now there were two toothbrushes, a drinking cup, and the toothpaste on the ceiling.

"It just started, oh, I don't know, half-an-hour, forty-five minutes ago. He came into my bedroom and said he felt sick and that he was leaking light. Then he threw up, and this poltergeist stuff started. He got a little better and I put him in his bed and it started all over again. I don't know what else to do, Jack. The water helps, but he can't stay in the tub forever. What am I going to do? What in God's name am I going to do?"

Jack spoke slowly, shaking his head. "I don't know—maybe—do you have anything from Faerie? Didn't you say Valeria left a charm, like a crib mobile—maybe it has magic to protect him?"

"The star. I'll be back—here, keep washing his face." Ben ran to his bedroom, trying to remember where he had hidden the star. He dumped out his sock drawer, his shirts, underwear. No star. In the closet? No, his trunk, where he kept all his sweaters—and there, in the bottom, was a lumpy leather pouch. Ben pulled the drawstrings and dumped out the silver-grey twelve-pointed star Valeria had left swinging over Malachi's crib. It felt heavy and cool in his hand.

Clinching his fist around the talisman, Ben ran back to the bathroom, dodging tornadoes, shoving through a tangle of light-snakes and kicking aside light balls the size of soccer balls on the floor. Jack looked up and then stepped back, knotting the washcloth in his hands. Very gently Ben slid the star's silver chain over Malachi's head. For a moment, nothing changed. The star lay flat on Malachi's wet chest. Then, one by one, each of the star's twelve points started to glow and shine, as if the silver were polished metal and not wood. Ben could have sworn he heard a faint humming— Jack? No, it was the star. Then the entire star shone and the humming grew louder and louder. The toothbrushes fell to the floor. Then, the drinking cup and the toothpaste. The light balls stopped bouncing and then, in ones, then twos, then threes and fours, started winking out. The snakes faded, like smoke. The tornadoes stopped whirling as if they had suddenly lost power, and winked out. At last the humming stopped and it was quiet, except for the sound of the shower. Malachi was solid, his body was opaque.

Ben turned off the water and touched Malachi's forehead and cheeks with the back of his hand. "He's not hot anymore. It worked, Jack," he whispered

"Let's get him out of the water," Jack whispered in return. "Towels out here in the hall closet?"

"Yeah."

Ben picked Malachi up and wrapped the boy in the thick towels Jack handed him. *He feels so light, so light. Too light.* He carried Malachi across the hall and sat down in a rocking chair by the boy's bed. Jack sat down on the bed, yawning as he held his head with his hands.

"You know, Ben," Jack said, looking up as Ben slowly rocked, "Malachi's ears are pointed now. Valeria's were, weren't they?"

Ben nodded as he rocked his son back and forth.

"Have you told him everything?"

Ben got up from the rocker and laid Malachi in bed. He pulled the sheet over the boy and smoothed his son's hair. Fairy-knots, Ben thought.

"Yeah, I have. You know, he doesn't have to tell me when he's been flying. There's something extra in his eyes, they shine. Just like his mother. But knowing hasn't, won't, stop him from getting sick like this. And Jack, I think I've started seeing them again."

"Them?"

"C'mon in the living room. I don't want to wake him up," Ben said.

"Them?" Jack repeated when they were both sitting on the living room couch. The front door was open. A faint breeze came through the screen; the lawn was half in shadow and half in moonlight. "The Fomorii. Just out of the corners of my eyes stuff. Like a sudden shadow. I look and there's nothing there. I'm at the reference desk and I look up and see someone across the room with red eyes. I blink and they're gone. I smell that hot, wet smell. I feel how I felt when I woke up the night they first tried to kill Valeria. If they aren't back, they are on their way."

"He just turned ten—didn't she tell you something about puberty for fairy-children?"

"All she said was that he would manifest his feyness at puberty. And that he would have to learn to control what comes naturally to Daoine Sidhe children."

"He's a little early for a human, but I'd say puberty's here, Ben. You're going to have to take him to Faerie. We can't teach him how to be a fairy. And if the Fomorii are coming back, geez, man," Jack said softly.

"I know. Even if he hadn't gotten sick, I would have to. We have to find the nearest gate. God knows how we are going to do that."

After Jack left, Ben went down the hall to check on Malachi. He laid his hand on the boy's forehead: still cool. He sighed and sat down in the rocker. *I am so tired, but I don't think I can go to sleep just yet.*

"Dad?"

"Mal? How do you feel?"

Malachi looked up at his father, his eyes half-open, his voice low and weak. "It wasn't a dream, was it? What happened, I mean. I feel really sore and achy and really tired. What's this on my chest?" He held up the twelve-pointed star.

"No, it wasn't a dream. That was your mother's. She left it to protect you. It sure did tonight. Why don't you go on back to sleep, Mal. We can talk in the morning.

"Tell me the story again. How you and my mother met, okay?"

"*. . . Just to be on the safe side,*" *Jack had said, looking at me over his glasses. Tufts of his brown hair stuck up like little horns all over his head. "Fairies are known to be, well, mischievous." I think the clerk at the hardware store had all his suspicions about loony bookworms confirmed when I asked for just five nails.*

"*Small project at the library, Mr. Tyson?*" *he asked as he handed me the nails in a little paper bag. I smiled weakly, knowing I would think of a snappy comeback at three o'clock in the morning. My next stop was Food Lion, to buy an Angel Food cake and a bottle of white wine. Emma would have been proud of me, I thought as I walked home, even if the wine was on sale half-price at $4.59. Buying the cake and the wine was what she would have done the day after Vale-*

ria moved in. Then, with me grumbling, Emma would have gone over to Valeria's and knocked on her door. She wouldn't have waited three-and-a-half weeks, like I had. Emma would also have taken some of her kitchen herbs from the pots scattered all over the house: basil, savory, thyme, and rosemary, her favorite. She probably would have invited Valeria over for coffee. I would have stood behind her, grinning like some hopeless hebephrenic.

I grabbed the first Angel Food cake I saw. I didn't have any rosemary. Two nights after the funeral I had gotten good and drunk. Staggering drunk. Yelling-at-the-moon drunk. Pouring-wine-on-my-head drunk. Finally crying drunk and then I smashed every rosemary pot on the back stoop.

It was a three-minute walk from the Food Lion to Beichler Road and the little gateway into Sunset Hills, my development. From the Sunset Hills sign to 1411 was half-a-block, one more minute. I stood for what seemed like an hour in the street, rehearsing the lines Jack had suggested, trying to make them seem as casual as if they were really my own. Finally I walked up the blue flagstone path to the door. Feeling silly, I reached down in my pocket one more time and touched the nails. Then I knocked. I knew she had to be home; all the lights were on.

"Who is it?" a voice called from inside.

"Ben, from next door, 1413. Huh, I thought I'd drop by, say hello, be neighborly—if you aren't busy or anything." Unfortunately these weren't Jack's smooth opening lines.

Valeria opened the door and bright light washed out from the house.

"Like my light?" Malachi said, his eyes barely open, his words soft, slow, close together.

"Yes, just like yours," Ben said. Malachi was asleep, his breathing slow, regular. No light except from the lamp, which Ben turned off. He sat for a very long time in the dark, on the side of the bed, listening to Malachi breathe, watching him sleep.

Hazel

Hazel put her ear to Alexander's side as she carried him up the stairs to her bedroom. His motor was definitely running. She knew if she could see his face that the cat's bright blue eyes would be half-closed in complete bliss. Every day he waited for her by the dinner table until Hazel was finished and her grandparents said she could go. Or, more often, she would just push away her chair and leave. Her grandparents, engrossed in conversation, or both reading, wouldn't notice until they cleared the table, if then. Then Hazel would scoop up the grey-and-white part Siamese and the two of them went on their walk around the house, Alexander's purr getting deeper and more satisfied the longer the walk. The walk was another thing her grandparents rarely, if ever, noticed, even if Hazel went through the dining room and the kitchen two or three times.

The walk ended in Hazel's bedroom with Alexander curled up at the edge of Hazel's bed and Hazel sitting in front of her computer, cracking her knuckles and waiting for the date and time prompts to appear.

"08-01-91," Hazel said to herself as she typed. Three more weeks of summer vacation, then fifth grade. Next she keyed in 19:45, and then Hazel\Worldmaker. After a few beeps and chirps, the World-maker logo appeared: a map of the world growing one section at a time, as if an invisible hand was putting down puzzle pieces. When the map was complete, the screen faded to grey and then, slowly, as if they were emerging out of mist and smoke, a picture of a group of medieval men and women in a forest of white-barked trees. The Alexzelians. Hazel-Guinevere was their leader, with Alexander the Lion by her side. Hazel, without looking, reached over to rub the cat's head. In response, Alexander stood, stretched, and then climbed into Hazel's lap. He snuggled into the crook of Hazel's arm and closed his eyes. Hazel stroked Alexander's back as she thought.

"Not bad," she said to the cat. "What do you think? Should I add more trees? I think the forest needs to be thicker—"

Hazel stopped talking. The screen was growing, expanding. Hazel tried to press escape but she couldn't. The keyboard had disappeared. There was no chair or desk or bedroom or house. She was standing on the edge of the monitor, wavering, holding tight to Alexander, who was wide-awake and yowling in her arms. The Alexzelians were gone. The trees—Hazel could hear the wind murmuring in, no, *to* the trees. The trees murmured in return. She could feel the same wind on her face. Hazel took a step backward, reaching for where the edge of the monitor screen had been. Dry leaves crunched beneath her feet. Instead of the familiar metal of the monitor Hazel felt bark. She was touching one of her trees. The bark glowed. She set Alexander down and rubbed her hands over the smooth bark. Some of the bark's luminosity lingered on her palms, pale, ghostly streaks.

Hazel and Alexander stood at the edge of the forest. Facing Hazel was a meadow of tall grasses and in the center of the meadow was a dark lake. She took a step forward and felt something heavy and warm pushing against her leg. Hazel looked down to see Alexander, who while not a lion, was three times his normal size. He looked back up at her and held her gaze.

"Can you talk now, Alex?"

Alexander didn't reply except to push against her again, nudging her out into the meadow.

"Hey, boy, want me to go out there?" she asked and knelt down to hug him and scratch his head. Alexander licked her and nudged her again toward the meadow. "Out there, huh?" She paused before following the cat and looked back over her shoulder. Just trees, no metal window looking into her bedroom. Alexander nudged her a third time and Hazel let the cat lead her out into the meadow, into the tall grasses and the wild flowers. The flowers nearest her were white, like paperwhite narcissus. To her surprise she was barefoot—her shoes had disappeared along with the monitor, computer, and everything else.

The meadow greeted her.

Hazel felt a pressure against her feet. It was as if the earth was an enormous cat gently bumping her feet. Hazel rubbed the ground with one foot and felt the pressure again, still gentle, but insistent. She kept rubbing the ground and it vibrated in return.

"Hello ground, hello meadow," Hazel said. She wasn't surprised the vibrating grew louder in response. She had spoken to the meadow at the right moment . . .

Hazel shook her head and yawned. The cursor was blinking at her beneath a zero in the lower left-hand corner of the screen. The word Print was in the upper left-hand corner, and below was a list of commands, the first being Full Document. The printer's document tray was full. Hazel gathered up the pages and started to read. It was her dream: falling through the monitor, the glowing trees, the purring ground, and Alexander getting bigger. Hazel quickly looked at her cat. He didn't look any different—did he?

. . . *Hazel and Alexander found themselves at the edge of a meadow filled with white and yellow flowers. Tall, white-barked trees encircled the meadow, making the sky into a blue oval. The sun was high in the sky and bright, so bright, that the white of the trees and the flowers was almost too much to look at. The yellow flowers seemed to be on fire. There was a breeze blowing, a sweet breeze that seemed to be playing tag with the leaves.*

Hazel and Alexander were all alone, or so Hazel thought.

There was a pool in the meadow. The water in the pool was dark and still. As she walked toward the pool, the flowers began to change their color. The white became tinged with a line of dull bronze-yellow at first. The dull yellow made Hazel think of the Mexican coins she kept in a glass jar on her desk. Her grandfather said her parents had brought them home from a trip before Hazel was born. The Mexican coin-yellow grew brighter and brighter the closer she came to the pool, until the flowers growing at the water's edge were fire-yellow.

Hazel had no idea how long she and Alexander stood by the pool before the dragon flew out of the sky and landed on the other side of the water. She wasn't even surprised to see the creature in the air. A flying dragon was no stranger than the glowing colors or the breeze that seemed to be almost speaking with the trees. In fact, she was more surprised that she wasn't surprised. For such a large creature the dragon was graceful and light in the air, as if it were a huge, light bird, riding the thermals. When the dragon landed, its huge wings beating down the flowers around it, its long green neck stretching, Hazel thought it was one of the most beautiful creatures she had ever seen.

"Next to you, of course," she said to Alexander, who was butting her on the leg.

Then the dragon spoke to Hazel in a low, rumbling, gravelly voice, calling for her to come to it and not be afraid.

"Stay with me," she whispered to Alexander, who answered by rubbing the length of his body against her legs. "I think it's a nice dragon, but just the same," Hazel said, thinking of all the stories of dragons burning down cities and gobbling up princesses and knights. "Come on, let's go see what it wants."

The dragon said nothing as Hazel made her way around the pool, pushing aside the grasses and flowers. It only watched her with its brilliantly colored iridescent eyes; like green agates, Hazel thought. When she was close enough, it lowered its head so that Hazel could touch it. The dragon's head felt warm and smooth.

Then the dragon began speaking. It told Hazel she was needed here, in the world of the meadow and the white trees and the flowers. She was needed and was called to come home. Hazel told the dragon her home was somewhere else, back there, where she had been born, where her grandparents were. The dragon told her yes, she had been born there, but here, this place, was also hers.

"I don't get it," Hazel said. "Back home—" and she looked behind her to see the white trees and above her to see a sky whose blue she now could see was different, darker and deeper. "I live there, in a house, with my grandparents, and Alex, and I go to school. This is a dream. You're not real; dragons are fairy tales."

"It was your machine," the dragon said, "and your game. The machine knocked at the door and the game opened the door to this place; the machine answered a call from this place. It can talk to other machines, yes? Create invisible links of energy, of electricity? Such a link was made to here, which is beyond dreams (and you do not remember it, yet, but you have already been here in your dreams). We all travel when we sleep, although we forget quickly where we have been and what we have done. It is better so; there are some dream places that would haunt the waking too much."

"Nightmares?" Hazel asked.

"Sometimes. Sometimes it is just the opposite. Dreams show us places in our minds that when we are awake are disguised or obscured. Dreams remove masks and let us see the faces beneath. But this dream-which-is-not-a-dream you will remember and I am wearing no mask and neither are you. Your cat is larger than he was; you just can't see it yet," the dragon said. Smoke curled and twisted from the dragon's nostrils as it talked, surrounding its huge head in a small cloud. Its great tail twitched back and forth.

Then Hazel woke up. She was sitting in front of her computer. Her cat was asleep on her bed.

Hazel felt around the monitor and the hard drive and knocked on each one. Solid. She tested each connection. Nothing was loose. Every light in the room was on and the clock on her desk said it was past midnight, 12:51. If there had been a power failure, it would be blinking 12:00 over and over and over.

Had she been sleeping at her computer for over four hours? Dreaming? But—the story she had in her hand—had she written it in her sleep? Had her grandfather found her asleep and—that had to be it. Yes, her grandfather came in, found her asleep, wrote the story, and set things up so she would see the print screen and find the story in the printer.

Her grandfather had never written a story in his life. Somehow Hazel was sure of that

She did the only thing she knew to do: she went to bed. Alexander curled up beside her, his back pressed against her leg.

Russell

Russell woke suddenly in the middle of the hot August night. Someone had been calling his name, someone he knew.

"Mama?" he whispered into the darkness. Then, with some hesitation, "Daddy?" But even as Russell repeated both words he knew the voice was neither his mother nor his father. It couldn't be. His mother was in Arizona, or at least she had been two years ago. His father was nearer—down the hall—but he wouldn't be calling for Russell in the middle of the night.

Russell.

Miss McNeil. How could it be his first grade teacher? She was six years and half-a-continent away, in Lawton County, Oklahoma. How would she know where to find him in Raleigh? This trailer in Neuse Woods, out on Poole Road, was the fourth place Russell had lived since Lawton County—how could she possibly find him? Why would she come now, when there had been so many times before when Russell had wished for her, prayed for her? And it was in the middle of the night—would his first grade teacher be outside his window calling his name? *Yeah, right.*

Russell got up to look out the window anyway. Just maybe. Of course the Whites' backyard was empty: a broken swing set, a slide, a tire hanging from a tree. It was bright and clear and warm. The fan facing his bed rattled. The stars were tiny, white fires; the moon was a white crescent. The trailer next door shone as if it were silver.

"It sure sounded like Miz McNeil calling me," Russell said. Just the way she would call his name when she called the roll, or asked him to read or clean the erasers. *Daddy? Jeanie? Miz McNeil is in the backyard and she wants to talk to me.* His father's answer would be a quick backhand. Jeanie would just start whining about how hard she tried to be a good mother or some other crap. The way she had at supper when her parents had been over.

Today had been Jeanie's birthday and her folks had stayed after they brought him back from yard work to help celebrate. He supposed they had to come; she was their daughter, after all, but after working a good chunk of the summer as their yard boy he didn't like them and they didn't like him. The yard work had been Jeanie's idea. Get the boy out of the house, give him something to do, he's too big to lie around all summer watching TV. And if he had been working for anybody else, it would have been okay. Russell found he liked working with plants, the digging, the cutting, moving, setting out, watering.

Jeanie's folks were another matter. The old lady never shut up. If Russell didn't mend his ways, he was going to wind up in jail, or worse. Look what had happened to his mama—where was she? Apples don't fall far from the tree; he'd better watch his step. Don't you go smart-mouthing me, I'll jerk a knot in you so fast it'll make your head swim. And she preached. Was Russell right with God? He'd better get right, not like his mama, she worshipped idols, did he know that? Cathlicks prayed to statues and it says right here in the Bible that's a sin. She followed behind Russell, fussing about how he did one thing or another, didn't he have any sense? Russell wanted to kill her. The old man would have been all right if the old lady hadn't been around. Once or twice the old man had even said something halfway nice, but the old lady would snap at him not to get soft with the boy, and that would be the end of it.

The only way Russell had gotten through the summer without blowing up or telling the old lady to go to hell was when he remembered what he called his special dreams. They had started in May and he had them every two or three nights. Sometimes a week would pass, but that had been in the beginning. He would think about them while he worked and the old lady talked: the silvery-white trees, the sky with the two moons, the talking wind, and running, just running through the tall grasses and the glowing flowers. Standing in the meadow, watching and waiting as the flying horse flew down to talk to him, nuzzle his face with its warm breath.

The well-being, the secret happiness, of the dreams would linger most of the next day, enclosing Russell in a safe and close cloud that muffled the old lady's words and kept them from hurting quite so much. Today had been like that so that even when he knew the old lady and the old man were going to stay for dinner after they brought him it had been okay. The dream-feelings got him through what seemed like an interminable dinner; Russell was amazed at just how much mashed potatoes and fried chicken two old people could eat and still claim they had room for the big, white cake Jeanie brought out. Jeanie had picked it up that afternoon at the Food Lion where she worked. She had also set up a pink artificial Christmas tree.

"Mama and Daddy put up a tree on everybody's birthday, ever since I was a little girl," she had explained to Russell the first time she hauled the tree out, for his father's birthday last year. Russell had stared dumbfounded at Jeanie when she started putting the artificial tree together on the kitchen table. "This way," Jeanie had said, "we'll have Christmas three or four times a year—or at least a tree, anyway. Get me those little, white lights out of the Christmas box in the closet."

Having a Christmas tree up in August or March or May was, in Russell's opinion, stupid. Having Jeanie's parents over made it worse. But at least this time the old folks were only going to be around for a few hours, not the entire day the way they had been on the real Christmas. If he could just keep remembering his dreams, he'd could get through it and not get in trouble.

He had thought when he opened up the old folks' present for him at Christmas that maybe they had changed their mind about him. He had pulled bright, shiny fishing lures out of a box. The lures sparkled in the light from the tree lights and the sun coming through the picture window, as he held them up, turning them this way and that. Maybe Daddy will go with me this spring, Russell thought, if he asked the right way, at the right time, if his daddy wasn't on a job, if he hadn't had too many beers . . . Then the old lady had noticed Russell's Nativity under the tree. Russell winced, remembering. Why did he have to remember the bad things, too? He had made sure for this August Christmas tree his Nativity scene was in his room, safe and sound. The Nativity was the only thing he had left from Mama, the only person he was sure would listen to his dreams. If he told her, Russell knew what she would say: *Silver-white trees, with golden leaves? I used to dream about them, too, honey. They reminded me a little of the church I went to when I was a little girl. Not the way the church looked so much as how it felt. You know, Russ-honey, quiet, peaceful, safe. There was a little corner of the church where candles burned all the time in little, blue glasses.* She told him her dreams as bedtime stories, her voice soft and low, the window open to the hot, still Oklahoma night. Her eyes, he remembered now, had glowed green in the darkness, just like a cat's. Just the way he had thought his own eyes had been glowing.

"Well, Jeanie, I'm glad you didn't let the boy put out that Cathlick thing under your tree, the way he done at Christmas. Thou shalt not make graven images, that thy days may be long in the land of the Lord. And everybody knows there weren't no fox at the manger," Jeanie's mother had said, interrupting Russell's reverie. The white cake was cut and the presents were opened. Crumpled pieces of bright-colored wrapping paper lay on the floor like bits and pieces of a magpie's nest.

Russell looked hard at her and, for the first time, he could see colors all around the old lady: angry dark reds, oranges, purples flickering and flashing. There were lights around the old man, his daddy, and Jeanie—she had little silvery stars, sparkling and twinkling around her. He blinked, rubbed his eyes, and the lights were gone. And the lady was still going on about Cathlicks being little better than idol-worshippers, it was right in the Bible—

"My Catholic thing isn't under the tree because I don't want you near it, you hear me, old lady? Don't you ever touch any of my stuff and stop talking about Mama. You're just a mean, old lady. Mean, mean, mean. All summer long I've been working in your damn garden and your damn yard and you've not said one nice word to me, not a damn one. Making me eat on the back porch. I hate you, I hate you, *I hate you!*" Russell yelled in the old lady's face. He hadn't meant to yell; the words had just come out. He hadn't meant to say anything. Remember the dreams, smile, eat cake, nod at the right times. That had been his plan.

The plan hadn't worked.

"Jeanie! Do you hear the way this boy is talking to me? Cursing me, in my own daughter's house! You are one sorry good-for-nothing boy. Here we are trying to have a birthday party and you go and ruin it. I'm only trying to save you from that Cathlick idol worshipping. Your mama was a heathen, if not worse—to go off and leave her family like that. Of course I wouldn't have you in my house. I told Jeanie to make your daddy ship you off to your mama when they got married, I could tell the minute I laid eyes on you that you were trouble, but nobody knows where that worthless mama of yours is—"

"Now, Lillian, the boy has worked hard all summer long and he's not been any real trouble, you have to admit that now," the old man interrupted.

"Shut up, you old fool, the boy is nothing but trouble, trouble, trouble."

"You shut up, you old hag, just shut up, shut up, shut up!"

"Russell!"

"Boy, when you are going to learn to keep your fool mouth shut? Jeanie, goddamit, I thought you quit smoking—the damn trashcan is on fire," his daddy yelled and backhanded Russell so hard he jerked back against his chair. Dark smoke rolled out of the kitchen trashcan. His daddy seemed to almost be on fire as well, with dark red, black-edged lights—and so did everybody else, for that matter. In the midst of the blood, the fire, the smoke, and the yelling, Russell ran to his room, cursing himself for letting the old lady get to him, jerk his mouth open, and drag out those stupid, stupid words. God, he *was* stupid, just like they all said. He scooped up the little Nativity scene from his dresser and quickly hid it in the back of his closet. He heard his daddy cursing about the fire and now the whole damn kitchen was going to smell of smoke and it was a good thing he saw it before the trailer went up. Jeanie was cursing back—it wasn't her fault, she had quit smoking, months ago. And the old lady yelling: they could have burned up, they could have just burned up.

When the Nativity was safe, Russell made himself sit on his bed.

He knew what was coming next. When all the excitement about the fire was over, somebody would remember Russell and then his daddy would slam the door open and backhand him again or make him drop his pants and wallop him with a belt. And then drag him out to say he was sorry.

Stupid, stupid, stupid.

After the whipping and the apology, his daddy made Russell spend the rest of the evening in the living room with Jeanie and her parents. *Need to learn how to be civilized, boy.* No birthday cake. And listening to the old lady, with her lights now more a dark yellow than red, tell Jeanie she ought to call the law on him: "I don't know how you put up with this young 'un, Jeanie. I really don't. He's not even yours. When your babies come, you'll see the difference; it'll be like night and day. I know some folks at church called the law on one of theirs. Sheriff came and hauled him off. He wasn't the same after a night in Stony Lonesome, I'll tell you what. Couldn't hurt. Cut me another piece of cake, honey; it's pretty good for store-bought. I never bake cakes anymore myself. Why bother messing up all them bowls, you just have to wash when you can run down to the grocery store and pick up one. Larry, it sure is a good thing you saw that fire, I wonder how it started, since nobody smokes . . ."

Russell had almost bit off his tongue then. He wanted to tell her he'd get all the cake he wanted after she left; he didn't care if Jeanie had thrown his piece out the back door. He took a deep breath and made himself think of his dreams.

All that had been just a few hours ago. He could only imagine what Jeanie's mama would say if he told her he was hearing voices in the middle of the night. Might as well go to the bathroom, he thought. Maybe somebody was in there, whispering his name. Of course the room was empty. Feeling foolish, he checked behind the shower curtain and inside the clothes hamper and the medicine cabinet. When he closed the cabinet door, he found himself staring into his own face: a thin, red-haired boy, with hazel eyes, tufts of hair sticking up like little red feathers. And Russell saw his own lights: a dark flickering red, edged with black, and was that a touch of green? He rubbed his eyes, flicked the overhead light on and off—and the colored lights were gone.

Russell went back to bed, shaking his head. Colored lights. Special dreams. Voices. What the hell was going on? Was he crazy—he didn't feel crazy. But could someone who was really crazy know they were? Never mind, he thought, tomorrow would be better. No more gardening for Jeanie's folks.

"Need you at home, boy, packing and stuff," his daddy said. The Whites were moving in a few weeks, before school started and before Jeanie's babies were due. His daddy had said they would still be living on Poole Road, but closer to town. Russell would be in a new school for the fifth grade.

Maybe the new school next fall would be different. Ha. Maybe if he went back to sleep again, he would hear Miz McNeil and he would be able to hear more than his name. Maybe he would hear the voice tell him what it wanted him to do.

The night before the Whites moved out of Neuse Woods, Russell had gone to bed early. He knew his father would have them up at dawn to load the truck and the car. Jim Beam, Old Crow, and Johnny Walker boxes were stacked around his bed. Russell's closet and his chest of drawers were empty. Only the clothes he was going to wear tomorrow were out. *He stood before a tall, white house in the country, surrounded by taller trees and a patchy rough yard. Behind the house were more and more trees, a forest, thick and dark and green. The house was calling to Russell, telling him to come in, to come home. He followed the voice up the front steps and eased open the front door and shouted hello. The word echoed and bounced, like a tossed ball, in and out of empty rooms, until the house's silence caught it and gobbled it up.*

Russell, come further up.

Russell stepped into what looked like a short hallway. To his left was what looked like a living room. On the far side of the living room he could see what had to be the dining room, as there was an empty table in the middle, surrounded by chairs. Beyond the dining room he could see what looked like a kitchen; the white tiles shone in the light.

This is a big, big house.

Russell.

He followed the voice upstairs to another hallway, lined with doors. The first door was a bedroom, the second a closet, the third a bathroom. But the voice was calling from the last door, at the hall's end. The door opened by itself, slowly opening and revealing an attic, long and narrow, with a slanting roof and cedar wood floors. The attic ran the front length of the house, and two windows punctuated its slanted roof. Each window had wide sills, wide enough for someone to sit in and stretch out their legs.

This is my room. This place is meant for me.

Outside the window Russell didn't see the tall trees and lawn and the woods he had seen outside the house. There were the trees, silver-white, with golden leaves, from his other dreams. Russell unlatched the window and crawled out on the roof. The sky was black. The white trees swayed back and forth in a wind that was pulling at Russell, wrapping invisible hands around his legs. Russell let the wind slowly pull him to the roof's edge, and, then, as if it were something he had done all his life, Russell dove out into the wind and flew.

"Get up, boy. Time's a-wasting."

Russell looked up, dazed, from the floor at his daddy, who had just flipped over Russell's bed. "Get yer clothes on and then put this bed in the truck. Get moving," his daddy said and then clicked on the light. "Go on, now."

Russell covered his face against the bare light bulb in the ceiling and stood. Outside it was still dark. He could still see a few stars in the sky and the fading moon. Why'd they have to get up so early? Sometimes his daddy did stuff just for meanness' sake.

"Everything is already on the trucks," Russell muttered. He could see his father's pickup, his father's best friend's pickup, and his stepmother's station wagon. There was just enough room in the back of the station wagon for Russell to squeeze in. Russell's bed was to be tied to the top of one of the pickups.

Russell sighed and pulled a T-shirt over his head and then felt around on the floor for his pants. He had slept in his underwear. He could hear his father and stepmother yelling at each other about hurrying up and getting something to eat at Hardee's. *I bet the only reason we are moving like this is so we can be gone before the landlord comes to collect the late rent. This new house must be awfully cheap.* As he was pulling his shoes on, Jeanie started yelling for Russell to hurry the hell up and had he stripped the bed yet? Rolled up the mattress? Got his own personal box, put it in the car? Was he asleep or what?

An hour later, after packing up the last few things and biscuits at Hardee's, they were at the new house. Russell couldn't see it until his father opened up the back of the station wagon and let him climb out, holding tight to his Old Crow box. The box was filled with Russell's things: the Nativity scene, his mother's picture, the red fox Miz McNeil had given him.

It was a white, two-story frame house, with two roof windows. It was the house in Russell's dream. Beneath the slanting roof he knew he would find his attic bedroom. The woods he had seen behind the house were where they were supposed to be, even though the trees were ordinary oaks, sweetgums, pines, poplars, maples. No silver trees with golden leaves. The yard, to Russell's surprise, was bigger than he had dreamed. Lush, thick greenness spread out around the house: tall, thick grass, Queen Anne's lace, patches of red clay—red clay islands and continents in a wild sea. Russell imagined running and running over that green ocean and then falling to roll, over and over and over, until he would lie still, his head spinning, staring up at the sky. The house stood alone. Its nearest neighbors were about a half-mile down the road, Greenwood Estates. Russell had seen the sign when they had driven past it. He had caught just a glimpse of Greenwood: brick houses, mostly, trimmed yards, bicycles, shiny cars.

"Get a move on, Russell. Grab some boxes and take them inside. I don't want you running off until everything is in the house. Your daddy tells me there's a creek back in the woods. I don't want you going near it until I get the clothesline up and the washer hooked up. I do hope Larry remembered to call CP&L; I don't want to sit in the dark and sweat," Jeanie said.

A creek? I wonder if it's deep enough to swim in and has fish. Nobody mentioned a creek.

Russell went to bed early that night, in the attic bedroom. He lay motionless on his bed in the darkness, listening. The night-sounds were different from the trailer. A floor fan pushed air over him and outside, through the two open attic windows, Russell could hear, faintly, wilder noises than he had ever heard.

Learning the night-sounds was something Russell had done in every place he had ever lived in: the trailer, and the string of houses in Oklahoma and Kansas. For the first three or four nights Russell focused on knowing all the night-sounds before falling asleep. He had to learn the new words of the wind and the trees and if the house said anything in reply. Though muted, he could hear, right under his bed, the dull sound of a chair being dragged across some floor downstairs, probably the living room. The phone trilled like some distant bird.

Russell picked up a flashlight from the floor and clicked it on to read again the names he had found scrawled in magic marker and blue and black ink and pencil on the attic roof beams. Robert, 7-17-75; Donnie was here, 8-13-89; Sam, April 4, 1987. Tomorrow Russell would write his own name, below Donnie's. Russell wrote the letters of his name in the air with his flashlight. Then he turned it off and wrote his name again, using his fingers.

He was able to see, very faintly, the letters in what looked like blue skywriting, above his head.

Jeff

The day before the beginning of the new school year, Mrs. Clark took Jeff into Nottingham Heights Elementary. To meet Mrs. Bondurant, the guidance counselor there, she said. His social worker had requested it. What for, he had wondered. What could he possibly tell this woman that he hadn't told somebody else, that wasn't already written down in some folder somewhere.

"I'm going to talk with your teacher and then look around the library," Mrs. Clark said when she came out of Mrs. Bondurant's office. She had gone in first and Jeff had poked around the computer lab. The counselor's office was at the back of the lab. "This is Mrs. Bondurant."

Jeff eyed the woman warily as she got up from her desk to shake his hand. Mrs. Bondurant looked too young, with long, dark brown hair pulled back with a bright blue scarf. Dark brown eyes, a turtleneck, jeans.

"Thanks for coming in, Mrs. Clark. Jeff and I won't be long, maybe half-an-hour, forty-five minutes? Come in, Jeff, sit down for a minute, while I make some notes in this file, then we'll visit some."

She smiled a lot, Jeff thought, as he sat down stiffly in a chair by her desk, watching her as she wrote. Ever since he had come to live with the Clarks, everybody seemed to be writing something down all the time in little folders or notebooks and they wouldn't let him see any of it. They—the social workers, the police, the doctors, now this guidance counselor—were writing about what had happened and what he had said and hadn't said and what his saying or not saying meant. *It means I don't want to talk about it all the time.*

They all wanted him to talk, to express himself, tell them how he felt, what he was dreaming. This young Mrs. Bondurant with her long hair and smiles was going to want the same thing, he thought. Maybe.

Jeff looked around the room as Mrs. Bondurant wrote—boy, she was writing a lot. No, now she was reading something. Now she was frowning. Mrs. Clark must have told her everything.

Camille Bondurant was starting her fourth year as a school guidance counselor, a year that was to be split between Nottingham Heights Elementary and Marlborough Road Elementary. Mondays and

Tuesdays and every other Friday at Nottingham; Wednesdays and Thursdays and the other Friday at Marlborough. But even with two schools and a heavy caseload, Camille had never been not ready to talk with a new student. Until today. The principal at Marlborough, a singularly boring man, with sandy blond hair cropped close to his head, had gone on and on and on. She had just started skimming the Gates boy's file, her blue-green mug steeping a bag of Constant Comment, when his foster mother had knocked on the door. She knew a little about Jeff from a phone conversation with his DSS social worker—dinosaurs—but she needed to put him in context. Why he was seeing her, when, how, and what did he know about what had happened to him.

Gates, Jeffrey Arthur, age 10 . . . aggravated and protracted sexual abuse . . .

Now the boy was sitting three feet away and it was obvious he thought she was just one more person he had to tell his story to. About the right size for a ten-year-old, black hair that fell over his hazel eyes, slight body. Bored and detached? Yes, that was it, not quite present.

. . . father perpetrator . . . abuse began when Jeffrey was six years old, with mother's tacit consent . . . mother deserted family, has had no contact with Jeffrey for a year and seven months . . .

Detachment made perfect sense—how else would Jeff had gotten through four years of—what had the father said? *Servicing his sexual needs.* God. And the mother—the father blamed her, of course, after throwing him out of her bedroom. All her fault. In the next bedroom for three years, knowing what her husband was doing to their son. She had left a year ago, without warning. Fixed the boy's breakfast, got him ready for school, then drove away. No contact with the boy since. Camille felt like throwing her pencil across the room, followed by her stapler, coffee cup, and whatever else was within reach. She never got used to it—each time, each new case, she hurt all over. Now she wanted to take this little boy in her lap and rock him, tell him to cry, it wasn't his fault. Camille closed the file. Jeff had been told, she was sure, over and over and over, that it wasn't his fault, that he had done nothing wrong. Now she had to make him believe it. Those eyes—in a certain light, Jeff's eyes almost seem to be glowing, like two green fires.

Mrs. Bondurant's office was like most of the rooms Jeff had been in with adults who wrote things down and read folders and nodded and tapped their pencils. This one was a little different: there was an open chest in one corner and blocks, stuffed animals, plastic dinosaurs, and Transformers spilled out onto the floor, in an untidy heap. The floor was covered with a bright patchwork of carpet squares, reds, greens, yellows, blues, browns, whites.

"I hear you collect dinosaurs. See anything over there you like?" the woman asked, between sips of her tea. The tea bag label dangled out of her mug.

Jeff jumped, startled. The woman laughed. "Go on. Go on over and poke through the toys. They're for the kids who come here. Let me show you some of my favorites," she said and to add to Jeff's surprise, got up and walked over to the toy chest and started poking around herself. "Here, have you seen this one before?" she asked and held up a large, blue one with three horns.

"That's a triceratops. Everybody knows what they are," Jeff said. For a minute, he had thought she actually knew something about dinosaurs. But she was like all the others who had tried the same tricks to get him to talk.

The woman looked at him and laughed. "Yeah, you're right. I did know that. I bet you've had a whole bunch of people talk to you about dinosaurs, haven't you? And probably not a one knew a whole lot, did they? All right, I won't ask you about dinosaurs. You probably know more about them than I do, even if I did go to the library last night. Let's talk about something else."

Jeff nodded. He had to be careful. This woman was different.

"Mrs. Clark said you had a bad dream last night. Do you want to talk about it?" she asked and sat down on an old couch that was between the toy chest and her desk.

Jeff shook his hand. Not that dream, when he was trapped and it was dark and he couldn't move and there was nowhere to go. He had woken himself screaming and there, standing half in the yellow light of his lamp and half in shadow, had been a strange woman, her dark hair trailing down her back. Behind her was a man, hurriedly tying a knot in his white bathrobe. Jeff could see the man's hairy chest, a dark V between the white. Who were they and where was he? The wide bed wasn't his, nor were the sheets, decorated with Snoopy and Woodstock. His sheets were plain white. The dresser wasn't his. And what was in the strange darkness that he couldn't see? He was breathing hard, panting, his fists gripping the sheets. He had pushed away from the strangers, back against the wall—

"Jeff? What's the matter? Bad dream?"

Jeff looked at her, still breathing hard, pulling the sheet up to his neck. "You aren't my mother. You aren't my father," he had added to the man who was yawning as he sat down in a chair by the door.

The dark-haired woman had sat down very carefully and slowly in another chair by the strange bed. Jeff pressed back even harder against the wall, although he knew it wouldn't do any good. No matter how hard he had tried to get away, to push himself through the wall, it had never been enough. And sometimes he hadn't tried to escape through the wall. Sometimes he has just moved over and let his father slip into his bed. Sometimes Jeff would reach over and touch his father first. Things would hurt less, and would be over sooner.

That meant I wanted him to do it, doesn't it, he had once said to one of the adults with the pencils and the folders. *Doesn't it?*

No, no, no. You were just surviving, coping . . . That's what they all said.

"No, I'm not your mother and Fred isn't your father. Count to ten, think. Take a deep breath. I'm Ellen, and Fred, and this is our house. You live here now, remember?"

Jeff had nodded his head, slowly, his breathing slowing down. He had remembered everything.

Not that dream, he thought, and looked back at Mrs. Bondurant. He shook his head again. "Not that dream—that's the bad one."

"Well, do you have any dreams you can tell me about?"

"Well," Jeff said slowly, "I have been having other dreams, about another place."

"Tell me," Mrs. Bondurant said and leaned back on the couch, the triceratops still in her hand.

"Sometimes I dream about the same boys and the same girl. One boy has red hair and the other's hair is blond. The girl's hair is brown. And when I see them, I always see a blue fire around them. Sometimes I dream my dinosaurs, the ones at Mrs. Clark's house, are flying and leaving trails in the air, like a jet does, except blue. Last night I dreamed about the sea again."

He had stood alone on a sand dune, with a huge cliff at his back. Two moons shone in a starry sky. Someone, something, had called his name, and he had ran toward the voice, which came from the water.

"It was a dolphin calling my name. I woke up before I could get out to him."

"You've had this dream before—have you ever gotten to the dolphin?"

"Not yet."

"What do you think he wants? To play in the water?"

"Well," Jeff said, "I think he wants me. He wants me to come and be where he is, to his place."

As Jeff told me his sea-dream, his eyes seemed to become even greener and brighter. Alone, safe, the sea, the womb, the dolphin an animal guide, a protector—not too sure about the twin moons and the cliff. And the other dream—a reenactment of the abuse, no doubt, a return to the dark where he was hurt. But in his sea dream the dark is safe and wonderful and inviting and he isn't alone, the dolphin is there to help him, be his friend. Jeff also dreams of flying. The escape motif is dominant, coupled with the desire for safety . . . Funny, when he left, I would have sworn I smelled the ocean . . .

Benjamin Paul Tyson's journal, Monday night, August 26, 1991

The ceiling fan is beating down over my head. Outside I hear crickets and cicadas, cranking, cranking, cranking, their screeches reaching a crescendo, then gone. And again, and ebb and flow of noise. It's hot. Even with the fan on, I am sweating. I guess the computer generates more heat than I thought. At least the window units in the bedrooms are cranking right along with the insects.

Maybe I'll give in tomorrow and call the local AC boys and order central air. I can certainly afford it. Well, not tomorrow, since tomorrow is the first day of school and I am afraid for my son. He hasn't been fairy-sick since the first of the month, since Lughnasad, but I am certain there will be other bouts. What happens if he gets sick at school? Will his teacher whack out or call 911 or Dorothea Dix and have him taken away in a straitjacket?

I have been to Nottingham Heights, talked with the principal, a Miss Hallie Bigelow. A bit rough around the edges, but she cares passionately for her school, the children, education—a good woman. His teacher, Charlotte Collins, seemed a bit cold, but all right. Probably distracted, the first day and all.

Maybe I should put him in a private school. Ravenscroft is supposed to be one of the best. I can certainly afford that, too—I have barely touched the money Emma left me in her will. New cars every few years, yes. But mostly I have spent it on Malachi. To arrange for his forged birth certificate, immunization records, doctor's records, fake physicals.

And all the books and art prints. His mother loved art museums.

But Malachi is different enough. Putting him in a private school would mark him as even more set apart from the rest. No thanks.

Besides, it's not the school I am worried about so much. Notting-ham Heights feels like a good place. No, it's not the school—it's everything else. People are talking and whispering—not about Malachi—but it's like the very air has become charged, or the atmo-spheric energy has changed its voltage, AC to DC. The list of strangenesses gets longer and longer. Since Lughnasad, in Wake County alone, I have noted the following:

1. *Man found in tree in Pullen Park, swears he spontaneously levi-tated, placed under observation at Wake County Medical.*
2. *Sixteen sightings of UFOs: mostly balls of green and blue light. Three people claim they saw a dragon in flight; five, a winged horse.*
3. *Ghosts sighted at almost every graveyard in the county.*
4. *St. Raphael's Catholic Church petitions Archbishop for an exor-cism; claims education wing is infested with poltergeists.*
5. *As for poltergeists: incidents in bars, schools, playgrounds, offices, malls. One afternoon at Crabtree Valley Mall, the store security gates kept rising and falling, every five minutes, for two hours.*
6. *Librarians at Cameron Village arrive to find every book off the shelf, stacked in neat piles all over the library. A handful, like birds released from a cage, were flying about the room, hitting against doors as if trying to escape. Two librarians were placed on medical leave.*
7. *Power shortages, blackouts, appliances, cars going dead—repair-men and mechanics swamped with calls.*
8. *In the past two weeks, fifteen people have called in unicorn sight-ings, in gardens, backyards, front yards, highways.*

And I have seen the Fomorii—or rather their ghosts or shadows or projections. I've felt them: that sense of dread, of evil, of badness. Last week I'd swear one came in the library, looking for Malachi, a dark, scaly creature, those red eyes. Mal was sitting in the children's section, reading, and the thing was going straight toward him. I ran across the library, yelling.

Of course there was nothing there. Mrs. Carmichael thinks I need to see a doctor. I don't know—maybe Jack is right. He thinks I am projecting my own fears, conjuring up my own shadows. Regardless, I won't let Malachi take off the twelve-pointed star, even to bathe.

His mother could have blasted the thing with a fireball or some-thing. I don't know if Malachi could have or not. He is still just a ten-year-old boy, who is half-human as well as half-fairy.

Malachi continues to change, sometimes slowly, sometimes all at once. His eyes are golden now, and sometimes they glow in the dark. His ears are as pointed as his mother's, and like hers, nobody but me and Jack notice they are. He seems to have instinctively hidden them with fairy glamour. He can fly. He is psychokinetic and he can manipulate light and he is beginning to see auras. But Malachi can't count on any of his fairy-powers—his age? His human heritage? And while we have had no more crazy nights with wild lights, I know he doesn't feel well a lot of the time. He tires easily and his appetite is off; he's losing weight.

You know, there must be a lot of fairy DNA in the human genome. There have always been clairvoyants, witches, fortune-tellers, mediums, psychokinetics, levitators and bilocators, telepaths—the paranormal list goes on. Yes, a goodly number of these paranormals were and are fakes, but now, I believe the rest were and are real. All the changeling stories, the incubi and succubae, the pregnancies that "just happened"—they're true, or a lot are. But, doesn't this fly in the face of all we know about biology? How can two species, Homo magicus, and Homo sapiens, from two different rooms in the House of Creation, interbreed? Perhaps all we know are the operative words here, but even given that, I think there must be another explanation. I think the answer might be in another old story, one I don't know that well, and actually haven't read, but have only heard about. Adam was supposed to have had a first wife, Lilith, according to Jewish folklore. And Lilith, in other Semitic myths, was a demon, or had extraordinary powers. I remember in the Narnia stories Lilith was supposed to be a jinn, and the ancestress of the White Witch. Perhaps God originally had thought to give humankind magic, the paranormal, ESP, as a manifest part of our being. Did He change his mind? Did Lilith succumb to some sort of temptation, as Adam and Eve did? Or did God intend for Homo magicus and Homo sapiens to be separate all along and yet related and connected, cousin species, like dogs and wolves? Lilith left Adam or did he cast her out? I wish I knew the story. Whatever happened, I bet she left pregnant. And she just went next door, so to speak, through a door that has been, apparently, easy to open.

Now, Malachi thinks there is a difference in witches and fairies. Witches do magic, fairies are magic. Valeria never mentioned witches in Faerie—but then, did we talk about everything? Are witches something peculiar to our universe? Did Lilith leave a few of her children here?

I don't know.

☆　　☆　　☆

Malachi is telepathic now, too. It started a week after Lughnasad. We were going to Jack and Hilda's for dinner. I was in my bedroom, changing clothes and worrying about Hilda, about what Jack had told her, if he had told her, and how she would behave around Malachi. Some serious fretting.

Malachi came down the hall. "Dad, Hilda's okay. Jack hasn't told her about me yet, but she will be okay. Don't worry; it will be okay."

I stood there half-dressed, in my underwear and a Carolina T-shirt, and stared at him. "How did you know I was worrying about her?"

"I heard you."

"Mal, I wasn't talking out loud. I was thinking—you heard my thoughts." I sat down hard on the bed, with my head in my hands. Malachi came and sat down beside me on the bed.

Dad?

I looked up. "And you can—what mind-talk, too? Farspeak?"

"Dad, don't be mad at me; I didn't know; I didn't mean to listen in—"

He started crying and I hugged him. And we talked. About how people's thoughts—even his father's—are private and farspeaking is one thing, but listening in was no better than eavesdropping, and would he want everybody to hear his thoughts?

Like all his new fairy-senses or abilities, Malachi can't rely on his telepathy. But he's learning how to screen out other people—sort of like a background radio or TV, he said—and can really only pick up the thoughts of people really close to him. Mine, Jack's, mostly. Not Thomas, which surprised me at first, but then Thomas Ruggles is part of the strangeness, too. I don't want him near my son. Thomas is more than a little creepy and he smells wrong—not BO, really, but like a really old book or corners in deserted houses, an obscure spice. Thomas smells dark. And his eyes: they have become opaque and hard, like cold stones set in his head.

Thomas and Jack aren't talking.

Anyway.

I have to take him to Faerie; I know that, but I don't know how. I watch him—he's not well and he's not getting well. Being here, being half-fairy and having no real control over his feyness—if I don't get Malachi to Faerie, he's going to die.

I have stacks of books in my office on fairy lore, magic, Wicca, the occult, and I am going through them, painstakingly, looking for clues. In Ireland, there are fairy mounds and fairy rings. And the Cherokee have stories about gates between here and the Otherworld, which are behind waterfalls and under cliffs and beneath dark pools. To pass through into what sounds like Faerie—a world of little people, giants, humans with super powers, strange animals—one had to fast, bathe, and have a magical guide.

Which doesn't help me. Valeria was going to take a taxi to her gate, so it is near Garner and Raleigh. The next day the gates can be opened is Halloween or Samhain. I have two months to find her gate and take my son down the Straight Road to Faerie and save his life. In all the books, so far nothing, except the Cherokee stories, says North Carolina, let alone the eastern Piedmont.

Two months.

I lit a candle in church yesterday, after mass at St. Mary's. One of the tall, two-dollar ones. A new priest, fresh from seminary, Father Jamey Applewhite, gave the homily, on the Catholic perspective of the world as sacramental, as being imbued with the presence of God, and God as an ultimately unknowable mystery expressed in Creation. Accept the mystery, he said. There is no reason to be afraid of what we cannot hope to ever fully understand, at least in this world. The Celts accepted the mystery. They lived in a sacral world, numinous with spirits in trees, lakes, fountains, springs. Like Faerie.

I am afraid for my son, that his mystery will not be accepted, by the people around him, by the very earth itself.

Malachi keeps asking me to tell the story about his mother, over and over. Every detail again and again, about her, about Faerie. So I tell him the story over and over and over again . . .

The Chamber of the Dodecagon, The Library Tower, The White City, Faerie

After the rite and the feast were over, the Second remained behind to clean up and put everything in its proper place. Out of habit she repeated the healing words said to close the rite and seal the call to the changelings. She carefully gathered the salt from around the burning, white candles and took the bowl of water and rue off the table and after saying the appropriate words, emptied the bowl out the window. The White City could stand healing as well. Then she put the bowl back on the shelf by the window.

"This candle is the earth that is sorely wounded. By the power of the Light Beyond The Light, we abjure the wounds and call home those who were sent out, that their strength will strengthen the earth," the Second said and extinguished the north candle. The white shadows that played around her grew smaller and less distinct.

"This candle is the fire that heals as it burns, refines, and changes. By the power of The Light Beyond The Light, we dissolve the scars of the hurting flame and call home those who were sent out, that their souls will enkindle the flames of light and healing that are flickering," the Second said and extinguished the south candle.

"This candle is the wind that clears and sooths the mind, the heart, and the soul. By the power of The Light Beyond The Light, we ask for the wind of light, warmth, and sweetness; we call home those who were sent out, that their minds will make the very air clear and sharp and strong." She extinguished the east candle. The room grew smaller as the third white flame was put out.

"This last candle is the water that cleanses and nourishes away the dark. By the power of The Light Beyond The Light, we call for the water of life as we call home those were sent out, that they may bring new life."

When the west candle was out, the only light in the room, coming through the north and east windows, was that of White Moon, a silvery white outlining the tables and the chairs and candles and the shelves in sharp silhouette. The bowls on the shelves glowed. The Second stood at the north window for a long time, watching the moon and smelling the sea before she finally left, carefully leaving the door slightly ajar behind her.

III

Nottingham Heights Elementary School
Tuesday, August 27 - Saturday, September 21, 1991

Russell

RUSSELL STROKED THE GLOW-IN-THE-DARK BAT-man symbol on his new T-shirt as he rehearsed what he would say when he had to share his summer vacation with his new fifth grade class. *And where did you go on your summer vacation?* Russell rolled his eyes. He could just hear the teacher's sing-song first day nicey-nicey voice. As if by the time the twentieth kid told about a trip to the beach the teacher wasn't bored out of her mind. *I worked all summer for my stepmother's parents. They hate me; I hate them. I had a great summer. I hate my stepmother. She hates me.*

He looked over at Jeanie who was driving him to his first day at his new school, Nottingham Heights Elementary. She had taken Russell shopping for new school clothes on Saturday, at the Kmart in Garner. She had at first refused to let him get the Batman T-shirt, but had given in. Even so, this morning Jeanie had not been happy to see Russell wearing it.

"You are hell-bent on wearing that T-shirt on your first day, aren't you? Russell, we got you some nice clothes for school and you want to wear that. If that don't beat all. Haven't you got any sense? I swear, I don't know why I bother. I should have never let you talk me into buying it. I treat you as if you were my own . . ."

She had kept talking all through breakfast and out into the car. Not even another fire in the kitchen trash can, a small one this time, slowed her down. *Damn, if that wasn't the strangest thing—I wonder if there is something in the can's metal, maybe I should call the fire department—come on, Russell, let's go, it's out, get in the car . . .* Russell wondered if she slowed down to breathe. He was trying hard not to listen to anything she had to say to him on the way to school. Now she was talking about how tired she was with the twins coming and all and she couldn't always drive Russell to school, but since it was the first day and all, well. Russell nodded and uh-umed and tried to focus on the radio. It was on a top 40 station and he wanted to turn it up, but the last time he had done that in the car his father had popped him.

Focusing on the radio didn't work; he could still hear Jeanie talking. Maybe closing his eyes and trying to remember last night's dream would shut her out. He had had another good dream, not like the ones he usually had. Sometimes he would be in front of his class in his underwear or in nothing. Or the teacher would be yelling and yelling as he cowered under his desk. He would be sitting in a reading group, stumbling over words in the simplest book, words he knew he knew. Or his father would be chasing him through the house, the yard, into the woods. And lately there were dreams that left him with stained sheets in the morning. Russell looked over at Jeanie as casually as possible. Six months pregnant. She looked like she had swallowed half-a-watermelon. Looking at Jeanie and thinking about her being pregnant and how she got pregnant made Russell feel the way he felt when he woke up from the stained-sheet dreams. He hadn't been sure where each part fit but after discovering a stack of old *Playboy*s and *Penthouse*s in the corner of the attic, he now had a pretty good idea. Looking at the pictures and at Jeanie and thinking about her and his father made Russell want to touch himself. And that made him think of other things, of things that scared him, that it was the naked men in *Penthouse* that he had looked at the longest. No, he would just have to be sure he was looking at naked women the next time, that's all, that would do it. As for *who* was in the sheet-staining dreams—no, he *wouldn't* remember. He couldn't even get his mind around that. He was a boy, so it was impossible, end of story.

Russell shook his head. Last night's dream hadn't been one of the sheet-stainers. It had started with his father chasing him, yelling and throwing rocks. Russell had run into the woods and hadn't stopped running until he came to a meadow and could no longer hear his father's voice. And as he stood there, Russell knew he had escaped from a bad dream into a good one, as all around the edges of the meadow were the white trees. A winged horse stood in the meadow grass, waiting for him, and said for Russell to climb on his back. They had flown high above the trees and Russell could remember the cold air on his chest and in his hair. He could feel the horse's sides against his legs and hear the beating of the great wings. And the horse's voice: throaty and rough.

He had found bruises on the insides of his thighs this morning in the shower. Russell had examined them in amazement, even pushing at them to the point he had cried out in pain, as the water beat on his head.

I was really there.

"It's going to be another hot, sticky day, with highs in the mid-nineties, and lows tonight in the lower seventies . . ."

"We're there. Russell, at least run a comb through your hair," Jeanie said.

Russell blinked and sat up to read the neatly lettered sign on the hill just above where they were parked: NOTTINGHAM HEIGHTS ELEMENTARY SCHOOL. The building looked like every other school Russell had ever seen, in Oklahoma, Kansas, and North Carolina. It was one story, brick, with two wings spreading out from the center. A limp American flag hung on the flagpole. Tall pine trees grew around the building and brown needles and pine cones covered the side walk and the grass. Pine needle littered steps led up to the front door. Evergreen shrubbery lined the sidewalk and hugged the walls. *Maybe I'll tell them I went to the beach for two weeks and got up every day to go swimming and ride the waves and fish off the pier and look for sea shells and build sand castles and at night we'd go out to a seafood restaurant, Captain Bill's, for a big dinner and . . .*

"I swear, Russell, will you wake up? I ain't got all day," Jeanie snapped, her hands on her hips, from the top of the stairs. He tried to walk as fast as she was, but he couldn't. Russell was walking into a new school and each step was bringing him closer to the questioning and frowning teachers and the laughing and whispering students in his worst dreams. He wasn't entering a safe place. He almost bolted when the front door closed behind them.

"Wait here," Jeanie said, and after pushing back her blond hair, went into the office. Russell sat down at a round table between the front door and the office door and turned to face a line of kindergartners looking him over. Russell was sure they were whispering about how big his feet were. At least they didn't know he was twelve and in the fifth grade. The kindergarten teacher came back from wherever she had been and stood in front of the line, one hand high in the air, the other shushing. The kids copied her and trotted off obediently down the hall. Russell looked into the office. Jeanie was talking with a small, dark woman, her hands moving like birds just startled by a hunter. If Jeanie's hands were cut off, Russell thought, she wouldn't be able to talk.

He could her muffled voice through the glass. "You know, Miz Bigelow, the child failed kindergarten and first grade 'cause his daddy and mama split up. That woman drove his daddy crazy, what with all her boyfriends and one day she just up and took the baby and left, didn't say kiss my foot . . ."

Looking straight down I could see into the forest. The golden and silvery leaves and the white trunks were shining in the moonlight. A few trees, like dark flowers in the silver and white, had green leaves, so dark a green they were black. Here and there, I saw fir trees, sort of like spruces, blue-green-silver. Two moons shone in the sky . . .

Finally Jeanie stopped talking and started filling out and signing forms. A few minutes later, she and the small, dark lady came out into the lobby. "Russell, this is Miss Bigelow, the principal here," Jeanie said. "She'll tell you which bus to take to get home. You know where the key is. Stay inside and do your homework when you get home. I'll get home about when your daddy does, around six or so. Behave yourself, bye."

Russell rolled his eyes when she finally left for Food Lion. He let himself relax the tiniest bit—but not too much. He couldn't in a school; he wasn't safe. Miss Bigelow closed the door behind Jeanie and turned to face Russell. He was alone with her and the silence. The halls were empty. Inside the office, a black lady, Trudy Anderson according to her name plate, sat behind a paper-cluttered desk and typed, the phone cradled on her shoulder. Russell looked up at Miss Bigelow, his hands tight in his lap beneath the table. She really was little; Russell could tell he was already taller. She had short, streaked blond hair that somebody seemed to have whacked off and leathery skin. Miss Bigelow had a clipboard in one hand and a pencil in the other and she was nodding her head as she gave Russell a sharp appraising look.

"Well, now that we have checked each other out, are you ready to go to your new classroom?" Miss Bigelow asked in a quick voice. "I'm not gonna bite you and you aren't gonna bite me—you aren't, are you? Ready?"

"Uh, no, I mean, I'm ready. Yeah, let's go," he said. Russell followed Miss Bigelow down the hall. She talked a mile a minute about the school: here was the library, over here was the computer lab, the art room, this was a second grade, and Nottingham children were expected to behave, walk on the right side of the hall, and when a teacher raised her hand, that was the signal to be quiet. Got that? Her tennis shoes made no sound on the linoleum. (Russell had never seen any teacher, let alone a principal, wear tennis shoes at school.) All he could hear was her voice until she opened a door at the end of the hall, Mrs. Collins's fifth grade, here we are.

Russell felt like an idiot standing in front of the class while the principal and Mrs. Collins huddled together over his thick folder. He knew every kid in the room was watching him. *So look at something else, huh? Stare out the window, why doncha? Just leave me alone, okay?* Russell stared back, especially at a brown-haired girl wearing glasses in the second row. She was small and slight and looked really smart. You could tell. After she looked away, Russell knew he could make her miserable. It would be easy.

A very small blond-haired boy looked at Russell in frank recognition, as if he had always known Russell and had just seen him the day before. Russell had never seen anybody with eyes like the boy had, almost the color of a dog's, a golden brown.

"Third new one this morning, Mrs. Collins. Mrs. Markham got the first one, filled her up, you got the last two. Have a good first day, Russell; I'll check on you this afternoon," Miss Bigelow said and she left, closing the door behind her.

"Class, we just met Malachi; this is Russell White. Russell, why don't you sit over there by Malachi in the third row. Mrs. Perry, could you get Russell his books?" Mrs. Collins said. Russell saw an older, grey-haired, heavy woman, in a bright flowered dress, heave herself up out of her chair in the back of the room. She smiled in his direction and he sat down by the funny-eyed Malachi who was very intently reading his spelling book.

Mrs. Perry looked like Miss McNeil, Russell thought. Almost just like her. He wondered if she would be as nice as Miss McNeil. *From Thanksgiving to Easter, in first grade, Miss McNeil had been Russell's teacher. She was a big, dark-haired woman who was constantly dieting. She ate celery sticks and peanut butter for snacks and Carnation Breakfast bars for lunch. Russell and his little brother had then been living with their grandmother. She took Russell to school his first day.*

"This is my daughter's boy, Russell," his grandmother had said and left Russell at the door. (He had written his grandmother once after moving to North Carolina. The card had come back marked Addressee Deceased. He had sent a birthday card to his mother in

Arizona at the same time; that card had come back marked Addressee Moved, No Forwarding Address.) Russell stood in the doorway for a long moment until Miss McNeil crossed the room and took him by the hand.

"Russell. Did you know your name means red-haired, like a fox? And your hair sure is red. We're studying names right now. Let me show you a picture of a fox in this book. See, he lost his tail and he's trying to get it back. He has to ask three people to help," she said and she sat down in a small chair in front of the blackboard. She patted a chair beside her and Russell sat down. "After Christmas, when we study Indians—there are lots of Indians in Oklahoma, you know—you can be Red Fox." Russell leaned over to look at the book. He inhaled her peanut butter aroma.

Each day had been like that. Russell would wake up early and be out the door, zooming through breakfast to catch the bus. The wait on the playground before the first bell took forever. Miss McNeil was always there when he raced in the classroom door. He signed Red Fox on all his papers, printing in big block letters—

"Russell. Russell? You need to open your social studies book now. Put the rest in your desk. Now. Let's get off to a good start, shall we?"

Russell sighed. Mrs. Collins was staring fixedly at him from her desk. He looked away quickly and pulled his social studies book out of the stack still on top of his desk. Her eyes were hard and cold and dark.

"First page, the bottom," someone whispered.

It was the golden-eyed boy. Russell managed a half-smile in thanks and opened his book.

Jeff

Jeff's seat was in the back of the room. Mrs. Markham, his new teacher, had been very apologetic about having to put him at the very back, but Jeff didn't care. He liked it in the back, especially today his first day in a new school, the first day after summer vacation. He had sat in the back at his last school and the school before that. Jeff could be invisible in the back and dissolve into the pale green wall, where no one and nothing could touch him. When the teacher asked a question, she wouldn't even see him. His last teacher hadn't, until everything had happened, of course, and everybody knew. After that, he would look up to find her watching him. She would look away quickly, sighing guiltily.

He was pretty sure Mrs. Markham knew, too, but she wasn't sneaking looks at him as if he were some strange bug dropped in her class.

Mrs. Markham's class was having art. Earlier in the morning, Mrs. Markham had had sharing so everybody could tell the class about at least one thing they had done for summer vacation. When she had looked at Jeff, he had shook his head: no. It wasn't that his foster parents, the Clarks, hadn't taken Jeff swimming and to the movies, and even for one week, to the beach; rather it was that Jeff didn't want to talk. Besides, for the rest of the summer, after leaving his father, Jeff had felt as if he were watching a very long, long movie, one in which his character seemed to have a very small part.

Jeff watched the art teacher, Miss Melton, as she passed out huge sheets of white drawing paper. He liked how smooth and clean the paper felt. Jeff carefully printed his name in the lower left-hand corner. She handed out crayons next and then started explaining just what today's art project was . . . *Jeff stood on the sand, on the crest of a dune; he was on the same beach. Above him was the same star-crowded sky as before. Jeff inhaled and then exhaled in a loud whoosh. In, out, in, out. There. Finally he started walking through the sand and the dune grass; he liked the wet way the grass licked at his leg.*

"I wonder how this place looks in daylight," Jeff whispered. He had never felt so safe as on this beach, but still Jeff knew things hid in the shadows and the corners and came out when the sun was down. And once they were out, there was no way to send the things back.

What was that shadow—*a dragon, a flying dragon? Yes. Great bursts of yellow and orange flame shot out of the shadow's mouth and its huge black wings blocked the stars. The dragon circled the beach and then landed half-way between the dunes and the surf. A black tidal pool was between the dragon and Jeff. He watched as the dragon settled down, folding its wings and tucking in its tail. Its eyes glowed molten gold and bright sparks fell out of its mouth. He could hear some of the sparks hissing on the wet sand.*

Jeff had no idea how long he stood there, watching the dragon watch him, its hot eyes half-open, hazy smoke from its nostrils blurring the air. There was nowhere to run—and how could he outrun a creature that could fly and breathe fire? The only place he could begin to be safe was in the water and the dragon lay right beside the pool and between Jeff and the sea. The dragon's tail had come untucked and twitched back and forth, the way a cat's tail would, drawing huge patterns in the sand. Its green scales glittered in the double moonlight and starlight.

Finally he made his way down the dune, slipping and sliding until he was on the hard-packed wet sand. He took another deep breath and walked toward the dragon—this was a dream, after all, wasn't it? He couldn't be hurt in a dream, could he? Not really, right? The water in the tidal pool came up to his knees and felt warm on his feet, like bath water. The dragon watched him as he waded across the pool. Jeff stopped, still in the pool, but now less than ten feet from the monster. Jeff was sure the dragon knew his name and all about him—even what had happened in the dark. How and why, Jeff had no idea.

"Okay, dragon, here I am. You aren't going to eat me, are you?"

When the dragon spoke, its voice sounded the only way Jeff had thought a dragon could sound: low and deep, like slow thunder. "No, Human Boy, I am not going to eat you. I want you to look down in the water. What do you see?"

Jeff looked down to see his face in the dark water and wavery reflections of the two moons. He saw his black hair, all shaggy and rough about his face. The face that looked back was pale and his hazel eyes looked greener and deeper. His ears—what had happened to his ears? Both his ears were pointed. Jeff touched each point gently, pulled at each one—they were real. He traced the shapes of his ears with his fingers—what? His ears felt smooth—yet looked pointed. And he had felt the points.

"Dragon," Jeff said and held up his hand to ask a question. The monster nodded and Jeff took a step forward and fell into the pool and kept falling. And falling, falling, through the water, through a close darkness. He couldn't see or hear or touch anything, not even his hands, his own face. He tried to scream but found he had no voice or even a mouth. His corporeal self was gone. Finally, Jeff heard a sound, a loud tearing, and with a thud, he hit the floor and he could find his hands and feet, his head, and he could see. He was in his bedroom, on the floor, surrounded by his dinosaurs . . .

"You must be the new boy Mrs. Markham was telling me about."

Jeff looked up to see the art teacher standing over him. A blue pencil stuck out of her hair and green and red chalk was smeared on her cheek.

"May I see your drawing, Jeff? I don't think I have ever seen anything quite like it."

Jeff handed her his drawing and the woman held it out at arm's length.

"Tell me about it, Jeff. Have you been to this beach before?"

"Just once, this summer, for the first time," Jeff said very slowly. "I just drew what I remembered and added the dragon for fun."

Please don't ask me any more questions, just give me my drawing back. Or you can have it; just don't ask me any more questions.

"May I put this up for the rest of the class to see? It's really good."

Jeff shrugged; it didn't matter what she did or what he might say. Adults always did whatever they wanted. Jeff sank back in his seat and watched as the art teacher showed the drawing to the class, talking about its strong colors and shapes and imagination. Jeff wanted to drop through the floor.

Russell

Monday morning the second week of school Russell woke up in the afterglow of another special dream: the white trees, the meadow, a flying horse, a centaur. The centaur had told him to do something; it would help him understand if he did it. Russell tried to remember as he stretched out in bed, light half on his face from the window, his feet pushing against the sheets, but the centaur's words were gone. He got up and stretched again and looked out the attic window into a sky of grey and black clouds, pregnant with rain. If only he could remember.

Trying hard to remember, so hard he didn't watch where he was going on the bus got Russell into a fight. And every bit of the glowy feeling left by the dream was gone when he found himself across the desk from Miss Bigelow. She was on the phone when the driver brought Russell into the office and gestured him into a chair where he sat and waited, staring around her office. A dark blue Duke mug with cold coffee sat on the corner of a coffee-stained desk calendar. File trays flanked the heavily written-on calendar on both sides. Papers and manila folders spilled out of the trays like magazines on a living room table. File cabinets, two or three umbrellas, a coat hanging on a rack. An enormous Blue Devil poster on the wall, and framed photographs of teachers standing on the front steps of the school. The phone call went on and on—an unhappy parent, the bus hadn't even slowed down—and Russell started squirming in the chair. What would she do if he just got up and ran?

"Don't even think about it, Russell, sit right there. No, no, not you, Mrs. McHannahan. I'll take care of this, I'll talk to the driver this afternoon. You're welcome. Good-bye."

Miss Bigelow hung up the phone and pushed back in her chair, picked up the bus discipline report, and then looked at Russell. "Well, this isn't getting off to a good start, now, is it?" Miss Bigelow said, glaring at him over her dark-rimmed glasses. "It looks like you're up to your old tricks again, now, doesn't it? I've got a thick handful here of old bus disciplinary reports from your last two schools," she added and flipped the current one onto her desk.

"Do you think your parents will be pleased to hear about this? And I am going to call them, Russell, I promise you that. We don't have this kind of behavior at Nottingham Heights, Russell. Two more of these and you'll be walking to school. Follow me?" She leaned further back in her chair, her hands steepled together. Russell wondered if she leaned back any further if the chair would flip over and send old Miz Bigelow flying through the window.

"Yeah." *Please don't call Daddy. Maybe he won't be home; maybe he will be out on a job. Maybe I can get home before he does and erase the answering machine and he'll never know.*

"Yeah what?"

"Yeah, you're making yourself clear, Miz Bigelow."

"Yes ma'am is what I was looking for. Go on to class, Russell."

She didn't even ask me what happened. She didn't even ask me if it was my fault. That other kid started it. Same old crap.

Things didn't get better in the classroom. Russell had left his homework on his night-table. He had been too busy trying to remember what the centaur had told him to do. He didn't try to explain to Mrs. Collins, he didn't think she would believe him, and besides, she was too busy delivering a speech on being responsible and getting off on the right foot and fulfilling one's potential. She repeated a mind is a terrible thing to waste about three times. Russell sat stony-faced as she went on and on. He had heard it all before, even the wasted mind. Teachers must all read the same book. God, he hated her and this was only his fifth day in her room. If he had a cream pie to throw at her or maybe a trip wire between her desk and the door. Or a bucket of water on top of the door.

In the library Russell tried to trip Hazel to make himself feel better.

"First, last, and only warning, Russell," Mrs. Perkins, the librarian said, her hands on her hips. When he yelled at the yellow-eyed boy with the funny name for looking at him, she blessed him out in front of the entire class. She was so hot and bothered by what Russell had done that she was sweating. But, then, Russell thought, not listening, waiting for his chance to speak, *I'm sweating, too. It got real hot in here all of a sudden.*

"But he was looking funny at me! He was—I swear he was, as if he knew me! You're not being fair—"

The smoke alarm over the library door went off—so loud and

piercing that everyone, including Mrs. Perkins, winced in pain, covered their ears. A few of the kids started crying and kept crying as the kids were herded out into the hall and back to their classroom.

But even with a reprieve in the library, by the end of the day Russell's name was on the board with three checks beside it, thus guaranteeing a U for his weekly conduct grade ("And it's only Monday and the second week of school, Russell; am I going to have to put you in a cage for the rest of the year?") and a whipping from his father, phone call or no phone call. But the truly worst thing was that all the magical afterglow of the dream was gone, gone, gone. And he couldn't even remember how the centaur sounded, let alone his words.

"I'm going to call your mother at work this afternoon, Russell. I will certainly have a lot to tell her," Mrs. Collins said with a thin smile when his bus was called.

She's my stepmother, you bitch. She's not my real mother. I hate her and I hate you.

Russell thought Jeanie sounded a lot like Mrs. Collins that night at the dinner table. Jeanie probably memorized everything Mrs. Collins said word for word, he thought, as he pushed his food around his plate. "She said the boy is angry all the time, Larry. He talks back and is *dis*-ruptive in the classroom and gets into alterca— fights and he got in trouble on the bus today, too. He's gotta ride that bus, Larry. I can't run him out to school every day. I'm already late for work when I get sick in the mornings . . ."

"He don't need no coun-ser-lor," his daddy said when Jeanie finally ran out of Mrs. Collins's words. "Boy, got anything to say for yerself? Don't you know the hell how to behave? You wanna walk yer sorry ass to school? Huh? Answer me boy."

"No."

Even though this time his daddy used the buckle end of the belt Russell still managed not to cry out. He knew that not crying made his daddy hit him all the harder, but if Russell could keep back the tears until he was safe up in his attic room it would be a small victory. When he did finally get upstairs, Russell let himself cry until he was weak and tired. Then he sat up and gingerly walked over to his dresser and his Nativity scene. Outside he could see it was raining. The sky brightened every few minutes with lightning, throwing the trees into sharp, black silhouettes. The rumbling thunder sounded like rocks rolling down a mountain. He took each statue out. First the fox, then the two sheep, the cow, and the donkey. The shepherds, the three kings, and Mary and Joseph. The Baby he left in the manger.

I hate him. Russell put the shepherds and kings back in. *Why didn't she take me instead of Adam? I loved her the best. I've got homework to do.* Then the sheep, the donkey. The cows and the fox. *I hate him.* Mary and Joseph. *I think I have a test tomorrow. I hate him. Why is it so hot in here? The windows are open. It's pouring down rain. It smells hot. Why can't I remember what the centaur said?* Time for some fresh grass for the manger.

"Well, Russell, to what do I owe the honor of this unexpected visit?" the librarian asked, her arms folded tightly across her chest. "Didn't you tell me yesterday you would never set foot in a library again as long as you lived?"

Russell sighed. He knew this was going to happen. He considered telling her why he wanted some books. Russell shook his head. Mrs. Perkins wouldn't believe he had had dreams two nights in a row in which a centaur had told him to go find books about his magic dreams.

"Miz Perkins, I'm sorry about yesterday; I apologize," Russell said. Did she know there was a big stain on the carpet? "And, well, I want to read some books about centaurs and flying horses and dragons." Russell finally looked up. Mrs. Perkins was smiling. She almost looked pretty when she smiled. Maybe she wasn't going to give him too hard a time.

"Centaurs? Flying horses? Russell White, as I live and breathe, I never would have guessed it."

"I really am sorry about yesterday, really. I really am."

The librarian raised one eye skeptically. Finally she shook her head and laughed. Russell laughed, too, nervously.

"Okay, Russell. Centaurs, flying horses, and dragons. I think I have just the book for you. Let's go over to the L's in fiction."

Russell followed her across the room, wishing he were invisible. He was sure the girls over by the dictionary, who were both in his room, were talking about him. One of them was that Hazel Richards who thought she was so smart. *She* had skipped a grade. They were probably telling each other Russell White was such a dummy he had failed two grades. He wished he had worn a clean T-shirt and jeans without holes in the knees. Or shorts—maybe he wouldn't feel so hot then. But he had to wear jeans—so no one would see the bruises and cuts on his legs. The girls would laugh if they had seen: he's so bad his daddy beats him. He had tried to wear his glow-in-the-dark Batman T-shirt but Jeanie had insisted it be washed. He pressed down his cowlick for the millionth time and listened to Mrs. Perkins.

"Here, Russell, try these two first: *The Lion, The Witch, and The Wardrobe* and *Prince Caspian.* They are the first two in a series. Let me see, I thought so. Here is something about centaurs in *Prince Caspian.* I'll just stick this marker here for you. You don't think they will be too hard, do you?"

"No, I don't think so," Russell said as he leafed through the books, mentally cringing at how many words he saw. If I go slow, I'll be okay, he thought. "The librarian at my last school, she read us some Greek stories and showed us *The Hobbit* at Christmas. I know a little about these kinds of stories." *I dream them all the time now.*

"Well, good. Now, when you've finished these, I have some more I can show you about the same things. The Greek stories are over there in the 292's," she said, pointing toward a near corner.

"Thanks a lot for helping me."

"You're very welcome, Russell. And Russell, please wash your hands before you read, won't you?"

Russell bit his lip to keep his quick, hot words inside. If he had been Red Fox the Indian he could have whacked her with a tomahawk. The animal Red Fox would have chomped on her leg. For a minute he had been liking her.

"Russell—what *is* wrong with that thing? Everybody out—go on, I'll fix it, go on, hurry. Just hand me the cards, Russell, I'll take care of them . . ."

The smoke alarm had gone off again. Beads of sweat trickled down Mrs. Perkins's forehead.

Russell started reading the books as soon as he got back to class, opening *Prince Caspian* where Mrs. Perkins had put the bookmark. He read slowly, his lips moving as he sounded out the unfamiliar words: *". . . and after a pause, Caspian heard the sound of hoofs . . ."*

"Russell. I think you have morning work to do, don't you? Spelling sentences. Put the book up and get to work. I don't want to have to tell you more than once."

". . . there came in sight the noblest creature Caspian had yet seen, the great Centaur, Glenstorm . . . His flanks were glossy chestnut and the beard that covered his chest was golden red . . ." Just like in the dreams—

"Russell White, did you hear me? Put the book up and get to work. Now."

"But, Miz Collins, it's all in here, just like I dreamed—" Russell swallowed down the rest of his words.

"Russell. Put. The. Book. Up. Now."

"All right, all right, I heard you the first time. I was just trying to read my books. You let Hazel read her books, why can't I read mine, huh?" Russell glared hard at Hazel who quickly looked away and down into her library book, one hand covering her face. "And you let him, Mal-what's-his-name, Yellow Eyes, read his book." This time it was Russell who looked away first; for a moment Malachi's funny eyes looked even harder than Miz Collins's did.

"Hazel and Malachi happen to be done with their morning work. Put the book up."

Russell slammed the two books into the bottom of his desk and jerked out his spelling book. He dropped it on the desktop.

"You aren't fair," he muttered and pulled out a sheet of notebook paper and slapped it down by the spelling book. He looked up at Mrs. Collins. Just how mad was she? Uh oh, she was standing up— now she was leaning over her desk. A strand of her blond hair fell across her very red face. The entire room was silent. Everybody was watching her and Russell, back and forth, like the tennis matches on TV. Russell felt the back of his neck get warm. He was sweating— why was he so hot?

"Russell, I have already given you fair warning."

"I haven't done anything, Miz Collins. I put up my library books and I got out my spelling book and a piece of paper, see? Now I'm gonna do my spelling, see?"

"Russell, I've had it. Put your name on the board with a check beside it. That makes twice this week, doesn't it? Thank goodness you start Resource soon."

He scrawled his name in big, droopy letters and then drew a lazy check by it. *I hate you Miz Collins. I hate you I hate you I hate you. I just wanted to read a book. You don't yell at anybody else for reading. That goody-goody Hazel gets away with everything.* Russell stomped back to his seat and flipped open the spelling book. He wrote his name in the upper right hand corner, then Spelling, and September 4, 1991. There was a smudge on his notebook paper. He looked at his hands: they were dirty, after all. Russell carefully made a few more smudges in his spelling book. Then, even more carefully, he copied the fill-in-the-blank sentence from the book. *I've got to be good. I want her to let me go back to the library.*

Russell slipped out of the kitchen in the middle of his father and stepmother's arguing over how clean she didn't keep the house. His father had started banging on the table as Russell closed the kitchen door. It was an old argument and Russell wondered why his father cared so much about how clean the house was when his work room was a trash heap. Larry White sometimes even wore the same T-shirt for over a week and his pickup truck was a nest of gum and candy wrappers, old beer and soft drink cans, and cigarette butts, which had spilled out of the ash tray. And tonight, as he banged on the table, Larry White had on a T-shirt yellow with brick dust and dirt ringed the fingernails on the banging fist. So what if he had found the Styrofoam container from the stew beef on the kitchen counter in a drying pool of blood?

Each step up the stairs made the bickering grow fainter and when Russell closed his own door, it was like stepping into a cocoon of silence. First he went over to his dresser and checked to be sure everything was still there in his Nativity. He moved the red fox a little closer to the sheep and then, after some thought, moved a camel closer to the Baby's head. Then he picked up *The Lion, The Witch, and The Wardrobe* and opened it to the first page. Here, he thought, was proof, confirmation, that his magic dreams were real: somebody else had had the same dreams years ago and had written them down as stories. Just like the centaur had said he would find in the library.

Russell read slowly out loud. *Chapter One. Lucy Looks Into a Wardrobe. Once there were four children whose names were Peter, Susan, Edmund, and Lucy. This story is about something that happened to them when they were sent away from London during the war because of the air raids . . .*

Hazel

Hazel wondered how somebody knew if they were going crazy or not. It was almost six o'clock and in a minute, either her grandfather or her grandmother was going to call her down for dinner. When she had sat down at her computer to play Worldmaker, she had just gotten home from school—a little after three-thirty.

Two-and-a-half hours ago.

"Alexander, do you think we are both going crazy? I mean, you were there, too, with the dragon and everything," Hazel asked her cat who only looked back at her through half-open eyes.

"Don't look at me like that. And you know, I think you are bigger. Hmm, I can test that out," Hazel said. She went over to her desk and hunted out a piece of white paper and an ink pad. Her grandmother had given her a name stamp for a stocking stuffer at Christmas. Hazel smoothed the paper out on her desk and opened the ink pad. Then she scooped up the cat (he seemed to feel heavier) and took him over to the desk and carefully made a paw print. She put the protesting Alexander down and then dated the print 9-5-91.

"Tomorrow we'll do it again," she told the cat. "And I can do one more experiment." She took a Polaroid camera out from a desk drawer. After focusing and carefully balancing the camera on her shoulder in front of the closet mirror, she snapped her picture. "Tomorrow we'll see if my eyes are more grey than blue."

Should she tell her grandparents about the dreams and the changes? About what the Worldmaker game had turned into? What would her grandparents do—send her to a doctor? Hazel shook her head. *That* would depend on her getting them to focus on her. Hazel sighed. Doing that sometimes required too much effort.

"Hazel! Dinner's ready, come down," her grandfather yelled.

"Coming!" Hazel ran from the room. Downstairs, she knew, at the dinner table, with her grandparents chattering, the food being passed back and forth, glasses and silverware clinking, it would be safe and normal. Upstairs would be a dream.

Hazel took the stairs two at a time.

Jeff

Jeff looked at the Resource teacher, Miss Findlay. She wanted him to write about his dreams. She wanted him to write a story about his dreams and make a book. Everybody in the school was supposed to write a book for Young Writers. The whole school was part of the Young Writers Project and they were all going to write a story and illustrate it and make a cover and everything.

It was going to be *fun.*

Jeff sighed. Which dream should he write about? The ones with the centaur and the dragon and the swimmers? Or the other ones— the ones the doctor Mrs. Clark took him to see twice a week kept asking about? Jeff so far had told the doctor nothing. He wanted to forget what happened; why couldn't they figure that out?

The doctor wants me to say it, to tell the secret. But I already have—twice before, and look what happened. Dad's gone; Mom's gone; I'm not at home. Why doesn't the doctor just tell me he already knows the secret? I told before and everything went crazy. I didn't have these magic dreams before I told. If I told again . . .

He sharpened his pencil and started writing. *I met a—*

"Miss Findlay, how do you spell centaur?"

"Centaur. First time anyone's ever asked me how to spell that.

Let me look it up." She pulled the dictionary into her lap and flipped through the pages. "C-E-N-T-A-U-R. Centaur. Do you know what one is? Where did you learn that word?"

"I met one," Jeff said and kept writing.

Malachi

There was a note on the medicine cabinet mirror from his father when Malachi got home Friday afternoon. *Meet me and Uncle Jack at the Kuntry Kitchen, six, dinner.* Okay, Malachi thought, and tossed the paper into the waste basket. He looked back into the mirror, something, he realized, he had been doing a lot lately. Were his eyes any more different than yesterday? More golden, more bronze-colored? Malachi had noticed they were changing early in May, just around the edges, as if a stain was slowly spreading through his irises.

He snapped his fingers and there was a quick flash of white light and a sudden rush of air, and the balled up note floated up to rest in his open palm.

And now, today, something new, something different, and a little scary. Malachi was glad his father was still at the library; this way he had an hour-and-a-half to think and try and figure things out. Today he had felt the thoughts of the other new kids. He had figured out how to tune out other people's thoughts weeks ago. Now, just these three. Not very clearly, more like when he and his dad were in the car listening to the radio and they were leaving a station's range. The sound would pop and skip, static replaced words. But still, he had felt Russell's anger, Hazel's bewilderment and fear, and the very dark fear of Jeff, the boy across the hall, in Mrs. Markham's room. Then there was the other thing. He had dreamed of these three kids. They were all in his dreams of the magical place, with all the strange creatures, the place where his mother was from, Faerie. He had seen Jeff on the beach and Russell and Hazel, in the meadow in Faerie.

Malachi shook his head. Now he felt hot and flushed and his hands hurt from making the hot flash and the air rush. His hands really hurt. This pain was new, too, as if with each change, he had to pay a price. He sat down on the tub, suddenly feeling very, very tired. Carefully he pulled out of his shirt the charm his dad had given him in August.

"Your mother wanted you to have it when you reached a certain age. I am thinking you are that age now, son. Puberty. A little earlier than most kids, but maybe fairies mature faster," his dad had said when he had finished telling Malachi about the night of and the day after his birth. "I don't want you to ever take it off—not even to take a bath. Promise me."

"I promise, Dad. Do you think the Fomorii are going to come back?"

"Yes."

Malachi turned the charm over in his hand. It felt heavier—at least he thought it did. And it tingled, sort of, when he moved it. Or had it? He shook his head. The twelve-pointed star was more than just a charm, but what else, he wasn't quite sure.

God, he was tired. Maybe Uncle Jack was home—they could walk over to the Kuntry Kitchen together. Malachi slowly got up and went down to his dad's study, to look out the window and see if Uncle Jack's car was in the driveway. No, just Uncle Jack's new wife's car. Hilda. She wanted him to call her Aunt Hilda, but he couldn't quite it do it, and Mrs. Ruggles sounded too formal. She was all right, Malachi thought, although Thomas hated her. But then Thomas hated everybody these days.

He could walk over to the Kuntry Kitchen with her and Uncle Jack—he'd be home from State in—all of sudden, a high tide of fatigue rushed in. It was as if between one moment and the next, Malachi had done some incredible exercise, like run the track fifty times or pick up a car. It was all he could to get from the window sill to his dad's desk chair and sit down. It had been doing the magic, what else could it have been? But it was such a little amount; it didn't seem fair.

In about fifteen minutes Uncle Jack would come home and he and Hilda would walk over to the restaurant. In fifteen minutes his dad would go out the back door of the library and stroll across the open field between the library and the shopping center. They would all think he was with the other, until they all sat down at the Kuntry Kitchen. Malachi gave his dad about five minutes after that before he would rush home.

Twenty minutes.

That wasn't so long to wait and the phone was so far away—he wasn't sure he could even make it into the kitchen in twenty minutes. *I'll just sit here, put my head on the desk—*

Ohhh, now he was sick. Could he make to the bathroom before puking—not quite so far as the phone?

Malachi stood slowly, pushing himself up against the desk and then, holding first to the chair, then the bookcase, the wall, Malachi made it to the study door.

The pain pushed him down to the floor. The wind began to rise then, a low moaning in the hallway. Behind him loose papers on his dad's desk began to scatter. The bathroom door was ten feet down the hall, past his father's bedroom, across from his.

The other three—the kids he had first seen in his dreams, and now at school—they would be four together. Just like the dreams said: earth, air, water, and fire. In the dreams they had all been together, linked, the four quarters making the whole. Would he be as sick if they were altogether?

Eight feet to go. The wind was moaning now, and flowing up and down the hall, a quick warm air river.

It's because I'm half-fairy, he thought. That's why this is happening. A whole fairy would know how to handle magic. But the others—he was sure they didn't have fairy mothers—

Stop thinking. Get to the bathroom. Five feet. Push against the wind. No, just be still, let the wind go, let the light ooze out of his nose, his eyes, his ears. His dad would be home soon. He lay flat on the floor, waiting for his dad's footsteps on Beichler Road, hurried, quick. Then he would feel his dad's fear, the fear that his dad would be riding like a great dark horse. The door would open and his dad's aura, his dad's arms, would reach out and take him in.

Thomas

Thomas looked up from his computer, a bank-account application form in his hand. From the center, where Thomas was, he could see the entire room, all twenty-five other workstations, most busily doing what he was doing. One man was taking a coffee break, his cup in both hands, as he stared off into space. Two women, also on break, were laughing over something one of them had found in the *News and Observer*. Right beside him was another woman, frowning at the form in her hand. Thomas tried to remember her name. Amy? Andrea, no—Angela, Angela Hughes. She had just started at the bank last week. Dark red hair, darker hazel eyes. She was, he thought, as good a person as any to experiment with—just another of the masses, the expendable ones, as the high priestess called them. Pick one, or another, the high priestess had told him, practice the magic, the power that is yours, second-degree witch, Wicca Initiate, practitioner of the Old Religion.

"The more you use magic, Thomas," the high priestess had said, "the easier it will be to keep using and the more you will want to. Think of it as a stain permeating every cell. The heart and aura you ate—a catalyst to make the stain penetrate deeper . . ."

Thomas touched the amulet around his neck, pressing it hard

against his bare skin, the coldness of the metal a welcome sensation. He pressed it again, hard enough for the amulet to cut his skin. Just a drop of his own blood on the metal was enough to jolt him, give him a taste of magic: bitter, pungent, strong. He looked at Angela again and now, like a blush around her body, Thomas could see her aura, a pale, pale yellow. Thomas lifted his finger and, as if it were cigarette smoke in a bar, a tendril of the yellow drifted up and curled through the air. He let it wrap itself around his finger.

Look up, say yes.

"Yes? Is something the matter?" she said, looking puzzled.

After that it was easy.

Lunch, dinner, a movie, then coffee. And Angela was in Thomas's living room, lying against him, her head on his shoulder. Thomas undid her hair, loosing the long braid crowning her head, into a dark red fall. Each touch was like another nibble on the yellow, another taste. He reached down and pulled off her shoes, then her stockings, stopping to stroke all that bare flesh. Then, the blouse, one button at a time, one shoulder, then the next, and a quick bite, just a nip. Her body with his touches, her yeses part of each movement. He unhooked her bra and her breasts fell into his hands, her nipples hard as he licked and sucked each, drinking in the yellow. Then the skirt, her panties, and her entire body glowed.

Now me.

She started with his shoes and socks, and then his shirt, sliding it up his chest, and then over his head, and then back to his chest. When she sucked and licked his erect nipples, Thomas felt his skin sucking in return, taking in still more of the yellow. She paused at the amulet, and then kissed each one of the star's five points. Thomas groaned, a low guttural cry, and his entire body quivered. Angela moved down to his pants and undid his belt, unzipped, and peeled down his pants and shorts. She ran her fingers over his penis, lightly, her nails like the claws of a small bird. Then her mouth, wet, warm. Then up his chest, to his mouth, and they were together and off the couch and she opened and he entered.

At Mabon Thomas would take her heart. And the Dark Ones would be plain and visible, no longer creatures of the periphery of his vision, at the edges of his dreams.

Russell

Russell started Resource on September 9, the Monday of the third week of school. Miss Findlay came to get him personally. He was a little scared of her when she walked in the room and asked for him.

Russell could tell this tall, thin black woman wouldn't take any mess off anybody.

"Russell. Go with Miss Findlay. You can correct your test when you get back. You'll be going to her trailer every day at about this time," Mrs. Collins said from where she sat in reading group. "You'll have reading with her; take your book with you."

Russell had done exactly as she had said, not wanting Miss Findlay to wait a minute more than she had to. She stood in the classroom door, arms folded across her chest, watching, as he hurriedly got his things together.

"Ready? Let's go. You're late starting Resource here — paperwork and all that mess," she said as she closed the classroom door behind them. Russell felt drab beside her. Miss Findlay had a bright, multi-colored scarf around her head, and her dress flowed and swirled about her, looking at first red, then pink, then orange. "Let me fill you in on what the class project is: we are, each one of us, making a book. In fact, everybody in school is or will be for the Young Writers Conference. I'm just getting a head start . . ."

Resource at Nottingham Heights was in a narrow, rusty trailer parked between three or four pine trees and some pyracantha bushes on one side and the faculty parking lot on the other. Inside the trailer was something like an obstacle course, with file cabinets jutting out at odd angles, crammed book cases overflowing on the floor. Russell followed Miss Findlay into the trailer to a seat near her desk. She kept talking the whole time about this book she wanted him and the rest of the kids to write. There were five other boys and two girls already writing, their desks all in a row, their backs to the windows. Half were from Mrs. Collins's class. Russell guessed the others were Mrs. Markham's kids.

"We are writing stories from dreams. Here is a list of dreams the class came up with — if you can't remember any of your own. Now the rest of the class got started last week so I want you to work hard today to catch up. Try and get something on paper today before you leave. Are you with me, Russell? We'll do reading in a while. Russell?" Miss Findlay said as she sat down, pulling her swirling dress in.

"Yeah, I think so," Russell said. Writing about a dream would be easy. He took out a piece of paper, and started writing: *One night I had a dream. I was standing in a big, grassy meadow in the middle of the night. The sky was filled with stars and there were two moons in the sky . . .*

"Russell, I do believe you wrote enough today to have caught up with the others," Miss Findlay said when Resource was over. "I bet you will be able to have your first draft done by Friday. Good work. Now, class . . ."

Russell was surprised at how easy the story came that week. For the first time ever the words just came and he could trust them to be right and true. They didn't twist and distort themselves on the paper. The story began with the flying horse and ended with the centaurs, just as he planned, just as he had dreamed. His hands even seemed to be working smoothly—his pencil didn't snap and fly across the room or jab and tear the paper. There were lots of misspelled words, Russell was sure of that, but they weren't scrawled all over the paper or smeared from being erased and rewritten over and over. When Friday came he handed in the story with the rest of the Resource class, sure he had done a good job and his hands hadn't betrayed him. It was a good story.

The next Monday morning when Russell walked into Mrs. Collins's room, she told him to go see Miss Findlay immediately. *Hey, maybe she's read my story and she loved it. She wants to get it published and let everybody read it. I'll get to read it over the intercom—*

Miss Findlay glared at Russell when he stepped into the trailer. She was tapping her long fingernails on the desk.

What have I done now? I just got off the bus and I went straight down the hall and then I came straight here. I haven't done anything. She won't believe me whatever it is. She's like all the rest—why did I think she would be different? Boy, I was sure dumb. And the feeling was the same: bitter, angry, and hard, all tied together with overwhelming sadness. No matter how many times he promised himself he would never let himself like a teacher, let alone trust one, he did. Over and over and over.

"Russell. Let me get straight to the point. I read your story last night and I wanted to talk to you first before I do anything else." She opened his folder on her desk and motioned for Russell to come and sit beside her.

"Is something wrong with it? I worked really hard on it. I know a lot of the words are misspelled, but you said not to worry about that right now. Didn't you like it?" Russell asked as he sat down. He could smell Miss Findlay's perfume, light and sweet.

"Russell, I liked your story all right. I liked it the first time I read it, when I read Jeffrey Gates's story. Except for some rearranging of the order and a few details, same story. And you and Jeff have never written anything as good before. I even called your old teachers, just to be sure. I talked to Mrs. Perkins this morning and she told me both of you have come in and checked out fairy tales. What do you have to say for yourself? Tell me the truth: you copied this from a book in the library, didn't you?" She stared at Russell with The Look.

Jeff Gates? Oh, yeah, that shrimpy little kid in Miz Markham's class. He sits three chairs from me here and he never talks.

"I didn't copy my story from nobody. I wrote it all myself. I worked really hard at it." *Why is it so hot in here?*

"Russell. Please," Miss Findlay interrupted, her voice sharp and cutting. "You could not possibly have written anything like this. I know you and Jeff live close to each other. You even ride the same bus. Now, tell me the truth."

"I am telling you the truth. I didn't copy anything! Did you ask Jeff? What did he say? I've never even talked to Jeff. I did it all myself." Russell gripped the seat of his chair with both hands. It was really hot in the trailer. Russell could see sweat beads on Miss Findlay's forehead.

"Don't raise your voice at me, young man. Jeff isn't in school today; I'll deal with him when he gets back. Neither one of you is capable of work of this quality—it's just too good. You're getting off to a bad start, Russell—Mrs. Collins wasn't even surprised that you did this. I am very disappointed in you."

"Miz Collins is a liar and she hates me. I've never copied anybody's work ever and I wrote every word of that story myself. It's my dream! It's the best work I've ever done in school and you think I cheated. I didn't." Russell stood. He wished he could take back every word he said, every word he had written; he wished he had stayed in bed, safe in the warm darkness, the covers over his head.

"I told you not to raise your voice at me. Very well. Russell, you leave me no choice. I will have to give you a zero and call your father. *This* goes in the trash," Miss Findlay said and held his folder over the can.

"Don't throw my story away!" He jerked the folder out of the startled woman's hand and bolted for the door. Russell made his face as tight as he could; if he let go for a second, he knew he would bawl his head off.

"Russell White, you come back here this instant. Don't you dare run away from me."

Russell tripped right at the door and looked up to see Miss Findlay, her hair, wet with sweat, falling about her face, her bra transparent through her wet blouse.

"Get up. Now. You don't look hurt to me."

"No, let me go, don't touch me," Russell yelled and pushed her hands away, as she tried to pull him to his feet. He pulled away, his back to the metal door, breathing hard, and sweating. He was drenched with sweat and the air was close and hot, so hot it almost hurt to breathe.

"I said: get up, boy. If you lay a hand on me, you will be sorrier than you ever have been."

"I didn't touch you, leave me alone. Please, just leave me alone, I didn't cheat." He scrambled to his feet and pressed himself as flat as he could against the door and watched Miss Findlay. The only person he had ever seen as angry had been his daddy. She took a step closer and raised her hand.

"No," and Russell held his own hand up to stop her and he hit the air. It was as if the air in front of him had suddenly acquired substance and heat. The spongy, hard air was hot—really hot. He pushed the air when she took another step toward him and to both his and Miss Findlay's astonishment, the hard air knocked Miss Findlay down, sprawling on the trailer floor. Now Russell could see the hard air—it was glowing white-yellow and it looked like fire. It flew over Miss Findlay, as she tried to stand, singeing her hair. When she ducked, the air-fire smashed into the bookcase behind her desk. The books, the papers, the wooden shelves, the games— everything burst into flames. Miss Findlay half-stood, her back to Russell, staring in total disbelief at the burning bookcase.

Russell ran.

He didn't look back to see if she was coming after him, if she was fighting the fire; Russell just ran. He threw himself against the trailer door and took the steps down in one leap, gasping as he felt the cooler outside air. He ran to the building, banged the door open, and then, took one look back. There Miss Findlay was, staggering dazed out the door, smoke coming out with her. He couldn't see inside the trailer—only smoke, thick, black, and everywhere.

Russell turned and ran across the hall to the opposite door that faced the playground. Once outside again, Russell took off, kicking up blue gravel. The hounds were after the Red Fox. He barked as he ran past the surprised PE teacher who was taking a kindergarten class out. The fox raced down the hill and across the playground and into the woods surrounding the school. A fox could hide anywhere: under a log, in a thicket, just lay still, panting, while the hounds ran around like crazy. But the hounds could smell, maybe the fox should find a creek . . .

Branches slapped and scratched Russell's face and he was a boy again. Foxes didn't get popped on the forehead by a dogwood or get spider webs caught in their hair. And foxes didn't trip over logs. Russell slammed against the ground, twisting his ankle as he fell. He dropped his folder and the pages of his story flew everywhere. After what seemed like a long time, Russell started crying. There was the fire alarm, and the siren and the fire truck horns. He had burned up the Resource trailer. Miss Bigelow was going to kill him. It was bad enough he had pushed a teacher—he could hear the principal's machine gun voice repeating those words and over—but he had burned up the trailer. She would never believe him that it had been an accident, he hadn't meant to, and had no idea how the fire had started, it just had.

Magic—it had to be magic. Yeah, right, magic.

"Russell? Are you all right? What in the hell happened? Everybody's outside, the fire trucks are here, Margaret Mary—Miss Findlay—is—and you, out here. What in the hell did you do? Have you lost your mind?"

Russell rolled over and sat up to see Miss Montague, the PE teacher, coming through the trees. "I think I sprained my ankle. Can you help me walk?" Russell asked. He figured trying to explain what happened was not worth the trouble.

"You must have lost your mind. Come on, child, let me help you. Let's go, Russ," she said and they started back to the building, leaving his story behind in the leaves and pine needles.

Russell sat outside the office for a long time, waiting until the fire was out and the trucks, the police, and the WRAL Channel 5 Action News van had left and everybody was back inside. He had never felt so tired in his life and wanted nothing more but to go home and crawl into bed and sleep, sleep, sleep. But his ankle hurt too much and the scratches from the tree branches stung. Even so, he did nod off once, but woke up when his head drooped. Finally after what seemed like days, Mrs. Anderson came out of the office and told Russell Miss Bigelow was ready to see him.

"Now, be smart, boy," Mrs. Anderson said, shaking her head. "You are in a world of trouble—just say yes ma'am and no ma'am. Don't you even dream of talking back. Now, just stand there until they tell you to come in."

Miss Findlay was talking when Russell stepped inside Miss Bigelow's office. "Bad wiring in that old trailer, Hallie. What else could it have been to blaze up like that?"

"You're probably right—but there has to be some sort of investigation, insurance, the fire department. We'll put Resource in the computer room until we can get a new trailer. Russell, come in," Miss Bigelow said, shaking her head. She leaned back in her chair, her glasses in one hand, the other rubbing the bridge of her nose.

Russell leaned against a bookcase as the women talked to him. He was afraid to look any of them in the eye, so he stared at the floor and took Mrs. Anderson's advice: no ma'am, yes ma'am, I don't know, ma'am. He refused to admit he had copied part of his story from any book. His unacceptable behavior, his poor attitude, and his lack of concern for his school work were all discussed in detail.

"Don't you understand, Russell?" Miss Bigelow said. "Don't you see we just want the best for you? All of us—Mrs. Collins, Miss Findlay, myself?"

"Yes ma'am, I understand, I see," Russell said, wishing he could sit down. His ankle was really hurting now.

"We do care, Russell. But you have to care, too, or it doesn't make any difference," Miss Bigelow said. Miss Findlay nodded her head in agreement. Russell wondered how the hot, hard air had felt when it hit her and he wondered how to do it again. He had felt *something* when he had *pushed*—he had felt strong. Really strong. And when the fire had started—

"What do you have to say for yourself? Well?" Miss Bigelow asked. "Don't you at least have something to say to Miss Findlay? Russell?"

"I'm sorry, Miss Findlay," Russell said and then looked directly at Mrs. Collins. She looked back at him as if she were looking at crap on the floor. What the hell. He was already in trouble up to his neck. "But Miz Collins, she hates me. She never listens to me and— uuuhh—" Russell stepped on his bad ankle.

"That's enough. I'm going to suspend you for the rest of the week. I've already called your father; he's on his way—what's the matter?"

"My ankle. I fell in the woods."

"Come on, Russell. Let's go into the health room. Why didn't you say something?" Miss Bigelow stood up, looking exasperated.

I hate you I hate all of you the first time I do a good job and . . .

Russell hobbled behind Miss Bigelow. He didn't look back at either Mrs. Collins or Miss Findlay.

Russell sat in the lobby again, his sprained ankle propped on a chair, with a bag of crushed ice on it. There was a little pool of water on the floor beneath his foot. His schoolbooks for the rest of the week were stacked at his side, along with a detailed list of assignments tucked in the top book. Miss Findlay had left explicit instructions how Russell was to rewrite his story. He watched out the front, waiting for his daddy to come, wanting him to hurry up and get it over with.

There was the pickup pulling up. He couldn't see his daddy's face until he was halfway up the sidewalk. Miss Bigelow must have called him at work, at the construction site. Larry White was wearing a sweat-stained, holey T-shirt and mortar-spattered jeans. There was more mortar in his daddy's hair, little white pieces, like snow. Mr. White barely looked at Russell when he came in, just a quick flick of his eyes as he went into the office.

That was enough. Russell knew what his daddy was going to do when they got home: another whipping, a long and hard one this time. No supper. Grounded. Restricted to his room. No TV. Same old thing.

Russell went slowly up the stairs after his daddy left to go back to work. *At least I don't have to go back to school for the rest of the week. Nobody'll see the bruises and cuts.* He was careful not to let the bag of ice, newly filled, drip on the floor. It was a relief to close his bedroom door and lie down gingerly on the bed. The ice felt pretty good on his ankle and the bed felt soft to his rear and his back. Russell closed his eyes. He didn't want to read, to think, to watch TV, to do anything. He just wanted to be quiet on his bed and let the silence hold him and keep him safe.

I wonder what ol' Miss Findlay said to Jeff. Did she call his folks? I've never even talked to him. He's in the very front, right next to Miss Findlay's desk. Needs a haircut, all that hair in his face. How'd he write the same story as me? We'd have to have had the same dream.

We'd have to have had the same dream.

Russell sat up, no longer tired or wishing for stillness. He knew what stop Jeff got off the bus and he was pretty sure which house was his. It wasn't far; Russell could walk if he had to. He looked down at his ankle: still swollen, still throbbing some. Crutches. From once before, when he had broken his leg. They were in the downstairs closet. Russell got up slowly and half-hopped, half-hobbled to the door. He stopped by his dresser and first touched the red fox, then the Baby for good luck. His mother used to do that.

From the front steps of Russell's house to the front door of Jeff's house, was, Russell thought, between a quarter and a half-mile. It might as well have been ten. He only fell two or three times on the crutches before he got used to them, but each fall made his ankle hurt worse. By the time he got to the road, Russell's T-shirt was again glued to his body. The welts on his back and rear stung from the sweat. The ones on his legs started bleeding again, streaking red through the dirt.

"The Red Fox wouldn't let a little sprained ankle stop him," Russell told himself, panting, when he got to the end of his driveway. He could see the entrance to Greenwood Estates—at least it was downhill. "Jeff had the same dream. There's gotta be a reason."

The Red Fox set off.

Russell and Jeff

Jeff woke up Monday morning while it was still dark, and for too long a moment, he had not known where he was. He had tried to scream, but a hand covered his mouth, shoving his scream back through his teeth, down his throat. Only when he tried to pull the hand away did he realize it was his own hand and he was in the Clarks' house, the same house he had woken up in since May. He was safe.

Jeff looked at the clock on the dresser. 5:14. As he watched, the last red digit slowly changed from a four to a five. The Clarks got up most mornings around 6:30 or so. They took turns showering and using the bathroom and then came and got him up. Getting him up, Mrs. Clark had told him yesterday, eyeing him over her coffee, lately had been like waking the dead.

Not this morning, Jeff thought. After that dream, he didn't want to go back to sleep. It had been some weeks since he had had such a dream. Before, he had had them almost every night—alone in the dark and knowing he wasn't alone, that someone was just beyond his reach, waiting, and was going to put a hand over Jeff's mouth and . . . He had dreaded sleep. Now, there were the other dreams: the centaur, the swimmers, the sea beneath two moons. But going back to sleep now was too risky, there was no guarantee which dream would be waiting for him.

After checking to be sure the dinosaurs he had brought from his father's house were still on his dresser, Jeff went out in the hall, into its silence. No light made a line beneath the Clarks' bedroom door and the bathroom door was open. Jeff tiptoed into the bathroom and closed and locked the door behind him. He flicked on the light and blinked at the sudden brightness and the colors' sudden shift from shades of grey to sand-colored tiles, beige walls, and a white curtain over the window. The transparent shower curtain was covered with big red and blue fish. Taking a shower was sort of like being inside an aquarium.

Jeff loved showers, the longer the better, with torrents of hot water pouring over his head and swirling around his feet. He kept the plug in so he could pretend to be swimming in the rain. The water could get just deep enough so he could lay on the bottom of the tub and be underwater, the multicolored fish over his head.

Jeff peeled off his pajamas and got in the tub and carefully pulled the curtain so there was as little space between the plastic and the wall as possible. He turned on the water, twisted the shower knob, and grabbed the shampoo. Rivers of shampoo, Pert Plus, lather, hung all over his body like sea foam, like snow, like cotton candy. Water beat on his head. Lather frothed at his feet. He lay down and stretched as the water rained all over and around him. And nobody came to stop him, to pound on the door, find a key to the lock, come in. Nobody.

Now he was safe in the shower; for too long a time, he hadn't been.

Finally, reluctantly, Jeff turned off the water and got out of the shower, shivering at the sudden touch of cooler air. He wrapped himself in a huge towel, as if he were an Arab in a desert robe. As he enjoyed the feel of the soft towel on his skin, he noticed his ears. He straightened up to dry his hair and looked into the mirror.

"My ears," Jeff said and with a corner of his towel, wiped the fog off the medicine cabinet mirror, and looked again. His ears were pointed, like the swimmers and the centaur. He tapped the mirror: solid real glass. He pinched himself—definitely awake—and touched his ears, running a finger on the outer edges. He turned his head to the left and the right: both ears were pointed. Unmistakably pointed. Could he cover them with his hair? Jeff heard, as he fumbled through a drawer looking for a comb, the seemingly faraway tinny ringing of the Clarks' alarm clock.

Uh-oh.

Mr. Clark would call a doctor, or the social worker, and Mrs. Clark—what would she do? Jeff had no idea, but he didn't want to find out. He grabbed his pajamas and darted back to his room, closing the door just in time, as he heard the Clarks' door open. Jeff pulled his covers over his head and lay very still. Deep breath, take a deep breath, he told himself, think. He had half-an-hour before one of the Clarks would come and shake him awake. And see his ears. He felt them again to be sure: still pointed. There was no way he was going to school like this. Sick—he would just have to be sick today. Jeff would tell the Clarks his stomach hurt and he felt too sick to go and . . .

Mr. Clark came to wake Jeff up. Jeff could tell by the heavy sound of the footsteps in the room. "Jeff? Time to get up."

Jeff groaned. "I don't feel good. My stomach hurts. And my head. They both hurt," Jeff said, his voice muffled by the bedspread and the sheet. He groaned again and pulled himself into a ball in the middle of the bed. "Can I stay here today?"

"Ellen? Jeff says he's sick. His stomach and his head. I don't know if he has a temperature; I haven't touched him."

Mrs. Clark was there in a minute.

"Jeff, let me see if you have a fever. Let me feel your forehead."

"No, don' touch me, please. I told you I don't feel good. My stomach hurts and my head hurts." Jeff could feel the two of them hesitating. He was sure they were looking at each other the way grownups did, with raised eyebrows and crossed arms. He groaned again, just to be on the safe side. Then the Clarks walked out of the room to talk; Jeff could hear them whispering in the hall. Then one of them, Mrs. Clark, walked away, and Mr. Clark came back in Jeff's room.

"Okay, Jeff, maybe you'd better not go to school today. Ellen's going to stay with you—"

"I can stay by myself."

"No, you can't. You may be almost eleven, but you are not staying here by yourself. Ellen will stay here this morning and I'll bring some work home this afternoon, work in the study. Now, go back to sleep."

The door to his room closed and Jeff listened to Mr. Clark's footsteps down the hall and into the kitchen. Then the hall door closed, cutting off almost all sound from the kitchen—he could just hear their voices, the radio, the clatter of dishes . . .

That afternoon, when the doorbell rang, Jeff was so deep in a saurian struggle he didn't hear it the first or the second time. When the chimes echoed for a third time, Jeff jumped. The clock on his dresser said 3:31. Mrs. Clark wouldn't be home until five-thirty and Mr. Clark wouldn't come out of his study until then, either.

"Jeff, is someone at the door? If it is a salesman, tell him we don't want whatever it is," Mr. Clark yelled, his voice muffled.

"I'll go see," Jeff yelled back, giving up the last pretense of being sick. He knew they were on to him and couldn't quite figure out why they had let him get away with it. At least he had managed to keep his ears hidden when Mrs. Clark had taken his temperature in the morning. She had stared hard at the thermometer, gave him a small smile, and had left the room. Adults were just plain crazy sometimes. Now, who was there? A salesman, or maybe JWs, Jehovah's Witnesses, like those who came by his parents' all the time. Or two Mormons, with their bicycles behind them, in their skinny, black ties and starched, white shirts, their faces shining as if they had scrubbed them clean before each house. Or Baha'is, with their broken record on peace and oneness. Magazine salesmen, maybe. Baha'i, Mormon, JW, or whatever, Jeff wanted them to go away. If he stayed quiet and made no dinosaur noises, maybe they would decide nobody was at home, stuff their tracts in the door, and leave.

The door bell chimed a fourth time and then whoever it was started knocking. Jehovah's Witnesses, Baha'is, and Mormons didn't pound on the door. Neither did salesmen. Jeff put down the allosaurus and the plesiosaur and ran to the front door.

"I'm coming, I'm coming," he called, but the knocking got louder and louder. The door bell rang again as Jeff finally jerked the door open.

"Russell White? What are you doing here?"

Jeff knew who Russell was from Resource, but he had never spoken to the older and bigger boy; he had never even said the boy's name. Russell was a head taller than Jeff, and Russell was twelve, almost thirteen, and Jeff wasn't quite eleven. Russell's red hair looked ragged, with little spikes jutting up in odd places on his head. Jeff was surprised to see Russell's eyes were as green as his own. Russell leaned on the porch railing, crutches under his arm. His face was flushed and sweat dripped from his forehead. One foot was wrapped in an Ace bandage.

"You don't look sick. Yer not even wearing your pajamas," Russell finally said. Jeff grinned in spite of himself. He had on a tyrannosaurus T-shirt, bright orange with a brilliant cherry red rex, another gift from the Clarks. Trying not to look obvious, Jeff smoothed his own shaggy hair just to be sure his ears were still covered.

"Jeff, who's there?"

Russell froze and Jeff jerked around. Mr. Clark stood in the living room doorway, his glasses in one hand, a sheaf of papers in the other.

"Russell White, from school."

"I brought him his homework," Russell said quickly. "I, uh, live close by. I sprained my ankle."

Mr. Clark looked first at Jeff, then at Russell, then back at Jeff again, and shrugged.

"That was awfully nice of you to do that on a sprained ankle. Let me know when you want to go home. I'll drive you. Just come and get me in the study, Jeff."

"Okay, Mr. Clark."

Russell waited until Mr. Clark had gone down the hall and they both had heard the door closed.

"Yer not sick. And he knows it, too."

"Well, I feel a whole lot better. I'll probably be back at school—soon," Jeff said hastily. "What happened to your foot? And what are you doing here? Why aren't you at school? You didn't bring me my homework—we aren't even in the same class, except for Resource."

"I fell this morning at school. In the woods behind the playground. I was running away."

"Running away? From school? Are you running away now?"

"No, I came to see you. Gotta question I need to ask. It's important," Russell said. "Uh, could I sit down? Just for a minute. My ankle really hurts and it's kinda hot out here. My daddy would really be fussing if I were standing around with the front door open, letting all the cool air out. If we had air conditioning, that is. Gotta lotta fans."

"Yeah, okay, I guess so."

"Why do you call your folks Mr. and Mrs. Clark? Isn't your name Gates?"

Jeff made no reply except to open the front door as wide as possible and to step back and let Russell limp into the living room. Russell sat down gingerly and then lifted his foot up on the couch.

"My daddy whipped me pretty hard 'cause I got in trouble in school and they had to call him to come get me. The reason I got in trouble is why I came to see you."

"I don't know if Mrs. Clark would want you to put your feet up on the couch like that," Jeff said slowly, as he looked around the room. He wasn't sure if Mrs. Clark would care or not about feet on the furniture. His mother couldn't stand it. Her living room had been kept like a church: quiet, still, and unsullied. This living room was different. Where his mother had five magazines, no more, no less, fanned out on the coffee table, Mrs. Clark had six or seven, dog-eared and coffee-stained, lying every which-away. His mother had wall-to-wall carpets, Mrs. Clark had throw rugs on wood floors. Where his mother had—

"Why do you call your mama and daddy Mr. and Mrs. Clark? Aren't they yer real folks?"

"No, they're my foster parents. How'd you get in trouble? What do you want to ask me?" Jeff said quickly as he sat down in a chair across the room. For a long moment Russell didn't answer. He wrinkled up his face as if he were thinking really hard and picking out each word separately.

"Okay," Russell finally said. "Remember that story we hafta write for Miss Findlay? The book we're supposed to make?"

"What about it?"

"Well, I got into big trouble over mine today," Russell said, giving Jeff a curious look. "Miz Findlay said I copied mine out of a fairy tale book and that it was just like yours. She said you musta copied yers from the same place since they were about almost exactly the same thing."

"I didn't copy my story," Jeff said, wishing he hadn't let Russell in the house.

"I didn't copy mine, either. I got it in a dream. Didya have the same dream? Ya gotta tell me, because if you did—"

"What kind of dream?" Jeff said quickly and got up from his seat and went to the picture window, and started pulling the curtain drawstrings. The room grew light, then dark, then light. He could see Russell's face reflected in the glass, then it would disappear, reappear. Maybe if he stood there long enough, Russell would give up and hobble home. "The dreams you got yer stories from. About the flying horse, the dragon, the centaur, Roth."

"His name wasn't Roth, it was Thorfin—"

"But you met him in that meadow, right? It was night-time and there were all those stars, tons more than here at night, and two moons, right? You did, you did, I can tell by the way yer looking away. I knew it!" Russell crowed, shaking both fists over his head like a boxer. "I just knew it. Did you see the monsters, too—the red-eyed monsters?"

"Red-eyed monsters?"

"Yeah, right before waking up sometimes, real quick, with fire-whips," Russell said impatiently.

"I've dreamed about the centaur, the dragon, the flying horse, and the swimmers, mostly the swimmers. No red-eyed monsters."

"None? Oh well, maybe, I just see 'em and nobody else. Swimmers I haven't seen yet. Anyway, I think all of it, all of them, are real, just like here is real."

"Real?"

"Yeah, real. I woke up with a glowing white flower once, that left glowing dust on my hand—it was real," Russell said and Jeff nodded. He, too, had awakened in the middle of the night with a luminous bloom on his pillow.

"There's something else," Jeff said, feeling both enormous relief and surprise. He would have never guessed in a million years Russell to be the one he would tell his dreams to, but it didn't matter. It felt good to finally be telling someone. Maybe he was glad Russell had come over after all. "This is why I pretended to be sick today." Jeff walked over to the couch and sat down by Russell. "Look," he said, and pushed back the hair covering his pointed ears.

"Just like the centaur's ears," Russell whispered. Jeff sat very still while Russell touched each ear, tracing the point with his fingers. Then Russell felt his own ears. "Still round."

"I bet they'll start changing soon. I just noticed mine this morning in the bathroom. Do you feel, well, different, since you started having the dreams?"

"This morning," Russell said slowly, "before I ran away, when I was with Miss Findlay, I pushed her away without touching her, and, I think I started a fire—the trailer burned up. Man, Jeff, what are we gonna do?"

"A fire? Wow. I thought about running away, too," Jeff said with a shrug. "You know every other kid in school is going to laugh at us. The teachers will probably call the doctor or Social Services or something. I wish we could go there, where the dreams are—why couldn't we, if it's real?" Jeff said. He was almost, but not quite, sure he could trust Russell. After all, *this* Russell who was sitting on the couch with him, his feet propped up on one of Mrs. Clark's embroidered pillows, didn't seem to be quite the same person who got into so much trouble at school all the time.

"I think we can, Jeff, but we just have to figure out how. I've been trying to. I'm reading this book about Peter and Lucy and how they went to Narnia. They went in through a wardrobe one time, and the other time a magic horn called them—"

"What's a wardrobe? Narnia? What are you talking about?" Jeff asked.

"A wardrobe is sorta big closet for yer clothes, but it's not built into the wall. A big box, sorta—I have one—and in the book the wardrobe is magic and they go inside and keep on going and going until they're there. And Narnia, man, it's so much like our dreamplace—there are centaurs and . . ."

Jeff listened, amazed, as Russell told him the story. Russell, reading? In Resource, when Miss Findlay asked him to read, Russell would refuse until she fussed him out. Then he would read very slowly, as if each word was something he was seeing for the first time.

"But we don't have a magic wardrobe or a magic horn. We aren't even there together in our dreams—"

"I know. Hey, I know what we can do, Jeff," Russell interrupted, talking fast. "We'll sleep in the same room, go to bed thinking about there, and I bet we'll be in the dream-place together—but I can't go anywhere for two weeks 'cause of what happened at school—"

"I could come over to your house, Russell," Jeff said. "Would that be okay? I think the Clarks would let me. They want me to make friends," Jeff said and quickly looked away. Were he and this big, loud troublemaker boy going to be friends? "But they will want to meet your folks."

Russell shook his head. "No way my daddy's gonna let me haf company while I'm grounded. Lissen, can you sneak out, without telling the Clarks? How 'bout this Friday, we could do it this Friday, you could come over after seven and before nine—they're going over to Jeanie's folks house—and I'll be looking for you, get a flashlight, blink it three times at my window, any one of the windows on the roof on the side facing the trees—"

"And I'll wear black and my moccasins—"

"Yeah, all right, gimme five, man," Russell said and Jeff laughed and slapped Russell's open hand. "We're gonna go there, it'll happen—oww—"

"What's the matter? Your ankle?"

"My back and my butt. Where my daddy hit me—I told you he whipped me. I moved too quick just then. It ain't nothing." Russell leaned back into the couch.

"Your dad beats you?"

"Yeah, all the time—hey, show me your room," Russell said quickly, changing the subject. "Ya gotta lotta neat stuff?"

Jeff laughed when he opened his bedroom door and Russell gasped. Dinosaurs were everywhere. The shelves lining the far wall were crawling with dinosaurs of all shapes, sizes, and colors. A two-foot green tyrannosaurus towered over plastic and metal and stuffed dinosaurs. A herd of triceratops roamed across Jeff's desk. A poster of diving plesiosaurs covered another wall and a mobile of five more plesiosaurs floated above the desk. Another mobile of swooping pterodactyls slowly turned over the bed. Some dinosaurs were wind-up toys and some were carefully built models. Some were paperweights and eraserheads. Dinosaur books and comics spilled off the desk onto the floor. A blue apatosaurus sat in the desk chair, poking its head out of a shoe box.

"The plesiosaurs are my favorites. The Clarks gave me the apatosaurus when I came to stay with them in April."

"Wow. Where'd you get so many?"

"I've been collecting them ever since kindergarten. Birthdays, Christmas, and, other—times my dad just got them for me. But, I left a lot of the ones he gave me there. I know all the kinds there are," Jeff said and reeled off a long list of polysyllabic names. He hoped the names would make Russell forget what he had just said about his dad and the dinosaurs left behind.

"I thought you weren't any good at school stuff," Russell said when Jeff finished his recitation with ankylosaurus. "Howdya remember all those long names?"

"I can remember what I hear and my dad and my mom would read me the names. Mr. Clark reads them to me now. I can't write them down too good; I get all the letters tangled up. Hey, there's the bus," Jeff said and pointed out the window. His dad had always brought home a new dinosaur the day after, either as a reward or an apology—Jeff wasn't quite sure. *It's your mother's fault, son, don't you see that? If she hadn't left, I wouldn't need to. None of it. Here, you were a good boy last night, here's a new dinosaur . . .* Jeff shook his head, hoping the memory would somehow tumble out of his head and break on the floor.

"Well," Russell said, "if the bus is here, it's already gone past my house. I'd better get on home before Daddy or Jeanie get back. Whatcha going to do about your ears tomorrow? You can't stay home all week." Russell picked up his crutches and started out toward the living room and the front door.

"I'll wear a headband or something," Jeff said. "Can you ride a bike with your ankle? You're never going to get home on time in crutches. Let me get Mr. Clark; he really won't mind driving you home."

"Nah, I'd better go by myself. Gotta bike?" They were at the front door and already Russell was sweating.

"No, but the Clarks do. They keep lots of stuff around for different foster kids. Got a whole closet full of girl stuff. I'll go get the bike; you wait on the front steps."

Jeff ran around to the back of the house and came back wheeling a bicycle. He watched as Russell climbed on, wincing when he saw the pain in Russell's face when he started pedaling.

"It hurts some, but I'll be okay. I'll hide it under the house and you can ride it back on Saturday morning. Can you hide the crutches until Friday? I don't think I can carry them. A headband, huh? Like the tennis players on TV? What are you gonna say to Miss Findlay about your story?"

"I won't push her like you did—I don't know; I'll think of something. See you Friday?"

"Yeah," and Russell took off.

I'll just pull my dumb kid routine, Jeff thought. *Miss Findlay will go on and on and I'll just nod my head and say yes ma'am and no ma'am. She would eventually get tired of talking and then she'll tell me I'm going to get a zero and that she was going to call my parents.*

"I wonder what the Clarks will say," Jeff said out loud, remembering his mom and dad had never done anything when teachers called. Somehow he doubted the Clarks would be the same. He stood on the stoop, watching until Russell was out of sight. Jeff shook his head. Had he really just agreed to sneak out of the house late at night, go down the road and sneak into somebody else's house, spend the night—and repeat it all to get back into his bed before the Clarks found out?

He had and he was going to do it.

It rained all day, a constant deadening downpour. Even Narnia paled by late afternoon, especially when Russell reached Chapter Fourteen. Reading about Aslan getting killed by the White Witch was more than a little depressing. And it made him think for the first time of what else might be happening to him. The dreams about the centaur, the flying horse, and the dragon were wonderful and he had found them all in Narnia and in the other fairy tales. But there were other creatures in the stories as well: "*. . . such people! Ogres with monstrous teeth, and wolves, and bull-headed men; spirits of evil trees and poisonous plants; and other creatures . . . Cruels and Hags and Incubuses, Wraiths, Horrors, Efreets, Sprites, Wooses, and Ettins . . . and the Witch herself.*

Russell shuddered. He wished Jeff could come right then and just be there, someone else nearby, another voice to take his attention away from the drumming rain and the shadows inside and outside. At least he hadn't seen any creatures like the Narnian monsters in his dreams. Not yet, anyway. But if the good things were real, then the bad things were probably real, too. Even the Garden of Eden had had snakes. Finally Russell got up, closed the book, and the Red Fox haunted the house, trapped, trying to find a way out before the hunter came in his pickup. It sniffed and clawed at the doors, poked its nose in all the closets, growing more frantic by the minute. Finally the beast collapsed in front of the TV, its tongue hanging out.

When Russell's stepmother put supper on the table it was still raining—a heavy rain, splattering, splashing on the windows, running off the roof, making waterfalls from the gutters to the ground. The weatherman said on the evening news the rain was probably going to last all night, bringing welcome relief from the August heat. The farmers sure needed it. *I don't care about the farmers—now, Jeff won't come. He won't come. Why would he want to come to my house anyway—*

"Eat, Russell. Stop playing with your food," his father snapped.

Maybe the rain is making him grumpy, too, Russell thought, as he carefully scooped up some mashed potatoes. *Or it is because he and Jeanie have to go over to her folks' house to pick up some baby clothes and meet Jeanie's sister's fiancé. Daddy doesn't like Jeanie's folks any more than I do.*

Being grounded did have some advantages. Russell always felt like a caged animal at Jeanie's folks' house, a very small and very neat, too neat, place. Her mother had a cabinet of little china figurines that she was always dusting. Little lace doilies covered the couch and the chairs and were beneath every lamp. Russell had broken a china shepherdess once and the old lady had scowled at him ever since, even though he had apologized a hundred times over. He had even tried to glue the shepherdess back together. Spilling the glue hadn't helped. Maybe that was why she had let Russell in only as far as the porch all summer.

When his father and Jeanie had finally left, Russell started washing the supper dishes, alternating with each plate or cup: he's gonna come, he's not gonna come. He jammed the last one in the drainer, not gonna come. Okay, I'll fix that, he thought and held the plate high over his head. It made a satisfying crash when it hit the floor. Russell thought about dropping a few more but decided sweeping all the pieces wasn't worth the trouble. Or having Jeanie wonder just what was happening to her dishes.

He sat down with *The Lion, The Witch, and The Wardrobe* in the kitchen. That was the door Russell had told Jeff to use. Maybe Narnia wouldn't be so spooky now, even though it was still raining and a wind was rising.

"*Chapter Fifteen. Deeper Magic From Before The Dawn of Time. While the two girls crouched in the bushes with their heads covering their faces, they heard the voice of the Witch calling out . . . I hope no one who reads this book has been quite as miserable as Susan and Lucy were that night; but if you have been—"*

There was a knock and before Russell could jump up, Jeff came in, carrying the crutches and a flashlight and covered from head to toe in a dripping, black poncho. He grinned at Russell, laid the crutches on the floor and pulled the poncho over his head.

"You came; you're here," Russell said, getting sprayed as Jeff shook out the poncho, surprised at just how happy he was to see the other boy.

"Of course I'm here; I told you I was coming. It was kind of scary coming down here; I hope the Clarks don't check the lump in my bed. Can I hang this up somewhere?" Jeff said.

"Yeah, you did tell—yeah, in my room, upstairs. C'mon, let's go. And I don't need the crutches anymore, see? Let me put 'em back in the upstairs closet. C'mon. I thought you were going to blink your flashlight three times," Russell said over his shoulder.

"I forgot. Hurry up, I'm dripping everywhere."

Russell hesitated at the door to his bedroom before opening it. What would Jeff think of his narrow, little iron cot, his banged-up dresser, and the yard sale lamp and table? And his old wardrobe with the cracked mirror on the inside door, the big, brown rug Russell had found in a dumpster? There was plenty of time for Jeff to turn around and go home.

"Is the door stuck, Russ?" Jeff asked and reached around him to shove the door open. "Where am I going to sleep? Two of us can't fit in your bed; it's too small. Where'd you get this manger scene? You can sit in your window, cool. You have an alarm clock? Great, I have to get back before the Clarks wake up."

Russell ran and got extra blankets, a pillow, and a sleeping bag. When he got back to his room he dumped everything on the rug and they made a bed there.

"Are you sleepy? What time is it?" Jeff asked as he sat down to pull off his wet shoes and socks. "Should we go ahead and go to sleep? I'm not sleepy, are you? Are there any spells in your books we're supposed to say? I heard a door slam downstairs—your folks back?"

"It's 'bout 9:30. I'll set the alarm for 6:30—there. I'm not sleepy, either. Yeah, that's them. They went over to Jeanie's—she's my step-mother—mama's house. We'll hafta whisper."

"Are they going to check on you? I could hide in that big closet of yours—is that the wardrobe you were telling me about?"

"Yeah, that's it. Nah, they won't come up. I wish we had gotten some food from downstairs, though."

"Hey, I brought some stuff. I got a box of cinnamon graham crackers and a bag of popcorn in my knapsack here," Jeff said and pulled the food out. "And half-a-liter of Pepsi."

"All right; let's eat."

As they ate and drank, passing the bottle back and forth to take swigs out of it, Russell read aloud from *The Lion, The Witch, and The Wardrobe*. He didn't look at Jeff as he read, afraid again of Jeff laughing. Jeff said nothing. Instead he rolled over on his back to listen, and dropped popcorn in his mouth, one kernel at a time.

"Wanna read some?" Russell asked, his mouth full of graham crackers.

"Russell, I wasn't kidding when I told you I had a hard time reading. You read fine. I bet if Miss Findlay or Mrs. Collins heard you they'd be amazed and you'd never have to go to Resource again. I don't read aloud, remember? *I'm* the dummy."

Russell nodded. He had forgotten what had happened just last week when Miss Findlay asked Jeff to read. The silence had gone on forever and Jeff had turned to stone.

"I'm not a really good reader, either, though, like Hazel or that Malachi in my class. Yer not a dummy—remember Miss Findlay said being in Resource wasn't being dumb? Anybody who knows as much about dinosaurs as you do isn't dumb."

"Maybe. You're the first kid I ever told about my dinosaurs. I kept them a secret. Want some more popcorn? Keep reading."

Russell grabbed another handful and read on, slowly turning the pages, his voice filling up the room, a softer counterpoint to the steady, metallic beat of the rain on the tin roof. Finally his words became slow and heavy and he found himself squinting and yawning at the same time.

"Ready to go to sleep?" Russell asked, looking down at Jeff through half-closed eyes. "Gotta go to the bathroom? Next door—but be real quiet."

After they both had sneaked in and out of the bathroom, they got into bed, Jeff snuggling deep into the sleeping bag, Russell into his cot. He had to get back out and check the door and cut off the light, but finally he could roll over to talk to Jeff, until finally their voices became disembodied in the dark, loose and drifting. One voice told the other good night and the other answered and the room was quiet except for the steady rain and the soft, soft sounds of rhythmic breathing.

✳   ✳   ✳

At first Jeff could see nothing. Feel nothing. He knew Russell was
near, just beyond the tips of his fingers, but he could not reach him.
He had nothing with which to reach. Then, as if his arms, his legs,
his entire body, had all been asleep, Jeff felt a tingling all over and
stumbled into cool air and wet grass. There was Russell, less than an
arm length away. They were standing in tall grass at the edge of
some woods. Jeff could see, not far away, where the land dropped
away, and beyond was his sea, painted with silver and gold and white
and the light of the two moons. A salty wind blew away the thickness
in his head. He inhaled and exhaled and shook himself. Behind
them was the yellow road Russell had dreamed and his glowing
white trees.

"Hey, Russ, are you all right?" Jeff shouted over the wind.

"Yeah, I'm okay. We're here; we made it," Russell shouted back.
"It's true: magic is real. We have on the same clothes we wore to bed.
I've got my NC State tank top and yer wearing underwear."

"Well, I can't go back and get my clothes." Jeff thought he would
be embarrassed to be caught in his underwear, but he wasn't.

"Nope, no going home now. At least for a while. We're here, Jeff.
In Narnia—or some place just like it. Fairyland," Russell said and
punched Jeff on the arm. "I haven't been right here before, but this
is your sea, isn't? I smelled it back in the meadow, where we met the
centaurs and the dragon. I think I saw it when I rode the flying
horse—look! Jeff, look down there! Do you see?" Russell had
stepped a few feet away and stood at the edge of the cliff. "Come
look. You hafta look Jeff; it's really something to see down there."

The cliff didn't drop straight down into the ocean. A few feet
from where Russell and Jeff were standing rough steps had been cut
into the stone. The steps broadened and became stairs that hugged
the cliff wall as they zigzagged down to the beach. The stairs ended
in a dark pool, which was separated from the sea by a jumble of
rocks. Waves slapped and broke on the rocks, spewing foam into the
air. Beyond the rocks, in the open sea, people looked up at the two
boys. Jeff could see the round, shiny heads of dolphins and the
crested heads of the swimmers. Farther out a lone dolphin jumped
in a long graceful arc, its body shimmering in the moonlight.

"There are the swimmers I told you about, Russ. C'mon, they are
waiting for us; they want us to swim with them," Jeff said, not knowing how he knew, but even so sure he was right.

There was a swimmer waiting for them by the tidal pool when
Jeff and Russell reached the bottom. He was a boy, a little older than

Russell, Jeff thought, but then who knew how to tell the ages of any-one here? The swimmer was only a little taller than Russell and his hands and feet were like a frog's, long and webbed. A crest divided the swimmer-boy's skull and ran down his spine. He shook his head as he stood there, shaking water out of his long, black-green hair. Soft, feathery growths on the boy's neck fluttered as he stood there, as if there were tiny birds in his throat. The swimmer-boy looked as if he were wearing a dolphin's skin: sleek, smooth, and black and blue and green and grey, like the sea. The colors seemed to move as he did, as he came down from the rocks and waded through the pools to where Russell and Jeff waited at the foot of the cliff stairs.

"Did I swim with you before?" Jeff asked. "This is Russell. We came together this time, to swim—can we?"

"That's why I'm here, to take you both swimming," the swim-mer-boy said, his words sounding wet, as if waves linked the syllables together.

"Out there?" Russell said. They could hear, mixed with the sounds of the waves and the wind, voices calling and dolphins squeaking.

"Where else but there?" the boy said, laughing. Then the boy took Jeff's right hand and Russell's left hand and led them up and over the rocks and down to the beach. Russell gasped when they came down to the sand. Jeff laughed, remembering how the sea and the beach looked to him the first time he had dreamed. It was as if the sand were a huge, white carpet unrolled at their feet, curving out and out and around and then disappearing far away into the night. Foam made a white line separating the sea from the earth. The water glittered and shone. It had been bright from the cliff but from the beach it was as if there was light beneath the water, a submarine moon shining up to meet its sky sisters. Dolphins and swimmers were everywhere and way, way out, was that a whale's spout shooting out water?

"The water is warm. You don't need clothes," the swimmer-boy said and ran out in the water. When it was up to his waist, he jumped out in a long, low dive. A minute later, the boy surfaced and called for Russell and Jeff to come on, come and go swimming. Jeff looked at Russell, shrugged and peeled off his undershirt and stepped out of his underwear. He ran into the water and turned back to wait for Russell.

Russell didn't move. Would the swimmer and Jeff be able to see his body in the moonlight? Could he trust his body not to react the

way it had in his wet dreams, the way he found himself some mornings? But he couldn't stay here, on shore. Russell gulped and pulled
his shirt over his head and dropped it and his shorts on top of
Jeff's clothes. He looked down his legs: they were crisscrossed with
faint red and white lines. There were more scars on his back and
scabbed lines, fresh from earlier in the week. Long, angry streaks
striped his buttocks. Once his daddy had been so mad he had started
beating Russell in the shower. Russell wished for a cloud to cover at
least one of the moons.

"Hey, Russ, what are you waiting for? C'mon. The water is really
warm; it's like a bathtub."

Jeff had waded out until the water was up to his chest, the waves
parting around his body. The water will hide my scars, Russell
thought, and he walked into the sea.

"Catch me, Russell!" Jeff yelled and dived backward into a wave
and was gone. Russell ran, then, yelling and splashing, and a wave
slapped him in the face and flipped him over, up, and down. He
stood up, spitting out water, his feet barely touching the ground.
The cuts on his back smarted and the salt burned the insides of his
mouth and stung his eyes. Where was Jeff? There, with the swimmer-boy, diving into another wave, and a dolphin, no, two, three,
four. Another swimmer. Russell looked back and saw the cliff rising
sharply above the beach, a dark silver wall. The forest crowned it in
black shadows. As far as Russell could see, the cliff divided the land
from the beach and the sea. He turned and started swimming, calling for Jeff to wait up, he was coming, *hey, waaiiitt uuuppp.*

Something bumped Russell gently on his side, then it nipped on
his legs with tiny, sharp teeth. Russell rolled over and found himself face to face with a dolphin. It was squeaking excitedly. *What are
you saying? I can almost understand—you want me—*The dolphin
nudged Russell again and turned so he could grab its back fin.
When Russell had both hands tightly on the fin, the dolphin leaped
straight up into the air. It curved and twisted and dove down and
Russell fell off. When he came up again, sputtering and spitting,
shaking his head to get the water out of his ears, the dolphin was
waiting for him to jump again.

"Russell! Russell! Look!"

Russell, one hand on his dolphin, turned to face Jeff on the back
of another dolphin arching above the water. The dolphin flipped
and Jeff went flying, legs and arms everywhere. He came up a few
feet away from Russell. Between them, apparently content for the
moment to float, was another darker dolphin. Russell's dolphin

squeaked and nuzzled the darker one. Russell strained to listen—if he could just listen a little harder, a little longer—he would know what they were saying.

"They're saying it's time to ride and jump again, to go farther out, where Tasos—the swimmer-boy—is waiting with other swimmers. See, out there, Russ," Jeff said, gasping and laughing at the same time and pointed to the open sea, shimmering between light and dark before them.

"Jeff, you know what they're saying? You know what their squeaks mean?"

"Don't you? It's like—" But the dolphins wouldn't let Jeff finish. In the next minute Russell and Jeff were airborne again, and then, down, down, into the water, and up again. Down again, past the warm into the dark coolness. Russell could just see Jeff's body, milky white against the grey-black dolphin. Bright-colored fish, some glowing as if they had fires inside, swam around and between and over and under them. The dolphins, too, seemed to glow suddenly, as if a fire flamed inside, then, just as suddenly, the flames went out. The swimmer-boy—was it Tasos? Another? Russell couldn't tell, as there were three, no, five, no two, no—four? swimmers with them and the fish and the dolphins. Again and again they went up into the air and its quick coolness and down through the warm into the cold dark.

Finally, after how long neither could later guess, Russell and Jeff were floating on their backs, looking at the night sky. They were alone: all the dolphins and swimmers had disappeared. The sea was calm. Russell felt he was beginning to know this night sky—he was sure he recognized the huge, bright star to the left of the bigger moon from his last dream. Below the big star were five yellow stars in a circle. The two moons had faces, just like the moon back home. Back home? If he walked far enough, Russell thought, would he eventually be able to reach his house? But he had only read of places like this in books, in fairy tales: the swimmers, the dragon, the flying horse, the centaurs. He was in Faerie. Russell wished he could learn the magic rather than dreaming it. Then he could be here whenever he wanted. Here was safe. He could hear faintly the waves breaking on the beach. How far away was that and how deep was the water where they were?

"Where'd everybody go?" Russell asked sleepily. If he fell asleep here, would he dream of home, but he was in a dream now, wasn't he? If somebody came upstairs and shook him awake, where would he be?

"I don't know, but Tasos is coming, look—and two dolphins. I heard them in the water—here they are," Jeff said. With a splash, the swimmer-boy came to the surface. The two dolphins started bumping Russell and Jeff with their heads, like great sea cats. Bright pictures flashed in Russell's head: dolphins leaping, diving, racing through the water, far, far from any land. The swimmers were with them and all around was only the sea and the sky and laughing, laughing, everyone was laughing, laughing, laughing.

"They have all gone home," Tasos said. The bright pictures vanished. "It's time for you both to go home and you have to be on land for your dream to finish. Russell, you ride Akeakamai; Jeff, you ride Puka. Straddle them like a horse. That's right. They won't jump; I made them promise."

"We have to go now? Can we come back later?" Russell asked. He wanted one more leap in the air on a dolphin's back so he could let go and drop, a naked cannonball, into the ocean.

"Yes, if you can find the way here without dreaming. There will be no more dreams," Tasos said, his webbed hand resting lightly on Akeakamai's head.

"How? Where do we look?"

"You are looking in the old stories, yes? That is all I know to tell you. I would tell you more if I could but I am too young to know those mysteries. Akeakamai and Puka know more but I don't know how to translate what they know into words or even images you could understand. You have to go now. I will look for you again." Tasos slapped each dolphin, and then slipped under the water and was gone.

Neither Russell or Jeff spoke as the dolphins slowly swam them back to shore. When they could see the sand below them, they slid off and started swimming. The dolphins bumped them one last time and Russell had one quick, bright picture to flash again: him, Jeff, the two dolphins in a faraway sea. Then the dolphins disappeared.

"We can touch bottom now," Jeff said and turned to look again for the dolphins and the swimmers. There was only the sea. He paused again when they reached the beach, this time to look up at the night sky. "You know, I never really looked at the stars before. Not here or back there. Sometimes I hate the night back there."

"There are so many more stars here," Russell whispered. The smaller moon was directly over their heads. The larger moon was low and just above where sea and sky met. Russell thought a tidal wave might be able to slap it into the water. The two moons gave them two shadows, like ink stains on the sand. Both their bodies looked very pale, as if they were ghosts.

"C'mon, we gotta go," Russell finally said and touched Jeff lightly on the arm. He looked away from Jeff then, at the sand, the surf. "Where are our clothes, anyway?" Part of him wanted to cover himself—he was certain now in the light of the two moons there would be no way Jeff could not see his scars. He felt as if they were all blinking red, like ribbons of Christmas lights under his skin. *Maybe he won't notice, or if he does, he won't say anything. I wish I could peel them off, like sunburned skin.*

"Over there, see," Jeff said and turned away from the sky and ran up the beach, toward the rocks. Russell could see a small, white lump just past the tideline. Jeff turned back to wave his white undershirt like a flag. "They're full of sand. Here's yours."

Russell sighed and walked over and picked up his clothes to shake them out. He wondered, as he dried himself with his T-shirt, that if he hadn't, would he wake up naked and wet on Saturday morning? "I guess we should go back to the cliff, huh?"

"Yeah, I guess so—look, Russ, out there," Jeff said and pointed to the ocean. Outlined in moonlight they could see one lone dolphin jumping high in the air. For a long moment, the dolphin seemed frozen, a gilded silhouette. Then there was only the sea.

"That was for us," Jeff said.

"Yeah. It was Puka," Russell said. There had been another bright flash of recognition. "Akeakamai's below the water, but she's not far away." The first brightness had been followed by another, each one like a mallet striking a xylophone, one clear note, then another.

"Your ears are pointed now, Russ," Jeff said as he bent over to pull his underwear on.

Hilda Ruggles

"Of course I will meet you for lunch, Thomas," Hilda Ruggles had said early Saturday morning. "Where? The Art Museum? What a lovely idea. Twelve? See you there." Hilda hung up the phone, feeling very satisfied. She hated Jack and his only son being estranged to the point of no contact: no phone calls, visits, nothing. *If having lunch with Thomas could begin a reconciliation between father and son, and if she could bring it about—My gift to you, Jack,* she thought.

She glanced at the clock. Eleven-thirty. By the time she drove from Garner to the museum it would be just about twelve. Hilda gathered her handbag from the bedroom and stopped one last time, in front of the bathroom mirror. Not bad for a forty-something woman, she thought. No grey, body in shape, minimum number of crow's feet around the eyes. Hilda ran a brush through her light brown hair. She looked good in this simple green summer dress, sandals and bag to match. All this effort for a sulky stepson. But it would make Jack happy and making Jack happy made her happy. Good enough reason.

Hilda paused a second time on the way out. Should she call Jack? Let him know what she was up to? Jack had left early in the morning for his office at State, to grade papers, he had said. *No, I want this to be a surprise. And if it doesn't work, no false hopes.*

Hilda Alice Palmer had met Jack Ruggles a year ago one July afternoon, in a bar on Hillsborough Street. Jack had been sitting on a stool at one corner of the bar counter, nursing a Michelob draft as he graded English 112 essays with a green felt-tip pen, totally oblivious to the world. Hilda had come by after work, hot and tired and bothered. She worked as a lab manager for State's chemistry department. Hilda hated her job and hated her professor-boss. Hilda wasn't too keen on academics in general, not after her first husband, a religion professor at Meredith, had traded her in for one of his nubile undergraduates. She longed to get a job in private industry; then she could tell all these PhD so-and-sos to go to hell.

When Hilda sat down two stools over from Jack and realized who he was, Jack Ruggles, English prof and the author of two rather obscure labyrinthine novels she couldn't understand, Hilda had almost got up and walked out. What the hell and, hey, she had as much right to sit at the bar as anyone else, including Dr. Ruggles, thank you very much. And as much as she hated to admit it, Jack didn't look half-bad. She sighed—was she hopelessly attracted to professors?

It was the sigh that got Jack's attention. He looked up from an essay bleeding green and smiled.

"Bad day, huh?"

"You don't know the half of it," Hilda had said and took her beer and sat by Jack, thinking she must be crazy. But that hair—she wanted to run her fingers through it, smooth down the back cowlick.

She met Ben Tyson and his son, Malachi, on her fourth date with Jack, at what was evidently one of their haunts, the Kuntry Kitchen in Garner. It didn't take Hilda much more than a few sips of sweet ice tea to realize that meeting Ben and his towheaded son with the curious golden-yellow-brown eyes, was meeting almost all of Jack's family.

"Why didn't you tell me Ben is The Friend, practically your brother, and that Malachi's your godson, Jack?" Hilda said later that evening.

"I didn't want you to feel like you were being inspected," Jack said sheepishly.

"But I was, wasn't I? Well, did I pass?"

"With flying colors. And tomorrow, I want you to meet my son, Thomas."

Hilda and Jack had gotten married at Christmas, with blessings from Ben and Malachi, the NCSU English Department (the chair had sidled up to Hilda at the reception to whisper they were all counting on her to make Jack behave), and from Hilda's two children.

Thomas had come late to the wedding; he didn't stay for the reception.

I'm not going to give up getting that boy to like me, Hilda thought as she rode the glass elevator down to the lower level of the North Carolina Art Museum. *Not yet, anyway. Get him and his father to make peace. At least that wasn't her fault.* Hilda thought of herself as good with children. Her own kids had turned out pretty well, despite their father's predilection for sweet young things. And she got along well with Ben's little boy, although she did wish Jack would go ahead and tell her what was wrong with the child. Why was he getting sick all the time and why did Ben look so worried and—well, afraid?

Well, he will tell me eventually, Hilda thought as she looked out through the walls of the glass elevator. She loved being able to see the green lawn spreading out from the Museum. True, the clear view of the state correctional center for juvenile delinquents, barbed wire fence and all, did take some away from the scene's charm. Hilda smoothed her hair one more time and then went in the Museum restaurant. There was Thomas at a table, with two glasses of tea, lemon slices in each.

"I thought you might be hot driving over here and all," Thomas said smiling, and handed her a glass when she sat down. "It's Red Zinger, with lemon and mint. One of your favorites, right?"

"Yes, Thomas, it is. How'd you know?" Hilda said and studied Thomas when the waiter came over to take their order. He looked very little like his father; Jack had said his son was practically a clone of his first wife. Black hair and dark, deep-set eyes, sallow skin. Too many hours at computer terminals for Central Carolina Bank, she thought as she sipped her tea. Just the way she liked it. And he's nervous, too. But then Thomas had always seemed nervous, like a cat ready to run, ever since she met him.

"Well, Thomas," Hilda said when the waiter had left. "Here I am. What do you—want—to—ta—a—a—" It was as if suddenly Hilda was trying to walk and talk underwater. She could barely get her mouth open, move her hand. "Tho—helll—"

Hilda tried to move her hand and knocked over her tea. Thomas was saying something, he was shouting, and other people were getting up, moving shadows, and the waiter, what was he doing? She tried to open her mouth again and fell across the table.

Thomas

It had been too easy. His plan had worked to perfection, even down to the last detail, when he had simply stepped into the crowd of people around Hilda and walked away. A simple masking spell—he didn't become invisible, he just became unnoticed and unremembered. Someone would, eventually, call his father; he could handle the rest—just as Thomas wanted him to do. Talking to the doctors at the hospital, filling out the paperwork, sitting by her bed. Not that it would do any good, he thought as he pressed up on the elevator. After a week of a deep coma, Hilda Ruggles would simply die. The poison was slow but irreversibly fatal—and wouldn't show up on any blood test. Thomas stepped into the elevator just as the paramedics came racing down the stairs. Her heart would beat slower and slower, with the rests in between longer and longer, until, finally, her heart would stop. And he, Thomas, an adept at the black arts, would have the power of her life-force in him, seeping in, as it seeped from her. And he would grow stronger and stronger and stronger, until one day he wouldn't need poison anymore—he would be able to suck the life out himself, like a vampire.

He had to kill her. It had to be the deliberate and rehearsed murder of someone close and not close, of his family and not of his family. The life had to be stolen and done with malice and the stealing had to be slow and measured. The better to savor it, of course. Later, with more power, the sudden, quick feedings would be the way. And with each life, Thomas would receive power, pure, unadulterated power. Even now he could taste the hint of Hilda's life, her energy a bittersweet, almost yellow flavor. Just the hint of what he would have when she finally died.

Thomas stopped at the Museum Shop to buy postcards and a kaleidoscope. Innocent things. He made small talk with the sales clerk and then waited as the paramedic, carrying a stretcher and Hilda, rushed past him and out in the waiting ambulance. He watched it race away, sirens first a moan, then a full wail, and then, a casual stroll to his car. Tonight, he thought, as he backed his car out, he would take control of the coven. They would all bend the knee to him, the High Priest of the Dark Ones, the soul-vampire of soul-vampires, the Witch King, the Herald of The Change. Taking the boy, when the time came, would be so easy. And with the boy under his control, the boy's soul a conduit of energy, then Thomas could, well . . .

From the journal of Ben Tyson,
Late Saturday night, September 21, 1991

Jack called me from Rex this afternoon and told me about Hilda and Thomas. He was crying.

"Ben, it had to have been Thomas—some of his black witchcraft. The museum waiter described him perfectly. He just left her there, Ben, passed out on the table. My own son. And she won't wake up. The doctors are running test after test and she won't wake up—"

Jack ran out of words then; he was crying too hard.

"I'm coming," I told him. "I'll get Malachi and we'll be right there."

"My own son is evil. Just like those damn Fomorii. Thomas is a monster."

I asked Malachi about Thomas on the way to Rex Hospital. Had he noticed anything?

"Dad, I don't remember the Fomorii, not like you do. You saw them when I was a baby. But sometimes I think they are shadows in my dreams—the dreams where I see the three others—"

"You didn't tell me you were dreaming about the Fomorii."

"I didn't want to worry you and I am not sure, Dad. Just sometimes when I dream of Faerie, there are shadows there, red-eyed shadows."

"And Thomas?" I asked, quickly looking at Malachi. He looked as tired as he sounded. He had lost more weight and there were dark bruises on his arms and his skin seemed paler and more translucent. His hair was definitely paler, whiter. And his eyes. My son's eyes weren't golden-brown-yellow anymore. They are golden-bronze and luminous and they glow, even in the daytime.

People are starting to notice.

"He feels bad, Dad. Just being around him is like being inside a cold shadow."

"When have you been around him? Has he been around the house lately? Mal, you've got to stop keeping all this stuff secret," I blurted, my fear and anger and love twisting into one knot in my stomach. I am not going to let someone else I love die because of my stupidity and ignorance.

"No, no, not for some time. Just in the dreams."

We stayed at the hospital with Jack most of the afternoon, until Hilda's son arrived from Charlotte and her daughter from Wilmington. We sat in her room and watched her, the IV dripping into her arm, the monitors showing that somewhere in that deep, deep sleep Hilda was alive. Barely.

It was a long afternoon. I tried to talk to Jack, about what the doctors said and then about anything else I could think of. His class, new books at the library, whether State could beat Carolina in basketball this fall. I gave up after a while; Jack just wasn't talking anymore. He didn't cry, not then. He looked beaten, empty, as if it was all he could do to sit there in that chair and hold Hilda's hand.

Malachi slept for most of the time. But when Hilda's son arrived, he woke up and just as we were about to leave, he touched her on the forehead. For an instant, his hand glowed against her skin. Then, just as quickly, a pulsing light shone around Hilda's head, then it was gone.

I was the only one who noticed.

He told me in the elevator Hilda was going to die.

"Her aura is getting dimmer and colder. Dad, pretty soon it's going to wink out and she'll be gone."

"Can you do anything?" I said, remembering when his mother had shown me my aura years ago and how far that light had extended from my body, shimmering and vibrating.

"I'm just a kid, Dad, and half-human," Malachi said and took my hand.

I felt like an idiot. Yes, my half-human half-Daoine Sidhe son, my first-born, my only child, can fly and has psychokinetic powers. Telepathic, too, I guess. But he's just ten; he won't be eleven until March.

We drove straight from the hospital to St. Mary's, for the Saturday evening vigil mass. Somehow I felt it was important for us to be there, to light another candle for Hilda, to make the sign of the cross and kneel and pray. To rise and sing when the priest came in, pray again, *and sing the Gloria. Each part of the mass, in its right place and at its right time, felt so familiar and comforting. Outside the world seems to be unraveling, changing, metamorphosing. But inside I knew when to kneel and when to stand, when to sing and to pray, and when to listen.*

The celebrant was Father Jamey Applewhite and this time he didn't speak of the mystery. Rather he spoke of loving one another, and using love as an enabling force, a power, a strength.

Is love enough to combat the Fomorii who haunt me and my son? To stop Thomas, the evil son of my best friend? Is love enough to stop the accelerating craziness? Is there anything else strong enough? Love hadn't saved Emma twelve years ago. Love hadn't saved Valeria ten years ago. And love won't keep Hilda alive.

When we shook hands in front of the church, I told Father Jamey I might want to talk to him, if that would be okay, if he was going to be around St. Mary's. I usually went to St. Anthony's—well, I had been going, kind of—

"It's okay," he said, laughing. "Call me anytime. Nice to meet you, and you, too, Malachi."

What will I say to this priest? That I am scared and desperate and haven't yet found the nearest gate?

I don't know.

Malachi had a nightmare. The Fomorii had cornered him and were getting closer and closer, their eyes on fire, their fangs and claws dripping blood. He screamed and I ran in there and shook him and held him. He was leaking light all over the place. He insisted I tell him the story again—

Malachi fell asleep before I finished. Now I am going to lie down beside my son and try to sleep.

IV

Mabon to Michaelmas: Becoming Magic
Sunday, September 22 - Sunday, September 29, 1991

Russell and Jeff

JEFF WOKE EARLY SUNDAY MORNING FROM A BAD dream to still more rain drumming on the roof. Outside cars went by, tires hissing on the pavement. Jeff sighed. He loved rain, but he had planned to go and visit Russell in the afternoon, while the Clarks hunkered down in the living room to read the Sunday papers, do the crossword puzzles, and nap. But even with them distracted, it would be difficult to hide any wet clothes—and he had barely managed to get away with sneaking out Friday and back in on Saturday morning. He knew if he asked, they would have taken him over there—but then they would have to meet Russell's parents, and Russell was afraid of what would happen if they did. Besides, Russell was still grounded. Jeff thought about praying to God to sort things out, but no. Jeff shook his head. His dad had made him go to church every Sunday and every Sunday Jeff had prayed for things to stop and everything to be as it was. It had taken God three years to answer the first part of his prayer and being with the Clarks wasn't how things had been.

But never mind that, Jeff thought, as he leaned against the window. Maybe it would fair off later. Then he remembered Mr. Clark saying it was supposed to rain all day Sunday.

I'll call him tomorrow—I mean later today, Jeff thought, still leaning against the window. He looked back at the clock on his dresser. 3:11 A.M. Waaay too early to call anybody, he thought. But he was wide-awake and he didn't want to go back to sleep. Sometimes if he woke up and it was still night and went back to sleep, he would have the same dream again, as if it had been waiting for him, just the other side of being awake. He had been in bed and had been frozen. He had been cold and still, with ice on his skin and all around him. And Someone had been in the room, waiting in a dark corner, just beyond where Jeff could see. But *this* dream had been different. When Someone had started walking across the room, his feet heavy on the wooden floor, Jeff had finally been able to do something. He couldn't move, but he had been able to make one of his dinosaurs move: the big one-foot-tall bright red T-rex. T-rex had floated up from Jeff's desk and smashed into Someone. And again and again and again until Someone had fled, howling.

Jeff had woken up when Someone had started howling and running away.

"I did that," he whispered to himself. "I made that dinosaur *move.*"

But it had been just another bad dream, right? But now he knew dreams were real—after all, his ears were pointed and if he looked into the mirror he would see his eyes were greener and almost luminous.

Okay, let's see. Jeff stood up from the window, turned on the lamp by his bed, and looked around the room. There was a heap of dinosaurs on the floor. A purple pterodactyl was on the top. In the dream it had been like completing an equation, or completing a puzzle. This here, that there. For a long moment, nothing moved, except the rain outside the window. Then, with a quick jerk, the pterodactyl shot straight up, hit the ceiling and fell back down on the pile.

"Okay, I'm getting there," Jeff said and grabbed the pterodactyl and held it over his head. "Dreams are real," he reminded himself and tossed the pterodactyl up in the air. This time when it hit the ceiling it stayed. *Yeeessss. Just like in the dream.* The dinosaur banked to the left and zoomed around the room, in and out of the white light of the lamp. He made it do cartwheels, somersaults, figure eight's, loop-de-loops, barrel rolls. *Now: here.* And the pterodactyl landed on Jeff's open palm.

For the next half-hour dinosaurs flew everywhere. Jeff's comic books joined them in flight, becoming big paper birds with flapping wing-pages. The lamp flicked on and off, on and off, on and off, over and over again.

"I can't wait to tell Russell," Jeff said as he lay on his bed, hands behind his head, watching an apatosaurus spinning right above his head. Three triceratops whizzed around the room, swooping and diving low over the bed. A brachiosaurus hovered by the window, looking for all the world as if it were watching the rain outside. The air-trails the toys left behind became a web of blue, an azure net cast over the room.

"Maybe I *can* tell Russell now," Jeff said and sat up. All the dinosaurs fell down then, banging on the floor, flopping on the bed. "If I can *move* my dinosaurs—" He pushed up the window, and then the storm window and screen, and jumped back almost immediately as the rain and wind hit him in the face. "Sure—" and he *pushed* back the rain and the wind. The air between Jeff and the outside sparkled and shimmered and no rain and no wind came in the window. "Now a test pilot." He tossed the brach up and out and *caught* it before it hit the grass. Then the green toy flew in widening circles around the backyard, around the trees, under and over the swings.

"Come back," he called and the brach turned and floated back to his hand.

I can do this, I know I can do this.

Jeff closed the screen and storm window and the glass window and then, feeling more wide-awake than he sometimes felt in the daytime, Jeff snuck out of his room and down the hall and out the back door to the deck. He climbed up on the porch railing and stood there for a moment, balancing himself, his eyes closed. *I'm getting soaked—hey, if I can push the rain back out the window—There—* Now the faintly sparkling air surrounded Jeff; it moved as he moved, as if it were a separate skin. And he couldn't feel the rain or the wind. *All right. Just like moving the dinosaurs, pushing back the rain, except it's me. One, two, three—* Jeff flew, the wind and the rain parting before him, the night all around him like a black glove. He flew faster and faster, his eyes still closed, until he ran headlong into a pine tree. The sparkling air disappeared as if it had been cut off. Branches slapped his face and ripped a long tear in his shirt and down his back. Crying and wet, Jeff fell, breaking more branches until he hit the ground with a thud.

He sat unmoving, water soaking through his shorts to his skin, rain on his head, running down his nose, into his eyes, down his back. At least the rain was slowing down a little. He gingerly moved each arm and leg. Nothing broken. His back was a little sore and when he reached behind him, Jeff felt something warm and wet. In the light from the deck Jeff could see a dark streak on his hand. He shrugged and wiped the blood on his shorts. He stood up slowly, pulling a few twigs and needles out of his hair. A trail of broken branches marked his path down the tree.

"Okay, let's try again with eyes open and away from trees. First, the sparkly air," Jeff said. The annoying rain disappeared. Satisfied, Jeff glanced toward the house: no sign of the Clarks. Good, they hadn't heard him crash into the tree.

Onetwothree . . .

Jeff flew straight up, not stopping until he was high above the trees and power lines. Then Jeff floated on his stomach, his arms spread out like Superman. The cars looked no bigger than the Matchbox cars he had left at his parents' house. Their headlights seemed to be running in front of them, white shadows pushing back the black. Jeff let himself drift for a long time. He floated on his back, pretending he was in an invisible hammock, swaying back and forth. Flying was just how he had dreamed it would be.

"Okay, Russ," Jeff said and flew up and over the trees and other houses and streets between his house and Russell's. The night was amazingly dark: no moon, no stars, only the heavy clouds and the rain. At least it was beginning to taper off, and the wind was almost a breeze. He wished the clouds would go away and let the moon and stars come out. Then the night and everything in it would be all his—for right now, as he flew, there was no one in the whole world but Jeff. He was almost disappointed to reach Russell's house. Down Poole, and then left here, down the Whites' driveway. There was the house, standing alone in the middle of its big, ragged going-to-weed yard. Jeff landed on the roof, just outside Russell's window. He could see Russell's manger scene through the glass.

"Windows lock on the inside," Jeff muttered. *Just like the dinosaurs.* Even so, moving the metal lock was harder and required more concentration. Jeff closed his eyes and scrunched up his face. He felt the sparkling air wavering around him and he felt just a hint of the cool, wet night. *There.* The lock *moved* and Jeff shoved the window up. He carefully set aside the little manger and the statues, and crawled inside. He let the sparkling air fade away.

"Russell. Russ, wake up. It's me, Jeff. Wake up," Jeff whispered and shook the lump beneath the spread.

"Huh? Jeff? Watterya doing here in th' middle of night? How'dya get in?" Russell finally rolled over and pulled the covers back from his head. He looked up at Jeff, his face still heavy with sleep.

"I flew here from the Clarks."

"Huh? You did what?"

"Wake up, Russ. It's like what you did when you *shoved* Mrs. Findlay at school. I, we, can *move* stuff. I had my dinosaurs flying all over the place and I *moved* me. We can fly and stay warm and dry—I mean—Russ, are you awake? Watch me." Jeff floated straight up to the ceiling and then came down slowly to stand on Russell's furry rug. Then, slowly, the spread peeled itself off Russell and clumped at the foot of the bed.

"Now hit me," Jeff said and the air shimmered and glowed around him.

"Hit you?"

"Hit me. Go ahead. You are awake, aren't you? It's okay, hit me. Go on. It won't hurt."

Russell got out of bed and slowly swung his hand toward Jeff's face. His hand stopped a few inches away. He pressed hard and still he couldn't reach Jeff's face.

"Man, I can't—but—this is more magic, isn't it? And you said you flew here, right?" Russell asked. "Can you show me how?" He sat down on his bed and pulled his spread around him. He was wearing only his State gym shorts.

Jeff sat down beside him, still wrapped inside his shimmering air shield. "I think so. I can see, when this air is around me, lights all around you, layers of light. Close your eyes and hold my hand."

Russell nodded and closed his eyes. He couldn't quite get his hand around Jeff's; instead, he was holding the shimmering air. His hand tingled, and then for a long moment, nothing happened. He could hear Jeff breathing and his own breathing. Then small, white stars appeared behind his eyes. The stars grew bigger and brighter until there was nothing but brightness and it hurt and yet felt good and funny and warm and too hot and cold and—it was gone. And Russell could feel Jeff's hand, each finger, and he *knew*.

"Well?" Jeff said when Russell opened his eyes. Russell got up and opened his wardrobe and looked into the mirror. He was surrounded by the same shimmering, twinkling light as Jeff was—no, Russell's light was more the color of fire, a yellow streaked with orange and red. The light rippled in his red hair, making it like a living flame. Jeff's light was cooler and more subdued. It was the color of ice: blue, white, and streaked with pale green. Jeff's light was wet, Russell thought, if a light could be wet. *His* light burned.

"Ready to fly?" Jeff asked. He stood by the now-open window. Russell hesitated. All he could see behind Jeff was night.

"Here, Russ, hold my hand for a little while," Jeff said and they climbed out the window and onto the roof. "One, two, three, blastoff!"

For a few seconds Russell knew he was a weight, dragging Jeff down. Then, it came to him, as if someone had flicked a switch, or pulled curtains back to let light in. He *saw* what Jeff had been trying to make him see. At first, a strange, intricate pattern, convoluted, intertwined, sparking, shifting colors, then, he could see the pattern, trace it, and there it was, he *saw*. Russell let go of Jeff's hand and flew past him, straight up, the fiery light around him crackling and sparking and hissing in the air.

"I'm flying, I'm flying! C'mon, Jeff, let's race, let's do something, anything. *We can fly.*"

Jeff caught up with Russell when they were a good hundred feet above Russell's house. Russell was floating on his back and laughing. Jeff flew up and under him and flipped him over and darted away, a quick air-fish.

"I'm gonna get you!"

And they flew, one after the other, two small comets in the sky, one blue-green, the other yellow-orange.

Russell wondered, as he turned and banked to chase Jeff over the trees if this was the same Jeff who had been so terrified on the cliff above the swimmers' sea. The same Jeff who tried to be invisible in school? And yes, he thought, the same Jeff who swam like a fish and rode on dolphins' backs. Each one was Jeff, whose eyes were like twin green stoplights. *I bet my eyes are like that: green lights.* He shook off his questions. There was too much happening all at once for Russell to even get close to any answers. Below and behind him was his house, but it didn't look like his house anymore. It was a white box receding into the shadows of the forest, which was all dark and green and black. Jeff's neighborhood looked like a patchwork quilt made of uneven squares and rectangles. Russell caught Jeff when they crossed Poole Road and they flew side by side, their arms outstretched, a hand's width apart. Russell flew a little closer and tapped Jeff on the hand.

"Tag. Yer it."

"Wait, I've got a better idea," Jeff said, laughing. "Let's go to the school, to the playground. I want to try something. When we get there, let's play follow-the-leader. I'll be leader first, okay?"

"Sure," Russell said with a shrug.

The school came into sight within a few minutes' flying time. Jeff turned his head and grinned. "Are you ready?" Russell nodded. When they cleared the trees enclosing the playground, Jeff dove straight down. It was like riding a roller coaster: a long, long, sharp dive, and down, down, down, down, to skim the ground; then straight up and back down again. And up again, making a corkscrew in the air. Then Jeff led him in great circles around and around the playground.

"Okay, now we go this way, toward that pond over there," Jeff shouted and banked left.

"What are we gonna do there?" Russell shouted back, wondering why they were shouting. Jeff was only a few feet away.

"You'll see."

When they got to the small pond, Jeff dove straight down again, slicing into the water with a quick splash. Russell could see Jeff's blue-green-white shape streaking below the pond's dark surface, like some great racing fish. He burst through the water on the far side and flew up, the water streaming off his light-skin.

"We're still playing follow-the-leader, Russ. You aren't scared, are you?"

"I'm not scared," Russell snapped. He'd show Jeff who was tougher. He let his light-skin wink out and before he could begin to feel the night air and the now-misty rain, dove into the pond. The water was like a sudden slap, very cold and very hard, and then he was under, shooting just below the surface as fast as he could go. The water exploded in front of him and he shot up in the air, a wet comet.

"You lost your shorts," Jeff yelled, laughing and pointing.

Russell looked down. He was naked, forty feet up in the air. And he was wet and shivering. Chattering and with some effort, he turned back on his light-skin full strength. At least the cold went away. He flew down slowly, in wide circles, to look for his shorts. There was the dark water of the pond. No shorts. Russell flew back up, shaking his head. Jeff laughed again and dove down into the water. He skimmed the surface this time, as if he were a skipping stone, and then up, stopping to hover in front of Russell.

"Here they are, you goof. Can't you see? You'd better put them back on," Jeff said and handed the dripping shorts to Russell.

"What for? Who's going to look up in the air in the middle of the night? This is like swimming with the swimmers, remember?" Russell said and let his gym shorts fall back in the water. They weren't his favorites, anyway.

"I guess you're right," Jeff agreed and peeled his clothes off and dropped them in the pond. "This *is* like when we were with the swimmers and the dolphins. C'mon, let's race." Jeff flew off, with Russell at first behind and then right beside him.

Sometime later they stopped racing and diving and floated, like dandelion fluff on a light breeze. They lay on their backs, with their arms outstretched, over the trees between Russell's and Jeff's houses. By then it was almost morning. The clouds were gone and the sky was changing from purple-black to blue-grey.

"I could live up here forever," Russell said, his eyes closed.

"Me, too. The sun's going to come up soon, Russ. Look over there. See the light just starting behind those trees?"

"Yeah, I see it. I guess we should go home soon before somebody on their way to early church does look up and see us up here with no clothes on."

"You're right," Jeff said a few minutes later, yawning. "There's the sun, just over the trees," he added. The faint glow had become a golden fire. "There's the Clarks' house. I'd better go. Call me later, if you can."

"Okay, see you later," Russell said, wondering if either one of them would be able to sleep when they were home, if they would just lie in bed, remembering flying. Russell watched as Jeff flew down and landed in the backyard and then ran into the house, disappearing into the back door, a white shadow on the green grass. Russell flew back to his own house and landed on the roof. The floor felt odd to his feet as he put the manger scene back in the window. He crawled back in bed and the sheet and spread lay heavy on his skin. For a little while the pillow felt hard. And then, completely under the covers, Russell let his fire-colored light-skin go out.

Malachi

Malachi stayed out of school three more days, until the middle of the week. He had wanted to go back on Monday but his father had insisted he stay home, sleep, get back his strength. Thursday was soon enough.

"Dad, I'm going to get behind," Malachi grumped Monday morning as his father stood meditatively over his open briefcase, pondering what to put in next.

"I'll call your teacher and get your assignments. I'll drive over there this afternoon and get your books. I'll tell her the doctor said you were to stay in bed for a few days. The flu. No, don't ask me again. You're staying at home. And how in the world could we explain how you look?" Ben said and selected two books he needed to review. Then he scooped a stack of the manila file folders. He wasn't on the public desk until the afternoon; maybe he could get all these done today. Well, at least two or three of them. "I don't think there are any other kids at Nottingham Heights Elementary that have light-smoke drifting out of their pointed ears. Do. You? Besides. You're. Still. Tired."

"When Mrs. Collins gets mad she has smoke coming out of her ears—never mind," Malachi said. Whenever his father spoke each word as if it was a single sentence he knew the argument was over and done with. And he *was* still leaking light. Tendrils oozed slowly out of his skin pores, his ears. As his father closed his briefcase, another thin stream came out of his nose. Malachi watched as it drifted slowly up in the air, twisting and turning near the living room ceiling until it faded away.

"Case in point," his dad said, watching Malachi's nose smoke in the air. "Your mother could turn the light on and off. I wish I knew how to tell you to do it, too, son. Try concentrating on it, visualizing the light going off. You can do it—you were born to," Ben said. "You glowed all over when you were a little baby. I wish I could take you to a doctor about being so tired."

"I've never been to a doctor," Malachi said. He raised one hand and the door opened in front of his father.

"You've never been sick before, either. Never caught anything like measles or mumps. But even if you weren't leaking light, I couldn't take you. Who knows what would show up on a blood test and your normal temp is 100. I arranged for all the paperwork the schools needed—but never mind that. I'll be home for lunch. I love you, son," his dad said and kissed Malachi on the forehead and went out the door.

"I love you, too, Dad," Malachi called after him as he closed the door.

It was a long three days, even though Malachi spent most of them sleeping—deep, heavy sleep. His father had been right. Getting up for breakfast, eating, reading, doing whatever schoolwork Mrs. Collins had given his father took him to mid-morning. Then Malachi would be bone dead tired again, so tired he would fall asleep where he was, on the couch, in an armchair, at the kitchen table. By Tuesday night he began to feel stronger and the light discharges stopped. Malachi had wanted to be able to tell his father he had stopped them, but he couldn't. They just stopped.

In the afternoons, after the morning nap, lunch, and another nap, Malachi practiced his levitation and psychokinesis. By Wednesday morning Malachi was able to keep a circle of balls moving over his head, like a revolving halo. He drifted about the house, from room to room, and walked up walls and on the ceiling. It was a relief to be able to practice magic and not have to hide it from his father. All his father had said when saw the balls in the air was to be careful and let no one else see what he was doing.

"Be sure you draw the drapes, son. And no going outside. I just have a funny feeling they aren't far away."

They were the Fomorii—the red-eyed ones who sometimes lurked in dark corners in his dreams. He knew the monsters terrified his father. Malachi was able to pick up enough of his father's thoughts to know that. It wasn't actual mind-reading or listening— rather it was as if the emotions that were part of his father's thoughts —fear, worry over Malachi—were being projected. And even if he couldn't pick up his father's emotions, Malachi could tell his father was worried and afraid by the colors in his aura. The usual warm white-yellow of his father's aura was streaked with dulling browns, black, and greys. He wanted his father to tell him about the Fomorii: who were they, really and did they come from Faerie, too, and what did they want so badly? Uncle Jack had been of no help.

"The Fomorii? Those red-eyed monsters, huh? No, Malachi, that story your dad has to tell you, not me," Jack had said.

On Thursday morning, his father, grumbling that Malachi could have waited until Friday, drove Malachi to school. Malachi had wanted to ride the bus, but his father had been adamant. "Malachi, are you sure you're up to this?" his father asked when they were stopped in front of the school.

"I'm fine, Dad, really," Malachi said, one hand on the door handle.

"Well all right, but you be sure you tell the teacher to call me if you get tired," his father and kissed Malachi on the forehead.

"I'll be fine, Dad." He wanted to ask his father right then about the Fomorii. The physical contact—lips on forehead—had been an instant download and this time not just emotions, but images. The Fomorii, their eyes, fire whips, in the middle of the night, and his father, afraid, afraid for his son, his wife—and deep, sharp grief. Then his dad had pulled away. "I'll be okay, Dad; I have her charm, remember? See you at three." *You are going to have to tell me and soon. I need to know.*

Malachi waited at the top of the school steps until his father's car was out of sight. Then he turned and faced the school and took a deep breath. Malachi could just vaguely sense the other kids' feelings, as if they were a distant thunderstorm. When a girl bumped him as he stood there, it was like having someone throw cold water on him in the shower. He pulled away, gasping. She was—her dad had—no, no—she hadn't wanted him to—And she was gone. Malachi counted to ten and then, keeping himself as close to the wall as he could, went in. He wasn't leaking light, and as long as he didn't touch anyone, it would be safe.

That feeling of safety lasted until he got to his classroom. Hazel's mind practically slapped Malachi in the face when he stepped through the door. She was sitting at her seat, reading and fiddling with her long, brown braid. Hazel was outlined in layers of light: a pale blue close, then rainbow colors, yellow, and more rainbow colors. What looked like small fires burned at the top of her head, her neck, and her heart. Hazel's ears were pointed; her eyes glowed silver. Malachi blinked and she looked like she always did, except she wore a headband over her ears. Hazel looked up then and Malachi saw recognition in her face: he knew she had seen him in her dreams.

Two, Malachi thought, and went in the room, chatted with Mrs. Collins, and then sat down with the work sheet for morning work. *I'll talk to her at lunch, maybe PE. She's scared, too, and kind of glad—*

The air crackled and snapped and Malachi felt a sudden heat on his face and rain on his head. He looked up. Russell White stood in the doorway, talking with his buddy, Jeff, who was in Mrs. Markham's room across the hall. Both of them had headbands wrapped around their ears. Malachi could see the layers of color in Russell's aura all the way to the fine burning gold edge. Small fires burned on the top of Russell's fiery red hair, his neck, his heart, the middle of his torso, his belly, his crotch. His eyes glowed green. Jeff's eyes were as green as Russell's, but his aura was cool: white, blue, and green. A rose-colored vine of light grew out of each of their hearts, linking the two boys together.

Three and four. Russell, he thought, hadn't been the same since his suspension two weeks ago. The usually cantankerous boy had come back quiet and subdued and suddenly best friends with a boy who was no longer quiet or subdued. And somehow Malachi was sure Russell's new quiet wasn't just because of the fire and the trailer and the new Resource teacher. Malachi quickly looked back at the work sheet on his desk as Russell walked past him to his desk, feeling like a faint brush across his back the boy's dislike and distrust.

At least he doesn't out and out hate me. And he and Jeff and Hazel are the other kids I have dreamed about. Now, what do I do? I know

*them and I don't. I know they are becoming like me and we are sup-
posed to be together, the four of us —*

"Ow," Malachi said out loud, for the moment forgetting the
other three. He had brushed his bare arm against the steel desk sup-
port. There was a long, angry red welt where the metal had touched
his skin and his arm hurt. He pressed his right hand against his
mother's charm and felt an answering surge and the welt faded. A
ward, he thought; Dad had talked about her setting wards like force
fields. And iron, how iron was poisonous to her —

"Malachi? Do you feel well? Did you hurt your arm?"

He looked up to see Mrs. Perry leaning over him.

"Just tired. I've finished my morning work. Here it is, and here's
what I did when I was home and . . ."

Then Mrs. Collins began quizzing Russell about his headband.

"Is it some sort of club you and Jeff have, or something one of
you saw on TV? Well, Russell?" she asked, tapping her pencil on
her desk. Malachi looked up to see Mrs. Collins's aura as well, a
dull, rusty brown that kept flickering on and off, as if whatever bat-
teries powering it were weak.

"We just wanted to wear them, that's all. No club, no special reason. Besides, Hazel has one on, see?" Russell said. Mrs. Collins
turned from Russell to look at Hazel and her mouth dropped open.

"Hazel? Why are you wearing a headband?"

"Uh, I, uh —"

Malachi dropped all his books on the floor and everybody in the
class jumped and looked away from Russell and Hazel. Jeff slipped
out the door and Russell took his seat. Hazel buried herself in her
spelling book. Malachi busily and loudly picked everything up.

Hazel

Hazel looked up from her spelling book when everyone had settled
down. Russell, still scowling, looked intent on his morning work.
Malachi had finally secured all his books beneath his desk and it
looked like he was doing math. Hazel could tell by the red cover of
his book. Was he the boy she had seen in her dreams in the country
of the dragon and the white trees? She couldn't be sure — not of that
or anything else now.

The morning had been bad for Hazel. She had turned around
from the water fountain to find Russell White standing directly
behind her, glaring, with his arms folded across his chest. Jeff Gates
stood a little behind him, tugging at Russell's arm. Russell shrugged

him off. Hazel took a step backward. Russell scared her. Hazel had looked frantically up and down the hall. Where were all the teachers? The teacher's assistants?

"Why are you wearing a headband, Hazel? Huh? Are you trying to make fun of me and Jeff? Is that it, you little goody-goody teacher's pet? Hazel, will you please take this to the office? Hazel, your story was sooo good I want you to read to the class. Take it off," Russell ordered and reached out to jerk the headband off.

"No, Russell, don't," Hazel cried, stepping back even further until she was pressing against the water fountain. "I'm not making fun of you. I promise. Leave me alone. I didn't even know y'all were going to wear them today. Leave me alone; I have to go to the bathroom." The girls' bathroom door was right behind Russell, a few feet away. He wouldn't follow her in there, would he? Or maybe she should just make a break for the classroom. Mrs. Collins was probably there, or Mrs. Perry. She should have caught a ride with her grandfather, skipped the bus, gotten to school sooner.

"Russ, leave her alone. Hazel's all right. C'mon," Jeff had said and jerked Russell's arm again. Hazel ran when Russell turned away from her, as fast as she could down the hall. She didn't look back until she got to the door. Mrs. Hoban, a second grade teacher's assistant, was talking to Russell. She could see Mrs. Hoban wagging her finger in Russell's face.

Hazel looked away from Russell quickly, before she made eye contact and took out her math book. At least numbers were a constant; they didn't change. Not like her ears had. And Russell, too, she had thought. He hadn't been mean to her for over a week. When school started Russell had picked on her almost every day: her hair, her size, her glasses, being Mrs. Collins's pet. Hazel had wanted to kill him. Then he had gotten into really big trouble and there had been the trailer fire and Miss Findlay; Russell had been suspended for a week. When he came back he seemed like a different boy. Until today.

Twenty-eight plus forty-four would always be seventy-two. She wrote the answer neatly on her paper. And today was computer lab day and for the first time ever she dreaded going. All her dreams of the other place began with the computer and the Worldmaker game and the Valley of the Alexzeli—but that was the computer at home. It would be different at school; it had to be.

Mrs. Perry started taking the class down the hall to the computer lab in the middle of the morning. She had everybody count off by fives and Hazel's group, the ones, went first. She reached into her book bag to take out two new math games her grandfather had given her. She knew the class's games would be boring and she also knew Mrs. Perry wouldn't care.

"I like seeing a young girl stretch her mind," Mrs. Perry had said when Hazel first asked if she could bring computer games from home. "I wish I had someone like your grandfather when I was coming along."

What would Mrs. Perry say if Hazel told her that sometimes she wished her grandfather—and grandmother—were different? She did love the computer games, but still, they were only another way for her to be invisible.

Hazel got into line and sighed. There was Russell; three people up—how did he get to be a one? She liked it better when they went by math or reading groups. Maybe he had gone back to his new quiet self and would leave her alone. Anyway, she thought, Mrs. Perry could handle Russell and a lot better than Mrs. Collins could. Hazel could see the relief plain and visible on Mrs. Collins's face as the students passed her going out.

Hazel chose the computer farthest away from everybody else, especially Russell. She didn't want a partner. Besides, they wouldn't get her grandfather's games anyway. When she sat down in the hard-backed little chair, the computer blinked on. What? No, someone had to have left it on. Behind her she heard Mrs. Perry telling Russell how proud she was that he was behaving so well lately. *She didn't see him stop me at the water fountain,* Hazel thought, and started to slide her diskette into the A drive. A claw snagged it and pulled it in with a quick pop.

Hazel froze, blinked, and then slowly looked around the room. Everybody was doing what they were supposed to be doing. She poked her finger into the A drive. No claw, but when she touched the little A drive slot again, the room became instantly silent. Whatever Russell said back to Mrs. Perry and whatever the two girls two computers away were arguing about was lost. Hazel couldn't hear them, nor could she hear the hum of the computer in front of her. There was no mathematics game menu on the screen—and she heard a loud tearing noise. The screen, the pale green cinderblock walls, the school, was ripped away.

Hazel stood at the edge of the meadow, a few steps out of the forest of white glowing trees. The tall meadow grass brushed against her legs, as the wind made the meadow into a green sea. She could and did reach up to touch a low branch over her head, pull off a leaf, and press it to her cheek. And there, wings outstretched, gliding down over the trees to the grass, was a flying horse. Hazel watched and waited, her arms crossed, the leaf in one hand, as the horse landed a few yards in front of her. It pawed the grass and bent to take a mouthful. Then it lifted its head, folded down its wings, and came to her. Hazel kept very still until the horse was so close she could feel its warm breath. She touched its nose with the tips of her fingers and then let it eat the leaf out of her hand. Then the horse nuzzled, blowing more warm horsy air on her face until Hazel laughed.

"Put your hand in my mane and walk with me," the horse said. "I want you to talk and walk with me—but I will do most of the talking." Hazel nodded and wrapped part of the horse's thick, silvery-grey mane around her hand.

The horse talked for a long time. It talked about dreams and gates and time and space being like a house with many rooms. Dreams removed the walls between the rooms and let one remember what was forgotten. Dreams let souls travel.

"I don't understand what you mean—is this a dream or it is real? Where are we?" Hazel asked.

"Elfhome. Faerie. Tir Mar, the Great Land. Tir Na n'Og, the Summer Country—this place has many names. Think of your house at home—you have your room and your grandparents another and a room to eat in and to cook in, yes?"

"But I can just get up and walk into other rooms at home. And I was sitting in front of a computer at school—just, just a little while ago. And before, when I met the dragon, I was in my bedroom."

"The machine is a dream-gate. The story you are telling yourself is the one I am telling you and the one the dragon told you."

"I don't get it."

"Hazel, wake up; wake up, honey. Earth to Hazel, come in, Hazel, over," Mrs. Perry said.

Hazel jumped. Her computer mouse fell and banged against the metal desk leg. Mrs. Perry was standing right behind her. Hazel looked up at the woman, feeling dazed and flushed. On the screen in front of her was the math game's menu. The cursor blinked at Hazel, a tiny, amber eye at the bottom of the screen. The other kids giggled. Russell hee-hawed like a donkey.

"Russell, that's enough. Y'all line behind Tommy and go on back to the room. Tommy, tell Mrs. Collins to send the next group in about ten minutes," Mrs. Perry said and turned back to Hazel. "Hazel Richards, do you mean to tell me you have just been sitting here sleeping the entire time? Russell, go on, and mind your own business. Hazel-honey, do you feel all right?"

Right now she wanted to curl up in Mrs. Perry's lap, snuggle up, inhale the sweet scent of the vanilla or lilac hand lotion, and tell her everything so Mrs. Perry would stroke her hair and tell her it was all going to be all right. She knew she could never do that with her grandmother. Hazel shrugged; Mrs. Perry would never believe her —and neither would her own grandmother, for that matter.

"Hazel? Are you not feeling well? It's not like you to sleep in class."

"I'm fine, Mrs. Perry, really I am. I'm just—really tired; I couldn't sleep last night. I'll be all right." If Mrs. Perry wasn't going to take Hazel into her lap, couldn't she just go away? Hazel's head felt thick and heavy, as if she had gotten a really bad head cold.

"Insomnia? That explains it, because you don't look fine and you certainly aren't acting fine. Go on to the health room and lie down for a minute. Maybe you're coming down with something. I'll be up in a minute and take your temp. Is your grandmother at home today? Never mind, now go on—don't try and argue with me—go on. I'll be there directly."

Hazel nodded and got up. Maybe Mrs. Perry was right. Maybe she was sick. *Hazel, you aren't sick. That is what I am trying to tell you. You are not sick and you are not crazy. Dreams are real.* Hazel stopped in the middle of the hall and looked around. Where had that voice, the winged horse's voice, come from? She could hear Mrs. Perkins's voice coming from the open library door. She was reading a story. The phone was ringing in the school office, just up the hall. Behind her Hazel could hear Mrs. Perry moving chairs in the computer lab. The horse's voice seemed to have come right out of the wall beside her.

Hazel?

Now Hazel could see the winged horse. And Mrs. Perkins holding her book and the kindergartners sitting on the floor in front of her. She saw the meadow and the white grass. The tall grasses stirred and rippled from the warm breeze. The white trees moved, their leaves whispering. The kindergarten teacher sat at a table, her head bent over papers. Hazel laid her hand on the nearest wall. It was made of solid, smooth, yellow cinder blocks. But when she pushed, she felt her hand go through the wall until she felt the hard, white wood of a tree. Hazel jerked her hand back and there, like a huge scar, was a glowing white streak. Beneath her feet, shifting and moving, as if reflections in water, were grass, earth, flowers, and the tiled floor.

Hazel?

"Hazel? Are you all right? I thought I told you to go to the health room. Hazel? Can you hear me?"

Mrs. Perry and the winged horse were standing in the same space and they were speaking at the same time. The horse's wings rose and fell, and for a moment, Mrs. Perry looked winged, and did Hazel see the woman's grey hair rise and fall in the wing-made breeze? The skin in the palm of her hand glowed even brighter. Hazel cried out and reached for the horse's mane, for Mrs. Perry's hand, and fell and fell and fell.

"She's waking up now. Normal pulse and blood pressure and her heart sounds fine. How are you feeling, Hazel?"

Hazel opened her eyes and looked into the face of a strange woman. Hazel lay flat on her back and the dark-haired woman was leaning over her. The woman who was wearing a white coat, like a doctor—she *was* a doctor, Hazel realized—holding a stethoscope to Hazel's chest. Hazel closed and reopened her eyes. She wasn't in school—in the doctor's office? A hospital, she decided. She was lying in a hospital bed, with long rails on either side. A crisp, white sheet covered her up to the waist.

"Grand-dad? Grandma?"

"We're right here," her grandmother said, moving into view. Her grandmother was wearing one of her work smocks, dusty with clay and spattered with paint and glaze. Brown clay made smudges on her forehead and cheeks. Behind her grandmother was her grandfather. He looked like he had been in his lab. He had on a white coat and his IBM ID dangled from one pocket.

"Mrs. Richards, Dr. Richards. If you could both step out with me for a moment," the doctor said, and Hazel watched her grandparents follow the doctor out. The doctor was a loud talker. "She's going to be all right, but I would like to keep her overnight. This afternoon we'll run those tests I told you about. It's really unusual for a healthy nine-year-old to pass out like this and stay out for so long. I'll be right back with the forms for you to sign."

"What was she talking about?" Hazel asked slowly after the doctor had left, and her grandparents had come back into the room. A long, yellow curtain hung from runners on the ceiling. One side of the bed was a little table with a pitcher of water and a small box of Kleenex. Beyond the table Hazel could see out a window into a parking lot. A TV looked down at her from the opposite wall. "How did I get here?"

"Haze," her grandmother said, with a rare use of a diminutive for Hazel, as she reached down awkwardly to stroke her hair, "we're in Wake County Hospital, not too far from your school. You came here on a field trip last year, remember? I was with you."

"You felt sick at school—don't you remember?" her grandfather said, walking around to stand on the opposite side of the bed. "You were in the computer lab and you fell asleep and—" He stopped and looked at her grandmother.

"Go ahead, Hawthorne, you tell her."

"Haze, you may have had a seizure. Remember the boy in your class last year who was epileptic? The doctor wants to give you some medical tests to see if you really did have a seizure. You passed out again in the hall and you didn't wake up until now."

Hazel remembered the boy. Charlie Baggott had fallen out of his seat in the middle of science. His whole body started jerking and twitching and his eyes rolled back in his head. A lot of kids screamed and ran. An ambulance came, with a siren, and quick people shouting directions at each other. Everybody talked about it for days.

"It wasn't a seizure, Grand-dad. It's the game, Worldmaker. It's not a game anymore; it's real and—" Hazel stopped at the expression on both her grandparents' faces.

"You were delirious in the hall and in the ambulance—a winged horse? That was a dream, Hazel-honey, you were dreaming, that's all," her grandmother said. "Just a very vivid dream."

"But—never mind." Hazel knew it was useless to argue. And maybe they were right. Maybe her game and her dreams had gotten mixed up and she really had been sick, with a fever or something. A virus, like the doctors always said. But she was positive she wasn't sick the way Charlie had been. And the horse had told her and told her it wasn't a dream.

"But what?" her grandfather asked.

"Nothing. I'm just tired."

The doctor came back in then, with forms for her grandparents to sign. An electroencephalograph, blood work, some X-rays, a psych consult (just to be sure), the doctor said. Insurance forms.

"I don't think there is anything to really worry about, but I just want to be sure there's nothing I missed," the doctor said as Dr. Richards signed each form. "We'll get these started right after lunch and she should be able to go home tomorrow morning . . ."

The tests took most of the afternoon. First the electroencephalograph and the X-rays, then some man took little tubes of blood from her finger. Another doctor examined her eyes and then asked her question after question: did she ever have headaches? Any other dizzy spells? Hear voices, have bad dreams? Either her grandmother or her grandfather stayed with her, until finally Hazel was back in

the room with the yellow curtain. Her grandmother sent her grandfather home to get clothes for both Hazel and her and Hazel ate
bland food from a plastic tray. Her grandmother was at her best at
times like this. Hazel knew that when she was better, her grandmother's attention would refocus downstairs on her pots and the
wheel and the clay, and Hazel would be back on the edges. But, for
now, Hazel's grandmother's attention was on her.

Her grandmother fell asleep first and it made Hazel feel better
to watch her sleep, her chest rising and falling, wisps of hair floating
up and down as she breathed. It was as if her grandmother's breathing was a soft and very faint lullaby and Hazel felt herself slowly,
slowly, falling down, down into sleep. As she turned over, stretching
against the crisp hospital sheets, Hazel heard her name and the
voice, low and dark, was a familiar one, one she had heard before. It
caught her right between diving into a great warm pool of sleep, and
being awake, listening to the hospital sounds, the voices outside, the
distant metallic sounds. Hazel tried to wake up to answer the voice,
but she couldn't. She could brush the bright underside of wakeful-
ness with the tips of her fingers.

I'm not there; I'm here.

Grandma? (and she knew she was asleep, as the words came
without her mouth moving, with her tongue still)

No, over here.

It was the dragon in the meadow. Its yellow eyes were like two
fires in the room's darkness.

*I know they told you were dreaming or hallucinating. They are
wrong. Everything that happened was real, even though your body
slept. You were in Faerie.*

*Where am I now? I can see you and the bed and Grandma and
the curtain and behind you, the white trees.*

*Between. I am going to give you proof, proof that won't go away.
Here, take this.*

Something small and shiny fell onto the white hospital bedspread.

And one last proof: open your right hand.

The white streak was still there, luminous in the darkened room.
Then, the dragon leaned, shot out its forked tongue, and licked her
hand.

"It burns—and the white—" The white winked out, leaving
behind two glowing, thin blue streaks.

*No one can see that unless they are like you and have been here
and belong with you.*

The dragon began to dissolve then, as if it were turning into its own smoke and when Hazel reached for it, it was gone.

Wait—I want to ask you—I need to know—

Hazel sat up in bed, breathing hard and fully awake and alone in the dark of the room. Her grandmother, a darker shadow in the chair, stirred and murmured something in her sleep.

Hazel opened and closed her right hand, dimming and brightening the streaks, like little lines of blue fire across her palm. She laid the luminous green scale against the blue. It was the size of a saucer and pliable; Hazel could bend it back and forth.

"Grandma?"

Her grandmother moved again, smacked her lips as if she had just eaten something pleasing in her dreams, and then was still. Hazel could hear her grandmother breathing. She lay back in the bed, pulling the spread up to her neck. She rolled over and opened her right hand on the pillow: two flashes of blue fire. She pulled the scale out from under the covers and laid it on the sheet: a soft glowing green.

It was true then, all of it.

The doctor let Hazel go the next afternoon.

"All her tests came out fine. She's a perfectly healthy nine-year-old, who seems to be putting herself under a lot of stress. She needs to relax. Here is the name of a good child psychologist. You should call her if there is another episode—and you might want to call anyway," the doctor said and handed Hazel's grandfather a business card.

"Can she go back to school?" her grandfather asked, as he stuffed the card into his shirt pocket. Hazel said nothing.

"Let her have the rest of the week off. Relax. Stay home and play, watch TV, read a good book—"

"But I want to go to school tomorrow," Hazel interrupted.

"Hazel, give yourself a break," the doctor said, smiling. "Please call me if you need to."

Hazel smiled back and stood when her grandparents did. *It's not school; it's the magic. If I told you I'd be in trouble; you wouldn't believe me, anyway. But I have a dragon scale in my pocket and two dragon tongue marks on my hand that glow blue in the dark.* Hazel shook the doctor's hand and then let her grandfather wheel her out of the hospital, her grandmother trailing behind.

Hazel wanted to see Alexander the minute she got home. Even before her grandfather had the car in the garage, she was out and calling the cat's name. He wasn't in the house. She grabbed a can of Pounce from the kitchen and ran outside to look for him, shaking the can and yelling *Al-lex, Al-lexxxx*. Hazel ignored her grand-mother's protests to take it easy. She wished she could yell back she wasn't sick and she had never been sick. *It's magic.*

"She's fine, Annie, just look at her. She's fine," her grandfather said. "Let her go. Remember what the doctor said . . ." Her grand-father's usually loud voice dropped into a whisper. It didn't matter what they were saying, Hazel thought as she made her way through the bushes that separated the Richards' backyard from the neigh-bors. It didn't matter.

"Alex, there you are. Why didn't you come when I called?" Hazel said. There was the cat, crouched by the neighbor's goldfish pond. He stared intently into the dark green water. He looked poised to strike, one paw half-raised. Hazel quietly knelt down beside the cat.

"What do you see, Alex, a goldfish?"

The cat turned and looked at her, his dark blue eyes intent on her face, his head bent to one side, listening.

"Here, have a Pounce," Hazel said. She couldn't see any gold-fish: just her face and Alex. Was he bigger than he was the day before? Maybe. But what Hazel could see without mistake was her ears. Pointed.

Alex touched her thigh with one paw. She sat back on her heels, and then lay down on the grass, her arms outstretched, her feet touching the edge of the walk outlining the pool.

"Hey, boy, do you see my ears? I bet you do," Hazel whispered. "Here, have a Pounce. The cat leaned down to scarf up the tuna-flavored snack. Then he reached out with his paw again, this time to lick her hand, his rough tongue right on the two marks. In the shadow of the neighbor's house they glowed. Then he sat back and meowed and, for a moment, looked as if he were trying to talk.

Alex

ShetasteswhatIsmellfeel
SheknowsmeIknowher
TongueIcantshapethesesoundsheadsounds
HazullmeIammynameAlexxxIknow
Iknowmyname
Alexxx
IknowmynameAlexxxIknowyourname: Hazull

Hearmyname
HearmynameIknowIam

Becoming Magic: Malachi and Hazel

Friday morning, the day Hazel went back to school over her grand-parents' protests, Mrs. Collins sent both Malachi and Hazel to the library on an errand. She gave them a long list of books to find for her. The library was empty when they got there, except for Mrs. Perkins. She sat at her desk in her glass box office, typing carefully. Malachi and Hazel went there first, and stood waiting until she finally looked up.

"Mrs. Perkins? Mrs. Collins wants us—"

"It's okay, Malachi. Y'all go ahead; Mrs. Collins told me she was going to send the two of you up here this morning. If you need any help, let me know."

"Here, Hazel," Malachi said when they were standing in front of the 398's, the fairy tale section. "You take the first half of the list, it starts here, I think, and I'll take the other half—" He stopped and looked at Hazel's open right hand. The blue streaks glowed.

"You can see them?" she asked, whispering even though Mrs. Perkins couldn't possibly hear through the glass walls of her office. "The dragon said only those like me and who belong with me would be able to—only those who had been there, where the dragon is."

"I've seen your face, reflected back at me, in water in the other place, with the white trees." *And your thoughts like a murmur in my head therecanyouhearME?*

YesIcanhearYOUears&eyes?

Malachi pushed back his hair and smiled.

We'reNotaloneanymoreShowme.

Hazel pulled her headband down to her neck.

ThatfeelsbetterHURTSmyearsYoureyes are gold.

YoureyesaresilverAndYOURcat, too? "Hey, you don't need the headband anymore, Hazel. Nobody but people like us can see our ears are pointed. Well, my dad can, and Uncle Jack. I think the priest at our church can, too. Glamour is what Dad calls it: a fairy magic to hide things in plain sight. What about your cat?"

"Yeah, my cat," Hazel said, sounding infinitely relieved, "bigger and his eyes—well, it's hard to tell if they are glowing, cats' eyes look so funny in the dark anyway, but he's smarter, too. Everything, all this, our ears, the cat—"

"It's real. I'm still trying to figure it all out, but it's all real. My mother—she was from there—the place in our dreams, where the dragons and the centaurs are. My dad told me she was Daoine Sidhe, a fairy. There are—two others—I think," Malachi said softly, looking around the library. Mrs. Perkins had left her typewriter and was at her desk, buried in a catalog. There was nobody in the hall. The other nearest person was Mrs. Anderson, the school secretary. He could see her over Hazel's shoulder, through the glass display case. Mrs. Anderson was on the phone. And the goldfish in the library aquarium, swishing their long tails in and out of dreamy green water ferns.

"We'd better start getting Mrs. Collins's books before she sends somebody to look for us," Haze said. "Who are the other two?"

"Yeah, I guess you're right. Most of these are in the 500's," Malachi said. "We can talk while we get the books—I'll tell you who I think they are as we get these ones Mrs. Collins wants. Here is the first one," Malachi said and pulled down a book on eagles and handed it to Hazel. When their hands touched there was a spark and a pop and for a moment, both their bodies glowed, a barely visible luminescence. Above them the lights flickered and one of the fluorescent tubes sputtered and went dead. Balls of light the size of a ping-pong ball shot out from the dead tube and ricocheted around the library, caroming off walls, bouncing off tables. The air glittered and sparkled with trails of light.

"Malachi, stop it, Mrs. Perkins, she'll see," Hazel yelled and ducked as the ball zoomed over her head, to smash into the biographies, raining down glowing glitter that fizzed and popped and disappeared on the library's green carpet.

"I can't; I don't know how," Malachi said as he began crying, big glowing tears that left luminous trails down his face. One of the balls struck the glass wall of Mrs. Perkins's office and bounced back straight at them. Trying to hide behind chairs or under a table did no good—the ball was like a guided missile: it paused and hovered and bounced again as Malachi and Hazel moved. Finally the ball shot forward and zipped through a chair and then through Malachi, from shoulder to shoulder, then in and out of Hazel. They both shook as sparks flew from their fingers, their toes, ears, eyes. Then, everything stopped. The dead fluorescent tube over their head hummed back to life. The tear-streaks on Malachi's face grew pale and then winked out.

"What did you do, say abracadabra or shazam or something?" Hazel whispered. She wanted very much to run as fast and as far as she could. She forced herself to be still—running, no matter how far, wouldn't change anything.

"No, Hazel. We aren't becoming magicians or witches. They can work magic, make it do stuff. They know the words. Us, no, we are becoming—we are magical. You, me, the other two."

"Here, let's get the books together," Hazel said and crawled out from under the table. "Who are the other two? And what do we do now?" Hazel stood and picked up half the books. How had all that happened without Mrs. Perkins seeing anything? Or maybe the lady had, Hazel thought, as she stared through the glass walls of the librarian's office. Mrs. Perkins was at her desk, her glasses off, and her face in her hands. "Do you think she saw?"

"If she did, she will never admit it. Anyway, there have always been four of us in my dreams," Malachi said as he picked up his half. "You, me, and Russell and Jeff."

Hazel shuddered. "I hate Russell White and he hates me. Come on, let's check out these books. Not Russell, Malachi. I don't know Jeff, but he seems okay. Russell is mean."

Malachi shook his head. "It has to be Jeff and Russell. All four of us are being called as a group; a quartet, I guess. You know, I can *move* these books—see?" Malachi said and the first three books on his stack floated a few inches up into the air. Then, wobbling, they floated past the aquarium to drop on the circulation desk. Then, with a smoother flight, the rest of the books Malachi was holding floated over to the desk. "You can do that, Hazel, I bet you can or will soon. It *has* to be Russell; he'll be all right. A centaur told me that in a dream."

Hazel nodded her head as she followed him to the circulation desk. "I know," she said, sighing. "I dreamed about him and Jeff both. I just don't like him. And besides being mean, he's gross. His clothes are always dirty. I wasn't really surprised to see them both wearing headbands. So, what do we do now? That all the books?"

"Yes, they are all checked out."

Above them all the lights in the library flickered, popped, and went out.

There was only the sunlight from the tall library windows, broken into long rectangles by the venetian blinds. The library was in grey shadows for a long, long moment, then as if they were odd gumball machines, the light fixtures started popping out glowing white ping-pong balls that bounced and bounced and bounced. Behind them someone screamed, and they turned and saw Mrs.

Perkins's office was filled with the glowing balls and she was surrounded by them, trying to knock them away.

"We have to help her—can you make them go away—too late." While Hazel was watching, Mrs. Perkins dropped out of sight.

"I can't stop it—I can't—I need all of us to be here," Malachi yelled as the balls began exploding. It was like being inside Fourth of July fireworks as all around and above and under and through the library was filled with showers of stars.

Tetrad

Jeff and Russell stopped in the hall outside the cafeteria to examine the pictures hanging on the wall. They were looking at the fifth grade pictures, which made a long line from the cafeteria to the teacher's lounge, then all the way to the health room. They had found Russell's and they were looking for Jeff's. They were supposed to be on their way to Resource.

"Russ, I still think we need to ask Hazel about her headband. I am positive her ears are pointed, too," Jeff said stubbornly. *Russ, you can be such a pain in the butt, you know that? Don't you see that three are stronger than two? Three have a better chance of finding the way to Faerie than two?* "She's not wearing it for decoration."

They had been arguing about Hazel ever since she had gotten sick at school.

"I told ya, I don't care if she has two headbands and horns growing out of her head, like those faun guys. She's never been nice to me or to you before. Tell me one time—see, you can't think of one. Hazel Richards hasn't said good morning to me since I started coming to Nottingham Heights," Russell said, his face darkening. "And another thing—"

Russell stood still for a moment and held his stomach, as if he had a sudden pain. Then all the pictures flapped up and down, as if a sudden warm wind had come and gone. A faint smell of heat lingered in the wind's aftermath. Behind them a tiny, white ball of light rolled down the hall and out the front door.

"Russ. We agreed not to show off at school," Jeff grumbled and the pictures stopped flapping. "Do you think she meant *bad morning* when she spoke to you? C'mon, Russ, give her a chance. She's trying. Before you got suspended, you picked on her all the time."

Russell frowned and clenched and unclenched his fists.

"Nothing's the same anymore, Russ. You know that. You and me

—we've changed. You know what I heard Miss Dorman said to Miss Bigelow yesterday?"

Mrs. Markham had sent Jeff to the office to deliver the morning lunch count and to get a nine by twelve envelope from the secretary. While he waited for Mrs. Anderson to get off the phone, Jeff heard his name and Russell's. It was Miss Dorman, the new Resource teacher, in the principal's office. Miss Findlay had quit two days after the fire, telling everyone as loudly as possible that she had had enough. Miss Dorman stood just inside the door, her back to Jeff and the secretary. Miss Dorman waved her hand as she talked, as if she were drawing circles in the air.

"She said she couldn't believe how we had changed—she said she had read our files from cover to cover and we weren't the boys she had expected us to be. She thought maybe it was because we had became friends. You aren't getting into fights or talking back to your teachers and you've been coming to class looking happy. She went on and on at how talkative I've become—she had expected me to be practically a deaf-mute—can't talk, can't hear."

"I knew what the deaf part was," Russell muttered, looking down at the floor. "Maybe you're right about you and me. But, Jeff, you were like a ghost; nobody ever saw you or anything. Nobody ever told you how horrible you were and what a bad kid you were and that your mama left because you were bad and she took the good kid with her. Kids like Hazel and that buddy of hers, Malachi, tell me stuff like that all that time. Or they did. Why should I be nice to her? She's always ignored me. Kids like her are the worst. They laugh at me, call me names, tell me I'm dirty and stupid. And if I called them names, I'd get in trouble, not them. Why, Russell White," he said in a falsetto, "do you think I'm going to believe you: little goody-goody started a fight? Hazel is one of them."

"She's scared," Jeff said. "Come on, let's go before Miss Dorman starts looking for us. Just think about what I said, okay?"

Russell grudgingly nodded as they went down the hall past the cafeteria to go outside to the brand-new Resource trailer.

But I do know, Russ, what it's like to be told that my mother is no good and if she had loved me and him, she wouldn't have left. And he wouldn't have to do what he did. I do know what it's like to feel dirty and bad and ashamed. I want to tell you, but I'm scared, too. Jeff wanted to tell Russell all that, but telling Russell teachers had noticed his good behavior and Jeff being talky was one thing; finding the words needed for the other was another thing and just too hard.

A little, white ball of light dropped out of a hole in the hall ceiling. It bounced once, twice, and then winked out.

The lights went out halfway through their Resource time. Miss Dorman was sitting at her desk, working with another kid, Kwame, from Jeff's class, on his Young Writers Book. Kwame and his book had been picked to represent Mrs. Markham's class at the county-wide conference. Jeff and Russell and the other kids were finishing up new versions of theirs—everybody's but Kwame's had burned up in the trailer fire, so Kwame was going to the Young Writers Conference. Miss Dorman whispered to Kwame, one hand on his book, the other fingering a cameo broach on her dress.

The lights overhead flickered and popped, quickly, as if popcorn had been trapped inside. Everybody stopped and looked up. The popping got louder and louder and then the lights got brighter and brighter and exploded into a shower of glass splinters and sparks and hundreds of little, white balls. Miss Dorman screamed as the balls rolled and rolled out of the light fixture, hitting the floor, desktops, bookshelves, to explode again, into tiny showers of stars. When a ball exploded on Kwame's head, he ran, batting the balls away, smashing them into stars, stars, and more stars.

"Kwame! Kids! Be calm, just be calm; nobody's hurt; everything will be all right. Get under your desks, I'll go get—" Miss Dorman fell to the floor when another shower of white balls fell on her, exploding on her head, her face, down her chest, her arms, her legs. Half the class bolted after Kwame, screaming and crying.

"Russ? Russ?" Jeff whispered under his desk. They were both lying on the floor, along with four other Resource kids—they were all too scared to run through the white balls.

"Russ, this is magic. Just like in the dreams. It's happening here—and neither one of us are doing it."

"I know, I know—what do we do now?"

JeffRussitsokaycometotheLibrary!

"Jeff, you say something? C'mon, let's get outta here—I think the balls have stopped—whoa," and Russ dived back under his desk as another shower of balls rolled out of the fixture.

"Boys? Come on, nobody's getting hurt, come on, get up. See? They explode and there's this dust, but nothing else," Miss Dorman said. She stood, slowly, and brushed away the now-grey residue.

IknowyoubothhavePointedEarsIT'SOkayweareintheLibrary.

"I thought you did—it was in our heads—"

"Don't whisper so loud, Jeff—"

"Boys. Let's go. Marty, Jeff, Russell. Thomas, you okay? Will? Jamey? Good, let's get out of here," Miss Dorman took Marty's hand and the rest followed, picking their way through unexploded balls on the floor, stepping on them so they would explode like a puff-ball filled with white stars and sparks. Miss Dorman's orderly departure might have worked if there hadn't been another shower of white balls that this time, instead of falling, zoomed and cavorted in the air, zipping over and around and through bodies, hands, arms, cameo broaches. Everybody bolted, including Miss Dorman.

"Russ, come on, this way," Jeff said and grabbed Russell's arm. "Not with them, this way, we have to follow the voice—he's in the school." Jeff took off running then. The rest of the class ran after Miss Dorman out into the teachers' parking lot. Jeff didn't look back; he knew Russell was following him.

Inside the school bouncing, vibrating, exploding ping-pong balls of light zoomed and ricocheted, caromed off walls, zipped in and out of ceilings. The balls kept exploding as they ran, the white stars raining on them, soft, warm, and then a fine, grey dust. The fire alarm was on, but Jeff could barely hear it. He dodged kids and ignored teachers yelling for everyone to be calm, line up at the door, or just yelling.

"This way, Russ, this way."

Jeff ran to the library. Once inside he stopped to catch his breath and wait for Russell, who was right behind him. When Russell closed the door, all the noise outside—the zipping balls of light, the running kids, the shouting teachers—stopped, as if a too-loud TV had finally been turned off. They stood and listened in the quiet, dark room and heard only the bubbling of the filter in the aquarium. Mrs. Perkins was gone. As they stood still a moment longer, they could hear each other's breathing beginning to slow down. The goldfish swam in their dreamy way, the biggest one close to the surface, delicately eating the last few flakes of food.

"Well, Jeff," Russ whispered. "What do we do now?"

"Back over there," Jeff said and pointed to the jumble behind Mrs. Perkins's glass-box office: the big laminator, a copier that was always breaking down, two VCR's, a 16-millimeter projector, the Chapter I reading teacher's desk. Jeff could not have explained to Russell how he knew the mental voice they had both heard was here in the library and specifically where he had just pointed. Here was the place.

"This way," Jeff said and taking Russell's hand, led him past the encyclopedias, the carts with unprocessed new books and the record bins, to a little space behind the laminator. Russell shook his head and let Jeff lead him, thinking he would have never let *anyone*, let alone another and smaller boy, lead him anywhere before.

Jeff dropped Russell's hand and pulled off his headband. Russell did the same. Sitting on the floor, with two small stacks of books on either side, were Hazel and Malachi. All four had pointed ears. All four had intensely glowing eyes. Malachi's eyes were a bronze-gold. Hazel's were a silvery grey-blue. Jeff's and Russell's burned green.

The Raleigh News and Observer
Friday, September 27, 1991
Carolina Power & Light officials are baffled by the bizarre electrical problem experienced at Nottingham Heights Elementary yesterday. A short circuit of some kind apparently generated a rare electrical phenomenon known as ball lightning in massive amounts. No students or staff were injured by the peculiar electrical malfunction, although several suffered minor cuts and bruises in the efforts to escape the building. The elementary school was closed by mid-day . . . Wake County School officials stated that only after all the wiring has been checked will the building be reopened . . . According to local meteorologists ball lightning is extremely rare and especially so in such a small size, that of a ping pong ball . . .

Jack

"Hilda? Hilda? Honey, can you hear me? It's me, Jack. Hilda?" Jack squeezed his wife's hand. No response. He looked up at all the medical machinery—the heart monitor, the respirator, the IV hookups—all the lights and numbers that said she was alive. Jack glanced at the clock on the wall. He squinted to see the numbers in the dim light: close to midnight, late Saturday. Hilda's heartbeat was too slow. Even with the drugs the doctors had given her, which were even now dripping into her, her heart was too slow. Or at least Jack thought so, watching the blips on the screen—shouldn't there be more of them? Shouldn't they be moving faster?

"We'll light a candle for Hilda tomorrow, Uncle Jack—one of the big two dollar ones. And ask Father Jamey to pray for her. He's the new priest." Malachi had said that afternoon, sounding for all the world like your regular run-of-the-mill ten-year-old who was a little on the short side. With some very strangely colored eyes.

Jack checked all the machines for what he was sure was the millionth time. Nothing new, no difference, no change. Ben had told him about all the other weird things that were making local, state, national, and now international news. Everybody was seeing UFO's; it was as if there was an invasion fleet scouting out the planet. And not a fleet of your usual flying saucers, but rather UFO's with huge, black batlike wings and breathing fire. Ancient rituals were being spontaneously revived and in broad daylight. Ping-pong balls of electricity had been flying around Malachi's school and now there were three more kids like the little golden-eyed boy. Well, almost: pointed ears and glowing eyes.

"At least he's not alone anymore, the only one like him. It all has to connect, Jack, you know—all of this is the same thing, I think. Malachi and his fairy magic and the light—" Ben started and stopped when the internist came back in Hilda's room.

"There's no discernable medical reason for this to be happening to your wife, Mr. Ruggles," the internist had said, repeating himself as he reviewed his clipboard. "We just can't wake her up. I don't get it; I'm sorry." Ben and Jack had looked at each other as the doctor left, shaking his head and thumping his clipboard on his hip. Of course there was no way to wake Hilda up. She was dying from magic.

That had been seven hours ago.

"My son—*my son*—killed her," Jack said to the machines. "*My son* killed her."

Jack squeezed Hilda's hand again and then put his open palm against her nose. He looked up at the heart monitor: the peaks were gone and a flat line traced itself across the screen.

Thomas

The young woman's name had been Marnie and she was a med tech at Rex Hospital and Thomas had picked her up in Bennigan's, on Six Forks Road two days ago. Now, naked and drugged, bound to the coven's altar, the fire's tongue-shaped shadows flickering over her body, she had no name. Thomas had removed her name when he had removed her clothing. Everything that made her Marnie—the dark blue dress her mother had given her, the matching shoes, her purse with its motley collection of lipstick (coral, pinky peach, touch of mauve), powder-and-mirror, Kleenex, movie stubs, car keys, wallet, money, NC Driver's License—had been given to the fire. She was now the Sacrifice, the offering to the Great Goddess and her consort, the Horned God, the requisite gift to their servants, the Lords of The Shadow, the Fomorii. Thomas stood beside the altar, with the high priestess at his right. The other coven members enclosed them in a hot, shifting naked circle. The cauldron, filled with a black liquid, bubbled and hissed above the fire.

Thomas looked at the high priestess, her long, black hair a mane down her back. Her nipples were hard, her body flushed from the fire. The same two days ago they had sat together at Bennigan's, drinking a beer. No one who would have seen her then would have guessed this woman beside Thomas was one and the same. No one in the bar would have even paid that much attention to the high priestess. She had not wanted them to see her, she had told Thomas, and a simple spell had done the trick, a small glamour of distraction, and their eyes strayed to the next person, the next thing. If she had wanted to be seen, she had added, she would have been seen and remembered.

After the beer and idle conversation, the priestess had given Thomas the shiny black belladonna berries and told him to mix them with blueberries, make a cobbler. But first he had to select the sacrifice.

"A woman, Thomas. The Goddess and the Horned God ask for it. You have taken the life of someone close to you, a family member—now take the life of a stranger—someone you pick up at this bar—any bar, for that matter. Complete the acquisition of power."

After she left, Thomas had put the belladonna berries into his briefcase and then sipped his Cuba Libre. Bit weak on the rum, he thought, and scanned the room. Bankers, secretaries, state government workers, maybe a doctor or two from Rex, he guessed. Some he knew from the bank, but none really seemed right for this. He thought back to work, doing a mental run through the building. The tellers? No—wait. That woman there, by herself, three tables over—hadn't she been looking at him, checking him out? He smiled at her over his beer—yes, she was smiling back. This was going to be easy.

The sacrifice and Thomas had had dessert a few hours ago, Saturday evening. She must have said a thousand times, he thought, how she couldn't believe she was having dessert at a guy's house she had met just two days ago. But they had talked so long the first night and the second, and well, here she was. It didn't take long for the belladonna to shut her up. After all, Marnie had eaten almost all belladonna. Just a few blueberries. Thomas had used all but a few blueberries in the other tarts, including the one he was eating. Small individual fruit tarts—the crusts from Harris Teeter—had been easier than a cobbler, and besides, this was his sacrifice, not the priestess's. Thomas finished his—not bad for a first time—and drained his coffee cup before he took her pulse: she was barely alive. There was no way out of her coma, even if Thomas had called 911 the minute she had fallen asleep. Eventually, no matter what happened, her heart would stop beating.

The high priestess began the sacrifice by touching Thomas with the blade of the athame: on his forehead, his chest, above his navel, his erect penis. Then she handed him the knife, black, carved handle first, and stepped back. Thomas inhaled deeply as he held the knife, drinking in the scents of the oil on his and all the other bodies: frankincense, cinnamon, bay, rosemary, and the almost overpowering musk. His skin glowed and tingled and as he looked at the hand that held the knife, he could see a subdermal luminescence shifting and turning, like a tiny, trapped ghost. Then Thomas listened: the cauldron, the fire, his own breathing, nothing else. The normal night sounds were gone; the forest was still. He was inside the magic now, in a time and space without minutes, without seconds and hours. And close, so close that Thomas knew he could touch it if he wanted: the others in the coven, the priestess, presences, pushing against his own.

Midnight.

"Now," Thomas said, feeling power flowing into him, into his blood, stronger, harder, darker, permeating his cells like an enormous ink stain. Thomas presented the knife to the coven, to the high priestess, to the fire and the cauldron, to the night sky. Then, he cut out her heart and held it up, the blood streaking his arm.

Father James Ronald Applewhite
St. Mary's Catholic Church, Garner, North Carolina
Sunday, September 29, 1991, 10 A.M. mass

"This is the Gospel of the Lord," Jamey said.

"Praise to you, Lord Jesus Christ," the congregation answered and in the soft rumble of bodies and fabric on wood, sat down.

"Today," he began slowly, as he scrutinized the congregation, his gaze roaming from pew to pew, lighting on first one face, then another and another, "today, I want to tell you a story." After two months, a few of the faces now had names—and a goodly number were familiar. Around a third, barely glimmering, he could see auras: golden, white, blue, green, red, brown, and purple. Faint ripples of light, flickering, appearing and reappearing, like a candle in a breeze.

Ah, there they were: the golden-eyed boy and his father. Their auras weren't faint or flickering—more like small fires, especially the boy's. White flames burned on the tips of the boy's pointed ears. Jamey carefully ran his fingers through his own dark red hair, lightly tracing his own pointed ears. Then he cleared his throat, shuffled his homily notes, and smiled out at the congregation.

"Today is Michaelmas, the Feast Day of St. Michael. According to the liturgical calendar today is the Feast Day of all the Holy Archangels, Michael, Gabriel, and Raphael. Only the fourth, Uriel, is left out—I couldn't find out why when I was looking all this up in the library at State. Probably should have driven over to the Divinity School at Duke. Anyway, by tradition this is St. Michael's Day. Who is he and why does the Church venerate him? What significance does St. Michael have for modern American Catholics in Garner, North Carolina, in the latter days of the twentieth century? In England, this is a day for roast goose. And don't pick any blackberries after Michaelmas Day. Any young animal born on this day is thought to be particularly rambunctious. Kittens are called blackberry kittens and if tortoiseshell, considered lucky. If you wish to have money in your pocket, put three leaves each of blackberry, bergamot, and bistort—I see you shaking your heads, I am not sure what the last two are, either—inside it on Michaelmas Day. Now, how many of you, not counting those who took St. Michael's name when you were confirmed, had any idea, until now, that today was St. Michael's Day, Michaelmas? Come on, raise your hands."

A scattering of hands rose nervously across the church. The parishioners of St. Mary's weren't used to being quizzed by the priest during the homily. Jamey noticed with no surprise that the golden-eyed boy, Malachi, and his father, raised their hands.

"I thought so." Jamey glanced quickly at his notes and cleared his throat, wishing he had thought to have a glass of water tucked away in the lectern. "Well, then, who is St. Michael? There is no historical figure anywhere in the Church's long two-thousand-year history that matches the St. Michael of tradition and story. But the Catholic Church believes in angels, and I do, too," Jamey added. He saw one woman in the back pew stand up, look hard at him and then at her watch, and then left. The auras of a dozen more glowed even brighter. He felt as if he could warm his hands by their fires.

"In Hebrew Michael means *who is like unto God*. In the Book of Daniel, we learn he is one of the chief princes of the heavenly host.

Indeed he is the great prince and the guardian of Israel; he is their patron angel. Michael is also the patron saint of soldiers and knights, and of the Catholic Church herself. Michael is the great captain and the slayer of dragons, according to Revelation 12: 7-9. He is the helper of the Church's armies against the heathen. He is the Prince of Light."

Jamey paused and shuffled his notes. A couple, three pews from the rear, slipped out the back door, their exit opening and closing a brief box of white light.

"You are, I know, wondering why I am telling you all this in this morning's homily. More than a few of you are trying to look at your watch without anybody seeing you. Yes, this homily is a little longer than what you're used to. But I do have a purpose and it is one that I feel is important, especially today, now, here, in Garner and Raleigh, in North Carolina. I will explain—but let me get back to Michael. In Acts 7:38 there is mention of the tradition that he gave Moses the Ten Commandments on Sinai. When Michael is portrayed in art, he is a young man, strong, in full armor, but bare-legged, and wearing sandals. Often as not his sword is drawn and a dragon is prostrate at his feet. But Michael is not just God's chief warrior. There is more."

Someone cleared his or her throat. Two other people coughed. A woman two pews back from the front sneezed.

"Michael is the patron saint of soldiers. But he is more than that: Michael is an angel considered so powerful that his intercession can rescue a soul from Hell. This is reflected, surprisingly, in the song we all sang at summer camp: *Michael, row the boat ashore*, Michael, the saver of souls. High places are sacred to Michael; there are churches and chapels across Europe built on hilltops consecrated to the saint, the most famous being Mont-St. Michel in France. Any hilltop is sacred to Michael." Jamey cleared his throat and again wished for water. Nobody was leaving; they were all watching him intently. A few, he was sure, were wondering if this new, young priest had gone over the edge. After all, Garner was a flat, little town, with no hills worthy of the name. The Southeast Regional Branch of the county public library system, which had replaced the old Garner Public Library a few years ago, was built on a slight rise—hardly a hill. St. Mary's was on very flat ground—so flat Jamey had been reminded of the beach.

"So, St. Michael is the warrior-archangel, one of the chief princes of the Heavenly Host. Now, you have some context for Michael, context for what I want to talk about now, what I think is important to us here at St. Mary's today. Michael is not far from God in Heaven. He knows the secret of the mighty word, by the utterance of which God created heaven and earth. A lot of you are thinking right now: so? Well, we all read the newspapers and watch the news, listen to it on the car radio. Most of us either saw or heard President Bush speak last night. Surely most of you read about his speech in the paper this morning; it was the front-page headline story in the *News and Observer*. How many of us believe what he said was true? Go ahead, raise your hand."

Jamey waited as a sprinkling of hands raised in the sanctuary.

"I thought so. What did the president say—it's sunspots or atmospheric phenomena, NASA is going to send up a shuttle to investigate? But we know better: *something* out of the ordinary is happening. Things we would normally call impossible, out of fairy tales, have and are happening, and are witnessed by thousands of sober, reliable people. And not just the happy magical things from fairy tales, but the bad, dark things. The New Agers are proclaiming the Age of Aquarius. I don't think so. I think it is this, friends in Christ—that God is changing the pronunciation of the secret word of creation that Michael knows. The world, the universe, is transforming.

"It scares me.

"I know it scares you. I can hear it in your voices in confession; I see it in your faces—even from up here. So, my message for this Sunday morning, this Michaelmas, before we take communion, is to remember God loves you. He sent Jesus who loves you. And because God loves us, we must love one another. Love is, I believe, the single most powerful force in the universe and when we love and accept love, we are the closest to God we will ever be in our lives. Love will get us through these crazy dark-and-light times we are in. It's going to get crazier folks, darker and lighter. But if we love one another, as Christ taught us to, we will survive. Remember the words in the creed we recite every Sunday:

"We believe in one Lord, Jesus Christ,
The only Son of God,
Eternally begotten of the Father,
God from God, Light from Light,
True God from true God,
Begotten, not made, one in Being with the Father.
Through him all things were made."

Jamey counted to ten, took a deep breath and let it out slowly. At least they were listening; some were nodding in agreement; others looking as if he were completely crazy. Maybe he was. But he had told them what they needed to know, given them the armor to protect themselves in the coming craziness. Most of them would get through it in one piece. More or less.

"God from God, Light from Light. Through him *all things* were made. All that is happening now—the banshee wails in the night, the shadows of dragons, the flickerings of light and shadow through which we see no place on this earth—all this comes from God. It is a mystery as to why they come with fear and darkness, but they do. And what isn't from God, the evil, the malevolent, the wicked—we must resist with love, the force, the strength, the power of love. Jesus is this love incarnate; we must remember this. There is no other way. God is changing the pronunciation of the Word. We must remember to call on the saints like Michael to shield us with love, to help us fight the wicked and be who God meant us to be. In the name of the Father, the Son, and the Holy Spirit, Amen."

From the journal of Ben Tyson
Tuesday morning, October 1, 1991

Yesterday went on forever. I should be in bed—getting some sleep before I have to go to work this afternoon, instead of sitting here in front of this computer, babbling on. I envy Malachi tonight—being ten-going-on-eleven, being a boy, no matter how unusual a boy he is. We spent the day with Jack in Charlotte, at Hilda's funeral, got home late last night and after futzing around the house and grazing in the kitchen, he asked me to tell him again Valeria's story.

"Again?" I asked him.

"Yeah, I want to memorize it, okay, Dad?"

"Sure."

So I told the story again.

"I dreamed about the swimmers, Dad," Malachi said sleepily, interrupting the story. "They aren't really big frogs, you know."

"Yeah, but that's how I picture them," I said and tapped my head. "Anyway, then . . . And you're still a pretty good looking boy," I said at the end, "now go to sleep."

"Night, Dad."

I watched him as he slept. He looks so small—light and little, like a bird. He's still losing weight. I wish—what do I wish? That he would stay ten forever and that none of this had ever happened—that I wouldn't have to keep telling him his mother's story, that he was a human boy and not half-Daoine Sidhe? That when I turned off the lights in his bedroom, I wouldn't be able to see light leaking from his fingers, his nose, his ears, his eyes—tiny flecks of light on his eyelashes? Not see the tiny snakes of light twisting through his hair, like tendrils of ghost ivy?

I don't know what I wish except that I could go to sleep as easily as he does, and not pace the house, rearranging magazines, the salt and pepper shakers, the bottles in the medicine cabinet. Or sit down and write everything out, while sipping on Sleepytime tea.

He was worried about me when I drove him to school this morning—that I was too sleepy, that I wouldn't be okay driving home alone. I'll be fine, I told him, you go on. I'll be fine.

So I came home to sit down and write. Taking my thoughts and making them into concrete, tangible words appearing one after the other on a computer screen or a piece of paper makes them real and manageable. I worry out problems by writing down questions for myself, possible solutions, alternatives. Anne Morrow Lindbergh once wrote that "writing is more than living; it is being conscious of living."

I believe she's right.

I got up early this morning, before Malachi did, and went to the six o'clock mass at St. Mary's. I liked the walk—few cars, a sky with a few stars left, a fading moon. I felt foolish, though, to be going to early morning mass on a weekday. Most of the people there were little blue-haired old ladies, clutching rosaries. I never went to early mass at St. Anthony's with Father Mark. Emma wasn't a morning person, and after moving to Garner, well, it was just too far to drive into Raleigh.

Jack has asked me why I still keep going to church.

For Malachi, I told him, but he wouldn't have it. "Come on, Ben—it's more than that. Why don't you convert to Wicca, then, or whatever faith Valeria professed?"

"Because Val said they were all the same."

"Yeah, right."

He asked me again, yesterday, at Hilda's funeral. And here I am, Tuesday morning, trying to come up with a good answer. They are all the same, but there is more to it than that.

I was raised a Presbyterian in a little country Orange County church whose roots go back over two hundred and fifty years to a group of Scotch-Irish settlers coming down from Pennsylvania looking for farmland in the Carolinas. The Scotch-Irish are from Ulster and were supposed to be pretty hardcore Presbyterian—I imagine my Presbyterian forebears spinned in their graves when I was confirmed a Catholic.

I started attending Catholic confirmation classes (Jack always said RCIA: Rite of Christian Initiation of Adults, sounded like joining some fraternity or lodge, where you had to eat raw eggs or something to be initiated. So speaks the confirmed agnostic—and I told him it wasn't raw eggs: it was the fresh blood of a chicken) just to make Emma and her parents happy. But after we were married, and I was attending church regularly, I found the mass to be poetry, rich, tex- tured, symbolic poetry that struck a chord in my soul that the Presbyterian services of my childhood never did. Religion is, after all, imagination before it is anything else: to believe in God, you first have to be able to imagine the concept of a god or gods, something greater and larger than yourself. Instead of just pleasing Emma, the faith journey became mine and to my surprise, I stuck with RCIA and on Easter a year after we were married, I was confirmed and took my first communion as a Catholic.

And I stayed Catholic, more or less, after she died, because of the poetry.

So, this morning I went to the 6 A.M. mass. I wanted to talk with Father Jamey, especially after his Sunday homily. He knows. He looks at Malachi and sees more than his yellow eyes. He sees the pointed ears and the glow in the eyes, the sometimes too-visible shifting lights of Malachi's aura. And that all that is happening is not, as President Bush tried to explain, a result of sunspots, disturbances in the iono- sphere—no, not causes, symptoms.

Okay, okay, I know the president is trying to calm and reassure everybody, take away some of the fear I see in almost everybody's eyes. Just Saturday, at the library, Mrs. Carmichael told me she sleeps with all her lights on: "I don't know, Ben, but the lights do keep away the dark and, well, things have just been so strange at night lately. Every- body on my street keep their lights on—like Christmas. It is more than just being scared of the dark; this dark is different. I know that sounds crazy, but the dark does seem, well, alive and purposeful."

Alive and purposeful? Yes, with the Fomorii and their minions.

I lit a candle this morning and then knelt in a pew near the front. I prayed for strength and wisdom and love and that my son be safe and that he live. And I felt guilty: are my prayers selfish, do I say the same things all the time, am I—Father Jamey talked about love being the force we need to get us through, to sustain us for what is coming. And what is that? I have to get Malachi to Faerie before he dies and I still don't know how to and where to go—when, Halloween, I guess, Samhain. Is it the call to come home, to return to Faerie that is causing all the weird stuff? It has to be.

I talked to Father Jamey after mass. He came by to visit after I got back from taking Malachi to school. He seemed to know the wards Valeria left around the house were there. He pushed to enter the house, paused, as if waiting for the magic to recognize him, and then, a sudden pop, and he was in.

Father Jamey sat at the kitchen table as I poured coffee, and then put milk on the table, spoons, checked the sugar bowl to see if it was full.

"So, Ben, what do you want to talk with me about?"

"Your Sunday homily, I guess, the craziness, all the strange things," I said as I sat down across from him and spooned in sugar and then milk.

"Tell me what you know—like why is there an invisible electrical fence around your house. The Jehovah's Witnesses and Mormons aren't that bad in this neighborhood, are they?"

"There are only a handful of people who can feel that fence," I said slowly and looked at the priest for a long moment, long enough for the lights in the kitchen to shift and change color. His dark red hair grew suddenly brighter and the freckles on his face glowed. His eyes—I am sure they were blue. Now, they were a silvery-grey, like polished pewter. I would have guessed Father Jamey Applewhite to be about my age, late thirties, but now, in this new and unexpected light, he was no age, like Valeria, ancient young Valeria, who had no age. Father Jamey's aura shimmered around him, a pale blue shot through with gold. His ears poked out of his hair.

"You're one of them, too; you're a changeling," I said slowly. "You're the first adult I've met—and there haven't been any JW's or Mormons about in a long time."

Father Jamey sipped his coffee and looked back and slowly smiled, "Of course you would be able to see past the fairy glamour, wouldn't you? It started back the first of May—"

"Beltaine," I said.

"Yes, and that was about the time the Diocese told me I was coming to St. Mary's here. But I started having dreams about Malachi before that—and three other children, and the dark ones," Father Jamey said. "Got any more coffee?"

"Some instant dessert flavored stuff, Café Vienna, Italian Cappuccino—I'll get it—I can nuke it in the microwave. Which flavor?"

"The Vienna. You weren't raised Catholic, were you?" he asked as I first spooned in the coffee, added water, and set the microwave for two minutes, ten seconds.

"No, how can you tell?"

"Oh, you don't have that pre-Vatican II parochial school look about you. No scars on your hands from those nuns' sharp rulers. Anyway, by the time I came here, I was seeing auras; I could levitate—not much—and move things. You know, you are the first person I've been able to tell all this."

The plastic milk jug on the table rose up and floated over to Father Jamey's hand. The microwave chimed and the door opened and the cup floated over to land in front of the priest.

"I knew when I met you and your son that you both knew, but I thought maybe it would be better if you sought me out. Protect your privacy—not expose you, you know. Ben, I don't know the purpose of our coming together here, but we are supposed to; I feel sure of that. My fate and yours and your son's and his three friends are tied together in all this."

"But, Father," I asked, wanting this priest, this priest-who-looked-too-young, to give me an answer that would explain everything. "This can't be just about my son. Yes, he is entering puberty and I have to get him to Faerie; I know that. But he is only one half-fairy child. Your mother isn't a fairy—these three other kids—they're human. I saw the ghost of a unicorn running down Vandora Springs Road last night. You are all being called, you are all becoming magical—why?" And I told him everything: Valeria, the dreams, the light-sicknesses, the Fomorii, everything I could think of.

Give me an answer. You have to know. You're a priest.

"You and James Thurber?" he said and laughed. I laughed, too. "It's the call from Faerie all right—and from everything you are telling me, everything I have seen, what people are talking about—here, here (he slapped the kitchen table) is a locus. Malachi is like, a magnet, and the center of a huge rippling pool—which metaphor is better, I don't know. Fairyness, sexuality, puberty, not-quite human hormones, the call: powerful stuff to be in one place. But I don't know why I am being called—or even if I am. I haven't had those dreams like Malachi; I am just changing. Maybe it's because of the story in Genesis, what happened right before the Flood. And I don't think we are really becoming magical—I mean, I can't work spells. I don't even know any. Rather, it's as if our bodies are waking up to what they are meant to do. Witches are different. They can manipulate the unseen forces—God, that sounds corny—the Force? They are learning another language; we are becoming that language."

I nodded my head. "Malachi tried to explain all that to me, too."

"Genesis 6, verses 2 and 4: The sons of God seeing the daughters of men, that they were fair, took to themselves wives of all which they chose. Now giants were upon the earth in those days. For after the sons of God went in to the daughters of men, and they brought forth children, these are the mighty men, men of renown. *The story is in all the mythologies: humans bearing the children of the gods. Hercules, Perseus, Aeneas,"* he said, *and then raised his hand and his cup floated over to the pot and hovered as the pot poured him another cup. Then the cup sailed back to the priest's hand. "I've been practicing. There have been fairies mixing in the human gene pool since forever, Ben."*

"Valeria told me that Faerie-folk had been coming here for centuries. Now they need their descendants back—all of them, it seems."

"No, not all. Like I said: I haven't been called. I am to remain here. The crossing is soon, though, and the dark ones will do anything to stop it."

I shuddered. "Have you seen the Fomorii?"

"Yeah, I have," he said *and drained his cup and stood. He wasn't wearing his collar and he didn't look much like a priest. T-shirt, jeans, Nikes. "I've got to get back to St. Mary's. Ben, you'll know when to ask me for help. Be careful. They will kill you and Malachi if they have to, to prevent him crossing over. He's important."*

"He'll die if he stays here. Why is God letting this happen? Why is He letting evil run loose? Why is He changing the pronunciation of this universe's word of creation?"

Father Jamey had no answers.

The governor of North Carolina, according to National Public Radio, is considering declaring the state to be under martial law. He declared a state of emergency this morning. He has ordered the National Guard to mobilize, and is consulting with Senators Helms and Sanford and even the White House.

Malachi told me this morning, on the way to school, that he had had a dream of flying over North Carolina, being guided by the twelve-pointed star around his neck. He said the star was pulling him east.

V

Light and Dark
Thursday, October 3 - Tuesday, October 15

Jack

THREE DAYS AFTER HILDA'S FUNERAL BEN CAME looking for him.

"Jack, if you don't open this damn door, I will knock it down. I swear I will. I know you are in there."

Jack sighed, looking at the knife in his hand. He had waited too long. He knew Ben wouldn't go away and that Ben would knock down the damn door.

"The door's not locked; come in."

"You look like shit. You haven't been eating—damn, Jack, you haven't even changed your clothes since the funeral. And what in the hell are you doing with a knife? Give it to me," Ben snapped and threw the steak knife across the room. "Are you out of your fucking mind? I don't have time for you to be messing around with a damn knife. Now get up and get some clothes, you're coming with me. I know how it is—remember how I was when Valeria died? Hadn't been for you, and if I hadn't had a baby to look after—never mind, I'll get your clothes," Ben growled and stomped off down the hall.

"Valeria has been dead for ten years. You've had time to get over it; you've got Malachi," Jack said to Ben's retreating back. He was sitting in his living room, facing the television. He hadn't bathed or shaved, let alone changed clothes since coming back from Hilda's parents in Charlotte. Would he have used the knife? He *had* tested it against his skin; it *was* sharp enough.

Ben turned to stare hard at Jack. "No, I'll never get over it; I've just learned to live with it, and you can, too. And I know you haven't had ten years—but I need you now. Alive. Thomas isn't your fault. Where's that duffel bag of yours?"

"In the closet, top shelf. But you have her son. *My* son, my only son, killed Hilda. My only son is a murderer, a black witch, a practitioner of the dark arts and the whole fucking world is going crazy."

Ben came back in the living room, carrying a stuffed duffel bag. "This should be enough for a few days; we can get some more stuff later. Now, get up."

"Why?"

"Like I said: I need you. I can't do this alone. I can't protect Malachi and three other kids, and get them to the gate on Halloween—if we can find the gate—and now his teacher is calling. She wants to know why he's been out of school so much. Told me he's already missed too many days. Made some vague comment about reporting these absences, making sure Malachi was really all right. I told her where to get off. Now, come on."

"What do you want me to do? I can't do anything," Jack muttered, looking away from Ben. "I can't save my wife; I can't save my son. How can I save my best friend and his son? Who is going to save me?"

"I'm trying to. Now get the fuck up," Ben said. "Okay, I'll get you up." He grabbed Jack and pulled him to his feet. "Let's go."

Jack let Ben haul him next door, untie his tie, pull his jacket and shirt off, shuck off his shoes, and socks, and then shove him in a shower. ("You can take off your pants yourself.") After standing there, his pants and underwear soaked, water pooling at his feet, Jack started crying for the first time since the funeral. Jack slowly started peeling off his sodden clothes until he was naked. He leaned into the shower then, wanting nothing more than the water to keep beating his head, pounding its way into his brain. He cried for a long time.

That had been seven days ago and nothing had happened since the funeral. No more dragons were sighted in the air, no more unicorns wandered out of the woods. No more shadows moved without bodies, no more children disappeared. Schools reopened and parents started sending their children back to school. Jack met all his classes at State.

Men and women, calling themselves white witches, appeared on local television and warned the public whatever was happening wasn't over, that Samhain was coming, and people should get prepared.

"What," a bemused Channel Eleven reporter asked, "should we do? Wear garlic?"

"Yes, and rowan," one of the white witches said. "Burn marjoram; it will help people accept the changes that are coming—"

Psychiatrists also appeared on TV to talk about mob psychology and mass hallucination and to make fun of the white witches. Everywhere, most people sighed in relief and turned the TV off when the white witches came on the air. But garlic and marjoram weren't to be found on the shelves. Rowan trees lost a lot of leaves.

Jack met Ben at the library Thursday afternoon. "Did you see the *News and Observer* this morning? There was another white witch on TV last night and today the paper prints this article on mass psychosis and that everything is all over and we can go about our business as if nothing happened."

"I saw it; I even called the paper," Ben said, shaking his head. "I told them it wasn't over and everything really did happen and more is going to happen. The reporter wanted to know how I knew and didn't I think my kind of talk was just going to scare people. I said that people should be scared and that she was an idiot. Then I slammed the phone down. I should have told her that every day three children fly to my house—through the trees, hiding in clouds, walking at strategic points. They are all waiting for Samhain and for me to get to them to that gate. And today—"

"What happened today?" Jack asked.

"I got a call from Malachi's principal. Wants me to come in tomorrow. Very serious, she said, Malachi's welfare."

Jack looked around the library. Today was the first day it was crowded again. People were trying to believe what the newspaper had said and were coming out of their houses and doing more than just going back and forth to work. Even so, they looked wary, glancing over their shoulders and around the room from time to time. And the library's books on anything remotely connected to magic had to be put on two-hour building-use-only reserve, or the shelves would have been stripped. Staff had to start searching bags and purses and knapsacks at the door to be sure the reserve books were just being used in the building and not borrowed by "mistake."

"So we had a respite. We rested while the Fomorii and their people gathered their strength," Jack said.

Ben nodded.

Camille Bondurant

Camille found Malachi Tyson in one of the study carrels in the library asleep over a book. His class was at PE down on the playground.

"He has a doctor's note—but I have my doubts," Charlotte Collins had said to her that morning. Camille had been in her office, reviewing Russell White's thick file. Hallie Bigelow had asked her to. The boy was doing much better, Hallie had said, and he seemed to have finally made one friend, Jeff. *Jeff Gates, of all people. How did those two find each other? One wounded soul knows another?* Hallie had wondered if maybe she should just let well enough alone, but still, this change seemed a bit too quick. *Jeff certainly needs a friend, too. And here I am, reviewing a bad boy's file because he is now a good boy?* Camille had tried telling Charlotte that maybe if she expected Russell to be good, he might surprise her—kids live up or down to our expectations, she had said. Charlotte had ignored her. Camille tucked her brown hair behind her ears, and pushed her glasses back up her nose. Back to the bad-boy-gone-good's file—

"He has a doctor's name—but I have my doubts. Camille?"

Camille had jerked up from Russell's file, her glasses almost falling off. *Note: go to optician's today.* Charlotte Collins stood in the door of her office, a dark frown on her face—and her eyes—surely they weren't red. Odd the room seemed darker with her in it.

"Oh, I'm so sorry, Charlotte. I must have spaced out completely. Who has a doctor's note you doubt?"

That had been an hour ago. Camille Bondurant, school social worker, investigating—checking up—Hell. What parent would fake a doctor's name? Just to get a kid out of PE? To the point of faking doctor's stationery? She sighed and leaned down to gently shake Malachi awake. He felt so warm—could he be running a fever? *It's my job to investigate cases of neglect.* She shook Malachi's shoulder again.

"Malachi?"

He slowly looked up, rubbing the sleep out of his eyes.

"Mrs. Collins said you weren't feeling well and I just thought—"

Malachi looked hard at her, as if he could see something about her she couldn't. "You're not the nurse. You're the counselor."

"She just mentioned in the lounge and I had to come in the library to pick up a copy of—*Nana Upstairs and Downstairs*—for my grief group and I saw you." *God, I am a terrible liar and I have no idea if that is the right name for that book.*

"I have some sort of flu. My father said it's going around. I'm better; I just get tired easily."

"What sort of flu?"

"Stomach. I'm okay, Mrs. Bondurant. I just get tired easily."

"Why aren't you at home? What did the doctor say?"

"I felt okay this morning. My dad didn't want me to come anyway. I had to promise I would call him if I felt sick again."

Pretty quick with the answers. Rehearsed? And he didn't answer my question about the doctor. He seems to be hiding something. Am I getting paranoid or is Charlotte Collins?

"You feel warm; I think you'd better call him," Camille said. "You can't even keep your eyes open to read."

Malachi stared hard at her again, his odd eyes seemingly brighter. She finally had to look away, her skin prickling. *What is this child seeing? And why is he holding on so hard to this carrel? Like he would float away if he let go? What is going on with this kid?*

"Okay, if you think so."

Camille watched Malachi walk out of the library and down the hall to the office. Something was odd, but neglect? The doctor's note looked real. She just didn't know enough.

Above her the fluorescent lights popped and went out.

Ben, Hallie Bigelow, and Charlotte Collins

Hallie Bigelow frowned at the clock in her office. Friday, October 11, 7:45 A.M. In fifteen minutes, Ben Tyson would be sitting in one of the chairs facing her and so would Charlotte Collins, Ben's son's teacher. Hallie didn't want either of them in her office for the reason they were coming. Where was her coffee? She had put her mug down right here on her desk—was she losing her mind? Put something down for a minute and—there it was, below today's breakfast and lunch menu. Hallie picked up her dark blue Duke University mug and took a long swallow. She wondered if she had tried hard enough to talk Charlotte out of all this. At least the woman hadn't called DSS—or had she? Charlotte *had* gotten Camille Bondurant to talk to the boy, but all the social worker had said was that Malachi had thought he was better from some flu and came back to school too early—after arguing with his father. He should have stayed at home. Camille, when pressed, said something *was* odd, but what, she couldn't figure out. She was adamant that she had no proof of neglect. Hallie shook her head. Damn Charlotte Collins. The woman had always had a mean, self-righteous streak in her, Hallie thought, and she didn't like people brighter than she was—like Malachi and Ben Tyson. Or Hallie Bigelow, for that matter. *If only we paid teachers enough money.*

She took another swallow of her cold coffee. If Charlotte had called DSS, Hallie would be furious—just thinking about it made her more than a little irritated. Innocent until proven guilty, right? She got up to pace her office: a neat square enclosing her desk. She just couldn't believe Ben Tyson was guilty of criminal neglect in regard to his son. After Charlotte had talked to her, Hallie had made some calls. Well-respected librarian in Garner, been there for almost fifteen years, pillar of the community, regular church-goer, widower who doted on his only child. Not that any of these were guarantees, she reflected as she flicked open and closed the venetian blinds. Too many well-respected churchgoers had been guilty of child abuse. Hallie had met Ben when he came to check out the school and later, to enroll Malachi. She had been sure then Ben was a good man. And if Hallie Bigelow was anything, she was a good judge of character.

What had possessed Charlotte to even suggest Ben was hurting his child? Had she become one of those born-again fundamentalist Baptists who believed all Catholics were papist idolaters bound for hell? Hallie shook her head: too crazy. And surely she would have noticed that if it had happened to Charlotte. Charlotte didn't even go to church, Hallie remembered. Maybe the craziness that had infected the world had infected Charlotte Collins.

Hallie drained her coffee mug and glanced at her watch: 7:51. Nine more minutes. Her twelve days of grace were over. Nothing weird since the end of September. Until this morning. She had only been half-listening to the radio on her way into school when an excited reporter started describing what was happening between Norfolk and Elizabeth City. Monsters were crawling out of the Dismal Swamp. Godzilla-like monsters. Highway 64 in North Carolina and Highway 58 in Virginia were packed with people running scared, and heading west. She started pacing again, this time pausing to pick up and examine and put back down objects on her desk: the telephone, pencils, pens, a Blue Devil paperweight, the stapler, a Post-it packet identifying her as Boss Lady. Her grandmother had been right: there were unseen things in the world. Spirits and things that did go bump in the night. Never leave a candle to burn out, it brings bad luck. When Hallie had moved into her new house, a few months before her grandmother had died, the old woman had come over to give her a threshold blessing. Granny had hung three pinecones over the front door, and what had the inscription above them said? *Who comes to me, I keep /Who goes from me, I free /Yet against all I stand /Who do not carry my key.*

Maybe it was time to hang that inscription back up. People with glowing eyes. People flying, disappearing into thin air. They had never really gone away, had they? We just didn't see them for twelve days because we didn't want to, or we couldn't: shock overload. Just too much that couldn't be explained. Every morning she and her next-door neighbor left for work at the same time. Every morning they would smile at each other and wave as they got into their cars. Today her neighbor's eyes glowed green.

The governor was talking again about declaring martial law, by Saturday; the National Guard was placed on full alert, along with Fort Bragg and Pope Air Force Base and Seymour Johnson and Camp LeJeune. Not that tanks and guns could fight fairy tales. The whole northeast corner of the state was supposed to be in a total panic. The Navy had evacuated dependent families from Norfolk and evidently naval artillery and aircraft had been tried and failed. People were so on the edge, nerves frayed, that she was afraid they were going to fall off. The suicide rate had skyrocketed. So had physical assaults, random violence. Chaos within and without.

Hallie finally stopped pacing at her gift shelves, where she kept all the little things children had given her over the years. Ceramic apples, little school bells, Duke blue devils, dried flowers, clumsy clay handprint ashtrays. She glanced at her watch: 7:59. In a minute the parents of the gift-givers would start calling to tell her their kids were staying home.

There was a knock on the door. Hallie turned around to see the school secretary, Trudy Anderson, standing there, wearing a raincoat and carrying an umbrella.

"Good morning, Trudy. I didn't hear the weather report this morning. Rain?"

"I didn't, either, but the clouds are sure dark. Mr. Tyson's here, Hallie, and so is Mrs. Collins. Both of them are out in the lobby, standing about as far apart as two people can get and still be in the same space. And you should take a look at Charlotte, Hallie. She looks *really* strange," Trudy said in a low voice. Then the phone rang.

"You get the phone; I'll ask them in," Hallie said with a heavy sigh.

"Heard half the buses aren't running, either. Good morning, Nottingham Heights Elementary, can I help you?"

Hallie, wishing she had had at least one more cup of coffee, stepped out into the lobby. "Ben, thanks for coming over this morning. I wish you were here under happier circumstances. But, as I told you over the phone, Charlotte has called some things to my attention that we need to discuss. Come on in and let's sit down and talk. Yes, please, close the door, Charlotte. Thank you. Now, Ben, as I was saying—"

Charlotte did look really strange. What had she done with her hair—spilt a peroxide bottle on it? And her eyes—were they darker and redder?

"Hallie, this man is abusing his son. Call DSS; this little meeting of yours is a waste of time. Camille Bondurant told me the boy was too sick to be at school," Charlotte Collins said, cutting Hallie off with one slash of her hand. Ben froze, his hands on the chair arm, his body poised above the seat. "That child has been out of school two or three times a week since school started—he's already used up his quota to be able to pass the fifth grade. I am positive it's Mr. Tyson's neglect and maybe worse than that is keeping Malachi out of school—"

"Go ahead, Ben, sit down. Charlotte, stop. I talked to Camille, too. She also said that Malachi had felt better before he left home, persuaded his father he was okay, and then he felt worse," Hallie said, making an even sharper gesture with her hand. "Let me talk." What in the hell was going on? This wasn't how this meeting was supposed to go. What was the matter with Charlotte? Was she crazy? The woman had ten years of teaching experience; she knew better. "Ben, Mrs. Collins is concerned because of Malachi's high number of absences and his—well, deteriorating appearance. Just concerned, that's all."

"He's not behind. He always makes up his work. He did feel better the day Mrs. Collins is talking about. Why is the school social worker interrogating my son? What is going on?" Ben said slowly, not looking at Charlotte, his hands tight around the chair arms.

He looked wary, on guard. *My God*, Hallie thought, *maybe Charlotte hit a nerve. No, not Ben Tyson. He's pissed off—with good reason—for being accused of hurting his boy. I'd be pissed, too.*

"He has been having some health problems lately, but he's under a doctor's care, and the doctor assures me he is fine."

"What doctor, Mr. Tyson?" Charlotte asked. "I checked the name on Malachi's health forms—and while Dr. Todd Tilman does indeed practice right here in Raleigh, the receptionist told me there are no patient records for a Malachi Tyson in their files. I don't believe that child has even seen any doctor; you're just cooking up some perverted home remedy, some sort of bizarre ritual with your own son—"

"You are out of your mind and how dare you invade our privacy by calling the doctor's office. I take good care of my son. He saw Dr. Tilman, who is one of the most respected pediatricians in the city. God only knows who you talked to in his office—if you talked to anybody, that is. The receptionist wouldn't tell you that—you are lying. The person who is sick and perverted is you—"

Ben hesitated, just a little. Didn't he?

"Hallie, Miss Bigelow, this man is lying. He's not taking care of his son—you can look at the boy and tell that. The boy is ill and his father is guilty of criminal neglect and abuse. These medical records are fakes—I know that's against the law. If you'd let me call DSS immediately instead of insisting on this innocent until proven guilty crap, Malachi would be safe now."

"You will not take my son away from me." Ben stood and stepped back and away from Charlotte Collins, toward the office door. "You're working with the Fomorii, aren't you? You smell like evil, like one who's been to bed with evil. You're not touching my boy. Either that or you've gone completely crazy like everybody else."

"You are out of your fucking mind," Charlotte hissed, after a pause that was just a little too long.

"Will you both shut up?" Hallie shouted. "Ben, I don't know what the hell you are talking about, but wait, don't leave. Please." It will be all over school in a minute, she thought. "Can't we discuss this like adults—no fairy tales, no threats? Please, sit down. Ben." He stood by the door, one hand on the knob.

"Let him leave, Hallie," Charlotte said, her voice now cold and measured. "The charge of criminal neglect isn't going away. Or any other charge. I think DSS will want to know why Russell White, Jeff Gates, and Hazel Richards were seen leaving Mr. Tyson's house at odd hours of the night. And why Russell was wearing just a T-shirt and gym shorts. I don't think they will think *I* am the crazy one."

"What are you talking about? You are possessed—you are one of their lackeys, aren't you? They own you, body and soul, don't they? What was your price, Mrs. Collins? Remember what happens in the old stories to people who sell their souls?"

Charlotte flinched. Hallie was sure of it: Charlotte had flinched. *Had she really sold her soul to the Devil? What* am *I thinking? And*

Ben—did he pause or did he not, before he answered her—are those kids coming to his house?

Maybe *she* was going crazy.

"Go back to hell," Ben yelled, jerked the door open, and literally ran. Trudy stared in amazement, her hand frozen over the phone which was ringing and ringing and ringing.

"Charlotte, what the hell is going on? Trudy, get the damn phone. I thought we were going to discuss the child's health and you are accusing Ben Tyson of being a child molester? Are you crazy?" Hallie shouted, knowing she was shouting, wishing she wasn't shouting, and knowing she couldn't stop shouting. The phone started ringing again—this time Trudy got it on the second ring.

"Hallie Bigelow, you will be going to jail along with Mr. Tyson. I am going to go into the health room, pick up the phone, and call DSS," Charlotte said slowly and then, as slowly, she got up and walked out of the office and into the health room.

"Trudy: the health room line," Hallie shouted.

"I got it—I got it—" Trudy shouted back.

Charlotte stepped into the doorway between Trudy's office and the health room. Her eyes—they looked as if they were not just red; they looked like they were on fire.

"You can't stop me," she said and left.

"What just happened? Is everyone crazy?" Hallie said, shaking her head, as she watched Charlotte Collins walk down the hall to her classroom. "That was sure one hell of a waste of time."

"Yes, everybody is going crazy," Trudy said as she put the phone down. It started ringing again, almost instantly. "I have never seen anything like it. Nottingham Heights Elementary, please hold. Central Office called, by the way—this will really make your day— they're thinking of closing all the schools for good, until the crazy things stop. Emergency meeting of the school board this morning. Sit down, Hallie honey; let me get you some more coffee. Thank you for holding, may I help you? Yes, Mr. Parker, I will tell Miss Murphy that Danny isn't coming today, thank you. That makes—let me see, I've been keeping score—the fortieth call all about the same thing: why their kid isn't coming or they are coming to pick them up. Give me your cup and don't answer the phone."

"What time is it?"

"8:17."

All that had taken only seventeen minutes?

Hallie Bigelow stood very still by her desk, ignoring the ringing phone with its blinking lights. Forty kids and counting. If this kept up, the school would be closed regardless of what the school board did. Sighing, she picked up the phone.

Thomas

That afternoon, at four o'clock, the phone on Thomas Ruggles's desk at the bank rang only once before he picked it up. He looked quickly around the room. None of the other data processors seemed to be even aware of his existence, let alone what he was doing.

Fools.

"Well, what happened? What'd they say? A social worker will be sent out for a home visit? When? Monday? Why so late? Too many caseloads and the current emergency. Damn, I hate having to wait that long for DSS to get its act together. Yes, I am sure he is the one, Charlotte. Yes. No, I have no doubts he is the one promised to us. If we have him, we can open the gates wide for the Dark Ones. Much more so than the last three children. Their feyness was latent—just barely manifesting. It's all there in this one; Malachi is half-fairy. The other three—I discarded them. You don't want to know how I found out that Malachi is half-fairy or how I discarded the others. Four of them—damn, he is forming a tetrad. It makes all four stronger as a unit. Who are the other three, tell me about them, who's the weakest. Russell? Well, we will just go after him. If they have to defend Russell, the other three will get weaker. Malachi especially will get weaker and then we'll snag him. Yes. Hold on, I've got another call on my line—okay, I'll call you tonight. We may have to wait for DSS, but we can go ahead and call, say, Larry White? Exactly. Okay, bye. Central Carolina Bank, Thomas Ruggles speaking, how can I help you?"

Russell and Jeff

Russell reluctantly stepped off the bus Friday afternoon, and stood by the side of the road, watching until he could no longer see Jeff watching him back in the rear window. When Jeff waved, a blur through the yellow-dust-covered glass, Russell waved back. He didn't want to go home. He didn't want to leave Jeff, even though Jeff was coming over in a few minutes. He didn't want to be left alone at all. Even Jeanie, who was getting crankier and crankier the longer she was pregnant, would be okay company for a little while. Russell had overheard his dad say more than once that November 12 couldn't come soon enough, just to shut her up. Jeanie's back ached, her feet ached, her hands were swollen. She was so big she couldn't get up out of a chair by herself. She couldn't squeeze behind a steering wheel, so somebody had to drive her everywhere: to work, to the store, to the corner, everydamnwhere.

"And I'm carrying twin boys," Jeanie had complained to her mother. "Mama, I don't know if I can handle another White boy-child, let alone two, like Russell. I declare, if it isn't one thing, it's another. . . ."

Russell had drifted out of earshot then. He knew just what she was going to complain about—not that he hadn't changed. Russell hadn't gotten into trouble at school since the fire. He had stayed, for the most part, out of his father's way. He was being good. Of course, neither his father nor Jeanie noticed Russell's new behavior any more than they noticed his green eyes were greener and glowed in the dark, his pointed ears, or that his red hair was redder and every now and then, had flames of light flickering in the red. But, then, nobody but Jeff or Malachi or Hazel or Malachi's dad had noticed. Malachi had explained: the fairy glamour that hid things was an involuntary reaction, a protective camouflage that just turned on. Unless somebody was also changing, they wouldn't notice.

Besides, being good didn't stop the bad ones. The shadows, the red-eyed monsters, they weren't just whispering to him in dreams anymore. The dark ones wanted Russell; the whispers promised him things: fuel for that hard, little knot of black anger which wouldn't go away, no matter how much Russell changed, no matter how closer the changes brought him to the light. He had actually made a friend, Jeff, and now, maybe, another, no two: Hazel and Malachi.

But the anger remained. Russell couldn't quite trust Hazel, yet. She was too much like the kids who picked on him for being too old in the fifth grade, for being too big, for wearing clothes bought at Kmart, for wearing dirty T-shirts. The goody-goodies, who always had everything done on time and without mistakes, looked down their noses at those who didn't. Hazel was money and clean clothes and a nice house. So was Malachi; Russell had seen that when he met Malachi's father last Thursday. And he was sure Malachi's dad had looked at him and seen trailer trash, white trash, redneck.

Russell shook his head. He didn't want to believe all that, but it was hard not to. And thinking like that only made the whispers come back. The sky rumbled again, this time louder and louder, and a few raindrops splattered on Russell's head and his face. He started walking faster. At least, since they had gotten out of school early, he had the whole afternoon to himself. And maybe next week as well. From what the principal had said when she announced early dismissal, there might not be any school on Monday, either. Not with swamp monsters crawling across North Carolina. That had been what all the other kids talked about—that, and seeing people-less shadows.

The sky rumbled. Russell started walking faster down the driveway. He looked up into the dark grey clouds that had been there all day long. It looked as if the storm that had been promised since morning was finally here. Where was Jeff? Why wasn't he here yet? All he had to do was fly over; it took less than five minutes.

Lightning forked over his house, and the rain began, big fat drops. Russell started running, holding his books over his head. *No, this will just make Mrs. Collins mad.* He stuffed the books under his shirt.

"Hey, Russ! What are you doing?"

Russell stopped and looked around, the rain beating on his head, soaking his shirt, his pants. The books were going to get wet, no matter what he did.

"Up here."

Russell looked up to see Jeff hovering above him, completely dry, surrounded by a thin, barely visible envelope of white light.

"Forgotten how to do it? You can even dry everything off, too."

I am so stupid. I can't remember anything. "No, I haven't forgotten how to do it. I just forgot I could. There." He was no longer getting wet; his clothes and his books were dry. The rain, coming down harder, washed around and over him and off. Grinning, he slowly rose until he was at Jeff's height.

"Better? I had to talk to Ellen—Mrs. Clark—for a while. She had to tell me something about my dad. Come on; let's go to your house. Boy, it's like night out here."

They flew companionably down the driveway, almost drifting, in no hurry. From the Whites' house to the road was a five-minute walk, a one-minute flight at top speed. Today, with the hard rain and not being in a hurry, Russell and Jeff took almost ten minutes, talking about Malachi and his father and Hazel. Rain came down in sheets around them.

"You don't like Mal's dad? I do; I wish I had a father like that—Russell, look out!"

Out of the dark and the rain, a darker shadow formed, with long tendrils, twisting and uncurling, reaching out for each boy. The cool, wet air grew even colder, so cold Russell thought the rain would turn into snow. The shadow was familiar; he knew it. He knew what it was saying and what it wanted.

"Fly, Jeff, fly as fast as you can. It's me they want, not you—just me. I'm the evil one, the mean one—like my dad. I hurt; I hate. Get away, Jeff, are you crazy?" Russell screamed and shoved Jeff away, his aura growing brighter and hotter with each shove. The shadow shrank back, hissing.

Jeff shoved back. "Look, don't you see? It pulled away. You're not like that anymore, you know that. You were never really like that, Russ, not the real you, the you that has finally gotten its chance. Russell, look out!"

The shadow pounced, all its many legs wrapping around Russell, as if it were a net and had caught a huge fish. Russell screamed. The shadow tossed Russell up, and caught him in its cold claws, then up again, the second time catching the boy in its mouth. Russell's hot white aura went out and he felt colder and duller than he had ever felt in his life, too cold to shiver, too cold for his teeth to chatter. The cold was turning him into a stone, a stone to be juggled in the air.

He couldn't just let the thing eat Russell, make Russell into darkness, but what could he do? *I'm so little, so weak, so smaallll.* No, not this time. Not like before when Someone had come for him in the darkness and he had let the Someone do whatever he wanted. Not this time. Jeff flew straight at the monster, the rain hissing as it struck his aura, which was now a white flame. He struck the monster dead center in an explosion of incandescent white light.

Jeff opened his eyes and sat up.

The storm was gone.

The sky was clear, a pale grey-blue. The monster had disappeared. He was soaked and lying on soaked ground, in a mud puddle. Like a small ghost, some of his aura was still visible, tiny flickering white flames.

"Russell?"

Russell lay a few feet away, curled up in a tiny, tight ball. Jeff crawled over and laid a hand on Russell's head. Cold, cold, cold. But, beneath the cold, a bare trace of warmth. Russell was breathing—barely.

"He's alive," Jeff whispered. "He's far away, but he's there. He feels like he's pure fear." One of Jeff's still-flickering white flames flowed from his hand into Russell's wet, red hair, like water being absorbed by a paper towel. "He felt that—I felt him feel it—but he's too scared to come back. I can't get him back by myself."

Jeff closed his eyes, squinched up his face, and then stepped back as Russell's body floated up from the ground. Keeping his hand on Russell's head, Jeff took off, his feet barely touching the ground. After making sure neither of Russell's folks were home, he slowly rose up to the roof, Russell floating beneath his hand. With Russell still floating, Jeff raised Russell's bedroom window and then guided his friend's body inside and onto his bed.

Then Jeff called for Malachi and Hazel.

Ben

It had been a day. First that insane meeting at the school, then a weird conversation with his lawyer. Could Charlotte Collins make DSS do anything? Would there be social workers waiting at his door when he got home? The lawyer had no answers. What about the threat of a charge of child molestation? Yes, the other children had been at his house, but if he had tried to explain to Hallie why they were there, how they got there, she would have thought he was crazy. And he wasn't a good liar. Yes, he had told the doctor lie enough times that it felt true, but he hadn't had any practice defending himself against molestation charges. If he had explained to Hallie why he could never take Malachi to a doctor—yeah, right. And after that the county library director had called to talk about closing the entire system until the "emergency was over"—did Ben think that would be a good idea?

Ben shook his head. Why not close the library? So what if there were people coming there to hide—why they thought they would be safer surrounded by books, he didn't know. He doubted the schools would re-open on Monday, which was fine with him. Malachi didn't need to be riding on an unprotected bus. Not that it mattered if he ever went back, Ben thought. His son would be gone after Halloween. Gone forever? Gone was all Ben could think of, conceive of, right now. What would happen after they crossed over into Faerie, cured Malachi of his fairy-sickness—it was just too much to think that far ahead—and he still didn't know where the gate was.

What? Why is the air in here getting so hot? His office smelled of white heat. The air shimmered and tiny lightning bolts zigzagged across the room, making zapping electrical popping sounds, a whoosh of smoke, and there, perched on his desk, was Ben's son. For one brief wild moment, Malachi looked just like his mother: the glowing eyes, the golden-white hair, and the pointed ears. Ben felt his heart stop, squeeze, and then go on.

Coughing, Ben waved away the residual smoke, wishing Malachi would hurry up and grow out of the special effects stage. And didn't the boy ever think of the effect of others seeing him materialize in a puff of smoke in his father's office?

"I told you *not* to do this in public. And why aren't you in bed — you've been sick, remember?" Ben snapped, glowering. He glanced out his door — the few people he could see on the library's main floor didn't seem to have noticed the pyrotechnics in his office. Not that it really mattered. How could it? Stranger things were happening almost every day lately, things that had nothing to do with Malachi.

"Sorry, Dad, but I had to get here as fast as I could — neat trick with the smoke, huh? — and I really do feel much better and I've got to go help Russell, Jeff called me, Russell got attacked by a shadow, Hazel is already on her way —"

"Slow down. One word at a time. What's going on with Russell?" Ben asked, remembering what he had seen last week, when he had gone to pick up Malachi at Nottingham Heights after it had closed early. The other three had been waiting with Malachi outside the school, on the front walk. For a brief moment, before Ben was close enough to speak, he saw the auras of all four children, the different lights merging together, drawn into one greater aura by pink and red pulsing ropes of light.

They are closer to my son and will know him better than I will ever be able to. They are more like him than I can ever be.

"The Fomorii are after him. They attacked him during the storm — Dad — they need me. It will be all right; I promise."

And Malachi disappeared, winked out, leaving only the smell of heat in Ben's office and a thin, grey haze of vanishing smoke.

I don't know them, these other three. Who is this Russell, who looks so tough and mean? This Jeff, who looks like he wants to hide behind the next tree and Hazel, the most normal-looking of the bunch, yet her eyes glow, too.

Who are these three kids who are so attached to my son?

Oh, God, the Fomorii.

Jeff, Malachi, and Hazel

It was late afternoon, almost twilight. The sky was darkening again, but at least for now, the darkness was not ominous, just the forerunner of night. Nights were another matter. As the changes progressed and the barriers between universes continued to fracture, nights became more and more horrifying and dangerous. *Things* roamed in the darkness. The good weakened, or so it seemed. Good people stayed at home, with their doors locked, windows bolted. Crosses, Stars of David, Amish hex signs hung on doors, along with cloves of garlic, all charms against what might be loose between sunset and sunrise.

But that was night and this is afternoon, Jeff thought and looked at Malachi and Hazel, then at Russell. From below Jeff could hear movement, a TV, cabinet doors opening and closing, pots and pans banging. It was close to dinnertime. Russell's stepmother was home; his father would be soon. When everything was ready, would he come up the stairs and get Russell? What would Larry White do if he found his son in a magical coma, curled up in a tight, little ball, cold to the touch, and his son's best friends sitting around him? Jeff didn't want to find out. Larry White scared him almost as much as his own father did.

"Jeff, it has to be you to go in. He knows and trusts you far more than he does me or Malachi," Hazel said. She looked tired, Jeff thought, and for the first time her long, brown hair was unbraided; strands kept falling over her face like a shifting veil. Hazel had brought her cat, Alexander, with her. The Siamese, now as big as a Maine Coon cat, had first prowled around the room, sniffing one thing or another. Now he was sniffing Russell and licking his forehead and his hands.

"He loves you, Jeff. He can't say it and I know it's hard for you to say it, too. That means there isn't anybody else he will leave his fear for but you," Malachi said. Hazel looked tired. Malachi, on the other hand, looked sick and pale and worn out. Dark purple rings made his eyes look sunken and he was whispering, as if he didn't have enough energy to speak louder.

Jeff nodded, watching Alexander as he kneaded the quilt covering Russell and then curled up beside him, pressing his feline bulk against Russell. Hazel swore the cat could mind-speak. Jeff wasn't surprised. He wished Malachi hadn't said that about Russell loving him. His father had told Jeff he loved him. Love hurt. *But I do really like Russell a lot. When does like become love? Does love have to hurt? And he is a boy. Boys don't love other boys, do they?*

"Are you ready? We can't leave him there much longer, Jeff. Russ may never be able to come back and that would mean the Fomorii would have won. Our set of four, our tetrad, would be broken, and we won't be able to cross over on Samhain."

And you'll die, Jeff thought. I'll—I'll have to go back to live with my father. He had been about to tell Russell that when the shadow had attacked. The Clarks had told him yesterday after dinner.

"His psychiatrist thinks he has made enough progress to handle having you in the home again. His lawyer is petitioning the court and courts tend to favor the natural parents. We're trying to fight it, but it doesn't look good," Ellen Clark had said.

"Jeff? Hold my hand and Malachi's," Hazel said.

They completed the circle and closed their eyes. A slow, white flame-aura grew around all three of them, through them, and above them.

Malachi opened his eyes. "He's there."

"I know," Hazel said. "I felt him go."

They both looked at Jeff, whose eyes were still closed, as he sat between them, the light of his aura playing across his face.

Jeff and Russell

Jeff stood outside an elementary school, an enormous one with towering brick walls. It wasn't Nottingham Heights Elementary or Vandora Springs or any school in Raleigh Jeff had ever seen. Yellow dust was everywhere and the trees Jeff knew—pines, poplars, oaks, sweet gums—were replaced by scrub pines and trash oaks. The schoolyard seemed to go on forever, spreading out from the school into endless prairie.

The red of the brick and the yellow of the dust were bright, bright red and yellow, chrome red and yellow. The green of the grass was just as bright, but it was intermixed with splotches and streaks of white. It's a drawing, Jeff thought, colored with Crayolas. He could see where the red and the green and the yellow overlapped, and the sky was a scrawled pale-blue half-sky, marked here and there with purple streaks. A black line marked the edges of the school. In one corner of the half-sky was a yellow circle sun, with radiating orange lines. Below the blue was a pale cream color—manila, Jeff thought, which was what the teachers called that kind of drawing paper. Jeff was sure if he walked far enough he would come to where the manila-and-blue-and-purple sky and earth met. The sky felt close, as if it were a huge window screen someone had just pulled down.

"Russell," Jeff said out loud, "is inside. I have to go and get him and bring him back." His voice sounded strange and oddly flat. There were no other sounds: no cars passing, no wind in the prairie grass, no thunder in the sky's purple.

Only one door and a tiny line of windows broke the expanse of the brick wall. Jeff took a deep breath and walked across the yard and knocked on the door. He waited and knocked again, louder and harder. Finally Jeff pushed down the bar, shoved the door open, and went in.

The inside was even brighter than the outside. Jeff stood in a classroom in which each wall was a different color: red, green, blue, and yellow. The polished linoleum floors was a mosaic, a maze of patterns and shapes—spirals, ellipses, waxing and waning moons, comets with long, long tails—that were only hidden by rag rugs, with even more colors spinning out of the centers. A cheerful fire crackled in the hearth. A deep red couch was against the yellow wall. That part of the classroom was like a living room, with soft arm chairs to either side of the couch, a table, a reading lamp. Behind one armchair was a darker yellow door, slightly ajar. The rest of the classroom was like any other: desks, a blackboard, the teacher's desk, and a wall of windows overlooking a playground filled with jungle gyms, rope swings, and huge climbing mazes. Jeff wondered why the windows and the playground weren't visible from the outside. Each desk was a different color, as if someone had used the 64- or 128-color box: burnt sienna, raw umber, periwinkle, aquamarine, maize, goldenrod, peach, mauve. The color names were neatly printed in black square block letters on each desk. The only other difference was that all the furniture looked just a little too big, as if large-sized children were expected to use the room.

But the classroom had more than wild colors and off-sized furniture: Spices—cinnamon, nutmeg, clove—drifted in the air, rich and fragrant. He could even see spice-trails, shades of red and brown, tiny cloud snakes. And somewhere a woman was singing. Jeff followed the singing slowly across the room, touching each desk, the chairs, as he passed. The red couch smelled of strawberries; the yellow wall felt warm.

Jeff opened the dark-yellow door and stepped into a long, long white hallway. "Hello? Hello? Russell? It's me, Jeff. Where are you?"

Nobody answered. The woman kept singing, a familiar tune, and as Jeff listened, he remembered he had heard it from a babysitter years ago, when he was very small: *Down in the valley, the valley so low. Hang your head over, and hear the wind below . . .*

Jeff followed the singing down the long hall. The off-white walls of the hallway smelled of banana and when he rubbed his fingers on the wood and licked them, Jeff tasted banana. The hall floor was furry. Jeff wanted to take off his shoes and go barefoot. At the end of the hall was a closed purple door, the color of the clouds. The singing came from behind the purple door; so Jeff didn't knock, he just turned the knob and went in.

Hush, little baby, don't say a word, Mama's gonna buy you a mockingbird. And if that mockingbird don' sing, Mama's gonna buy you a diamond ring . . .

Jeff stood in a bedroom—Russell's bedroom. There was the wardrobe and the carpet Russell has salvaged from the dumpster. But this carpet was more than the ratty throwaway Russell had back home—Jeff's feet sank into the thickness of this lush, soft warmness that covered almost the entire floor. The carpet stopped by the window, exposing polished cedar planks and there the singer sat, a woman in a rocking chair. Behind her was Russell's manger. The star cast a white light on the Joseph and Mary and the Baby.

Jeff didn't recognize the woman. She didn't look at all like what he remembered of Russell's mother from the photograph on Russell's dresser. This woman was older and heavier. She wore glasses and a pencil stuck in her dark brown, grey-streaked curly hair. A little boy with red fox ears sat in her lap, his face pressed against her. His red fox tail twitched across her legs. At the woman's feet stood a large, long-necked glass jar, filled with a bubbly oily black fluid.

The woman stopped singing and frowned when she saw Jeff.

Jeff gulped and started talking as fast as he could: "Russell. It's time to go, to come back, I mean. We need you. I need you. I don't think I can finish this journey without you. I don't want to. And Malachi and Hazel need you. None of us can finish this journey without you. We're a linked group, a tetrad; Malachi says we all go or none of us go. Russell, c'mon."

"You must be Jeff," the woman said in a low, sweet voice. "Russell, my little, red foxy, told me you might be coming and that you would be asking him to go. He doesn't want to. He's afraid, and as long as he is with me, he won't be afraid. And those monsters—why should he have to fight those? They were so mean to him—they wanted him to let his anger out and then they were going to eat him up. I never. Russell can keep his anger in this nice jar where it will be safe and it won't hurt anyone. You run along now, honey," she said and smiled and started humming to herself, rocking back and forth.

"Who are you?" Jeff asked, wishing he could crawl into her lap, too.

"Why, I'm Miss McNeil, of course. Russell is in my first grade. Today we are learning lullabies. Russell said none of you really need him, anyway." She looked away and started rocking and singing: *I gave my love a cherry that had no stone . . .*

Jeff took a step closer. Should he grab Russell and run? Pull him off Miss McNeil's lap? No, that wouldn't work. There had to be another way to get Russell back. How had he gotten through before—and he had, Jeff realized, broken through the tough, bad boy to find the Russell who was his best friend. Talking? Listening? Was it that simple? It couldn't be or Jeff wouldn't be here, inside Russell's terrified imagination, talking to a long-ago memory in a school that Russell hadn't seen since he was six.

He sat down on Russell's bed, facing Miss McNeil and Russell and the rocking chair. Sunlight poured onto the bed, washing the white spreads and gold oak frame clean and bright. Russell didn't have a white spread, Jeff thought, and his bed is cast iron. He almost said nothing, but pointing out differences between reality and this other place probably wouldn't work. This other place didn't have shadows that came alive and tried to eat people. There was nothing in the room that Jeff thought he could use. The manger, with its Red Fox, the picture of Russell's mother, the wardrobe. Where *had* Jeff's imagination hidden him when he needed to hide? Maybe that was it. Maybe Jeff needed to tell Russell he was afraid and how he was leaving *his* safe place behind. Maybe.

Jeff cleared his throat. "Tell me where we are, Russell."

"Why, we are right here in Russell's bedroom, Jeff."

"No, I need to talk to Russell. You aren't real; you're a memory. I'm real and Russell's real and I need to talk to him."

"Well, I never. If you had been in *my* first grade, you would have learned better manners."

"Russell," Jeff said in a louder voice, "Where are we? Where's this bedroom? How do you eat here? Go to the bathroom?"

Still rocking, Miss McNeil looked away from Jeff, shaking her head. She turned to look out the window and started another song: *Rockabye baby in the tree tops, when the wind blows, the cradle will rock . . .*

The little fox-tailed boy said nothing.

"Russell, Red Fox, I know you can hear me, so just listen, okay?"

"Run along home, Jeff," Miss McNeil said. "Russell doesn't need you. He has me and that is enough."

"That's not true. Russell, it's the other way around: you don't need her or this place anymore. You don't have to come back here when you're scared. You—we—can take care of ourselves now. We've changed. We're different; we're strong. You don't have to be afraid of your father anymore. He can't hurt you. It's not just being magic, either; it's more than that. I don't know if I'm saying this right or not, but we've become, we're becoming—wait a minute, let me think—"

"It doesn't matter, Jeff. Russell is staying right here. Run along now."

Please let me find the right words.

"Russell, coming back here is saying you aren't strong. It's admitting all the bad things—all the bad names, all the times your dad beat you—are true and right."

Was it Jeff's imagination, or was Miss McNeil looking a little bit blurry around the edges? Okay, now for the really hard part. One, two, three, just say it all really fast:

"Russ, I was going to tell you something today before the monster came. When I got home from school Mrs. Clark told me my dad was out of jail, on parole for good behavior. His lawyer had made it happen and he wants me back; my dad wants me to come and live with him again. Mrs. Clark told me she didn't want that to happen and it won't, not right away, supervised visits first, but still, it might, eventually. I might have to go back to that house. I got so scared when she told me; I'm still scared. I almost went back to *my* secret place where I don't have a body and I can't be hurt, even though I can see what's happening, hear my dad telling that lump on the bed that it was all my fault, my mother's fault for leaving, a man has needs, and if I loved him, I'd help him out, and it's okay for fathers to love their little boys like that in the dark. And I'd be floating in the air, in the dark, and it would be all right. But I thought about you, telling you, and Malachi and Hazel, Mr. and Mrs. Clark, and Malachi's dad. I didn't go to my secret place. I came to see you. C'mon, Russ; it's time to go. I don't need my secret place anymore and neither do you."

Jeff stopped to slow down his breathing, to hold his hand against his chest, to slow down his heart.

"Now, Jeff—" Miss McNeil began, but the little boy in her lap sat up. His foxtail and ears had vanished. The boy climbed down and stood up and he got bigger and bigger until he was normal-sized and Miss McNeil began to fade away, her edges blurred, her features a scrawl, as was everything else around them.

"I guess I'm ready to go back," Russell said, sighing. "But I sure do like it here."

Jeff grinned and got up from the bed just as it vanished. Holding hands, they started to walk out of the dissolving bedroom when

Russell stopped and picked the glass jar filled with the black liquid. It was the only thing that remained solid. He looked at Jeff.

"What do I do with it? I've had this forever."

"Do you still need it?" Jeff asked.

"Well, sort of," Russell said, looking sheepish, "but not like this, all locked up in this jar, boiling like this." He unscrewed the top and emptied the jar onto the floor. The black liquid oozed and bubbled, forming little balls, which, as they dissolved, scattered and disappeared. "C'mon, let's get outta here, Jeff," Russell said and tossed the jar away, into the disappearing wall of the bedroom. "I won't listen to those monsters anymore. I'll try really hard not to, anyway."

By the time they got to the hallway, it was almost transparent. The hallway was all that was left, except for the blue sky and the purple clouds and the scrawled grass. The manila was fading into what Jeff could only call no color.

"I'm sorry your dad hurt you that way, Jeff. Why didn't you tell me before?" Russell asked as they stood in the schoolyard. Behind them the hallway collapsed, as if it had been plastic at the edge of a fire.

"I was too scared."

"Well, which way do we go from here?"

"There's only one way, Russ. The way you came in."

Jeff opened his eyes and yawned. The afternoon sunlight had gone; it was almost night. Russell pushed back the quilt and slowly sat up, a small, half-crooked smile on his face. Hazel and Malachi cheered. They could all smell the food downstairs: meatloaf, onions, bread. In a minute, Jeanie would be hollering up the stairs for Russell to come on down.

"I'm really hungry," Russell said shyly, and looked at the others as if he had been given new eyes.

Jeff

Sunday night Mrs. Clark came into Jeff's bedroom and sat down quietly on the edge of the bed. "Jeff, honey, I know you're scared about seeing your father and I don't blame you, but his psychiatrist has assured me he is making progress. Jeff, are you listening to me?"

Jeff was in bed, with his face turned to the wall. "Yes, I'm listening. My dad promised me he wouldn't touch me that way again lots and lots of times, and he broke his promise just as many times."

"This time will be different. He'll be supervised and so will you.

At first, you will stay here, and he will come visit once a week and we will always be here. Things will be different," she said and reached out to smooth Jeff's hair.

"My dad said the same thing every time he promised me it wouldn't happen again. And he said the same thing after each time he broke his promise: *I'm so sorry; it won't happen again, Jeff, I promise. I'll never do it again, I promise. Things are going to be different.* Every single time," Jeff said and turned from the wall into his pillow.

"You said you would try to stop this from happening. You said you would fight to keep me. You promised I would be safe. I'll hide when he comes here; I won't let him see me."

"Jeff, you will be safe." She waited a long pause for Jeff to answer her, then sighed, smoothed his hair again, and got up and left. Jeff lay very still for a long time, his face buried in his pillow. He wished he never had to leave his bed again, that he could stay hidden beneath his pillow forever.

"He'll find me, no matter where I hide," Jeff whispered to himself. "He found me before when I tried to hide from him at night. He always knew where to look: the closet, under the bed, the bathroom, the garage, under the house. He always found me."

But this time things were different: he could fly.

But where would he go? They were all supposed to go through the fairy-gate on Halloween—which was eighteen days away—if they found the gate, although Malachi was positive they would. Malachi was sick again—Jeff could barely feel Malachi's good night in his mind, a quick whisper that had become a nightly ritual the last week. And Russell. Russell's dad had yanked out the phone Saturday and Malachi was the only one who could mind-speak. Hazel? Maybe. No matter. Tomorrow, when his dad's dark red Honda Civic pulled into the Clarks' driveway for the first supervised visit, Jeff would be gone.

Monday morning breakfast had been strained and Jeff was relieved when it was over, even though Mr. Clark had fixed his favorite: pancakes and bacon, with hot maple syrup and Five-Alive Juice. And they had let him sleep late. The food had tasted wooden, but Jeff had eaten everything anyway, while the Clarks were relentlessly cheerful. Both had taken the day off and over pancakes and between cups of coffee, talked about what all they would do. The Art Museum downtown. Or Pullen Park. Drive to Chapel Hill to the Planetarium. Or to Durham, to the Life Science Museum, with the huge scale-model dinosaurs. Jeff would like that, wouldn't he? Of course, he would—Jeff *loved* dinosaurs.

The one thing nobody mentioned which for sure was going to happen was that Jeff's father was coming for his visit between three and four o'clock.

"Well, Jeff, what would you like to do this morning?" Mr. Clark asked for what Jeff thought must be the hundredth time. "Made up your mind?"

"I think I would like to stay right here," Jeff said slowly, pushing one last bit of pancake around in leftover syrup. "Play with my dinosaurs." *And fly away.* First, to Russell's. Then, maybe to Malachi's. And hide until Halloween. Yes, his dad would find him, as he had done before, but maybe, just maybe, with Malachi and Hazel and Russell with him, he would be safe. Finally and truly safe, as he was not even here with the Clarks. After all, they hadn't kept their promise, either. Maybe all four of them would just fly forever and ever, circling and swooping in the sky, playing tag in the clouds and never, never coming down to the earth. They wouldn't have to go to Faerie then—just into the sky.

Jeff felt the Clarks' eyes on him as he walked out of the kitchen and down the hall to his bedroom. It was also a relief to shut the door. Now, Jeff thought, as he stood in the middle of his room: which dinosaur shall I take with me? And when should I leave? He glanced at the clock on his desk: just after 9:30. At ten? Maybe 10:30—no later than that. If he waited over an hour, Jeff was sure the Clarks would come into his room and talk and try to keep him company. Be Good Foster Parents.

10:30 on the dot, Jeff decided. Just one more hour.

Malachi

Malachi ran out the back door, across the back yard, and jumped over the chain-link fence. Why oh why oh why had he not gone to the library when his dad and Uncle Jack had, just fifteen minutes ago? *I'll be safe for half-an-hour, Dad. Just thirty minutes. I have to talk to Jeff, Russell, and Hazel, okay? They might fly over. It won't matter if anybody sees them, not now. Yes, I know, it's still Monday morning rush hour, but, Dad, who is going to work? There won't be much of a rush hour. Half an hour, tops.*

After his dad and Uncle Jack had left, both reluctantly, Malachi had settled down on his bed, the twelve-pointed star in his hand, his eyes closed, his *seeking* tossed out before him as if he were a fisherman, casting out his line. Where was Russell? There—*there*. And angry and something was happening— It was then the knocking started, a loud and insistent pounding on the front door, and even on the walls of the house. Malachi's fishing line snapped and vanished and he was back, solid and present on his bed. The air smelled pungent, as if someone had just lit and blown out a match. The pounding got louder and louder.

They weren't pounding the door; they were pounding the magic barrier made by the talisman around Malachi's neck. He felt the pounding in the talisman itself: the star throbbed in his hand. Malachi squeezed the star so hard its points cut into his hand. *There.* He could *see* outside the house, who was there: the Fomorii, black and dark, reptilian, their red eyes, their yellow teeth, and sharp claws. And five humans, two men and three women. Thomas was one of the men, and one of the women was . . . Mrs. Collins. His teacher. Thomas moved his arms in slow circles, stopping after the third circle to toss what looked like dried leaves at the house. He talked the entire time, but his words were slurred and in a strange accent.

I should call 911. No, the police stopped answering those calls days ago. Too many and not enough police. Besides, if I did, would the police see the Fomorii? Or just five people in business clothes? Would they see Thomas working witchcraft?

The house shook and Malachi heard a cracking noise, and Thomas's voice higher and sharper.

He ran.

Once he had cleared the back fence, Malachi could hear them behind him, howling, crying out his name, yelling for him to stop, it was all right, they weren't going to hurt him, just protect him, keep him safe. *They're from Social Services, they are nice people; you can trust me, Malachi, I'm your teacher . . . I used to baby-sit for you, my dad is your Uncle Jack; our dads are best friends . . .*

By the time Malachi reached Vandora Springs Road and was airborne, he was completely luminous, a glowing boy-comet, trailing sparks behind him. He glanced once over his shoulders at the monsters and their human allies behind him: *They're eating the sparks, the light—they are drawing the light out of me.* Once across the street, Malachi turned and slapped the air back at them. A shimmering wave rolled across the street, knocking over a car and a truck, and the Fomorii and their five people down flat against the ground, like cornstalks after a hard rain.

Malachi didn't look back again. He flew as fast as he could to the library, landing in a hiss on the wet grass behind the staff entrance in the back. He stepped in, sparks popping and exploding in the air behind him. Mrs. Carmichael was the only one in the staff workroom, staring intently at a computer's blank screen. Malachi guessed his entrance must have shorted it out. Right above her head was a big calendar, with each day in October marked off by a pumpkin, except for today. No one had put a pumpkin on the 14th yet. He took a deep breath and his luminosity faded out. Only if someone looked really hard would they have been able to see the glowing light in his eyes.

"Mrs. Carmichael, where's my dad? I need to see him right away. It's kind of an emergency."

Mrs. Carmichael jumped and turned. "Lord, you scared me child," she said breathlessly, her hand on her chest. "Why aren't you in school? Does your daddy know you aren't in school?"

"Mrs. Carmichael, the schools closed this past Friday. They aren't open anywhere in North Carolina," Malachi said. She knew that; everybody in Wake County, in the whole state—probably the whole country, the world—knew that. It had been on every radio and TV station, in the *News and Observer*—everywhere.

Mrs. Carmichael looked puzzled. She took off her glasses and rubbed her eyes, looking then, Malachi thought, even older than she was. How old was she? Almost sixty? Probably over sixty.

"I've got to see him, Mrs. Carmichael. And Uncle Jack. Are they at the reference desk? I'll go look," Malachi said and started to walk past her.

"He's working. You shouldn't bother him right now. You know that; you used to be such a sweet little boy. Your daddy's probably with a patron. I don't know where Jack Ruggles is—poor, sad man. Why aren't you in school? Why—" She reached out to stop him, to hold him back.

Malachi stared at her. Mrs. Carmichael wasn't even looking at him as she talked. She was staring at the wall behind him, her head framed by small paper pumpkins. Her words sounded slow and thick, as if coming from under water, or through syrup.

"You can't. Bother. Him. Go—"

"I've got to see my dad and Uncle Jack before it's too late," Malachi said and rushed past her, pushing her hands away, feeling *them* pulling at him, sucking at his energy. In the few seconds it took for Malachi to run from the staff workroom to his father at the reference desk, he glowed again, trailing bits and pieces of fire that scorched the carpet.

"Dad, help, help, Dad—I can't hold it in anymore. They're try-ing to get it, get me, it's what they want—they eat it. Dad!"

"Leave your father alone, go home, go to school," Mrs. Carmichael cried out as she staggered out of the workroom, like a wind-up toy about to sputter out.

His father turned around, practically knocking down the woman who was asking him a question. Malachi couldn't quite make it across the room. He stopped a few feet away from the reference desk, wrapping his arms around himself, but it was too late. Everything was too late. He could see the Fomorii and Thomas and Mrs. Collins just outside, through the glass front library doors. Uncle Jack, who had been at the magazine racks, had started running across the room, yelling that he was coming, but he was too late. Malachi's arms unfolded their grip of his sides and lightning crack-led from his hands, blue-white forks leaping to the overhead fluorescent lights. The lights exploded in a rain of fire and plastic and glass. Then, the lightning, now a fire-snake, raced around the ceiling, the walls, in and out of windows, popping, breaking glass, scorching the air, leaving licking flames in its wake. Every light in the library went out. The fire alarms went off, beating the air with noise. The air reeked of ozone, of heat, of fire and smoke. People ran, screaming and crying, for the doors. One man ran so hard and so fast he knocked the glass out of the front door, shredding his hands and his face with broken glass.

"Oh my God, ohmyGod, omiGod," Mrs. Carmichael moaned, over and over, swaying back and forth, her hands covering her face. "He's the devil, that child is the devil—he's Satan—Saataaan . . ." Mrs. Carmichael's last word was lost in a long, sirenlike scream, rising and falling, in rhythm with the fire alarms. She turned, ran, and fell, as pieces of the roof fell, burning, around her.

"I can't stop, I can't stop it, they're pulling it out of me, help, help me," Malachi wailed. The lightning rippled down the walls and back up and down and into the carpet. The carpet started to smoke and then burst into flame, sending flames up the walls to meet those coming down.

Ben

Ben scooped up Malachi in his arms just as Jack reached them.

"Run, get the hell outta here, go, go, go," Jack said, pushing Ben on. By then the smoke was everywhere, thick and black.

"Go where? I can't see the doors and the fire—how do we get out of here? This smoke, . . ." Ben said, coughing.

"This way, I know it's this way," Jack yelled. "Follow me, we'll get out of here."

A book case fell then, and another, and Jack fell, Ben on top of him, dropping Malachi.

He looked up, coughing, and there they were: the monsters. Glowing red eyes, the fire whips. Thomas stood with them and a woman as well—Charlotte Collins. All of them, a frozen tableau, as the library burned around them, flaming books dropping off shelves. The Fomorii and Thomas and the woman stepped forward and one of the monsters snapped its whip, sparking into the smoke, at Malachi. Jack threw up his arm, deflecting the whip, his flesh scorching.

"Jack, don't—" Ben yelled, but too late. Jack tackled the monster, trying to wrestle it to the ground, until another Fomorii grabbed him and slung him toward the door. Ben stood slowly, his arms wrapped around his son, and stepped back. Did he hear sirens? What had taken the fire department so long—the Garner Volunteer Fire Department was less than a block away. He took another step back and screamed; a Fomorii was behind him.

"I'll take this," Thomas said and as the Fomorii peeled back Ben's arms, its claws sinking into his flesh, he took Malachi. "And this," he added as he ripped the star off Malachi's neck. He screamed then, dropping the boy. "Damn thing burns," Thomas snarled and tossed it in the direction his father had been thrown.

"Pick him up," Thomas said to a Fomorii. "Take him. Go."

Ben tried to move, but the Fomorii held him back.

"Too late, now it's your turn," Thomas said and gestured at the monster holding Ben. It threw him into a glass wall. The shattering was the last thing Ben heard.

Ben sat on the hood of a car in the library parking lot. How long had he been there? How long had he lain in the broken glass? When had Jack shaken him awake and got him to stand, to walk? When had the firemen come, one of them helping both him and Jack away from the fire? How long had Jack sat by him, picking glass out of Ben's hair, as they watched the firemen and their huge hoses trying to stop the inferno? When had Jack put the twelve-pointed star, its chain broken and bloodstained, into Ben's hands?

Ben looked down. The star glowed faintly against his skin, its even fainter vibration tingling.

He didn't ask Jack for any answers. He knew Jack wouldn't have any. The biggest question was the worst: where had Thomas and the Fomorii and that woman taken his son? They had disappeared into the smoke and the fire, carrying Malachi, using the light of his body to show them way out of the burning library. No, the biggest question was how would he get Malachi back?

Russell

Larry White swung. Russell jumped back, feeling the air move in front of his face. He had *moved*—very slightly—his father's hand aside. It was all he could do. Dodging his father's fists, with magic and by being quick on his feet, was taking more out of Russell than he thought. His sides hurt. He tasted blood from his lips and his eyes. One side of his face was already swelling and he couldn't see very well out of his right eye.

"You'd better hold still, boy, or it's gonna be worse when I do get holt of you. Just tell me why you let that goddamn faggot touch you. You a faggot just like him? I ain't having no faggot for a son; I'll kill you first. Tell me the truth, boy. Yer just like your whore mama, except you whore for boys." Larry White swung again, hitting air.

Two kitchen chairs lay on the floor. The salt shaker had rolled up against the refrigerator; the pepper shaker lay against the stove. The sugar bowl was in pieces and sugar was everywhere. Russell could hear the grains crunching beneath his and his father's shoes.

"He didn't touch me. Malachi's daddy is a good man," Russell said softly, stepping back just out of his father's reach. He flicked his right hand quickly: a small *push* against his father's chest. Larry White jerked, as if something had hit him, and stood still, breathing hard. "He's a better man than you'll ever be. I hate you, you son of a bitch."

"Don't talk to me that way, boy. Yer asking for me to beat the shit out of you. I've fed you, clothed you, took care of you when that sorry-ass whore mother of yours wouldn't. I ain't having no queer shit in my house; your teacher told me the truth about you going over to that queer's house, staying there real late with that other little fella, Jeff. He felt y'all up, didn't he? My son ain't gonna be no damn queer. Hell of a world—damn schools are closed, people are glowing like damn light bulbs everywhere you look—"

"You son of a bitch, that teacher is a damn liar, and you aren't ever going to hurt anybody ever again," Russell whispered as he retreated one more step. Then, he took a deep breath and *pushed*, harder and with more force than he had ever done before. His father, wide-eyed in shock, lifted up off the floor and slammed into the refrigerator door. Larry White hung there for a long second and then slid to the ground, his eyes closed, blood at the edge of his mouth. He didn't move.

Russell stood very still, waiting to be sure his father didn't get back up. He glanced at the clock in the microwave: ten. Jeanie would be home in two hours; she was only working half-days in the last weeks of her pregnancy.

Larry White still didn't move.

Russell ran, out of the kitchen and up the stairs to his bedroom. He grabbed the red fox from the manger and then *pushed* the window out of its frame, nails popping, wood splintering, the glass shattering and cascading down the roof. Then, with the fox safe in his pocket, Russell flew out the window.

Jeff and Russell

Jeff had just about decided to take the little blue rex and the stuffed apatosaurus when he heard a tapping at his window. He looked up to see a face—Russell's face—pressed against the glass. For an instant, Jeff didn't recognize Russell. When Russell *pushed* open the window and slowly crawled inside, Jeff saw why. One eye was swollen shut. A big, purple bruise covered one side of his face; dried blood made a dark mustache on his upper lip. His shirt was torn.

"Russ, what happened?" Jeff whispered. The blue rex that had been hovering above Jeff fell to his bed with a dull thump.

"I killed him. I think I killed him, Jeff. My dad. He wasn't moving when I left. I got my fox and I flew away. I came here. I waited outside for a long time—I wasn't sure you would want me like this, after what I did." Russell sat down on Jeff's bed by the blue rex.

"You killed your dad?"

"I don't know. I think so. I *pushed* him, Jeff, harder than I have ever *pushed* anything. He wasn't moving; there was blood. I don't know," Russell said. He spoke slowly, as if talking hurt his face and he talked to the floor, as if afraid to look Jeff in the eye.

"Maybe you just knocked him out."

"Maybe. What do we do now? I can't ever go—I won't ever go back there again."

"We can't stay here, either. I've been meaning to tell you, but, you know, with the shadows and you getting stuck back there in your head—my father is coming to visit me today. I was going to run away to *your* house or Malachi's—but he hasn't *spoken* to me this morning, either."

Russell frowned, looking up for the first time since he had

arrived. "Something isn't right. He always mind-speaks us—every day, every morning—"

They both felt it at the same time—a mind-scream: *help, help me, help me, the dark ones, the red-eyed . . .* The words slammed around in both their heads like sharp, tiny rocks caroming off the sides of their skulls. Then, as suddenly as they had come, the words were gone, swallowed into a deep silence.

"Let's go find Hazel," Jeff said. "And Malachi's dad. They can fix your face and check on your dad and tell us what to do. C'mon— here, hold my hand if you need to."

"Okay."

They flew out the window, followed by the blue rex.

Jeff, Russell, and Hazel

"Hazel, honey, doesn't that little blond-haired friend of yours, Malachi, live in Garner?" Mrs. Richards asked her granddaughter mid-morning Monday. Hazel and her grandmother were down in the studio. Hazel sat on the floor, reading as her grandmother worked at the wheel. A radio sat on a table near the wheel. Around Mrs. Richards's head was a thin black headphone, linked to the radio by an even thinner black wire, like a tiny snake. Alexander lay stretched out beside Hazel, snoozing.

Hazel looked up. "Yes, Malachi lives in Garner. His father is a librarian at the public library there. I told you that."

Her grandmother pulled off the headphones and looked at Hazel. She wiped her hands on her smock and came and sat down by her granddaughter on the floor. "He's on the news," she said gently, one hand on Hazel's shoulder. "The Garner public library burned down this morning and he's one of the people missing. No body, no nothing. His father won't speak to the reporters—won't even come to the door—"

"Malachi's not dead," Hazel said slowly, staring at her grand-mother's pottery wheel. Of that, she was certain. She would have *felt* his death, like a sudden chill, or a tremor in the earth and in her body. Now she *felt*: nothing. And that was almost scarier than Malachi being dead. Nothing. No whispery echo of his thoughts, no warm brightness, nothing.

Her grandmother pulled Hazel to her chest, her arms folded around her granddaughter. "Honey, I am so sorry. I know he was your friend, but the radio said the library burned to the ground. He was last seen inside; there was no way he could have escaped. Once

the ashes cool," she said softly into Hazel's hair, "they'll look again —
for his remains. There's always something left."

"No, Grandma," Hazel and pulled away and out of her grand-
mother's arms. "Malachi's not dead. I'm going to go up to my room."
She stood up and nudged the cat awake with her toe. "Come on,
Alexander."

Her grandmother sighed. "All right."

Hazel smiled at her grandmother and went upstairs, Alexander
bumping against her side. Alex must have his own fairy glamour,
Hazel thought. Otherwise, even though her grandparents were
equally oblivious to just about everything outside of pottery and
computers, they would surely see the beast bumping his head into
Hazel's legs was the size of a collie. Wouldn't they? She laid her
hand lightly on Alex's broad back, just enough to feel the vibrations
from his deep, low purring. And now he mind-talks, she thought,
looking down at the wide, flat head.

Then, as she came to the top of the second floor stairs, Hazel felt
the cat's mind touch hers, as gently as he touched her face with his
paws: *Waiting inside.*

"Who's waiting inside — inside my room? Can you tell me who?
Is it safe to go in?" Hazel asked just outside the door, which was
covered with a huge circuitry map, something her grandfather had
picked up at IBM. The door was closed and she knew she had left
it open.

Alex bumped her leg and looked up at her, the blue in his eyes
brighter than she could remember. *Inside. Waiting. Boys waiting
inside. Safe.*

Each word, sharp and clear, as if they had just been cut from
new paper.

I hear you, Alex, I hear you in —

Open door. Boys.

Hazel opened her bedroom door, and there, sitting in the middle of her bed, were Russell and Jeff. The window was open and
a touch of wind fluttered her white curtains. A big, purple bruise
covered one side of Russell's face. One eye was a smaller, darker
bruise inside the purple. His shirt was torn and Hazel could see
more bruises on Russell's chest. A blue T-rex hovered about Jeff's
head. Before anybody spoke, the dinosaur fell to the bed.

Golden boy trouble.

"I killed him, Haze, I killed him —"

"We ran away, they were going to make me see my dad, I don't
want to ever see him again —"

Golden boy hurt dark.

"Something's wrong with Malachi. What are we going to do—" Hazel slammed the door.

"Stop talking all at the same time. You, too," she added, glaring at Alex who stared hard at her for a moment and then sat down on his haunches and starting licking his forepaws. "I heard something bad happened in Garner, on the radio—I mean, my grandmother did—the library burned down. What happened—one at a time. Russ, who did you kill? Did you really *kill* somebody? You first, then Jeff. Let me sit down first, okay?" *How did I get to be leader all of a sudden,* Hazel thought as she turned her desk chair around to face the two boys on her bed. *Was I second-in-command after Malachi?* Somehow, knowing something bad had happened to Malachi and that now Hazel was the one expected to decide made everything more real and scarier. *Malachi hasn't been kidnapped by regular criminals; he was kidnapped by magic.* And whatever Russ had done, or thought he had done, was magic, too. *We need an adult—we're just kids.*

But for now, she was in charge.

"Okay, Russ, talk."

Hazel knew, from little things Jeff and Russell had said, that both came from families not at all like her own. But just how different was another matter. Listening to Russell tell how his father had hit him so many times for so long a time ("I don't really remember him ever not doing it, now that I think about it.") and all the things his father had said made Hazel feel as if she had stepped inside some dark and harsh and cold place, where no light came. Jeff's story of what his father had done and then seeing the scars on Russell's back and legs made Hazel feel ill. What must they feel like *here,* she wondered. Or was it that different here—where she would be invisible for days before either one of her grandparents noticed her? Her grandmother had spent the night in the hospital—but, once Hazel was well, she had become invisible again. But invisible or not, Hazel knew she was safe. It *was* different here. Was coming into her house a little like coming into the light? Into a church? And—for the first time— could she come back from Faerie once there? Russell and Jeff would never want to, she was sure of that. But, she knew she might. "What do we do now?" Jeff asked when he had finished talking. "Russell and me can't go back. We won't go back."

Golden boy man.

"Huh?" Russell jerked his head around to stare at Alexander. "Can he talk? Malachi's daddy—is that what the cat means? He can talk, can't he?"

"Telepathy. Mind-speech," Hazel said, wishing that for just a few minutes she could turn on her computer and call up her valley with its tall, white trees and big meadows and lie down in the sweet-smelling grasses and do nothing but stare up at the sky. Or better, because the valley was *there*, a nice, complicated computer game with good guys and bad guys and tunnels and secret passages and hidden doors and a treasure. A game that would last for a long time, so long she would be lost in it and nothing outside the game would or could possibly matter except when her grandmother or grandfather called her to come and eat.

"No, Alex can't talk—it's mind-speech, like I said, like Malachi does. He started—never mind. This is the clearest he has ever been. I think Alex means that Malachi's dad can help us find out what happened. And that we should go and find Malachi's daddy." *As soon as we can. Then an adult can be in charge and not me.*

"It's bad," Jeff said. "Whatever happened to Mal is really bad. I can feel it—"

"The red-eyed monsters. Those shadow-things," Russell said and shuddered. "They have him. And—they want all of us, all four of us—they need all four of us," he added.

"How do you know that?" Hazel said, wondering what she was going to tell her grandmother when she brought down two guests from her bedroom or that she and these two strange boys and Alex all had to fly away for a while. Really fly away. *Well, Grandma, you were so busy doing pottery downstairs I guess you didn't hear them come in. Can they stay? Oh, for a few days, for the rest of their lives.*

"I had a dream. I had a dream this morning," Russell said, shaking his head and looking at his hands. "In the dream all four of us were on a baseball diamond, each one of us on a base; Malachi was at home plate. It was night and there was a wind. Malachi raised his arms and this thin, blue light came out from each hand and drew a line in the air until it touched me. I was on first, you were on second; Jeff was on third. We all raised our hands and the light passed through all of us, and back around and through Malachi, over and over, getting brighter and stronger each time. It was like a web: the light passed between each of us—I mean, between you and Malachi, me and Jeff, me and you—until there was a blue web everywhere. The light got so bright I couldn't see the stars or the moon. And I *knew* each of you—I really knew you in ways and in places that I can't explain just yet," Russell said and glanced quickly at Jeff and then back to his hands. "We were safe as long as we were together, all four of us, and we were powerful. The red-eyed things want that power."

Jeff nodded his head. "I guess we find Malachi's dad then, and see about rescuing him. Right?"

"Right," Hazel agreed.

Gold boy father home now.

"Okay, Alex. I guess we just fly over there."

"Uh, before we go, can we have some lunch first?" Russell asked. "I'm starving."

Hazel thought a minute. Maybe she wouldn't have to tell her grandmother and grandfather anything. They could all fly over to Malachi's house, talk to Mr. Tyson, and Jeff and Russell could stay there—well, not tell her grandparents anything right away. Besides, her grandmother wasn't likely to come up from her studio until nightfall. Once she got going on a project, Mrs. Richards would single-mindedly follow it through, in voluntary self-exile with the wheel and the clay. Her grandfather was the same way around computers.

"Y'all stay here. I'll go get some bread and peanut butter and stuff. We'll fix something in here. Then we will go over to see Malachi's father."

Thomas

Thomas woke. He sat up in bed. Where was he? For a long moment, he couldn't remember: his head seemed filled with fog and wind. Then someone stirred beside him and Thomas looked to see Charlotte Collins, naked, her face buried in the pillow. She turned and looked at him with one eye, muttered something and went back to sleep.

Now he remembered: they were in her house, waiting for darkness. After capturing the boy at the Garner library, and after the Fomorii had left, he and Charlotte had come here.

"But why can't we go with you—where are you going?" Thomas had asked. It had been only minutes after taking the boy, and Thomas, Charlotte, and the Fomorii were just down the street, hidden inside the thick, black smoke that was all around them. Where were the DSS people—had they really been there? But he had seen them fall when Malachi had thrown the ball of hardened air. Thomas shook his head: that wasn't important. What *he* was doing now, what he had just done—that was important. Thomas could hear, faintly, the fire and police sirens and the shouting. It was as if a barrier, a curtain, had been pulled, between them and the rest of the world.

"It's not yet time. You have only the one child—the most powerful one, the key, yes, but we must try for the other three to complete the tetrad and thus have all the power. With all four we can be sure we can prevent the gates from opening on Samhain. They will all try to rescue him—we'll take the other three then. Until then, guard him," one Fomorii said in its thick voice.

"Where do we keep him?" Charlotte asked.

"Where you called us, where you drew the circle and lit the blue fire. Where you killed your husband and we feasted on his heart and brains," the second Fomorii said and touched Malachi lightly with one clawed hand. As if a switch had been flipped, a red light enveloped the unconscious child. Thomas could feel the redness against his own skin as he held Malachi on his shoulder; the light was surprisingly cold and rough. "That will hold him in stasis."

Then the Fomorii had vanished. The two creatures had grown more and more transparent until they dissolved into the smoke. Thomas rubbed his eyes and waved his free hand in front of him, feeling foolish; he should be used to magic by now. He was a witch, wasn't he? And walking away, Malachi on his shoulder, Charlotte beside him, getting into his car, and driving away—too simple. But it had worked. But then, Thomas thought, why not? Couldn't the Fomorii have just as easily cast a glamour over his car as well? Wouldn't he be able to do so himself, once he had the boy's power? It wasn't as if everything around the library wasn't in chaos: smoke, lingering fire, burnt people screaming, the wounded crying and moaning, firemen, policemen.

Thomas had never taken a woman as roughly as he had taken Charlotte when they got to her house. Nor had a woman ever treated him so roughly, Thomas thought, as he lightly touched the scratches and bites all over his arms, legs, and chest. But it had been as if they had been compelled. The very air had felt charged with sexual electricity, an overpowering current that was in, around, and through them, catching them both in an explosion of flesh.

How long ago had that been? Thomas couldn't remember, but their fucking had seemed to go on for hours. He got to his feet slowly, making sure Charlotte stayed asleep. He wasn't tired at all. Naked, Thomas paced the living room, the kitchen, in and out of the bedroom, touching the sleeping Charlotte, the bathroom, and finally, he stood over the sleeping child on his couch: Malachi the Golden-eyed One, the fulcrum, the lever, the key, the one who could seal the door. The shimmering red moved as if it were a second skin, shifting and stirring as the boy stirred in his sleep, rippling across his face like blood. Malachi was his, his, his, *his*. And when he had the other three—and Thomas had no doubt he would and soon, they would come like flies to honey—he, Thomas, would have the ultimate power. He would be able to open and close the gates between here and there, between this earth and the earth of the red-eyed ones, the Fomorii, and they would come and bend the knee to *him*, the King of Darkness.

From the journal of Ben Tyson, Tuesday night, October 15

I don't know where to begin. Once upon a time?

That's not true; I do know where to begin. I begin with what I know I must do next; what Hazel and Russell and Jeff and Jack told me we were all going to do next. We are going to rescue Malachi from Thomas and the forces of evil.

Once I would have cringed to write such a cliché: the forces of evil. But it's true. The forces of evil—Thomas Ruggles and Charlotte Collins and whomever else is in league with them and the Fomorii monsters—have Malachi and they are going to use him as some sort of energy source to both pry open the gates so the Fomorii can come here and seal the gates, so that the changelings cannot go home. They have to go home, Faerie needs them. And Malachi has to go home, or he will die. For the want of a nail, the kingdom was lost. Is that it? No. He's my son and I am going to save him. If I don't get Malachi through a gate at Samhain he will die. If I don't rescue him from Thomas, he will die.

Why is God letting this happen? God—God? Oh, God? Are You listening?

The monsters have my son. MY SON. The monsters have my son. They are hurting my son.

Russell and Jeff are here. I'm hiding them. Russell ran away from home after his dad tried to beat him up—kill him, Russell says—until Russell roughed him up with magic. Jeff ran away from his foster parents' home because he is afraid of even seeing his father again, who sexually abused him. I brought Jack home because his house is empty and he has nowhere else to go. Hazel ran back—no, flew back— home. She will be back.

I have Malachi's twelve-pointed star in my hand. It is glowing and pulsating and pulling. It knows where Malachi is—a tracker? A directional finder or a magical compass?

Jack wants to try and talk to Thomas one last time, to try and find the place inside where there is no evil, where the Thomas he remembers as a boy lives, the Thomas Valeria touched so many years ago. Jack insists such a place is there.

I don't think so.

So, this star will lead us to the child—but none of us are very wise.

I have accumulated signs of protection, amulets, charms, crystals—any and everything I could find that wards against black magic. I am thinking I should ask Father Jamey to come, with a barrel of holy water.

I will ask him tomorrow. After Jack tries to reach Thomas.

VI
Dark and Light
Wednesday, October 16 - Monday, October 28

Jack and Thomas

JACK GLANCED FOR THE THIRD TIME OUT THE WIN-dow of the Hillsborough Street Waffle House. He wanted to be pacing back and forth, moving, doing *something* to burn up this energy and anxiety. Take his arm with one fell swoop and clean off the table: sugar, Equal, Sweet 'N Low, syrup, menus, salt and pepper. Or smash the syrup bottle against the window—which would break—bottle or window or both? A big splat of maple brown on the window? No, not maple, boysenberry. Burgundy drops. What the hell was a boysenberry anyway—something Waffle House had made up? Drumming his fingers on the Formica just wasn't enough to ease his tension. Gulping down coffee heavily laced with Equal and little packets of non-fat non-dairy creamer, which littered the table in front of him, was only a minor distraction. Why in the hell was he bothering to use Equal and non-fat creamer anyway? If the entire world was falling apart, what did a few clogged arteries and some extra calories matter? Besides, he'd lost a few pounds since Hilda's death. Eating had just seemed sort of pointless. Ben forced him to eat, and he did, to avoid the lecture, not because he really wanted or cared to.

No, Jack thought and glanced out the window for the fourth time, as a car passed, not falling apart. Re-arranging, changing, transforming. He shook his head and took another sip of lukewarm coffee. He was tired of thinking about what was happening: the transformation of reality into something different. He wanted the change to be done, finished, over, and for life to go on, regardless of the shape it finally had. At least the Waffle House was still open, until sundown, anyway. Everything closed then—except for hospitals. The governor had tried to keep gas stations open at night, but the owners had simply refused. Folks could just buy their gas before dark—and besides, who was driving after dark, anyway. Jack looked out the window for the fifth time at the Amoco station across the street. The line of cars snaked down Hillsborough Street. It was sort of comforting to see people standing by the pumps, holding the gas hose and watching the price and gallons add up. Yes, they were in a hurry, but at least they were out.

According to President Bush, all this would be over in two weeks. As if anybody believed Bush anymore. His sunspots theory for explaining the monsters crawling out of the Great Dismal Swamp had been given just as much credence as his ozone theory as to why all the weirdness was happening in North Carolina. Bush's current theory was that North Carolina was suffering a mass psychosis. North Carolina was under quarantine and federal troops searched cars crossing state lines on the interstates. Cars, trucks, buses—any vehicle with North Carolina tags—were forced to turn around. *That* had made Governor Martin *really* happy.

Jack wondered idly if the other rumors were true. The lieutenant governor, supported by the North Carolina National Guard, was planning a coup. A Republican had gotten the state into this mess—only the second one since Reconstruction—about time a Democrat got into office to set things straight. A coup.

Yeah, right. Jack knew why everything in Raleigh was going to close down at sunset, why Raleigh and every other city in the state would become a ghost town after dark: the ghosts were real. Malachi was the reason. Ben's son was the focal point. And Thomas and his witch-friends and the red-eyed monsters had the boy. They were going to use Malachi like some sort of catalyst or energizer to control the gate opening for their own ends. Jack shuddered, and for a moment, wished he had brought Ben and the other three children with him so he wouldn't have to face Thomas alone. None of them even knew Jack had set up this meeting or what he was going to offer Thomas in exchange for the boy's life.

Ben wouldn't have agreed to come; he wouldn't have agreed to even try Jack's plan. As for the other children, Jack was sort of scared of them. Not Hazel so much, the little girl seemed almost normal, her long, light-brown hair in a thick braid bouncing behind her and her quick, sharp mind. She reminded Jack of Hilda and even a little of his first wife, Thomas's mother, Kathleen. He had been attracted to both women because of their keen intellects. Poor Kathleen. If she were alive—could she have stopped Thomas? Or would she have joined him? If half of what Thomas said happened when he was with her was true—but it was too late to undo that.

Jeff and Russell—the two boys—on the other hand, made Jack uncomfortable. They both seemed haunted, with their glowing green eyes, pointed ears, and now Russell's hair was becoming fire-colored: red, orange, and yellow. Yes, Hazel's eyes were silvery and luminous and she did have pointed ears, too. It wasn't how the boys looked so much. Rather it was how they used their magic so casually, flying and floating and moving things here and there. Jack knew Hazel flew to Ben's house, but she always knocked on the door. Maybe, Jack thought, it is more than just casual magic—rather the sense he had of the power each boy had, a power they weren't quite aware of yet, and would have no idea how to use, but was still there, waiting, like a huge cat, ready to pounce. Besides, the two boys were dangerous for Ben in far more normal ways. DSS and the police were looking for them, calling, asking questions—even, Jack was sure, following Ben around Garner—

"Warm up your coffee?"

Jack looked away from the window and nodded at the waitress. Worrying about DSS and the police was a waste of energy—at least it was right now. Thomas was his focus right now, and what Jack was going to say to him—

Thomas Ruggles, his only child, pushed the Waffle House door open and came inside. He stood still in front of the counter, scanning the restaurant for Jack. Jack was glad for the minute and that he had selected the booth farthest from the door. For just a brief while, he could really look at his son, the son Jack hadn't seen since Hilda's death. This boy—his son—the man—was thinner and paler. His eyes were turning red. Thomas's already dark brown hair was even darker, almost black—a dull, flat black. Were Thomas's ears pointed as well? *My God. Is my son turning into a Fomorii?* For who knew how many times, Jack wondered again what had gone wrong, what he had done wrong as a father. The divorce? But that had been over twelve years ago. Kathleen? Or had Thomas simply been predisposed toward evil from birth and it had only been a matter of where and when and how. But Jack couldn't remember any de-winged flies or turpentined cats. Why hadn't Valeria sensed all those years ago—weren't fairies supposed to be able to do that? Or had she and said nothing—this was how things were supposed to be. The thirteen-year-old Thomas had adored Valeria—did the man want her back in some weird way through her son? That was too simple—but wasn't Thomas being seduced by darkness just as simple? Jack wanted to blame Kathleen for what she had done to Thomas. But, even so, ultimately, Thomas had to have chosen this. He chose evil.

Thomas had seen him.

Jack made himself not look away as his son walked toward him, his almost-red eyes measuring him, adding, subtracting, dissecting. No, Valeria had no more power to see into a soul than any human—and that, Jack decided, was where the wrongness had to be, somewhere in the darkest nether regions of his son's soul. Had Thomas been born bad? Bad in the womb? Or made bad? God don't make junk, Jack remembered someone telling him. Then, why had God let this happen?

God didn't; Thomas chose this.

"Hello, Father, what do you want?" Thomas said as he sat down.

"You know what I want: Malachi back and before you can do some sort of irreparable harm to him." Father? Thomas had never called him that—he had always been Dad.

Thomas laughed and Jack felt as if he were being whipped by the sound.

"He's the promised one, Father. If we can control him, the changelings won't be able to get back to Faerie and their victory will mean nothing; they will wither and die. And when we finally triumph there, we will triumph here as well. Why should I give him to you?"

"Coffee?"

Thomas paused for a long moment before he answered the waitress. He stared at her with the same measuring and dissecting look. Jack wanted to hit him. *My son is gone, lost. I have no son; this thing here looks and sounds like him, but it's not my son. It's a monster. God lets monsters exist, doesn't he? It's what we do with them that matters.*

"Yes, coffee." Then Thomas turned back to Jack. "Well? Why should I give him back to you?"

"Malachi is dying, Thomas; you know that. If Ben can't get him and the others back to Faerie by Halloween, he'll die."

"So? After Halloween, I won't need him anymore. What could you give me for Malachi, anyway? What do you have that I want or need?"

Jack stared down into his coffee and then slowly looked up.

"You're wrong. I do have something you want and could use. Your power is fed by sacrifice—human sacrifice—isn't it?"

"The sacrifice of human cattle. No true person is put to the knife," Thomas said and sat back as the waitress sat down his cup.

"Cuppa coffee cream and sugar's on the table. Gitcha anythin' else?"

"No. Case in point, Father—see what I mean?"

The waitress shrugged and left. Everybody was crazy these days.

"I see a young woman trying to make a living—not a heifer," Jack said, his voice low and to his surprise, angry and almost savage.

Thomas laughed and held up his hands as if to block his father's words. "Easy, easy. There are other power sources," he said, glancing at the waitress as she wiped off the counter. "But sacrifice is the most powerful for covens—what did you have in mind? What can you offer me more powerful than Malachi?"

"A willing sacrifice—much more powerful than somebody drugged or magicked or whatever you do. The sacrifice of Abraham in reverse—that would be loaded with power, yes?" Jack tried to look at Thomas while he talked, but he couldn't face the red eyes.

"A willing sacrifice. Not drugged or enchanted. Alert and aware the entire time, even to the last moment? And Isaac and Abraham— yes, you've done your research. That would bring me great power. Enough to do what the dark ones want and need at Samhain. Enough to trade for Malachi? I don't know about that, Father. Let me think this over, ask the others. I'll call you tomorrow—"

"At Ben's house. I haven't lived at home since Hilda died."

"Tomorrow, then," Thomas said, with a slight wave of his hand to dismiss Hilda's death as the inconsequential act it was. Jack hated his son then, as if he had never hated anyone in his life. He had not known he could even hate this much. "Tell Ben to be careful: there are all kinds of monsters loose. Lousy coffee. Bye."

Jack watched him leave, trying to stop his hatred, his anger, knowing that what lay between them wasn't as wide a gap as he wanted to believe. *There but for the grace of God go I? But he is my son. No, he was my son. I have no son. He is my son and he has done—he is doing great evil. What did I do wrong? God, why is this happening to me? What have I done to deserve all this?*

Ben and Jack

"You did what? Are you crazy? Do you want to commit suicide? Thomas is a necromancer—a black witch—he kills people for power and you want to trade yourself for Malachi? Do you really think I am going to let you do this?"

"Don't yell at me, Ben," Jack said, looking away from him, away from breakfast and coffee and juice, not wanting to see the pity he was sure was there. Yes, he *did* want to sacrifice himself: for Hilda, for Malachi, for all the others dead or whose lives had been turned upside down because of his son and the evil his son had done. His son, whom he had raised—what had happened? Was it his fault? Could he have done anything to prevent all this? He kept coming back to the same questions, over and over again. Jack had taken down the family albums and the shoe boxes stuffed with photographs that needed to be sorted and put in albums and gone through them, over and over, examining them as if he were a jeweler, looking for flaws in a tiny diamond. Was the evil there in a photo of Tom at thirteen, wet and dripping by the pool? Or it was there in all the photos, an unseen shadow lurking, waiting, biding its time? He could find nothing: no clue, no one moment, no action of his. Had it happened in the years his wife had had custody? Just exactly what had happened in those three years? He would never know.

Ben had caught him and had yelled at him to stop: "It's not your fault. You were a good dad. Some people are just evil—or they choose it on their own." Ben repeated himself as he got up to get more coffee. "It's not your fault. Want some more coffee? Getting yourself killed won't help Malachi."

"Yeah, pour me another cup. And stop yelling at me—please," Jack said. *But my death might help. It might atone for everything.* But he didn't say that out loud to Ben.

The two men were sitting at the kitchen table early Thursday morning, listening to Morning Edition on National Public Radio, WUNC 91.5 FM, and a cautious David Molpus discussing the limbo in which North Carolina seemed stuck until Halloween. Molpus noted Halloween as the end point hadn't been figured out scientifically—but still everybody was sure that was the time all the events were leading to. Food and fuel shipments crossed the state's borders only during the day, on trains protected by troops. The state's airspace was closed. Perhaps, David Molpus said, as Jack and Ben glared at each other over the table, it's time to talk of magic as real—again or for the first time . . . As for the reaction abroad, NPR turned to Sylvia Paggioli at Stonehenge on the Salisbury Plain in England, where thousands of neo-Druids and pagans, would-be Druids and pagans, witches, and the curious had gathered . . .

"Yelling? Maybe if you said something that made sense I

wouldn't have to yell," Ben yelled as he set a fresh cup of coffee in front of Jack and then sat down himself. "I'm sorry I yelled. I know Thomas is your son and I know you love Malachi and want to do something. But Thomas can't be trusted and I don't want you to die, you idiot, for nothing. There has to be another answer, another way. Your life as atonement for your son's sins isn't the way to go," Ben said in softer, more even tones.

Jack sighed. "What then? Get Father Jamey down at St. Mary's to lead a charge holding a crucifix and spraying holy water?"

"Well, why not? It works against vampires, why not against the Fomorii and the black witches?" Ben asked. "And if the cross was made of iron, why not? Besides, even though Father Jamey is a changeling, he's a priest. In all the old stories about priests and fairies, priests—Catholic priests—had special powers. I remember Valeria telling me the Church cast out fairies in Ireland."

"Two middle-aged men, one priest, three children, no matter how magical or how special, against a coven of witches and God knows how many Fomorii?"

"I don't think the Fomorii are here yet—not in any significant numbers. Just a few. That's why they need Malachi: his life energy can be used to control all the doors at Samhain. Want another bagel?"

"Listen to me, Ben. No, I'm full. Just listen to me, okay? I know Thomas can't be trusted and I expect him to betray us—so, let's use that to get Malachi back. You know we have to do it in a few days or it will be too late. He is going to die if we don't get him back to Faerie and if they use him, his power, he will die all the more faster. They will literally burn up his life. Unless you have a better idea, I don't see how we have any other choice other than to use me as bait."

"The next few days is right," Ben muttered. "I had another call from DSS while you were gone last night. They want to come over, ask more questions—just a few more routine questions. When I asked them why couldn't we talk over the phone, the woman made some noise about confidentiality and the phones being unreliable lately and besides they needed to *see* Malachi—"

Jack snorted. "When?"

"Next week, Monday or Tuesday. She even managed to mention police and search warrant. I told the boys to stay at Hazel's permanently. They can hide there, down in her grandmother's studio or something. All right—you are right. Let's go talk to Father Jamey. I don't like it, but I'll do it," Ben said, glaring at Jack. "But no sacrifices, understand? Promise me, Jack, you won't do anything stupid. Promise me."

"I promise," Jack said, looking away from Ben. It didn't matter what he agreed to or promised. And it didn't matter what happened to him—what probably would happen to him—as long as Malachi was safe and Ben got him to Faerie in time. At least when it happened, it would all be over and he wouldn't have to feel anything anymore, anything at all. The constant sorrow would come to an end. *But I would like to have seen Faerie, see if it looks like Narnia or Middle-Earth.*

Father Jamey Applewhite

It was, Father Jamey thought, actually a good time to be a Catholic priest, although he wasn't sure the price being paid for full pews was worth it. Fear had brought the lapsed Catholics back to mass, not any sudden reconversion. *But, you take 'em where you find 'em.* He looked again at his morning schedule on his desk calendar. Decidedly full, now that he had penciled in the appointment with Ben and Jack. Ben had called five minutes ago and the two men were on their way. He had them down for an hour. After Ben and Jack, Janet Thompson. Her oldest child had disappeared and her grief was choking her. Next were Carrie Maxwell and Jeff Allamaok. Probably wanted to postpone their wedding. He would encourage them not to, but, instead, to choose life over fear.

He yawned. *God, am I tired. And whom am I kidding? I don't have any answers. Did I ever really have any?* People came to his office and to him as if he were an oracle of some kind or another. As if in all the books lining his walls, and the file cabinets filled with clippings and case histories and back issues of *The North Carolina Catholic, Commonweal,* and *The Catholic Digest* there was one right answer. *There isn't even one answer in the Bible—not one neat answer, anyway. Telling people to have faith, to trust God, to love, to follow Jesus' example—was any of that enough? But it had to be. What else was there?*

"Father Jamey?"

Jamey looked up to see Ben Tyson peering around the door. Behind him, looking very tired, was Ben's friend, Jack Ruggles. Jack hadn't shaved in what looked like a week and his hair looked as if more than a week had passed since a comb had gotten anywhere near his head. The priest stood and waved the two men into his office.

"Sit down, Ben, Jack. That couch looks like crap, but actually it's pretty comfortable. Just throw those papers on the floor. Coffee? Isn't the best—you know how hard it is to get really good coffee since the Weirdness started. I asked at the Harris Teeter, Farm Fresh, and at the Food Lion, and nobody knows why. The guy at the Food Lion thought it might have something to do with Santeria in Brazil, but—you are not here to listen to me babble about coffee."

"No coffee, thanks—I'm floating in it already. Put in enough sugar and milk and it tastes all right. Father, what are you doing on the 18th, this Friday night?" Ben said as he sat down on one side of the couch. Jack sat down beside him, and leaned back, clearly wanting Ben to do all the talking. *His face, so gaunt, tired. He's lost so much weight his clothes look two sizes too big.*

"The 18th?" Jamey glanced down at his calendar. Friday night was open: no counseling sessions, no rosary groups, no Bible studies. But then every night of the week was open. He had even moved up the Saturday evening vigil mass to four o'clock in the afternoon. People were not going out in the dark unless they had to. "Friday night? What have you two got cooked up? You know the nights aren't safe."

"Father, Malachi's gone. We know where he is, and if we don't get him back, the days won't be safe, either, let alone the nights. We need you to help us—" Ben paused, looked down at the floor, at Jack, then back at Jamey. "In all the fairy tales I have ever read—and I have read a lot—priests have powers. Special powers. And if the fairy tales are true, then that has to be true, too. Will you help us? You can do things Jack and I can't."

Jamey listened as Ben talked. Thomas Ruggles had the boy and evil had Thomas Ruggles. The boy was far more important than he had expected: not one, but two universes' fates hinged on what happened to Malachi. Jamey had known Malachi was special from the moment he had seen the boy. But not *this* important. The last stand of the Fomorii, already beaten in Faerie, but if the changelings did not return, there could be no recovery from the war, and the Fomorii would have won, there, after all. And a victory there would mean an eventual victory here. The two universes were forever linked; one could not survive if the other fell. The priest listened, pondering, as Ben explained what Thomas wanted and what they had planned to do with his help. Jack's face was taut with pain and fatigue and a grief so deep Jamey wondered if he could ever recover.

"I can see auras, Ben, and I can see through glamour and even make a little of it myself. And I can see those who are changing, even before they grow pointed ears or their eyes began glowing. And this." He made the Sign of the Cross and a Cross took shape, shining, pulsing with charged light that shot out green and white sparks into the air. The first time that had happened in church, he had been as surprised as the congregation. One woman had dropped to her knees, her rosary beads whipping through her fingers. A man had got up and walked out. The rest had just sat there in a stunned silence. And a handful had come after, to touch his robe.

"That cross might do the trick, Father. Priests cast fairies out in the old stories. With holy water and crucifixes," Ben said and went on to explain Jack was to be the bait. Thomas could gain great power by the blood-sacrifice of his father—maybe even more than control of Malachi offered.

"Jack thinks Thomas believes he will still get the boy anyway, so why not make a deal. I know he can't be trusted, and he certainly won't trust us," Ben said. "But it may buy us enough time to get Malachi to a gate by Halloween and back to Faerie. He'll die if he doesn't. I don't think Thomas knows that—or maybe he doesn't care."

Jack finally spoke up. He leaned forward and talked in a low voice, his words sounding as pained as his face. Jamey saw that, when juxtaposed with Ben's white and yellow aura, Jack's looked all the more grey-streaked and stained with brown and black. "I've told Thomas I will come alone to the place where he makes his sacrifices, his black altar. It's in Clemmons State Forest. He will have Malachi there—to use to channel and control the energy he will release by sacrificing his father, eating his father's heart. I go in alone. And when he turns his attention from Malachi to me, then you distract him with that cross and the holy water and whatever priestly magic you have. Ben will get Malachi and I think the other three children will be doing some magic of their own. I *may* be able to break free then."

"I'll help, but will that be enough?" Jamey asked. The plan sounded too simple. Making a cross glow in the air and having three changeling *children* doing magic seemed hardly enough to combat Thomas and his witch-friends.

Jack shrugged. "It's all we can do."

Faerie

Larissa, the Second, left the White City and went home for the first time since the Call to the changelings. She flew alone, leaving early in the morning, just as the sun began to burn its way up through the sea, turning the green golden, scarlet, and white, illuminating one last time the noctilucent *savva*. The birds became black shadows against the light. The far sky was still night-purple and Yellow Moon was still visible, although fading, behind distant clouds, as well as a dim handful of stars, a band of glowing dust. White Moon had set hours ago. The near sky's purple had almost turned to blue.

She had only told the Third she was leaving, wanting only the privacy of her thoughts and none of the questions or worries of the rest of the Dodecagon. The hungry thoughts of the gulls were more than enough. And the beach was empty—before the war there would have been children, up early to go with one of their four parents to fish, to collect shells, to give the rest back home a break. *This is only temporary*, she thought as she flew soft, following the bright white line of the surf for a while, and then, as she had done as a child, out over the ocean. *Fishing folk on the beach when I was a girl and swimmers in the ocean, and dolphins. They were always here, and if I knew them, I would dip down and fly through the water, in and out of the waves, over and under jumping dolphins, diving swimmers.* She had hoped they would come back once victory and peace had been declared, once the Call had been given, but only a few had, and none of the people who had lived below, on shore or off.

Peace. Victory, she thought as she flew closer to the water, wanting the spray to catch her face every now and then. *But at what price? There are so few of us left, so few complete tetrads. If the changelings do not come home, the Fomorii will have won anyway. And where is the First? The Prime Mover—will the Peace last, the changelings come—stay?—if she was not at the table? I know she is dead—why is it taking me so long and why is it so hard to say that out loud?*

Do the Fomorii know what happened to her? At the last meeting, when the surrender had been signed, the Fomorii lord had wanted to know where the First was—this was to be a meeting between equals, yes? He had towered over the Second, a huge creature whose black scales shed as he walked, leaving a trail of smelly darkness in his wake, patches of grass here and there withering, turning brown, desiccating into brittle dust. Had he been—smiling? Did Fomorii smile?

"No Valeria? No Prime Mover? Well. You say she is traveling in the other universes, taking her rest before coming home? How *interesting*, Lady. Will this journey be long enough to give her sufficient rest and renewal so she can rebuild Faerie? We are resting from the war as well. She will be home by Samhain? Of course," he had said, with a slight nod, "you must protect her privacy. May I have another drink? It has been some time since I have had the wine of the White City."

The Second had made a slight, quick gesture to the guard as she smiled and sat back in her seat. "Of course. I think I will join you. Two," she said to the silent guard . . .

Enough. I promised myself I would not replay every conversation, every gesture, every look and glance. They had talked of inconsequential things afterward, as they sipped the hot spiced wine the guard had carefully set before them, the tips of his ears a disapproving red. Now, as the Second banked toward the shore, her parents' home just ahead, she wondered about the rumors that the Fomorii had violated the terms of surrender: troop movement, illegal use of magic, interuniverse crossings. Samhain was only days away. The gates would be open then, releasing magical energy into both worlds. Enough to let the changelings return, and to let others cross as well—depending on who controlled the gates, by whose will the gates open. Enough magic to overturn the Peace, no matter that neither fairies nor Fomorii would survive a second war.

She dropped to the ground behind the house. She stood for a moment, listening and smelling, looking. Flowers bloomed all around her on vines laced through a fence, up and down tree trunks, in the trees, on low bushes, in neat rows and circles on the lawn. Red, pink, white, yellow, blue, purple, and various shades in between, and all the accompanying perfume and music, the latter, faint, soft, just at the touch of a breeze. All of it—color, smell, and sound—was woven together in a kaleidoscopic harmony. *They knew I was coming. They always set the garden to bloom for me.* Inside she heard voices, low and muted, behind the walls of the house. Mom and Mama, and Dad and Papa. Making morning bread, the sweet, sweet bread she had loved as a child.

How long have I been gone? Too long. She slowly walked to the house, the grass wet beneath her feet, as the orange and scarlet trumpet-lilies announced her arrival.

Malachi

For a long time after the fire in the Garner library Malachi was lost. He wasn't at home in his bedroom, next door to his father. Nor was he in Russell's attic bedroom or the dinosaur nest where Jeff slept.

Nor was he in the neat and orderly room Hazel kept, her computer in the middle of her desk, and Alexander, her overgrown Siamese, in the middle of her bed. He wasn't in Uncle Jack's, whose house, even after a major effort by his second wife, Hilda, looked like an attic the library used for storage. Nor was he in church, leaning back against the satiny wood of the pews, half-listening to the priest, as he looked up to count the tiny, star-like crosses on the church ceiling.

Nor was Malachi in the other place, the place of his dreams, with forests of white and silver trees and gold trees and the shining sea everywhere and the White City. Malachi had dreamed of the White City the most often, next to his dreams of his mother. The City was high on a promontory, looking down on the ocean, its walls growing out of the cliffs. In his dreams he had stood on the walls, almost drunk from the sea air and watched the ocean, just as he did on the annual summer trips he took with his father to Ocracoke. Malachi loved the tiny island twenty miles off the North Carolina coast, the two-hour ferry ride, and its long, empty beaches and the wild ponies. Malachi had never told anyone—not even his father or Uncle Jack, who stayed with them for at least a few days, sometimes the entire two weeks—but the ponies, once he was old enough to roam around by himself, had come up to him. Snuffling, nudging each other, nuzzling his hands and face, they let him pat their heads and feed them apples and carrots. Malachi loved Ocracoke, but he knew he would love the White City and its rocky cliffs even more.

Malachi had seen his mother for the first time in his dreams of walking the walls of the White City. He had started remembering her when he was five: a warm light peering down at him in his crib. He had tried asking his father about her then, and learned Valeria was forbidden territory. Now he knew his mother was dead. Had his dreams *not* been dreams after all, but real memories of her ghost visiting him? Where did people go after they died? He knew his father still dreamed of her. Malachi could tell by his father's eyes the next morning: they echoed the lights in his own when he began to see her just ahead of him on the walls of the City.

But Malachi was in none of those places; he was lost. There had been the fire and the smoke and his father and Uncle Jack and the Fomorii. They had chased him from his house, with Thomas and that woman—Mrs. Collins, his *teacher*. And the burning books falling all around, the glass shattering, and the fire. Where was he now? Even with the light oozing from his eyes, ears, nose, and fingers, Malachi saw only greyness. Had he been asleep? Sick? Why was it so hard to open his eyes? Why was everything so grey—was this yet another universe, one without light?

"Dad? Uncle Jack? Hazel? Russell? Jeff?" Malachi said slowly and softly.

No one answered.

Then Malachi remembered.

They had taken him.

He opened his eyes, even though doing so hurt, to look into Thomas's face. He tried to move, but something was holding his arms and legs in place. Even his head. Malachi couldn't move at all.

"He's awake," Thomas said, speaking to someone Malachi couldn't see. "No, don't try to move, Malachi. The binding spell will only constrict you even more; it will really hurt."

"He is so little—do you really think he has all this power?" Another voice, familiar—there, she had moved into his field of vision: Mrs. Collins. Then he hadn't imagined her chasing him with the others, just before the fire. The two adults bent down and for one moment, Malachi could see their faces clear and sharp, but then it was as if *he* had fallen, back first, into water. The colors and shapes blurred and smeared, as the sounds of their voices waxed and waned in loudness. Words and sentences disappeared, evaporated, between their mouths and his ears. More magic, he thought.

"Malachi . . . can . . . me?"

"I'm falling, everything is, it's hard to see, I can't hold on any longer." Malachi tried to reach up, to grab something, but there was nothing. He couldn't move. He wasn't even sure if he had spoken out loud. Then his vision cleared again: a living room, on a couch. Thomas's? A lamp, a table, chairs. Thomas and Mrs. Collins. The lamp was vibrating and glowing. It got brighter and brighter—now it was on fire. The two adults started yelling. The more the lamp burned, and now the table it was on, the clearer he could hear them speak. The fire, it seemed, was burning away whatever held him so close and in such fog.

"Throw something over it, get some water. Quick! I thought you could control him, Mr. Magician, Your Majesty, the Great Witch King. He's going to burn down this place just like he did the library. Fireballs! Tho—"

He slapped her so hard she fell. "I'm trying, you damn bitch. *You* get the damn water and let me take care of him. Let me try giving him another injection—there."

"There. The fire's stopped, the drug worked."

"Is he going to stay under control until Friday? He could burn us all up," Mrs. Collins said, standing, a bucket in her hand, by the smoldering lamp and table.

"I know," Thomas said. "But he's under control and he will stay under . . ."

Malachi closed his eyes and slept.

Jeff

For a long moment Jeff wanted to tell Mr. Tyson—Ben—Malachi's daddy—to stop the car and let him out. Anywhere on the side of the road; it didn't matter. Or maybe he would just *push* open the back of the station wagon they were in and launch himself out. He would just fly straight up into the air as high as he could go until the city of Raleigh and the town of Garner were a blanket of brightly glowing colored jewels below and above was only the night sky and the stars. He would just float on the winds forever and ever, never coming down, never again touching the earth. And the hard, tight lump in his stomach would come apart as if it were a loose granny knot.

Jeff said nothing. Even up there on the night wind, he knew the red-eyed monsters would eventually find him and he would never be able to get to the other place—Faerie—where he had gone in his dreams. That had been just two months ago. Malachi would die and so would Hazel and Russell and Mr. Tyson and his friend, Mr. Ruggles, and Father Jamey and the Clarks and then all the people Jeff loved would be dead and he might as well be, if that happened.

It would be like going to live with his father. His therapist had asked him, at his last appointment, if he loved his father. Jeff hadn't known what to say. Love his father? Once upon a time—before his mother had left—yes, he had. And did he love her?

"I don't know anymore," Jeff said after a long silence. "I don't know."

Finally Mr. Ruggles spoke. It was a relief to hear his voice. It sounded so ordinary, and it broke the memory of that last time at the therapist, and the other memories lying behind it, waiting, receded, went out to sea.

"We should be riding white horses, or be astride the back of a green dragon," Mr. Ruggles said from the car's front seat, where he sat beside Mr. Tyson.

"Well," Father Jamey said from the middle seat, "this *is* the church car I am letting you drive. St. Mary's Catholic Church in gold letters on both sides, and an outlined Dove of Peace and Mary herself—"

"There is a cross on the hood, too," Hazel said as she leaned her head on the priest's shoulder. Russell was in the back of the wagon with Jeff, staring out the side window.

"I put that there this morning, along with some holy water," Father Jamey said laughing, "so we have a blessed steed after all."

The others laughed and Jeff felt the knot in his stomach start to unravel. He felt, with the lightest of touches, both Russell and Hazel mentally reassuring him: *It's okay. It's going to be okay, you'll see.* Even without Malachi to complete their tetrad, they remained linked inside a gossamer web of thought.

Huh you think YOU'RE scaredJeff I'm almost crazyscared tooscared to talk about it . . .

They needed Malachi, who was the true golden-eyed telepath, to really mind-talk, but even so, sometimes Jeff could hear Russell's voice, clear and soft, as if Russell were whispering in his ear. Only Russell and neither Malachi nor Hazel could hear him. Jeff leaned over and squeezed Russell's hand.

And Russell could hear Jeff's voice as easily: *HeyRuss, Everybody's scared, but we practiced and PRACTICED, REMEMBER? And thecloserweget, the stronger Malachi will be and he'll help, he KNOWS we'recoming&what we are going to do.*

"We're just about there," Mr. Tyson said as he drove the car off the interstate and down an off-ramp. He slowed at the bottom of the short hill, but he didn't stop, even though the light was red. There were no other cars on the road. It was almost midnight—way too late for any sane person to be out. "There's the entrance to the state forest up ahead."

"It's showtime," Father Jamey said.

Jeff clenched his fists. This time Russell found and squeezed his hand.

"I feel him," Hazel said suddenly, sitting up straight. "I feel Malachi. He's not far away. He's sort of sleepy—weird-sleepy, but he knows we're here. He's expecting us—and if he can wake up enough, he will help us."

"He's drugged or enchanted or both," Mr. Ruggles muttered. "How can a ten-year-old boy help us—"

"Jack: we can do this," Mr. Tyson said as he turned off the highway onto a graveled road, the station wagon's tires crunching as he slowed the car down and parked it beneath a cedar tree. "We'll park here. Thomas wanted Jack to approach on foot."

Jeff wished the car's headlights were on bright. All he could see was the gravel road and dark trees and darker shadows and a small sign pointing the way to Parking. When Mr. Tyson cut the car's lights, the dark jumped at him, as if it had been waiting for that moment to pounce. For a long moment, after he had climbed out of the car after Russell, Jeff could see nothing at all. It was as if the darkness *had* eaten him, its mouth so large he hadn't even noticed he had been devoured, a huge land whale and a very small Jonah.

"Hold my hand," Russell said very softly and the darkness receded at the sound of Russell's voice. Jeff gripped Russell's hand in his, reassured by the solidity of flesh. He wasn't surprised when a few moments later Hazel took his other hand. Nor was Jeff surprised that, when she touched him, a quick current of energy rippled between all three of them. Now he could see the trees were just trees: cedars, pines, dogwoods, and with a sudden new clarity of night vision, maples, oaks, sweetgums, sycamores.

WhyIcan see the colors of the leaves I see theleaves the texture of the bark—

Hold onTIGHT everybody, I need you all to HOLD on . . .

"He wants us to hurry," Jeff said as the adults started getting out of the car. "He's really sick and keeping them out of his head and connecting to us—he's gone. I mean, the connection broke—there is something he is going to do and he's afraid Thomas might figure it out."

Hazel

The holy water Father Jamey sprinkled on everybody felt cool on Hazel's face. She kept a firm grip on Jeff's hand as she watched the priest pray. Everyone seemed on the edge of crazy with fear. No, just Mr. Ruggles, Uncle Jack, as the man kept insisting they call him —he was the only one visibly shaking. He had the hardest job: bait. He had to walk naked down a very dark road in the middle of the night to face a group of monsters waiting for him around a boiling black cauldron. And the head monster was his only son who wanted to cut out his father's still-beating heart and hold it up for all the others to see, blood running down his arm, his chest, his legs, and then eat the heart.

Hazel shuddered. She wished she were back home, in front of her computer, playing a very harmless and easy to control and understand computer game. So what if her grandparents ignored her most of the time—at least they weren't mean about it. Everything would be a lot neater and safe and the only chaos would be chaos she could manage. The dangers would be known and predictable, but—in a way she couldn't quite name, to be here was to be—more alive. And it did matter that she lived an invisible life. Hazel shook her head. Now wasn't the time for these mental wanderings. She wanted to go over to Mr. Ruggles and hug him—well, maybe not hug him if he was naked—but at least squeeze his hand. But he seemed to want no one to get close to him; his aura had turned ice-blue-white, encasing him inside as if he were frozen. Not even Malachi's dad, his best friend, could penetrate the cold.

Hazel wanted to speak, to shout, to say something to break the heaviness of the silence, weighed down even more by the dark. But she didn't know what to say.

"In the Name of the Father, the Son, and the Holy Spirit," Father Jamey said, his clear voice breaking the heavy silence—a silence, Hazel realized, as he prayed out loud, hadn't lasted more than the time needed for everyone to get out of the car. The sound of the priest's voice let her hear other sounds—it was as if his speech had knocked open a door. Jeff's and Russell's breathing. The crunch of Mr. Tyson's feet on the gravel. The snap of a twig as an animal moved in the trees. And the wind in the trees, sounding like the low muttering of a crowd.

"In the Name of Jesus Christ, our God and Lord, strengthened by the intercession of the Immaculate Virgin Mary, Mother of God, of Blessed Michael the Archangel, of the Blessed Apostles Peter and Paul and all the Saints. And powerful in the holy authority of our ministry, we confidently undertake to repulse the attacks and deceits of the devil. Amen. That's the abbreviated version of what to say during an exorcism—the closest to what we are doing here, I think. Now it really is showtime," Father Jamey said and starting with Mr. Tyson and ending with Jeff, blessed everyone individually, drawing wet crosses on their foreheads.

From the journal of Ben Tyson, early Saturday morning 19 October 1991

3:11 A.M.

I should be asleep; I need to be asleep. I need to be in a sleep so profound that I am past all dreams, past all remembering. I know that sleep will never come. I will remember and dream of what happened for the rest of my life.

Everybody else is asleep. The kids insisted on sleeping together in the same room, in the same bed. When I checked on them for the umpteenth time a few minutes ago Hazel and Malachi were sleeping

*back to back and Russell and Jeff were a jumble of legs and arms. The
tetradic link between them is still visible: ropes of multicolored light
woven around, under, over, and through them.*

*This must be how it is in Faerie: tetrads make a family/
sexual unit. But then how did Valeria come to me? Are there two other
people there with whom I would have shared with her?*

Never mind.

*I laid my hand gently on the talisman, the silver-grey twelve-
pointed star on Malachi's chest. It's glowing now—it's never glowed
before. It's vibrating, too; I feel it through my fingertips. With the
silver light of the star rippling across his face my son has never looked
more like his mother.*

*I smoothed his hair and put the back of my hand against his
cheek.*

*Jack is asleep. I pray he isn't dreaming. I put a cot in my bed-
room and after giving him a double dose of painkillers, shoved him
on it with a pillow and a blanket. He managed to strip down to his
underwear before he fell asleep. His back was still hot to the touch,
beneath the dressings on his burns. The bandage on his chest oozed
blood.*

*Father Jamey is surely asleep at the rectory. Or perhaps he is at St.
Mary's, praying. I can see him doing that now, the only person in the
empty sanctuary, in the corner by the pieta and the lit vigil candles,
rows of tiny, white singular flames, turned blue by the color of the
rows of blue glass jars. For what is he praying and to whom? I need to
ask him how he fits God and Jesus into all this, now that the Change
is upon us. Valeria told me of the Three Sons in Faerie, and the Four
Teachers, and the Good God, the Father, whose symbol was an enormous cornucopia, overflowing with good things, and the Great
Goddess, Triune, the oldest of them all. Aren't they all just different
syllables of the same name?*

*He said he kept praying the whole time we were out there, in his
heart, to himself—however he could. I'm glad he did.*

*I have tried to sleep. I have lain on my stomach, my back, and both
sides. I have walked and walked around this house, checking and
rechecking each room, each window, each door. Just the way Valeria
did almost every night as she set the protective wards. I have re-
arranged and re-rearranged the salt and the pepper shakers, the sugar
bowls, and the honey and the jelly jars. I have stacked and re-stacked
the fairy lore books beside my desk and I have written all this down
here, in my journal, and I have been staring at my words on the screen
for a good five minutes. I know what I have to do before I can sleep.*

I have to write down everything that happened tonight: what I saw, heard, smelled, did. And what the others did:

Jack took off his clothes and Russell and Jeff and Hazel disappeared somewhere over their heads, floating inside their nest of lights.

"I wish I could hear Malachi like they can," Jack muttered as he pulled his NCSU sweatshirt over his head.

"I hear the barest of whispers," Father Jamey said as he took each piece of Jack's clothes in his arms: sweatshirt, T-shirt, socks, shoes, jeans, underwear. "But it is a good sign. He's not completely under Thomas's control. He might be able to help us when the time comes. Now, let me bless you."

I heard no whispers, touches, nothing. My own son, nothing. It didn't seem quite fair. Jack seemed to be getting smaller the less clothes he had on. When he was finally naked, I could see how much weight he had lost. Jack's bare body looked shrunken, frail, and no match for a black witch. Or the Fomorii guards we saw ahead, their eyes malevolent coals. They would let us pass now, I knew that. But if our plan worked, would they let us pass as easily on the way out? *I reached down to reassure myself I had the iron fireplace poker hanging from my belt. I looked up to check the priest: a stainless steel butcher knife in a homemade sheath. And each of the kids had steak knives. In my pocket: a thin tube of iron filings. Just maybe—no, I told myself, just let it happen.*

"Might? Better make this a strong blessing, then, Father, and a warm one," Jack said, shivering. "And pray that nobody sees me wandering naked out here. Getting picked up for indecent exposure would definitely screw everything up."

The night air was cool and wet with the promise of rain. *I could see clouds gathering behind them, back toward the highway, back toward home. We would have to drive home in a storm—if we got to drive home. The wind was rising—the leaves were already turning over, the tree trunks beginning to sway. Lightning flashed in the clouds. An October thunderstorm? Just one more thing different this week, one more sign of the coming Change.*

"In the Name of the Father, the Son, and the Holy Spirit, amen," Father Jamey said in a soft voice and then drew a cross in the air. His hands glowed as he made the cross and the glow stayed in the air, a shimmering cruciform of light. "Take it inside you, Jack. It'll help you stay safe."

I wanted to say something, anything to make Jack stronger and safe, but I couldn't. I didn't have any words. Jack had never looked *more vulnerable than standing naked in the gravel parking lot of the Clemmons State Forest, his skin even paler against the gravel's blue, with the dark trees and the path into the forest behind him, the path to the waiting fire.*

Jack held out his arms and closed them around the cross, pulling it into his chest. It sparked and popped when it touched him. "It's warm—ahhh," Jack whispered as the cross sank into his flesh. "There. I feel like I just drank a cup of hot coffee, really fast."

"Jack?" I finally said, my voice breaking, "you're my best friend; I love you."

"I know. C'mon, it's showtime."

Once we were inside the forest, on the path that led to the coven and the fire, the wind of the coming storm died, as if the trees had swallowed it into their leaves. Father Jamey and I walked several paces behind Jack and I listened as they walked for what, I wasn't sure. All I could hear was the sound of shoes and feet on gravel, and then, when there was no gravel, shoes and feet on hard earth. And Jack muttering in relief that the gravel wasn't cutting into his bare feet. No branches stirred, no leaves rustled, no small unseen animal jumped or ran. Even the hands on my watch stopped moving. The watch's luminous glow disappeared, as if it were a candle snuffed out by wind—but there was no wind. This can't be Malachi's magic; he's too weak and sick. He could barely connect to the other kids and Father Jamey. Thomas did this; he made this empty space. Is this the sort of world Thomas wants to make? Still, silent, dark? God, those two Fomorii are scary and dark, dark, dark shadows in the night, a black darker than the night.

I felt the heat first, before I saw the fire, at first a slight warmth on my face, as if someone had touched hot metal and then touched my cheek. But the touch lingered and grew warmer: sunburn at the end of too much time on the beach. I started sweating. We walked past an enormous, old oak next, with a park sign on it and a box attached to its trunk. (White Oak, Quercus Alba. If I pressed the button on the box, I would be able to hear what the White Oak had to say—about what I couldn't then imagine. Did trees talk in Faerie? Were they "in-spirited" with a dryad? Narnian trees were, but Narnia and Middle-Earth are fictions; this was real.)

After White Oak, I could see the fire and the coven waiting for them, shadows around the flames.

"Jack, Ben, it's going to be all right," Father Jamey said and blessed Jack again and drew yet another glowing cross in the air.

"Right, Father. Ben, if I don't—take care of yourself," Jack said and squeezed my arm. I hugged him, naked as he was, and then Jack turned to face the coven and their fire and his son.

The fire was huge. Somehow Thomas had managed to get whole trees to burn: they formed a tipi-like structure, with the fire at its heart and crown, roaring, laughing, eating, talking. The coven stood around the flames, all of them naked, the fire making red shadows on white, black, brown, and yellow bodies.

"He has stolen a church altar. Or it was given to him," Father Jamey whispered to me. I wondered why he was whispering—surely nobody could have heard anything unless they were shouting above the fire's roar. Sweat had plastered the priest's dark hair to his head. It rolled down his forehead, dripped off his ears, soaked his white robe, now a wavery pink in the firelight. I nodded. I had seen the altar, too. The marble top had been placed over four rock cairns, forming a rough table. I gripped the silver star hard and tight; its points cut into my flesh. I felt a surge of power and warmth in return.

Thomas stood behind the altar, the fire at his back, facing the coven, which had stepped back to open the circle, to let Jack in. Malachi lay on the marble, spread-eagled, his arms and legs tied to the four corners of the altar. Black candles sputtered in each corner. One silver bowl had been placed at Malachi's head; another had been placed at his feet. Something burned inside each bowl, releasing a strange scent and a heavy, white smoke twisting and curling out of each bowl like snakes. The smoke oozed and slithered to the ground, weaving itself in and around the stone cairns and Thomas's feet. Thomas lifted a long, black knife, its blade reflecting fire, when he saw all of them. He alone of those around the fire wore clothes: a midnight-blue robe, marked with glowing pentagrams and twisting spirals.

"Of course I can hear you. And, of course it's a church altar, priest. But this is a different congregation than the sheep that listen to you every Sunday, isn't it? Or is it? You might recognize some of these faces, if you look closely," Thomas said. "But let's discuss such things another time. We all know why we are here tonight."

"We have a deal, Thomas," Jack said. "My life for the boy. Release him to his father and the priest and then I'm yours."

"Yes, we had a deal. Your life for his life, your heart for his heart," Thomas intoned and raised his arms. The coven, in one voice, started humming: aaaeeeiiiooouuu. They stepped closer, drawing the circle tighter. I could see, in the shadows, in the firelight, individual faces: Charlotte Collins, Malachi's teacher, a Baptist minister, the mechanic at a service station on South Saunders Street. I looked at the priest and saw him nodding—yes, there were members of his congregation here. And were those red eyes as well—were there even more Fomorii already here? Had the walls between rooms gotten so thin?

I was terrified.

Charlotte stepped out of the circle and stood behind Thomas. Her blond hair seemed to be part of the fire, as it writhed and twisted around her head—a medusa in flame. Her bare body glistened and shone and was marked with the same symbols as Thomas's midnight robe. She must be his witch queen. I knew she couldn't be trusted. She reached around Thomas's waist and pulled his robe back and then down his back, to pool at his feet. The same markings that covered his robe covered his body. His erect penis had been painted to match the color of his knife.

The humming grew louder. A log shifted and the fire jumped, flames curling up into the sky like unrolling streamers. The smell from the silver bowls grew thicker and more pungent and the white smoke spread, twisting itself through the legs of the coven. I felt the fire's heat on my face; I was soaked to the skin with sweat. I felt the terror growing, swelling and I wanted to run, yelling, knocking down the coven, Charlotte, Thomas, get Jack, get Malachi, get the hell out of here—but this was pretty close to hell. My best friend, my son.

"Don't. I know it's hard, Ben, but don't do anything," Father Jamey said softly, stepping closer to me, grabbing my arm. "Thomas is distracted and he's let go some of his binding on Malachi. Give Malachi a chance to feel this, to figure out what's going on."

"What the hell are you talking about?" I whispered back.

In answer, the priest gripped my arm tighter and with his free hand, pushed back the hair from his own pointed ears. "Wait, just wait. And keep praying. Saint Michael, defend us in our battle against principalities and powers, against the rulers of this world of darkness, against the spirits of wickedness in the high places. Wait."

Jack stepped to the altar and untied Malachi's left hand, then his right. Then Malachi's left foot, his right. Then, slowly, carefully, he leaned down to pick up the boy.

"No, stop," Thomas said, and pulled Jack back from Malachi, who seemed to be waking up, stirring slightly, as if he were pushing against the spells that had bound him on the marble slab.

"What do you mean: No? We had a deal: me for him. More power from the willing sacrifice of a parent," Jack said, pushing away Thomas's hands.

Thomas laughed and held up his knife. The blade shone in the fire-light. "But I would have even more power if I took both hearts, now, wouldn't I? And why should I keep a promise made to you, old man?"

Thomas slashed down, aiming at Jack's chest, as Charlotte and the rest screamed, and the fire leaped higher. Jack caught his arm as the blade bit into his chest, and pushed Thomas back again, the blade shifting and then sliding against the sweat on Jack's chest. It fell between the two naked men as they wrestled, the screaming louder and louder.

Malachi slowly set up, dazed, rubbing his eyes, straining to see where he was, who was around him. I started toward him, but the priest grabbed my arm again.

"No, Ben, wait one more second. Jack, this way, Jack—now," Father Jamey yelled. "Now!" He pulled something—a squirt gun—out of his robe. An Uzi-sized squirt gun, which he shot straight into Thomas's face and groin. Thomas screamed and jerked away from Jack, covering his face and his genitals, the smell of cayenne pepper pungent in the hot air.

"Go, Ben, get him, get Malachi," the priest yelled and ran with me. Jack still stood by the altar, the knife at his feet, watching his son writhe in pain from the pepper-saturated holy water. The coven and Charlotte stood still, as if something had been broken, whatever had moved them as one group.

As the priest yanked Jack out of his stupor, I picked my boy up and held him against my chest, the boy's body hot against my sweaty clothes. Oh, my baby boy, my little baby boy. Malachi glowed everywhere, and moaned, burying his face in my shoulder and throwing out his arms. Lightning erupted from each hand. One bolt smashed the table. Another melted the knife. The third zapped Charlotte Collins in the chest. She shuddered, swallowing a scream, and fell over, her body smoking. Her hair fell about her head, long and loose and burning. Already the air was rank with the smell.

"Run, go, run, now," Father Jamey screamed, and with one arm around Jack, dragged him from the fire, the altar, his writhing son. "Jack, run, run with me."

I took off, Malachi close to my chest, one hand cradling the boy's head, the other around his waist. The silence broke when we hit the graveled path. The wind rose behind me, pushing me and Jack and the priest, breaking the fire into a rain of burning wood. The rain came behind the wind.

"No, no, no, the boy is mine—the old man is mine. No, I won't have it!"

We stopped—Malachi, Jack, Father Jamey, and I—and turned. Thomas stood over Charlotte's body, his face contorted in pain, his arms high over his head.

"Don't look, run," someone yelled, I had no idea who. Thomas threw a fireball as they turned and hit Jack in the back and Jack fell right beside me, his back burning. Father Jamey threw Jack to the ground and rolled him on the gravel, beating at the fire.

"He's mine. He's MINE."

Then the Fomorii guards attacked, their fire whips singeing the air. For almost too long a moment, I froze, remembering that night, years ago, when they came to kill Valeria and Malachi. Not this time. I let Malachi slip to the ground and straddled him as I whipped out the poker and slashed into the dark. A whip caught one ankle and I tripped, the pain hot and sharp. Father Jamey, with Jack on the ground behind, yanked out his butcher knife and sliced through the fire whip. The Fomorii howled and jerked back, and I rolled over and up, and whacked the nearest one on its arm. This time the monster screamed. I hit him again and again and its arm broke off, the skin melting, dissolving. The other Fomorii snapped its whip and it cut through my sleeve, taking the hair off my arm.

Malachi whimpered and opened his eyes. Another bolt of lightning erupted from his hands, exploding at the Fomorii's feet. I remembered the iron filings then and clawed them out of my pockets, uncorked them, and with a sweep of my arm, the grey dust fell on both monsters, their faces, their chests. The one-armed one fell, writhing. The other fled.

"Now, Ben, get Malachi, go," Father Jamey gasped, as he jerked Jack to his feet.

I picked up Malachi and ran and the rain fell, sheets of rain, cold, lashing rain, laced with hail, rain that hurt. The fire sizzled and hissed and screamed as it died. The coven broke and ran: some down the path, pushing past me and Malachi, shoving aside Jack and the priest, some screaming into the woods.

Father Jamey made Jack run. I heard the priest yelling but what I had no idea, as the rain tore his words from his mouth and beat them into the ground. I felt the ground move and I stumbled, got up, and kept running. The trees started moving then, shaking, and one fell, beside me, another somewhere behind me.

I had no idea how long it took to get to the car.

I laid Malachi gently on the backseat and peeled off my shirt to cover him. He looked so small and weak. Light popped and sparked from his fingers. The star glowed on his chest. The rain fell, so hard *and so fast, I could only see a few feet in any direction. What had happened to Jack and Father Jamey? How in the world was I going to find the other three kids?*

"It worked. We woke him up and he used us to make the lightning, call the storm."

I jumped as Hazel tugged at his arm. Where had she come from? And Russell and Jeff standing beside her. I was shivering, teeth chattering, without a shirt in the rain, and they were all dry. I could see the rain sliding off the light around them.

"I know, I can't believe we did it. Where's Jack? Father Jamey?" I yelled, trying not to think about the pain in my ankle or Jack's back. I held the poker like a sword. Just two Fomorii guards seemed almost too good to be true.

"There they are," Jeff yelled and pointed toward the path. There they were. Father Jamey was helping Jack over a fallen tree. The priest had wrapped Jack in his cassock.

"Wait, we'll help," Russell said and he and Jeff ran across the parking lot. I could see their shields extending around the two men and the relief in the priest's face. I couldn't see poor Jack's face.

It was too good to be true. The third Fomorii dropped out of a tree, right behind Jack and at the priest, a black shadow behind the shimmer of the children's protective shields. It lashed its whip against the shield, throwing off sparks and bits of fire and heat.

"Father Jamey—look out—look out—behind you," I screamed and ran. The priest let Jack fall and turned and threw his knife. At that range, he couldn't miss. The Fomorii stopped, looking down at the blade in its chest, its skin dissolving and falling away in chunks around it, in total surprise. I don't think it thought we would fight back. I shoved past the kids and finished it off with my poker.

"Come on, let's go. Now," I said as the rain fell even harder, as Jack groaned on the ground, as Hazel cried, and the boys and Father Jamey noisily exhaled. "Get in the car, kids. C'mon, Father, let's get Jack up."

Once everyone was in the car, I cranked the heat on and drove home, the rain beating the roof, sliding down in sheets across the windshield, enclosing us in a grey, wet world.

Jeff

Jeff woke before the others late Saturday morning. He had been dreaming of a huge house, with many rooms and corridors, stairs, attics, and cellars. He had been in the house and couldn't find his way to the door, his way out. He had to get out—his father was somewhere in the house and Jeff knew he had to get out before his father found him. He could hear his father calling his name and telling him to wait, wait just a minute, everything was going to be all right, really it was. If Jeff would just wait a minute, everything would be all right, he'd see. Jeff ran up and down stairs, looking for the door to go out, a place to hide. He ran down another long flight of stairs, down into a dark basement, slamming doors behind him. But his father followed him and was pounding on the last door, pounding and pounding and pounding.

Jeff sat up, disentangling himself from Malachi and Russell and Hazel. What time was it? Where was Malachi's clock—there, on the dresser—had anybody remembered to wind it? 11:10 and someone was pounding at the front door. Jeff tiptoed to the window and carefully pulled back the curtain. There were two women and two men at the door. Both men had on sheriff uniforms—Jeff could see the six-pointed stars and the heavy gun holsters. One of them was the pounder. In the middle of Ben Tyson's driveway sat a sheriff's car. Another unfamiliar car was parked in the street in front of the house. The light at the top of the sheriff's car was on, throwing red light around the yard. Jeff could see across the street another curtain just pulled back and a handful of people standing on their porches, their arms crossed.

Had they come for him? Had his father sent them? The Clarks said he had to meet his dad—had the sheriffs come to take him? Or was it because of last night? Mrs. Collins sure looked dead.

Move, Jeff, do something. Don't just freeze there. I can do this, he told himself. No use in waking up Malachi, Russell, or Hazel. He ran down the hall and slammed open Mr. Tyson's bedroom door: "Mr. Tyson? Mr. Tyyyyssonnnnn!"

"Je—wha—whaissit? Whasswrong?" Mr. Tyson had been sleeping on his stomach, buried under the covers. Jeff couldn't even see his head.

"You have to get up," Jeff said and shook the bed. Mr. Tyson finally rolled over and pushed back the spread to stare at Jeff, his eyes dazed and unfocused.

"The sheriff's here. At the front door—that's him pounding. He's got a deputy with him—and they have guns. They are going to take me to my father. I just know it. I can't go; I won't go, I—"

"Jeff. Stop. Let me think a minute. Just let me think. No, don't wake up Jack—he needs to sleep—besides with all those painkillers, he won't easily wake up. Just let me think."

There was Mr. Ruggles, on a cot on the other side of Mr. Tyson's bed. He looked terrible: what Jeff could see of his face looked grey and pale. The bandages that were visible were stained with blood. He stirred and groaned.

"Go back to sleep, Jack," Mr. Tyson said and sat up, swinging his legs to the floor. "I will take care of this. Jeff, hand me my pants over there—and that sweatshirt—God, they are going to break the door in if they keep hammering it like that. Call Father Jamey at the rectory. Tell him it's an emergency, go."

"Dad?" Malachi's voice, just down the hall, sounded small and thin and weak.

"Jesus," Mr. Tyson muttered. "Use the phone in my study. Go, Jeff, now," he said and stood to pull his pants up, stumbling to get his feet in the right legs.

Jeff raced to the telephone. The rectory number was on a list by the phone. He punched in the numbers, as the sheriff started shouting. *Please, please, please answer.* The phone kept ringing and ringing. Finally someone picked up and Jeff heard a tired, sleepy hello.

"Father Jamey, we're in trouble. The sheriff is here and I don't know what to do. Mr. Tyson said to call you—"

"Where's Ben? Jack?"

"Huh—Mr. Ruggles is sick, hurt, I mean, but he's asleep, and—Mr. Tyson told me to call you—"

"Hello? Can I help you?"

Jeff froze, the receiver pressed to his ear. Mr. Tyson was in the living room and he had opened the door. The pounding and the yelling stopped.

"We have a warrant to search the premises."

"Jeff? Jeff, tell me what they are saying. Quick, tell me."

"A warrant, to search—"

"Get Russell and Hazel. Come here, now, the fastest way you know how. Do it. *Do it.*"

"Where are Russell White and Jeffrey Gates, Mr. Tyson?" one of the women asked, her voice sharp. "I have reason to believe you are harboring these runaway children and that you have been molesting them, along with your own son. That's what the warrant is for, to find these children and take them into protective custody."

"We should just shoot the goddamn sunuvabitch and be done with it," the deputy said, not bothering to whisper.

"Let me see that warrant—you have reason to believe nothing. And I think I should be allowed to call my lawyer before you do anything."

"Russell, Hazel, we have to go, now. Now, before they catch us here," Jeff said and yanked both of them off the bed. "Come on, the back door. We'll fly; Father Jamey is waiting for us at the church. Wake up. *Wake up*. We have to move *now*."

"Go, *go*," Malachi whispered and leaned over as if he were going to push at both Russell and Hazel. Both stood suddenly as someone had pulled them up by the backs of their necks. "Go, out Dad's window. I'm supposed to be here."

"I'm afraid you are going to have to step aside, Mr. Tyson, or I may have to arrest you. Do I make myself clear?"

"I still haven't seen that search warrant."

"This is ridiculous," the other woman hissed angrily. "The search warrant is valid."

"You said it, sister. Goddamn faggot, trying to tell us what we can and can't do," the deputy added.

Russell and Hazel were finally moving. Alexander helped, nipping at their heels to get them to go faster. "Okay, okay, stop, Alex, I'm awake," Hazel said, when they stumbled into Mr. Tyson's study.

"Well, the warrant *looks* valid. You can look, but my son is sick; I won't have you disturb him, and so is my neighbor, Jack Ruggles. He's been staying with us since his wife died."

"Yeah, I'm okay, I'm ready, let's take off," Russell said.

Jeff shoved the window up. "Russ, go first."

"Step aside, Mr. Tyson."

Russell climbed out the window and dived out and up into the air. Hazel was right behind him. Alex simply jumped out the window and took off running, his feet skimming the wet grass. *We made it*, Jeff thought and flew out behind them.

Father Jamey

It was the Saturday evening vigil mass. Father Jamey started down the altar to take his place to offer the Host. The two Eucharistic ministers flanking him held ciboriums, and the two behind him held chalices. The woman on his right stepped down first and positioned herself by the front pew. The man on the priest's left held his yellow ciborium by the steps to the sacristy. The man and the woman behind the first two, holding the wine-filled chalices, took places closer to the church's side doors. Father Jamey, as always, stood in the middle. He picked up a Host from his own ciborium and looked up to see Ben Tyson at the front of the line. Ben held Malachi in his arms, the boy's fair head resting on his shoulder. Jack stood behind them. Jack was clearly only up and moving on sheer will power and painkillers; Malachi was obviously ill: pale, flushed, sunken eyes.

"Body of Christ."

"Father, we're here. What do we do now? Where do we go? I got out of the warrant this morning because the boys and Hazel got away, but they're going to be back. A deputy followed us here—he's parked in front of the church."

"Listen to me," Father Jamey whispered back to Ben, who had his right hand open to take the Host. He motioned to the obviously impatient woman behind Jack to go to the female Eucharistic minister. Both Eucharistic ministers were staring at the priest. They stopped when the communicants started following the priest's insistent hand gestures and came to them to take the Host. "After you take the Host, go to my left to take the cup. Then, go up those stairs to the sacristy. From there, go downstairs to the choir rehearsal room. The other kids are already there. Got it? Malachi," the priest went on, raising his hand to touch the boy's head, "I bless you in the name of the Father, the Son, and the Holy Spirit, and ask their healing to be upon you." Malachi's hair was wet with sweat and he was hot with fever. "Ben, the Body of Christ. Got it?"

"Amen," Ben said as he glanced back at Jack, who looked perilously close to falling over. "Jack?"

"I heard him; it's okay," Jack whispered back.

"May the Lord bless us, keep us from all evil and bring us to everlasting life," Father Jamey said as he traced a cross on Jack's forehead.

"Amen," Jack said, his voice barely audible.

The Change has finally begun, Father Jamey thought, watching the three of them walk over to the Eucharistic minister holding the chalice. The grey-haired woman seemed unperturbed by the long delay, and offered first Ben, then Jack, the silver cup. It had been on the radio again this morning: more monsters in the Great Dismal Swamp, unseasonal storms, apparitions, dragons in flight, unicorns wandering in city and state parks. And the focal point, ground zero: North Carolina, Raleigh, Garner, Vandora Springs Road. The church was as packed as if it were Christmas or Easter. A dawn-to-dusk curfew was in effect. Martial law had been declared.

"Body of Christ, Ethel."

"Amen."

What is Your will here? What sort of world will we have when this is all over? What do You want us to learn, to do, to be? Do You want to show us, teach us that magic is real and afoot? There, Ben, Jack, and Malachi were safe in the sacristy.

"Body of Christ, Steve."

"Amen, Father."

Somehow Jamey knew that what he was doing right then: cele-
brating mass, giving sanctuary to the persecuted, was exactly what
God wanted him to do and keep doing, no matter what sort of
Change was coming.

"Body of Christ, Margaret."

"Amen."

The Raleigh News and Observer
Sunday, 20 October 1991

Gays, Lesbians, and the Left are to Blame?

"They *are the ones responsible for what's been happening here
in North Carolina. Gays, lesbians, the feminists, the pro-abortion left-
ies, the ACLU, all of them—they are bringing the Devil and his
minions into this state," television evangelist Jerry Falwell said yesterday, the final afternoon of his seven-day Raleigh crusade, a joint
project with Billy Graham, in Dorton Arena at the State Fairgrounds.
Joint crusader Billy Graham seemed to be in sharp disagreement, as
he walked off the podium in the middle of Falwell's attack . . .*

Ben

When Ben woke Sunday morning he had no idea where he was.
He sat up, blinking and rubbing his eyes. God, he felt stiff—like he
had slept on the floor. Ben looked around: he *had* slept on the floor.
He was on the floor in the choir room at St. Mary's. He had spent
the night there and so had everybody else: Jack, Malachi, Russell,
Jeff, and Hazel and her cat.

"I wonder if I can borrow a razor and some shaving cream from
Father Jamey," Ben muttered, rubbing his hand over the morning
stubble on his face. He glanced over at Jack, who was still asleep, flat
on his back and snoring. Jack, at least for the moment, seemed to
be getting better. Father Jamey had managed to change the dressing
on Jack's chest wound and the burns on his back. The burns looked
as if they were healing. The long cut on Jack's chest still oozed blood
and the flesh around it had blackened. It hurts and it burns, Jack had
said. Liberal amounts of Solarcaine—all Father Jamey had for burns
—only slightly alleviated the pain. At least Jack could sleep with a
glass of water and two pills left over from the priest's arthoscopic
knee surgery.

Ben stood, his legs creaking. *Friday, Saturday, and now, on*

Sunday morning, I don't have a home. I have to live in a church until Halloween—Samhain—and what then? Where do we go? How do we get there? I have looked and looked: in books, journals, upstairs, downstairs—and my lady is gone and I don't know which gate will take me to her chamber, which gate Valeria tried to take ten years ago.

He had watched her die, only minutes after she left the house, forbidding him to come to the door to see her off, a command he had ignored. One more Fomorii outside, waiting, the backup, in case the first two failed. He had almost died with her, along with a willow oak and a dogwood and a good chunk of the front yard. Grass refused to grow back where the trees had been. And for a long time thereafter, he might as well have been dead.

Ben pulled his pants on and then wriggled into a sweatshirt. He would have to ask Father Jamey to get him some clothes. Would the Wake County Sheriff's Department let a priest into his house? Ben shook his head. Too many things to think about. He glanced at his watch—six. And what the hell—heaven—*I am in a church*—was he doing up at six A.M.?

There were no alarm clocks, of course, anywhere in the choir room. The closest thing was a metronome on top of the piano and an old clock on the wall. The wall clock was broken: the glass was gone and somebody had managed to snap off the minute and hour hands. The second hand remained, stuck between four and five.

Jack didn't have an alarm wristwatch. None of the boys did, either. Nor Hazel. So, what had woken him up? What had rang?

"I must have been dreaming," Ben whispered and stepping over Jack, went to check on Malachi.

The four children lay together in a nest of bodies on the opposite side of the room from Ben and Jack. Ben could see Malachi's luminous bright head between Russell's reddy-gold and Jeff's brown, a darkening brown, almost black, Ben realized as he stood over the children. And Hazel's honey-brown—the same? The bruises on Russell's face were almost gone. The blue-grey cat *was* bigger. *Malachi glows all the time now, just like his mother did when she was pregnant.* The cat was awake and staring back at Ben through half-open eyes, bright blue slits that cast a thin, blue light on the worn carpet.

"Good morning, Alexander," Ben said and knelt down to rub the cat's big head. The beast had grown to the size of a German shepherd, but it still acted like a house cat. As Ben stroked Alexander's head and back, the cat started purring, sounding like the rumbling of a small engine. To Ben's surprise, it rolled over on its back and let him stroke the soft white-grey belly fur.

"You are something else, kitty-boy-oh-boy—"

Ben stopped mid-stroke. He had heard again the sound that had awakened him. It wasn't an alarm, but a bell, a single, clear bell rung once. It couldn't be the church—the earliest mass wasn't until seven—no, eight, Father Jamey had said. No one wanted to be out before the sun was good and up, even when there hadn't been a curfew.

All that was left was a bare patch of earth in the front yard. I planted bulbs of every kind, fertilized, watered, aerated, everything I could think of, and nothing grew.

Ben resumed his stroking and was rewarded with another note from the mysterious bell. This time he could localize it: the sound was right by him—right in front of him.

The bell rang again.

"You are a good boy, Alex," Ben whispered and walking on his hands and knees went around the cat. He knew where the bell was and it wasn't a bell.

Ben sat down beneath the window, by his son. He leaned back to press his back against the wall: that always took away some of the soreness. He gently stroked his son's hair, the warm light twisting around his fingers. "Malachi? Wake up, son, tell me what you're dreaming."

"Dad? What?" Malachi opened his eyes and looked up.

"Tell me what you're dreaming. Quick, before you forget—the star your mother left you—it was ringing—"

Malachi sat up, holding the star in his right hand. He eased himself into the crook of Ben's arm. "A circle without grass, like the one in the front yard, where Mama died, but bigger and not here, it's glowing, and I'm above it, high in the air. Dad, feel what happens when I move the star."

He's so frail and that fever is burning him up. There was nothing left to bury after Valeria and the Fomorii burned up in the front yard. Just that circle where nothing has grown since. There might be another place like that—near—but where? I know this; the name is in my head; I've read about it. But I've read so many books, looking for a clue, any clue—

The star rang again. Malachi moved the star to his left and it rang yet again. To his right: no sound.

"You dreamed of the gate, didn't you, son? Your mother's star is a compass—see, that long point glows when you move it to the left. And the star rings."

"Yes," Malachi said, whispering, as he leaned into his father. "That's the way to the gate—now we can find it."

"Don't say anything yet to the others. We have to be sure, son. It's just like a compass—if we only had a map—a map, *that's it*," Ben said half to himself, half to Malachi, "*a map*." But his road maps were in the car, outside, and it wasn't safe to go outside. Father Jamey had to have a map somewhere—in his car, the church, the rectory.

Father Jamey will be down here soon, with breakfast. I can wait until then to get the map. Malachi can sleep a little longer—he's already fallen asleep again, even with all this noise. He is so very hot. And he's so light; he feels like a bird. His arms, his wrists are so thin. His body seems to be melting away. Those golden eyes are enormous. Now I can get him home; I can save him. Jack? If he doesn't die first, the fairies must know how to save people with black magic wounds. What am I going to do without Jack? If I can get Malachi and Jack and Jeff and Hazel and Russell and that cat out of this church, past the sheriff, past Thomas and his witches—I know he hasn't given up—if.

Father Jamey brought in the North Carolina map he had fished out of the glove compartment of his car, and spread it out on the floor in the choir room. The children, all four awake by then, their questions squelched, followed Malachi's direction and each sat on one side of the map, Malachi to the north, Hazel to the south, Russell, the east, Jeff, the west. A very pale looking Jack sat behind Malachi, to the boy's right, on the piano bench, leaning back against the piano, as if he needed its weight to bear him. Ben sat on the floor, to his son's left. Malachi held the still-glowing silver-grey twelve-pointed star in his hand, the chain looped around his wrist.

"Well," the priest said, looking at each of them, "are you ready? Malachi? This is your show, sort of. Your mother left you the star."

Malachi nodded and unlooped the star and held it over the map, letting it sway like a pendulum. "Nothing's happening, and it's stopped glowing," he said, frowning and looking at his father.

"It's a compass," his father said. "Hold it flat in your hand, close to the map, see where it pulls."

Father Jamey watched as the star glowed back to life and *pulled* Malachi's hand over the map, east on 40, then south on 15-501, away from Durham, around Chapel Hill, and south again, and into Chatham County, into Pittsboro, around the Courthouse, and southwest on 902. Each road lit up on the map, as if someone was drawing with a luminous marker, as Malachi let the star *pull* his hand. And as each road lit up, the star rang, a sure sweet note that rose up above all of them, almost visible, a brightening in the air.

"It's warm," he whispered, looking up once at his father. "Just like that game. Hot or cold."

Ben nodded.

Over the Rocky River, then Dewitt Smith Road, NC 2176, over 421, and Bear Creek, another crossroads with a name, and streets, roads, all spinning out from it: Old US 421, Barker Road, Roscoe Road, Bonlee School Road, Bear Creek Church Road. Harpers Crossroad and Malachi and the star were still. A slight twitch, up, another stop, and the star rang. This time it sounded like a gong, a long, low tone, which reverberated, bouncing off the walls, and settling over them.

"Here it is, this is the place," Malachi said and bent over the map to read the words naming the road. "1100. Devil's Tramping Ground."

Of course. A perfect circle where nothing grows, has ever grown. I remember the stories—we read about it in school. If something is left on the path, anything, overnight, the path is clear the next day. The circle in the yard—that was all she left.

"Dad?"

Ben looked over at Father Jamey, who shook his head. "I'm not from North Carolina, Ben."

"I know the place. I've never been there, but I know it. A big circle in a grove of trees where nothing grows. It's the gate." Ben said.

"We can really get there—we can get to Faerie," Russell shouted and jumped up. "We can do it—we can go home."

"We're almost there," Jeff shouted, joining in Russell's chorus. Hazel, then Jeff and Russell, started playing tag with the cat, knocking over the chairs and music stands. Music sheets became airborne, sailing around the room, making great circles in the air. Jack didn't stand, but he managed to sit up and watch, one hand on his chest, the other waving in the air, as if he had a baton and was directing the show.

From the journal of Ben Tyson, Monday morning, 28 October 1991

Father Jamey was able to go back to the house yesterday afternoon, after the noon mass. He told me the house had been ransacked. The doors *had been knocked down, the windows smashed, the furniture turned over, torn apart. He said it was as if they were DEA agents looking for drug stashes. Cushions, pillows, and chair seats had been slashed open, foam and feathers torn out and scattered everywhere. Every plate, every glass, every cup and saucer—smashed. The kitchen floor crunched. Even the salt and pepper shakers, the sugar bowl, the jelly jars—smashed into a sticky mess. The computer, the TV, the stereo. Books with pages ripped out, spines broken.*

Everything.

I had wanted him to get one book—just one, *The Devil's Tramping Ground and Other North Carolina Mystery Stories. He had to go all the way into Raleigh, to the Cameron Village Public Library.*

"None of the books in your house, Ben, were salvageable."

Somehow the books hurt the most. I know I can't go back and get them—I know I will never go back to that house again. Where I am going to go—after Faerie—I don't know. Is there an after Faerie? Do I stay there? Can I? She's gone.

It wasn't just Thomas's goons or the sheriff's boys, Father Jamey said. *My neighbors helped. He caught a handful in the house taking things.*

"They're normals, Ben; their kids aren't Changing. They aren't Changing. They're scared."

Normals? Are there two kinds of humans now? The Changed and the normal? The magical and the mundane?

"I got some of your clothes and Malachi's. Those diskettes you wanted—maybe you can use the computer in the rectory office. Here are some of Jack's clothes. They wrecked his house, too, by the way. I stopped at Kmart on the way back from the library—got some clothes for Hazel, Jeff, and Russell," *he had said.*

He came back down a little while ago, to bring dinner. He was still wearing his robes from mass, white and made from rough cloth, a rope around his waist. He looked a bit medieval.

"Are you going to stay here tonight with us?" *I asked, afraid that the house wreckers would follow us here.*

"You are safe in this church, at least for now. You remember what you told me about priests having special powers in the old stories? You know I can make a Cross in the air," *he said and quickly drew another shimmering cruciform apparition.* "I'm Changing, too; I told you that. Look at my ears, my eyes."

The Change must take longer in adults. Besides his ears, there is just a touch of luminosity in his blue eyes—as if there were a light shimmering behind the blue, a bit of a ways off, flickering in some distant wind.

"Are you going with us?" I asked.

"No, I don't think so," Father Jamey said. "I'm not dreaming of a place with silver and golden-leafed trees with glowing white trunks and two moons in the sky. My dreams are—different. I'd better go on, get to the grocery store before the panic sets in. It's the darkness—sunset is almost an hour earlier than it's supposed to be; sunrise an hour later. You're safe here. I can do that much, combined with the inherent power of a sacred place. I might be able to do more—I'll tell you later."

I am in the music director's office right now. I told the others I wanted to be left alone for a while. Father Jamey tells me the music director he inherited when he became the pastor at St. Mary's was a gadget man, sort of like Hazel's grandfather, I guess. There is a complete computer set-up and a music synthesizer and a stereo deck like something off the Enterprise.

So I can keep up with my journal for now. But even as I write this, I wonder what for and why. Writing helps me think. Writing helps me release stress, work off tension. But who will read this when I am gone? Do I want anybody to read this? People will want a history of these times—won't they?

Never mind.

I still don't know how we are going to escape, to get to the gate, even now when we know where it is: the Devil's Tramping Ground.

It looks almost Edenic in the drawing in the book, a circle of earth surrounding a grassy lawn that is probably yellow with dandelions and buttercups in the spring. Trees grow close by the circle, a few almost on it, cedars, oaks, maples. According to John Harden, starting on page 54 in The Devil's Tramping Ground and Other North Carolina Ghost Stories:

> . . . the story is that the Devil goes there to walk in circles as he thinks of new means of causing troubles for humanity. There, sometime during the dark of night, the Majesty of the Underworld of Evil silently tramps around and around that bare circle—thinking, plotting, and planning against good, and in behalf of wrong.

> So far as is known, no person has ever spent the night there to disprove that this is what happens and that is this what keeps grass, weeds, and other vegetation worn clean and bare from the circle.

The cleared spot, surrounded by trees, comprises a perfect circle with a forty-foot diameter. The path itself is about a foot wide and is barren of any obstruction—growing or otherwise. A certain variety of wire grass grows inside the circle in a limited fashion (all right, cut the dandelions and buttercups) and residents of that neighborhood say any attempts to transplant any of it have met with failure. Broomsedge, moss, and grasses grow on the outer edge of the circular path, but not inside the circle.

Anything left on the path is always removed by the next day. The Devil kicks aside "the obstacles on his nightly perambulations." Or, a circle worn by the dancing feet of Indians? The path kept clear by God as a "monument to these faithful Indian braves"? A battle fought between Indians before the whites came, the survivors burying their chief, Croatan, and the "Great Spirit kept bare the circle, down through the years, in mourning for the loss of a faithful chief and a great leader." The soil is simply sterile? Or the spells that bind this gate between worlds have made a barrier that keeps out vegetation, preserving only the earth in a perfect circle? Nine times around, backward, at midnight on Samhain and the gate will open.

None of which helps me. How are we supposed to get there, escape from this church when demons and demon-possessed people are just outside? Father Jamey says he has a plan and not to worry.

Jack is only getting a little better. I make him eat and drink, but he hurts.

Malachi is dying.

Russell and Jeff are bored and scared and excited and are driving me crazy. Hazel is waiting for her turn to use the computer. Alex is asleep.

Samhain is three days away.

I can feel the demonic outside.

VII

The White City
Faerie

FOR A LONG MOMENT, THE SECOND—*I MUST THINK of myself as First, as Prime Mover, Valeria is dead. The others need me to accept this, accept me as Prime Mover*—didn't respond to the report that had just been delivered to the Dodecagon. Instead she stared out the nearest open window. The day had dawned without sun. Thick, thick roiling black clouds all but hid the bare minimum of light. The storm, thank the Three, was still far out to sea. She could not see the lightning, but rather its flashing glow on the grey water. Below she saw only a few people hurrying through the streets. Most had not left their houses, or were at the Temple.

"Sec—Prime Mover, please," a speaker for the Third-Born said, his hooves striking the floor.

They aren't quite used to me as Prime Mover, either.

"I know. I'm sorry," she said and turned away from the window. "The report is no surprise. The Peace has held for a year—almost a year. There have been—and continue to be—violations. The Fomorii know how weakened we are from the war. There are signs they may be planning a new war. And you want to know if our call to the changelings has borne fruit. In three days, on Samhain, we will know. There is nothing I can do to make Samhain come any sooner. No petitions in the Temple to the Good God, to the Goddess, the Teachers, no prayers to the Three. I cannot sound the call any louder or make its effects happen any sooner. You all know this," she said, looking slowly around the table, her bronze eyes glowing. She lifted her right hand and then, one by one, flicked a splash of light at each one, a warm, white wash that broke and flowed over foreheads, eyes, ears, mouths, spilling down throats.

"But will they wait those three days before they break the Peace?" a centaur asked, his arms folded across his chest, his tail swishing nervously back and forth. His left front hoof kept tapping the floor.

The Prime Mover resisted going over to grab it and hold it still.

"We and the dolphins think so," the swimmer said who sat beside the centaur. "They need the power of Samhain and the opening of the gates as much as we do." For the first time in years, a speaker for the swimmers had actually attended a session of the Dodecagon. His green-and-black body glistened wetly in the yellow candlelight. Water pooled at his feet. When the swimmer turned to look up at the centaur, moving his hands to make his point, water sprayed everywhere. The drops bounced off the auric shields of the others. The centaur had forgotten to manifest his shield—he sputtered and stepped away, his tail swishing even harder.

"Uh, sorry, I didn't mean to get you wet," the swimmer said and got up to try and brush the water off the centaur's chest and face. This, of course, made matters worse as he sprayed and dripped more water.

"Never mind," the centaur said and stepped back hastily, his tail swishing. "Prime Mover, can we wait three days, can we hold out if they attack beforehand?"

"He's right," she said. "They need the power from the gates as well—"

"Why don't we attack?" a dwarf interrupted, ignoring the sudden intake of breath and mutterings at his breach of accepted good manners and council protocol. "We have waited and waited for this silly experiment of the First-born to work and so far, no powerful changeling children. Are we going to let all that we lost during the war be a vain sacrifice to First-born pride?"

"How dare you say such a thing?" a First-born shouted, his fist pounding the table. Fireballs popped as he hit the table and bounced over the polished wood, leaving scorched trails behind.

"*Stop, both of you,*" The Prime Mover said, as the fireballs fizzled out on the stone floor. "All of you: STOP!" she said angrily, turning to glare at the other First-borns who were grumbling among themselves. "We will not sacrifice anything to anyone's pride. There was no other solution. We will not just sit and wait. I have placed our forces on alert; we are prepared for attack. But, even if the Fomorii weren't moving against us again, we still would have called the changelings home. We are just too weak after the war to go on without their new blood, energy, their new magic. If this experiment does not work, if the changelings do not come to Faerie, a renewal of the war by the Fomorii will only hasten the inevitable."

"Fair enough," the dwarf growled. "Damn First-born arrogance," he added, under his breath. The Prime Mover shook her head at the other First-born. *Let it go.*

"Now, if we can go on to other business? . . ."

On the Great Sea

"We will be off the coast of Tir Mar and the White City just before midnight on Samhain, as planned, Your Highness," the lieutenant said.

"Good," the prince answered, his fangs bared, his eyes glowing fires. "We will strike them at their weakest—when their call fails and when *we* draw on the energy of the changeling world, of those at the gate who cannot cross. The rule of the dark will last for millennia."

"Yes, my lord," the lieutenant said, and touched his forehead with his front claws in salute. "I know their souls will taste sweet."

Father Jamey

The phone rang.

"Hello, St. Mary's, Father Jamey speaking," he said, surprised the church phones were still working. The electricity in the air had caused half the phones in Wake County to go out. And the half that worked seemed to belong to all the Catholics in Garner with the same idea: call the church, find out what was going on, get some reassurance. He was sure, as he listened, that there was a goodly number in the sanctuary, praying or lighting vigil candles or slowly following the Stations of the Cross, muttering as they walked. How many, he wondered, had even been inside the church before everything had started?

Don't be so cynical. Take people where you find them. At least don't be cynical out loud.

"No, I don't know what's wrong with the phones." The lights in the room blinked then, popped, and then were out. Instantly everything in the room softened and dimmed, as only the grey light from outside was left. "Yes, my lights just went out, too—there, they are back on. Yours aren't? Maybe soon. Yes, the weather report is still calling for unseasonable storms. No, I am sure we are not facing an inland hurricane. I heard it on NPR this morning. The National Weather Service is researching the cloud formation even as we speak. Yes, I know there was some daylight early this morning—I guess that old saying isn't true anymore. Darkest before dawn. Never mind, you were saying? It is safe to go out—but I would stay home at night—and there is a dusk-to-dawn curfew anyway—you know that. Yes, of course, you can come to church—just stay put wherever you are after dark. Yes. This is all real. Yes. In the Name of the Father, the Son, and the Holy Spirit. Amen."

Father Jamey hung up and looked out his office window. It was just after nine—the visible daylight for the day was gone, the one brief break in the clouds just after dawn, replaced by a pervasive greyness and the darkening clouds, the occasional lightning only briefly adding any light of significance. That was the tenth phone call since he had gotten into his office. Now the wind was beginning to rise. According to NPR severe thunderstorms were up and down the Eastern Seaboard and there really was a late hurricane, Susanna, brewing out in the Caribbean. Chains of typhoons were supposedly spawning in the Indian Ocean, but overseas news was erratic at best, with all the interference. The worst storms seemed to be in North Carolina.

More lightning rippled across the sky, followed by explosive thunder, as if a chain of firecrackers had gone off above the earth. The church had been packed for the eight A.M. mass. He looked briefly from the window to the mirror that hung on the inside of his closet door: *I guess they found your face inspiring, bucko—dark circles, hair looking permanently electrified. No accounting for taste.*

"Well, prayer won't hurt. I bet it's actually helping—if I can get enough to pray tomorrow morning during that one bit of light, I think we can make it out of here, anyway. I should talk to Ben—tell him this should work—that I can do what I have to do, my own magic," he said to himself, as he turned back to staring out the window. He raised his right hand as he stood there and then slowly drew a cross in the air, light bleeding from his hand as it moved. Then, the cross, wavering, but finished, he drew a five-pointed star around it. Father Jamey took both hands and pulled at the sides of the star, as if to make it wider, to give the cross more room. More white light first fell out of the star's interior, dropping like a net around him and he disappeared. Almost. He could see in the closet-door mirror a faint whiteness, a blur.

"That will do, I think. Let me go tell Ben."

The phone rang again just as he got to his office door.

"Damn." *Now, remember why you became a priest, Jamey-boy. Ben and the kids and Jack and that big cat are not going anywhere.*

"Hello, St. Mary's, Father Jamey speaking."

Three calls later, the last one cut short by a white flash that must have fried the line, Father Jamey stepped out on the rectory's back porch steps, and then down into the yard. He stood there, pulling his overcoat tighter as he watched and listened. The wind was rising, a cold, wet wind, with a high whistle. Wolf-wind, he thought, remembering what he and his brothers had called such winds when they were children. Wolf-winds came down from the mountains, spreading snow far and wide, as they set howling wolves loose on the terrified populace. *I wish I had tried to call home before the phone went dead. God help us all if it snows.* Twisting and turning sheets of newspaper, brightly colored insert ads like huge odd fall leaves, unidentifiable bits of plastic flew through the air. An escaped umbrella rolled and bounced down Vandora Springs Road. The number of cars and trucks on the road didn't seem out of the ordinary, but then Father Jamey had never paid any attention to morning traffic. He was sure, however, that the cars and trucks passing loaded to the gills were not ordinary.

Where are you going? Where do you think you can go to escape all this? You know all the highways leading out of North Carolina are blocked and guarded by the Army.

Now, where are the watchers? Ah, right across the street was the Wake County Sheriff's squad car—*I wonder why they haven't gotten the Garner PD to help?* The others—Father Jamey couldn't see them, but he felt them, and today, as if this wind had carried the scents, he could *smell* them: bitter, metallic, harsh, sort of like zinc. Wait— there was one, skulking behind the oak tree near the squad car.

Might as well as try this now.

Father Jamey drew a luminous cross in the air and then, with a *shove*, released the glowing cruciform into the air. The cross wavered, shook, and for a moment, as it collapsed into itself, Father Jamey thought his new magic had failed. But the cross became a white ball, a small comet that streaked across the streets, its tail a white flame. The comet smashed into the tree and the shape screamed and ran. *Was that a man? Or a woman? Or worse?*

A Cherokee Scout rumbled down the street as Father Jamey turned to go back inside. He waved at the dour deputy who waved back. *Did he see the cross turn into a comet? Hit the tree? The shape? Never mind.* The rain started when he got to the back steps, cold, and heavy and laced with bits of ice.

"Ben's in the choir director's office," Hazel said, looking up from the piano. She was trying to teach herself how to play. "I have to do something, Father." She wasn't doing so badly, Father Jamey thought as he stood beside Hazel, listening as she picked her way through a simple tune. *But then, isn't music a magic by itself? Random sounds shaped and arranged into meaning?* The cat, which had been drowsing at Hazel's feet, got up, stretched, and then head-butted the priest's legs.

Pet me.

Okay, okay, I will. I thought you could talk, you big overgrown rug.

Head to tail. Rugs don't have claws, by the way.

"Okay, no more rug jokes," Father Jamey said and sat down beside Hazel to stroke and scratch the cat's massive head as Hazel finished the tune.

"Jack helped me some—he said he had piano lessons when he was a kid and took them again for a while after his divorce," she said, looking up when she was done. "Your eyes are getting all silvery, too, Father Jamey."

"I know. I figure I can give up trying to hide my ears—everybody will be too busy looking at my eyes. Play something else."

"Okay, but I only know two."

As Hazel started another simple tune, Father Jamey looked around for the others. Malachi lay beneath the window, on top of a pile of sleeping bags, covered by several blankets and a quilt scavenged from the rectory. He was sleeping, his face to the wall. Father Jamey could see his aura, a pale, sickly yellow, streaked with red. The lights intertwined in his hair and glowing beneath his skin were the same feverish red.

Hazel stopped playing. "He doesn't wake up much now, Father, except when Ben makes him drink something, eat some soup," she said softly. "He can still sort of mind-speak, but mostly it's all dreams about Faerie and the White City and the sea. And the four of us all there together. He's dying, isn't he?"

"Yes, he is. Unless we can get to the gate. I have an idea—not a great one, but an idea. Where is everybody else?"

"Jack's with Ben. I think Russell and Jeff are flying around in the church. They were reading for a while," Hazel said and pointed to the books scattered on the floor beside the sleeping bags and blankets. "Then they got bored. They sent Jeff's dinosaurs flying around here, but Ben got mad and sent them into the sanctuary. They woke up Malachi. I told Ben Malachi liked to have them around, but he didn't listen. What's your plan, Father Jamey?"

"Let me talk to Ben and Jack first," the priest said and looked up to see a stuffed purple apatosaurus and a cherry-red tyrannosaurus rex parked on the ceiling.

Jack was in pain. Father Jamey could see it in the man's grey face and how he lay very still on the couch by the computer, as if the wrong gesture or movement might be too much to bear. He lay under an embroidered quilt the priest's mother had given him when he had accepted the job at St. Mary's. *My first parish. Might be my last one, too.* Even a priest needs to have some nice things, vow of poverty or not, she had told him when she had brought it out to his car. *I hope Duncan called her, let her know I'm all right, despite being at the center of all the storms.* Duncan, the older of his two little brothers, had called last night and his voice had echoed in the phone, as if he were talking deep inside a well.

"Hey, Big Brother Father . . . I've been trying for days to get a line . . . what the hell is going on in North Carolina . . . Mama's worried sick about—"

The line popped and buzzed, as if there was something between Jamey and his brother, eating their words, gulping down their sounds. Duncan finally gave up after extracting a promise from Jamey to call home as soon as he could.

I wish Dunc were here.

"Hey, Father J, Earth to Father J," Ben said, snapping his fingers, as he turned his chair away from the keyboard and the monitor. "I was trying to get on the Internet, when the modem went dead. It's as if we are on an island in the middle of nowhere."

"Sorry, my mind was—never mind. We are on an island, sort of. North Carolina is the spawning ground for these storms that seem to be driving anything electrical insane. The phone lines go dead, they come back to life, they just went dead a bit ago, so no Internet access. The lights are on permanent blink, I think. All of which you already know. What are you trying to find on the net, anyway?" Father Jamey said as he took the chair beside Ben.

"Passing the time—"

"He was looking for more magic, as if we didn't have enough of it already. A spell or a charm or something," Jack said slowly, trying to sit up. "To heal this wound in my chest. The burns on my back are healing; I don't think my chest will ever heal." The priest could see, from where the quilt fell from Jack's chest, the faint pink stains coming through Jack's T-shirt.

"I should change your bandage again," Jamey said. "I know you should probably not travel, Jack, but I do have a plan now, to get us out of here and closer to the Devil's Tramping Ground."

There was a sudden flash of light, immediately followed by a cannon shot of thunder, so loud, it seemed to almost be on top of the church. The computer popped, sparked, and went dead, along with the rest of the room's lights.

"Guess that takes care of that. Okay, Father J, what's your plan?" Ben asked. "Where did you put those candles you brought yesterday?"

"Over there, by the door; I'll help you light them. I told you I could do some magic myself now. I showed you how I could make a luminous cross in the air. Today I used that cross to make one of the watchers leave—I don't know if it was from the cross, like with vampires, or just the fright of having it turn into a fireball that exploded right in front of the watcher. I can do that now. And I can make a glamour—an old word for a magic shield, like a cloak of invisibility, which will hide the church van. I told you that I could, I think. I'm the strongest in the morning, in that brief hour of light before the clouds close over. We can get to Chapel Hill in an hour—even in the van. I figure we should take that over the wagon: more room."

"The van's fine, but what after Chapel Hill? We still have to get to southwest Chatham County before midnight day after tomorrow," Ben said. The two of them moved about the room, setting out and lighting the candles. The soft candlelight pushed back some of the grey light coming in the window.

Jamey shook his head. He hadn't quite figured out that part of the plan yet. He was working on it. He had another idea, but wanted to wait and mull over it some more. They had to travel in the dark then—there was no way around that or hide in the woods by the Devil's Tramping Ground all day and that didn't seem like a good idea.

"Will your magic be enough?" Jack said. "Black magic is awfully strong and it's getting stronger and stronger. I can feel it—that's where these clouds and storms are from. Even with that glamour, the witches will chase us. Or the deputies or somebody."

"We've got to try. What other choice do we have?"

"Okay," Ben said, nodding his head. "It could work, but the next part is what worries me. Chapel Hill to Chatham—"

"I have a plan for that," Jack said, interrupting. "Give Thomas what he wants and then hightail it out of there—fast car, church van—whatever."

"What do you mean?" Ben asked. "Give Thomas what?"

"Me."

"Jack!" Jamey and Ben shouted at the same time, Ben coming to his feet.

"No, no way, no way in hell—or heaven—I won't let you do this, Jack. I won't. I'll take you with us—"

"I can't go—I'm not a changeling. You don't even know if you can go, Ben. This wound is going to kill me, anyway. I can feel it. This way, my death will do some good. Not the evil Thomas wants. Please, let me do this," Jack said as he struggled to sit up, each movement obviously causing him pain.

"No, Jack. You are not going to do this. Father J, you tell him. No, no, no, NO!" Ben yelled.

"Ben, stop. Jack, no, it's wrong. He'll still get his evil and—it's just wrong."

Jack slumped back down on the couch, his eyes closed. "All right, Ben. Father," he said, whispering. "I haven't got the strength to argue with you."

"There doesn't have to be a sacrifice," Jamey said. "There aren't many witches out in the day—and in the hour of light before the clouds close back in, there won't be any. And the glamour will hide the van. I'll douse the van with holy water, string it with garlic. We will be in Chapel Hill in an hour, a little more. Then, tomorrow night, we can do it again—or something. We will; I know it."

He knew it was true. They *would* think of another plan to get from Chapel Hill to the Devil's Tramping Ground, in the dark, in the storm. How and at what cost—well, what good did it do to worry over that part? Good always won over evil, didn't it? In the end, anyway, he had to remind himself, and the end was sometimes a long way from the beginning. But that wasn't true. Evil did win, sometimes, completely and thoroughly. Weren't there Nazis who went to their graves uncaught and unrepentant? Wasn't genocide a way to outline human history? Did something good truly come out of everything evil? If humanity learned anything from the Holocaust, then why had there been killing fields in Cambodia? Maybe this was supposed to end badly—Malachi, Jack dead, Thomas the victor. Evil triumphant.

Or maybe there was no God at all.

I don't know. I have to believe Good wins; I have to believe God cares, that Jesus was who he said he was. I have to believe that all of this has some purpose. That the Nazis had to answer for what they did in the next world, if not in this one.

Then, he sat down by Jack on the couch, took the man's too-cold hand and began to pray.

WUNC 91.5, Morning Edition, National Public Radio
Wednesday morning, October 30, 1991
David Molpus reporting, Chapel Hill, North Carolina

Usually at this time, most local stations break Morning Edition for state and local news. And I will, even though North Carolina is national news today and has been for a while. The National Weather Service at RDU Airport is at a loss to explain why the state is the focal point for the electrical storms now plaguing the country. Janet Carrollton, Weather Service spokesperson, said this morning that so far the storms seem to be connected to some sort of extreme ionization of the upper atmosphere. As to why central North Carolina should be the spawning ground of all these storms remains a mystery to meteorologists all over the country.

Electrical power and phone service has been disrupted throughout the state. This station is right now running on a generator. Of course, I have no idea who is hearing this broadcast, if anybody is, or if it is making it out of North Carolina to DC. Almost three-fourths of Raleigh is in the dark, and Chapel Hill and Durham are supposed to be totally without power. Heavy rains have caused local flooding and that, plus the high winds, has made most major highways impassable. Lightning strikes have been reported throughout the state—the greatest number in south Raleigh and Garner—

While the Weather Service cannot explain the reason for the electrical storms, there are people in the area who do have explanations. Yesterday I spoke with local church leaders, several of whom believe this is the Apocalypse, Armageddon, the End Time. Local pagan, Wiccan, and Old Faith groups have another version or vision of what is happening: they are saying the storms are harbingers for the coming Great Change, the end of one Millennium and the beginning of another, a time when magic will once again be set loose in the world. Jackson Turner, Chief Priest of the Chapel Hill Pagan Circle, said yesterday the world is at a critical juncture in history.

Turner: The world *is* coming to an end—just not quite the way doomsayers would have us believe. *This* world—this way of life, with its machines, cut off from the Great Mother, Earth—is ending. It's failed, run its course, run out of energy, and a world in which humans are truly an integral, responsible part, is about to begin. Gaea is coming.

Molpus: Why here in North Carolina? Why not some place like —oh, I don't know, Ireland, for example? And how do we know for sure this is going to be a positive change? What about black magic?

Turner: An enormous amount of *mana* or magic energy has been released over the last ten years. This energy, I think, has caused many of the storms. Magic, as a natural force, akin to gravity, has always been around, and now it's been tapped, so to speak. As for why here, I want to believe that is because there are so many Old Religionists here of one kind or another. I really don't know why North Carolina and that does scare me. Evil—well, the change itself is neutral; it is just change. Evil people can use this change for their own purposes. There is that danger. Black magic is just as real as white. I think evil is responsible for many of the storms, too.

Molpus: And may the Force be with you. So, witchcraft is going to make a comeback? And it may be black witchcraft? When will this happen?

Turner: You joke about the Force, but Lucas wasn't that far off. As for when, on October 31, or Samhain, of course.

Molpus: On Halloween? Are we going to see a whole host of goblins, beasties, and things that go bump in the night? Dragons in the air.

Turner: There already have been dragons in the air; you know that. It was recorded on film. What sorts of creatures are set free will depend on who controls the Changer, the Dark or the Light.

Molpus: The Changer?

Turner: Yes, the Changer . . .

Russell

Russell watched through a narrow window, at the top of the stairs that led from the sacristy down into the choir room, as the church van backed up to the choir room door that opened to the outside.

Father Jamey drove slowly, wanting to make the van's back as close to the building as possible. He wished the priest would go just a bit faster. Light was literally burning. The time between sunrise and the rising of the dark was short and shorter. No blue sky—there hadn't been any for days, but for now, brightness despite the grey and no wind and no rain and no lightning. For the moment, except for the sound of the van, the world was quiet. For Russell, the quiet right then, as Father Jamey finally got the van to where he wanted, was both interior and exterior.

In a few minutes, he knew they would be calling him to come on, to go. And he wanted to; he wanted them to hurry. And he didn't. Russell was safe by this window, on these stairs, in the church. He had but to turn around and he would be through the sacristy and onto the altar. Nothing could hurt him there. Outside the church, even in a holy water-blessed, magic herb-washed church van, inside a glamour cast by a changeling priest, the others, the dark ones, the red-eyed ones, were that much nearer. They had hurt him before. He could feel them at the edge of his aura, nibbling at him like rats, their teeth tearing at the light, their claws trying to shred the colors. He had known they were very close when he had gotten up, early, to go to the bathroom. In the bathroom mirror his hair looked redder than he had ever seen it and his eyes had been green fires. Now he could hear them, too, whispering to him: *Russell, angry Russell, come, anger is power, real power, true power, if you just come . . .*

Now, this morning, as he heard the others carrying things into the van, the voices were louder, and this time, they sounded like Miss McNeil:

Russell, Red Fox, my little red fox, foxy woxy, sweet, little red fox, what's a little boy like you doing with those bad people? Come on out, be with me. That's right, just one step at a time; they are so busy they won't even notice, not that they care. Take another step . . .

"Russ? Russell, don't go out there yet. Not by yourself. Jeff, help me—"

Russell had come down the stairs; he stood in the choir room. The door to the outside was open. Father Jamey was out there, and Ben and—

Red Fox? Come on, you are such a good boy, that's right, come on. You've always been such a good boy for me, remember? Nobody else believes that but me. Little Red Foxy-Loxy, Fox-in-socks, sir, do you remember that story, Russ? Do you remember?

"Haze? What is it? Ben and Father Jamey said we should come

on, as soon as they get Jack and Malachi settled, get whatever stuff you want to take—"

"Stop talking, Jeff, and help me, it's Russ, look at him, he's almost—"

Tell these bad children to just go away and leave you alone. Tell them I said so.

"You got him?"

"No, not yet, I can't reach in enough—link, link, take my hand—Haze, my father is out there. I hear him. He's promising to be good forever. He loves me, he really loves me—"

"Jeff, not you, too, oh and Malachi is too sick to help, Alex!"

Russell Red Fox Russell Of course I love you; I would never hurt you.

The cat leapt through the door to land on top of the three children who by then were all tangled and pulling and pushing each other. The chairs and music stands fell around them, banging and bumping on the floor. Russell was on the bottom, shoving and kicking. If he could just get these two off of him, he could go. Miss McNeil was waiting. Jeff was on the top and he had just gone limp, caught between trying to hold Russell and trying to escape from Hazel at the same time. She was fighting with both boys as a rope of light wove itself around all three. The rope kept winking on and off.

"Here, Russ, Jeff, Hazel—we're here," Ben yelled as he burst inside, Father Jamey at his heels. Russell shoved Jeff and Hazel off, and stood in fighting stance. Ben was an adult, but slow. Russell faked him out, dodged to the right and out and he ran right into Father Jamey who locked his arms around him. Hazel held Jeff, rocking him back and forth, as Alex licked his face.

"It's okay," Jeff whispered. "I don't hear him anymore. It's okay. Help Russ."

"Let me go, let me go, *let me go, you cocksucking sonuvabitch priest—LET ME GO—*"

"No, you are not going out there alone, you're not giving in, no, no, no," the priest said, and held on. Ben grabbed Russell from behind, and right then, at the touch of the second man, Russell felt everything—the dark voices, Miss McNeil, the shadows—slip away. And he slipped against the priest, his body limp, and so tired, so tired.

"I'm sorry, Father J, I didn't mean—"

"Hush. Ben, bring me some of that herbal mixture I sprinkled on the van. Hazel, go get a paper towel. Jeff, just be still."

"What's in this?" Hazel asked awhile later as the priest dipped the paper towel into the dark-colored, aromatic liquid Ben had brought him in a bucket.

"Garlic, laurel, mandrake, marjoram, mugwort, parsley, thyme —a few other things," Father Jamey said as he wiped Russell's face. "For protection, for strength, for courage. These herbs are like conduits."

"They're all from Valeria's garden; she planted it right after she found out she was pregnant. I've been growing them ever since and never knew really what to do with them," Ben said. "Jeff, are you all right, son? You should wash your face with this stuff, Hazel, you, too."

Jeff sat up. He ran his hands through his dark hair and shook his head. He looked up, first at Ben, then at Father Jamey and Russell. Russell looked asleep. "Yes, I'm all right" he said and slowly got up. "I don't hear my father anymore. I think he may be out there, with the others, in the shadows." He took the wet paper towel from the priest and ran it over his face and gave it to Hazel; he wasn't sure he liked the smell.

Father Jamey shifted Russell until he held him over his shoulder in a fireman's carry. "I think it's time to go. I'll put Russ in the van. Ben, get Malachi. You two stay with Russell. Then we will get Jack and go."

Russell woke to find himself covered by an old quilt, lying on a narrow mattress. Malachi lay beside him, still asleep. Russell leaned over and put his hand on Malachi's forehead. Alex lay on Malachi's other side. The cat looked up at Russell, his blue eyes glowing. Jack lay beside the cat on another narrow mattress, his face turned to the wall. Hazel and Jeff sat, facing him where the last row of van seats would have been; Ben and Father J were in the front. How long had he been asleep? How long until they got—where were they going, anyway?

"He's still hot," Russell whispered.

"Yeah, I know. How are you?" Jeff whispered back. "Come over here, so you won't wake him and Jack. They aren't doing too good."

Russell crawled over the mattress and the quilt and the blankets Hazel and Jeff were sitting on and eased himself against the back of the middle van seat, besides Jeff. He leaned into the smaller boy, knowing again that Jeff, in many ways, was much stronger and tougher than he was.

"Everybody all right back there?" Ben called, turning around.

"Fine. Russell's awake; he's up," Jeff called back.

"Russ? How are you feeling?" Father Jamey said over his shoulder.

"I'm all right. I'm just real tired."

For a while, no one spoke. There were only the low soft sounds of Jack and Malachi sleeping and the van's engine and the wind outside. Russell got up on his knees to look out a window into what seemed to be a white veil wrapped around the van. Through it he could see dimly the passing highway—somewhere on Interstate 40, heading west—the blur of trees, the darkening grey of the sky, the shadow of the approaching rain. How much longer did they have before this bit of sunlight was gone? Where were the other cars? The big tractor trailers? Had everyone gone to cover, hiding from whatever was happening, the storms, the darkness, the monsters? And *they* were nearby. Looking. He felt them, just barely on the edge of his aura, not a touch, but a flicker, like a light wind over grass.

"When do—where are we going?" Russell asked, as he sat back against Jeff, suddenly tired again.

"Another church—south of Pittsboro, if we can make it there. So we won't have far to go tomorrow to get to the Devil's Tramping Ground," Hazel said. "That's what Father Jamey said. Depends on what happens when it gets dark again—which is any minute, I think."

Russell closed his eyes and leaned into Jeff. If he could just stay right where he was until they got to wherever whenever. Not move. Not think. Let Jeff hold him up. That was all Russell wanted.

Father Jamey

The glamour grew thin when the last of the sunlight faded and the rain and the lightning began. When the first lightning bolt struck in an eastbound lane, he knew the herbal magic was wearing thin, too. Not that there was a malevolent Zeus or Thor taking aim at the St. Mary's van, but that the circle of protection surrounding it was shrinking. Fire spurted and sizzled out of the cracked pavement and almost without a time lag, thunder smashed into the van, rocking it back and forth, pushing it onto the side of the road. For a long, long moment, the priest knew he was driving on two wheels. Then, with a hard thud and a bounce, the van tipped back onto all four.

He stopped; he had to, the rain was like gunfire on the roof and the sides. His heart was racing; his entire body shook with fear.

"Everybody all right? I'm calling roll, Ben?" Jamey said when he could finally speak.

He looked over at the passenger seat, where Ben sat, his head thrown back, breathing hard. "I'm okay, just really scared," Ben whispered. "Check on the kids, on Jack."

"We bounced around a lot, but we're okay," Jeff called, his voice shaky. "Me and Haze and Russ."

"What about Malachi and Jack?"

"They sort of fell on top of each other when the van tilted—still breathing, I just checked," Hazel said. "Still asleep—but they groaned a lot."

I'm fine I will look after them.

"Thanks, Alex. Okay, find something to hold onto, and don't let go. It's going to be rough and slow from here on in. We're just past the turnoff for the Durham Freeway, and the rain is so hard I can't go really fast—"

Lightning struck again, this time somewhere in the trees to their right. Fire again blazed up out of the greyness and the hammering rain.

"Let's go. I think we will have two more legs of this trip—to what we can find close to Chapel Hill now, and then again, tomorrow morning, to what we can find close to the Devil's Tramping Ground. I've got a map of North Carolina churches; I've got some in mind. Hang on."

By the time they got to Exit 276, Fayetteville Road and NCCU, the greyness had become darkness. And things in the air, riding the storm, had found them.

The things howled, they roared, they screamed, they wailed, louder and more piercingly than any banshee. They raked their claws on the now shredded and fading glamour, tearing off more chunks, the raking worse than any fingernails on any blackboard or piece of Styrofoam. The van swayed this way, that, as the things swooped, banged their tails, their heads, on the roof, the back door, the side. Somebody—was it Jeff, Russell?—screamed in the back—no, *oh, my God—it was Jack.* Somebody else was crying. Lightning kept flashing, striking the earth, exploding. Jamey shuddered, remembering the service station at the 276 exit, an Exxon station, roaring in flames. It had, at least, pushed back the dark.

"Ben," Jamey shouted, as the van swayed again. "You are going to have to drive—I need to try and strengthen the glamour, drive them off." *God, please help me do this. I am so scared.*

"Drive? Switch places?" Ben shouted back. "Are you crazy?"

"You have to. Come on, get over here, I will hold on until you take the wheel."

The van swayed again and swerved into the other lane and back, off the pavement, back on. A hard gust of wind slapped it back again, as some thing, screaming, ripped off a piece of the glamour. The van shuddered—something had struck the side—had the metal buckled? *God, please, give us time.*

"Okay, I got the wheel, now go do your magic," Ben yelled. Jamey lurched to the passenger seat, fell in, closed his eyes, reached out with one hand to take the handle above the window, and began to center in, find the place where the magic was, where the glamour had been grown.

Exit 273, Jordan Lake. 270, 15-501. Greensboro 50 miles.

Ben

A thing landed on the top of the van, then another, and another. They screamed, they snarled, and one ripped off the luggage rack, sending it banging into the rain and the wind and the dark. Then they flew off, and another hovered—*how can it do that in this wind?* —above the van, and swiped at it with its tail, knocking the van again and again. Ben wrestled with the steering wheel, cursing and praying at the same time. And he wrestled with his fear—no, he was way past fear, this was terror. Everything he had been afraid of since he was a kid had come back, including the dark, muttering monsters under the bed, big growling dogs, being lost in the dark. *Being scared and still going on, that's being brave. I can be brave. I am brave.*

"We are about to run out of Chapel Hill exits. Hurry up, Jamey," Ben yelled, trying to look over at the priest—*oh my God, had he fallen asleep—no, no, unconscious? God, please, please, help us.* "Jamey, wake the fuck up. Jamey!"

Jamey found the place, deep inside, where no wind howled, no rain fell, no monsters screamed. There was only the transparent white of the glamour.

Another thing, larger, heavier than all the rest, swooped out of the rain, its wings a blackness in and of themselves.

It was a dragon.

Flames splashed against the van, the window beside Ben cracked, behind him he heard other glass cracking. He wanted to run and run, as far away as he could.

"I've got to take this exit—266—Jamey—do it *now.*" Ben swerved off the interstate, the van almost skipping up the ramp, the dragon swooping, slapping at it with its tail, blistering the metal with its fire.

One slash of its claws tore off the spare on the back door. More lightning strikes, here, there, in the next lane, thunder almost incessant, an avalanche of sound.

Russell, Jeff, and Hazel

Malachi and Jack were scrunched together in one corner of the van, their bodies thrown side by side, the quilts and blankets all wrapped in and around them, the mattresses tight against each other. Alex lay against Malachi, who was on the outside, his claws dug in the mattress, pushing against the boy's body. Jack was pressed into the van wall, a pillow between him and the metal.

They weren't asleep, Russell could tell that. They weren't awake, either—more of a fever dream, a delirium he envied. He, Jeff, and Hazel were also scrunched together, wedged against the opposite van wall and the back of the seat, holding onto each other. Russell had one hand pressed against the van, the other locked with Jeff's. Jeff. Russell had never been this afraid. He had never given in to crying before, either. If the van crashed, or slid off the road—that was one thing. A wreck, big deal—how many times had his dad wrecked? But, if the things landing on the top broke through, they would be upon them, eating them, tearing out their hearts, their souls—his, Jeff's, everybody's. They would have had him back in Garner; they almost had. Russell leaned into Jeff again, pressing as close as he dared, into safety—knowing that even if the things broke through, this was a safe place. But he couldn't stop crying.

Jeff squeezed Russell's hand back, keeping his eyes tightly closed. He squeezed Hazel's on the other side. Like Russell, she was pressing into him, as close as she could, as if whatever he had was enough—enough for what? Jeff didn't know. At least his father wasn't with the things attacking the van. But the things *knew* his father—and they would take him to his father, if they could stop the van.

A bounce, a slide, and a jerk, as Ben righted the van, got it going straight down the interstate again.

If all of this would just be over. Please, let all of this just be over.

Hazel wanted her grandmother; she wanted her grandfather. She wanted to go home. But, if she did—what would happen if she asked Father Jamey to just stop the van, let her out? Let the storm pick her up, take the winds up, up, up, into the roiling clouds, and—

And the link between her, Malachi, Jeff, and Russell would be broken, perhaps forever. She would miss that. No. It would be more than mere missing. She would be incomplete. And how would her grandparents really miss her? Hazel shook her head; she didn't have an answer to that question, which, in a way, was an answer.

Something walloped the van, hard. The nearest window cracked, a spider web appearing out of nowhere in the glass.

The link was bigger than her grandparents—Hazel knew that. They would want her to be a part of it, tell her she was meant to be. Hazel knew that, too.

Malachi and Jack

He was in a—car? A truck? No, a van—was that it? Yes. He was holding onto—a man, and adult, who was this? Not his dad—Uncle Jack. And Malachi felt Uncle Jack's sickness, a dark fever akin to his own. Where were—right there: Hazel, Jeff, Russ. Still connected, terrified, tired, sleepy, asleep. *I have to hold on; that's all. I just have to hold on.*

Thomas? Where are you? Where's my little boy? Where's my sweet little boy? Is that you? You want me to come there, to come to you? Of course, I love you, son. I love you more than anything, you know that.

Ben

NC 86: Chapel Hill, to the left, Hillsborough to the right. The dragon wasn't going to let him turn left. And there were other *things* waiting at the light, at the bridge over 40. Writhing, screaming hydras. Ben swerved again to the right and down a hill, trying desperately to remember this stretch of road, what lay ahead. *Something* hit the roof—not the dragon, this time, too light, and Ben slammed on the brakes, and a fat scaly winged, black thing, about the size of a beach ball, bounced off the windshield, the hood, and lay still on the pavement. *One for our side,* and Ben gunned the van over the thing, and its body exploded, splattering the glass with pus-yellow blood. The wipers smeared the pus into the beating rain. Almost as soon as the pus was gone, another beach ball-sized thing attacked. This one Ben swerved to take out, the pus splashing the hood, with one wing speared by the radio antenna. The third beach ball-thing snapped off after impaling itself—thanks to more of Ben's swerves.

"Yeeeesss. That makes three," Ben crowed. "Jamey, wake up."

Ben was still terrified—more terrified than he had ever been in his entire life—but now, he was in the crazy zone. He wanted to laugh—and he did, loud, long, whooping laughter, just this side of hysterical.

"I'm back. Way to go, Ben," Jamey yelled. "And that gave me just enough time—"

Then the dragon, screaming, came back and slammed into the van, throwing Ben off the edge of the road. Just then, as Ben got back onto the asphalt, the van bouncing, as the dragon slapped the roof with its tail, Jamey began to glow, his body almost transparent, now filled with an intense, shimmering white. It poured out of his hand into the handle, and like a slow stain, into the van itself.

A trailer park, on fire from lightning strikes, down a hill, up, around a curve, a pond on the right, its rising water a froth.

The door beside Jamey glowed. The dragon blasted the van again with fire and somewhere Ben heard glass breaking and shattering. No more laughing, just insanely giddy—*wheee*—knowing he could falter, fall, into the whiplashing nightmares where the things waited with sharp teeth, where he would only be able to scream and scream and scream. *Hold on, I've got to hold on.* His fingers ached from the holding.

More trailers burning, a store, a white frame house—all on fire. Bouncing over a train track, over a creek, slooshing through the flood waters there, another curve.

The white oozed into the roof, the sliding door behind Jamey, into the instrument panel, and the more it oozed, the faster. *God, please let us make it.* The dragon swooped again—and this time, it screamed in pain, as if it had struck something hard and sharp.

Was that a sign for a church? New Hope Presbyterian, yes, on the left, a sharp turn, up a hill, a hill of running water, slowing the van, into the church parking lot, the cemetery on the right, a white house in flames on the left.

A side road, down to a side entrance, lightning striking the cemetery, an explosion of granite and marble and plastic flowers. Dark water swirling around the van's hubcaps. Coffins erupted out of the earth. The dragon attacked again and screamed again, in greater pain. The white glow filled the van, everything, everywhere, even Ben—glowing, glowing, shimmering.

Ben braked, the van slid, and he heard metal scraping brick and then the van stopped, right in front of a door.

From the journal of Ben Tyson
Wednesday night, October 30, 1991
New Hope Presbyterian Church
About seven miles from downtown Chapel Hill,
North Carolina

My hands hurt. And sitting here, writing with a pen, on paper, makes them hurt even more. I have bruises on the palms of my hands. I found some paper in a Sunday School classroom and here I sit, on the pale-green carpeted steps of the altar, in the sanctuary, candles beside me. Jamey says we will be the safest here, even if we had to carry Jack and Malachi up a flight of stairs. Besides, the downstairs is mid-calf-deep in water. And their mattresses, and quilts, everything. I had to carry Malachi myself; Jack was finally awake enough to sort of walk. He told me he had dreamed of Thomas when he was a little boy.

There are others here in the church; I thought there would be. Some families, couples, a few singles. We haven't talked to them much. I don't think they want to talk, really. I did ask about their minister, but she was in the parsonage—the manse, they said—when it was hit by lightning. They think she's dead. Probably. A man and his son helped us get the mattresses up the stairs, then they left us alone.

Jamey said he would keep my journal after we cross. Says it might help those changelings that don't. He thinks there might be many who don't.

The ceiling of this sanctuary—the nave, is that the right word?— is high and the wood is stained cedar, a reddish stain. The wood of the altar, the pulpit, the pews: light, blond, satiny—oak? And each window, frosted glass, turning the outside into an impressionist painting, not that there is much I can see tonight. The lights are out—but someone has put candles in each window and on the altar and lit each one. Single, white flickering lights. Behind the altar a huge window in the shape of a Celtic cross. I've walked around the church, too, quietly, on the carpet-lined stairs, in and out of Sunday School classrooms, with drawings and pictures and collages on the bulletin boards. The Boy Scout bulletin board downstairs in the water-filled fellowship hall, with the merit badge chart. The nursery with the big cardboard bricks, well-worn and loved stuffed animals everywhere, Lego's, Lincoln Logs, a spinning mobile above the crib. The preacher's office—a very orga-nized woman. Papers neatly stacked, folders labeled This Sunday's

Sermon, Last Sunday, Next Sunday. At a precise 45-degree angle on her blotter a picture of her two sons, one holding an overweight grey-and-white cat. *The huge, leather-bound King James Bible on the preaching lectern, the oversized large print Revised Standard Version on a shelf beneath it.*

I didn't speak to the others, those camping out in the classrooms. It's late, many are sleeping, and they are just so scared. My own fears are quiescent, just below this exhausted calm, this somewhere between shock and just too tired.

I wonder where the pastor is, those two boys, their fat cat, and if they burned up when their house was hit by lightning. She didn't have many notes in *This Sunday's Sermon* folder, just a few lines on God as mystery.

Malachi gets sicker and sicker, weaker and weaker. His body radiates the fever so much that he is bathed in a red light. He is becoming transparent—just at the edges, his finger tips, his ears. Jack has a fever, too, and that cut on his chest still trickles blood. Not to mention the bruises from being tossed around in the back of the van, and the burn on his back. Father Jamey's fairy herbs don't help much anymore. I remember reading somewhere in all the books I have read on fairy lore that a fairy-wound can't be cured by mortal means. That even if the wound is invisible, it still causes pain and a slow death.

There is nothing I can do to help my son and my best friend. Loving them isn't enough.

There doesn't seem to be much I can do about anything. I can sit with Jack and Malachi, hold them, wipe their foreheads with cool washcloths, and none of it helps. Jack is at least awake, and I can talk to him, but Malachi is lost in some fever-dream. Even the other kids can't get through anymore. They sense his dreams—and even, I think, take part in his dreams—but they can't wake him.

I know where we have to go tomorrow, what we have to do. Another mad ride in the van, down 86, straight through Chapel Hill, onto 15-501, over the Haw. (I wish I could show Malachi the big dam there—is it still there? Not split open by lightning?) Around the circle, around the courthouse in Pittsboro, until we hit 902. Across the Rocky River. Father J swears we will find a church somewhere around Bear Creek. And then we wait there until almost midnight— one last dash to the Devil's Tramping Ground. Then counter-clockwise, nine times, at midnight and the gate will be open and we will cross over and my son and my best friend will be saved. These children will be able to be what they could never be here.

What will I do there?

The witches and the dark things and the Fomorii will be there, too. We will have to get past them to walk on the circle. There will be others like us, changelings trying to cross over. Well, like them—I'm not changing.

Dear Lord, help us.

Jeff

Russell lay beside Jeff, on the quilt they had spread at the front of the sanctuary. He could unfold his arm and touch Russell, without sitting up, or stretching. Ben sat on the altar steps, candles on his left and right, writing. Hazel slept a body-length away, in the corner, by the door to the pastor's office. In the other corner, in front of the organ, Father Jamey and Alex slept with Malachi and Jack. Jeff could hear Russell breathing, slow, sure, steady. He seemed to have fallen like a stone into sleep, a safe sleep. Everyone was asleep, except Jeff and Ben. *Oh, no, don't*—but Ben blew out the candles and the darkness got closer. Jeff could hear and see Ben, as if he were a shadow, walking softly to the corner where Malachi was, checking on his son, then lying down.

Now, only Jeff was awake and afraid to sleep. Or rather go back to sleep. He had been so tired when they had finally gotten everything out of the van, through the water downstairs, and up the stairs to here, that when he and Russell had lain down, he had dropped right off, a falling stone like Russell. But Jeff's father had been waiting for him in his dreams: *first, just hands, one on my forehead, smoothing my hair, down my cheek, as if these hands are bathing my face. And a voice, very low, against my ear, as the body settles into bed beside me. The voice tells me I am Daddy's good little boy, that Daddy needs me, yes, Daddy needs me, as the hands slowly go down my shoulder and across my chest. I can't move; I am frozen; I have to take this. The hands take off my shirt and they press harder against my bare chest and back and pull me against the voice, against Daddy's hairy, bare chest. I can't move; I am frozen; I have to take this—*

No.

Jeff had woken with a start, breathing hard, and a shadow, was there another shadow, someone whispering—?

That had been—Jeff didn't know how long ago—before Ben had sat down to write. The candlelight had only marginally helped. *I should tell Ben Daddy's near. That he is outside. I feel him walking around, looking for a door that will let him in. But I am not supposed to tell. I told before and now Daddy hates me, and he is looking for me to love me, but he hates me, I made him do what he did, but I was being a good boy, he told me that, helping him out, it was her fault, if I told that meant I didn't love him, didn't I love him, didn't I love my daddy, wasn't I Daddy's favorite best little boy? Come home with me, Jeff, come back home and everything will be like it was, just you and me.*

No, no, no. And there *were* extra shadows in the room, Jeff was sure of it. And sounds, footsteps, just like before, just like all the nights before.

Daddy's here. Come home.

"No, no, NO, go away, GO AWAY, oh, I'm sorry, I didn't mean to wake up everybody, please, I'm sorry, I'm so sorry."

"Jeff? Are you okay, Jeff? Ben? Something's the matter with Jeff," Russell said, calling out, as he reached for Jeff, his hand on Jeff's shoulder a real, sure weight.

"I'm sorry, I'm sorry, I didn't mean to wake you up, but he's out there, he's right out there and he's going to take me, he wants me—"

Come home.

"Jeff, what's the matter?" Ben said, kneeling down besides Jeff, and pulling him into an easy embrace.

Daddy wants his little boy to come home.

"Daddy found me—I dreamed—and he's out there; he wants me to come home," Jeff said, crying, gasping out his words. He felt Russell move closer, his hand still on Jeff's shoulder.

"You're safe here. You're safe. I won't let him get you, I promise."

"I won't, either," Russell said very softly.

Ben relit the candles and found others and sat them all around Jeff and Russell's quilt, making a circle inscribed inside a pentagram of light. And he held Jeff until he was still and breathing regularly, telling Jeff over and over he was safe, with Russell's words a refrain and Hazel and Father J sleepy echoes.

Finally Jeff lay back down and this time, he snuggled against Russell's back and fell asleep inside Russell's warmth.

Malachi

Jeff, Hazel, Russell, and the cat are like ghosts—paler, fainter, almost transparent. They want to hold his hands, but it is so hard for a ghost to grasp anything real and solid. Malachi's hands are real—aren't they? Or is he the ghost—paler, fainter, almost transparent? He can almost see through his hands, see the grass and the rocks through his bones. Where is he? Not at home in Garner, or in school in Raleigh. Not at the public library—but that is gone—a big fire. Malachi remembers the fire and how fast it burned, the books falling as flames spread, shooting trailers as if they were being tossed in a parade. That happened. Where he is now they are all safe, but only a wall and flickering light are between them and darkness and dark things and dark people.

Malachi continued to dream.

VIII

Samhain
Thursday, October 31, 1991

A CHAPEL HILL HIGH SCHOOL TEACHER, A MEDIEVAL *professor at Carolina, and a Franklin Street car dealer were among many whom disappeared on the night of Samhain, when the storms stopped. The silence, for many, was as terrifying as the storms. No one was lured out to test the quiet. A few ventured to their porch, or stood behind curtains, waiting and watching, but no further than that. The high school teacher's husband was later found dead, from what look liked a wild animal attack. She had killed him with a single slash of her sharp claws, and then leaped through the window, glass raining behind her, shards falling from her now heavily furred body.*

A beast the size of a man, heavily furred, fanged, was later found at the wheel of a wrecked car on McCauley Street, behind the Carolina Inn. Other beasts were seen running south, down Columbia, over the bridge, down 15-501 toward the Chatham County line and Pittsboro.

The medieval professor fled into the woods near Battle Park, howling, shredding his clothes, and looking for others he knew he would find there: a former mayor, a Baptist preacher, a state senator, a beautician, a computer programmer, a high school tennis star. The pack then headed south with the others, a dark river flowing down the highway.

The things in the air came down to fly just above the packs, shrieking, their great wings beating the air. Fomorii rode on the backs of the largest, their fire whips shedding sparks as they struck the things for greater speed.

Some people went insane.

Some simply closed down: their brains could not take in and process any more changes or newness or fear. Fairy tales and horror stories were not supposed to ever become real, yet no amount of rationalization from the voices and faces they had trusted on the radio and television could convince them the stories had not come true. Nor could other voices and faces convince them the stories were true, and that they could handle this new reality. And now the radio and television were dead and the lights were gone and they huddled inside their dark houses, their dark minds.

Lightning struck the university bell tower: one, two, three, four bolts. The bricks split, fell, and the tower spouted flame, became a single flame. Lightning smashed the Planetarium, caught the Carolina Inn on fire, and brought down the WCHL and WUNC radio towers. There were other fires as the darkness became more palpable, pressing closer, closing heavy fingers around first one house, then another. A burning house made an awfully bright light, especially when fed by books, chair legs, window shutters, desks, and bed frames.

And the others, changelings, called to the gate, the circle where nothing grew in southwest Chatham, the Devil's Tramping Ground: the time had come at last for all their dreams to become real. Some rode in vans, others pickup trucks, station wagons, jeeps. Still others came on horseback or in farmers' wagons. Tonight, in the last hours, no one tried anymore to stop them on their journey. They no longer cared that their auras were so visible they glowed or that their ears were pointed or that their eyes were luminous. Some flew.

No one tried to stop them on October 31. The day before was another story. Many died.

The shrieking things and the werewolves and the Fomorii and the black witches gathered near the Devil's Tramping Ground, by the small, gravel parking lot that marked the site and where a narrow path led back through the pines to the Tramping Ground.

Jack

I will do this. I will do this. I will do this. I will do this.

Ben

At eleven P.M., October 31, the rain stopped. There was no moon and no stars; the night was India ink black. The rain hadn't gone away, just stopped—one look at the heavy, waterlogged clouds showed that. The air was charged as the bolts split and re-split the night sky, creating moments of sheer white light, freezing everyone and everything—as if the world turned into a long succession of black and white photographs.

Jesus H. Christ what have I done? What am I going to do when we get there? Why haven't I even thought about that until now? Last night was the first time.

After writing in his journal, Ben had awakened Father Jamey, who had been curled up under a borrowed choir robe, his head on a pillow snatched from the nursery, in one corner of the sanctuary. Ben had hesitated for only a minute. *Dammit, I need to talk.*

"Ben, what's wrong, what's happened?" Father Jamey said, turning over quickly after Ben shook him for the third or fourth time.

"I need to talk. I have been so focused on getting Malachi to the gate so he won't die, the other kids so they can really and truly live, that I haven't even thought of what I would do if we did make it. What am I going to do in a universe where everybody is magic except for me? Find some library somewhere and apply for a job? Do they even have libraries? What am I going to do with Jack—he certainly can't teach American lit over there—"

"Why not? You could both get married again—"

"I lost my first wife because of a stupid accident—Emma fell down the steps and banged her head. The Fomorii assassinated my second wife. Jack's son kills his second wife. His first wife thought life in Raleigh as the wife of a NC State English professor was too boring for words, and she turned out to be psychotic enough to kill herself. Father J, our marital track record is pretty poor, if you ask me. And why marry a human if you can have a fairy?"

"Ben, you are going to take Malachi, Jeff, Hazel and her cat, Russell, and Jack through that gate tomorrow night. And you'll live—you'll figure out how to live over there and you'll do it. Russell is twelve, the other three, eleven and ten—they'll need you and Jack to raise them."

"But, Father J—"

"Go to sleep."

And he had, a few hours later. There were no other answers the priest could give him, nor could anyone else, for that matter. The morning ride from New Hope to Merony United Methodist Church had been almost as bad as the trip from Garner to New Hope. They had had to siphon gas out of the car of someone hiding in the church; that had taken longer than they thought. The glamour and the herbs had protected the van in the lull after dawn all the way through Chapel Hill—seemingly another ghost town, like Garner, like probably almost every town in North Carolina—and around the traffic circle and the Chatham County Courthouse in Pittsboro. The things had returned that morning once on 902. They had taken sanctuary at Merony. Now it was time to leave their last sanctuary.

Ben picked up Malachi from where he slept in a pew in the sanctuary. The talisman was a silver fire on his son's chest, the light flickering across his body and Ben's as they went out to where the others waited, in the foyer, facing the road and the van.

"You're the last; everybody else is ready," Father Jamey said.

"How long can we drive before we meet with resistance? And where's Jack?"

"Right here, Ben. Are you afraid I'm going to make some sort of sacrifice on our last night on this Earth?" Jack asked. He was leaning against the wall, by the double doors into the sanctuary. He looked, Ben thought, a little stronger, a little better. If nothing else, he was strong enough to stand up.

"Yeah, that's just what I think," Ben snapped, then turned back to the priest. "How long do you think?"

"I think right until we get to the Devil's Tramping Ground. We won't be alone, though—I've felt others like us, heading this way. They are nearby, waiting like we are."

"Are y'all ready?" Ben said, turning to Jeff, Russell, and Hazel, who were standing beside Father Jamey. Alex was at Hazel's side, pressing close into her—he was, Ben thought, the size of a panther. Somehow it seemed anticlimactic: to just walk out the front door of Merony Methodist Church, get back in the van, and drive to the Devil's Tramping Ground.

Lightning struck the church.

One great bolt hit the steeple, blasting it off at the roof, heating the contorted metal white-hot as it fell onto the grass, scorching, burning, hissing. The next bolt forked and forked again and each new bolt struck a different part of the church's roof, exploding into streamers of flames that raced up, down, across, over.

"Look at the sanctuary," Jack breathed, stepping back. Fire burned down the walls, sudden hot streams, licking the pews, exploding again on the floor.

"Look? Are you crazy? C'mon, we're getting outta here now," Ben yelled, and holding Malachi against his shoulder with one

hand, jerked Jack away from the sanctuary door as hard as he could.
"Father J, get the kids to the van—"
They ran out into the October night, the flames roaring behind
them. The sudden coolness of the night air almost stunned them,
with the heat so close. The lightning fire was a beast and it was
consuming the white, wood-frame church. A strong wind came up
as they scrambled into the van. Ben shoved Jack into the back, and
then laid Malachi down beside him. Alex bounded into the van.
The other kids grabbed blankets and pillows to pad the spaces
around Malachi and Jack. The wind was so strong the van swayed
and the back door almost snapped off. The fire's heat quickly ate the
coolness, spitting it out in gobs of flame and sweat.
"You get the van started—I've got the door," Ben yelled at the
priest as he struggled with the door until it finally slammed shut.
The wind dropped bits and pieces of the burning church all around
him as he pushed against the wind to open the passenger door, get
inside, and close the door.
"The wind's pushing us—away from the fire—out onto the
road," the priest yelled, waving his hand at the windshield. Could
the wind finally be on their side—and not the bad guys? Ben didn't
know; he didn't want to ask. He leaned back into the passenger seat
and for a short moment, he closed his eyes, hoping to forestall the
return of yesterday's terror: the trip from Garner to New Hope.
Something joggled his memory, from the science fiction he had to
read for the library. From *Dune*. The Litany against Fear, he had
memorized it: *I must not fear. Fear is the mindkiller. Fear is the
little-death that brings total obliteration. I will face my fear. I will
permit it to pass over me and through me. And when it has gone past
I will turn the inner eye to see its path. Where the fear has gone there
will be nothing. Only I will remain.* There. He took a deep breath
as Father Jamey backed the van out.

Hazel

"Look—others, like us—flying," Hazel said, looking at Russell and
Jeff. They sat in the back of the van, as Father Jamey turned out of
the church parking lot onto 902. The Devil's Tramping Ground was
just down the road—a right turn, two more miles, and they would
be there. Midnight was less than an hour away. "I wish we could fly
there."
"Malachi can't," Russell muttered. "You know that. And Jack—"
"Don't worry about me," Jack whispered, but nobody heard him.

"I know," she said. "But I can hear them now. Can't you?"

"Hear them?" Russell asked.

"In my head. Can't you guys feel them? Here, take my hand."

"I don't want to hear any more voices," Russell muttered, but took her hand and then Jeff's. Jeff said nothing.

"Listen." For her, it was like entering a sub-current of unvocalized sounds, thoughts, intentions, wishes, and desires. Auras flared and flamed all around Hazel, Jeff, Russell, and Malachi, the cat, and Father Jamey. The van, she could tell, was no longer touching the ground—rather on this kind wind, and on this new coalescing strength of all the others in transit to the gate—it was skimming the earth.

Hazel and this is Russell, Jeff, Malachi, Father Jamey, my cat, Alex, who are you?

One voice: *Like you, I'm like you all, going to the same place, to the gate, to the place I have been dreaming of all my life.*

Another voice: *The call, I was called, we were all called to come here, to this place.*

Another voice: *. . . was drawn here like a magnet, pulled, I didn't even try to resist.*

Another voice: *My friend died yesterday—the lightning and the things—they got him. I saw him fall, drop, burning, like a falling star.*

The auric colors tumbled and fell and exploded and reformed in the back of the van, and then dropped into Malachi's still red aura, and for the first time in days, Hazel felt his fever drop.

Ben

Just ahead: the small, narrow, white sign said Devil's Tramping Ground and it pointed to the right, toward the small, gravel parking lot and dark trees and brambles and thick underbrush. Five North Carolina Highway Patrol cars waited in the middle of the road, two in front, three behind. Jack looked at his watch: 11:33. The blinking blue lights seemed unusually sharp and bright, blue fires in the night. Directly in front of the cars, in the middle of the road, was a fire, and what looked like a door, propped at each corner with cinderblocks—a hastily built altar. Behind the cars was a dark mass, a crowd of people and things and wolves. *All of it; them—I can see them a hundred yards away.* Behind and around the church van, a luminous mass of men, women, and children.

"The last battle? The metaphor is real: darkness versus light,"

Ben said, more to himself than anyone, but still loud enough for everyone to hear.

"Father, can you stop this thing? Thomas is up there. Stop the van!" Jack yelled, interrupting Ben's words, hammering his fists on the van's side.

"Stop? Thomas? Are you sure?" the priest yelled back over his shoulder.

"Stop, just stop. Please."

"Jack, what are you doing? You promised me you wouldn't do this, Jack—are you listening to me? Jack?" Ben yelled.

The van, already creeping, slowed even more, the wind beneath it began to die, and those in the air around it started to come down to the earth. The van touched the asphalt, bounced, once, twice, and then stopped.

"Ben: I never promised. I have to do this," Jack said as he threw open the van's back door. "I love you, I love you all," he said, and jumped out.

"Jack—wait—" Russell cried out.

"Jack, come back," Hazel said, Jeff's words a beat behind hers.

"He's gone?" Ben said, throwing open his door and jumping out. "Jaaacckk! Come back, oh come back, don't do this. Jaaack. Come back—I'm going after you—"

"Ben, don't—don't run after him," Father Jamey cried, running after Ben and grabbing him. "You can't stop him."

"You know what he is going to do."

"I know. I think this is something we have to let him do, Ben."

Ben, caught in the priest's hands, could only stare at the priest and then at Jack, who walked slowly across the no man's land.

The children walked up then, to stand beside the two men, all four of them, Malachi between Russell and Jeff, Hazel in the lead. Alex walked by Hazel, now, without question, a sleek blue-grey mountain lion, with Siamese markings. All five glowed, Malachi the brightest, and a rope of light moved in and around and through them. The twelve-pointed star, shining with a silvery light, pulsed on Malachi's chest.

"Dad?"

"Son?" Ben jerked back, caught again between his son and his best friend. "You're awake? You're all right?"

"It's the star—I feel strength coming in through it—from Russell, Jeff, Hazel, the others. I'm all right," Malachi said and looked past his father at Jack. "Dad, Father Jamey is right: Uncle Jack has to do this."

"I know, son," Ben said and gently pushed the priest's hands away and reached for his son to pick him up, hold him against his chest, the pulsing light of the star somehow reverberating in him as well. Ben glanced at his watch: 11:42. He wept.

Hazel

"Jack, come back," Hazel said again, this time so that no one could hear her. She wanted to run after him, take his hand, pull him back before it was too late. *He's going to let Thomas kill him. He's going to let Thomas cut out his heart. I don't want to see this. What am I doing here? I should be at home, in my bedroom, upstairs, with my computer, my Worldmaker game, my desk, my books, with my grandparents downstairs. I should be at home.*

Yes, you should be.

Hazel quickly looked around. Jeff, Russell, Malachi, Ben, and Father J were all looking at Jack and Thomas. Alex bumped against her leg, pushing his head into her hand. She couldn't see the faces of the people around Thomas. Behind her, the luminous faces of the other changelings were also all looking at Jack and Thomas.

I should be at home.

If you don't go home, your grandparents will forget you. And you will see Jack get his heart cut out. Nobody really needs you here.

Who are you?

Silence. No voices at all, none of the other changelings she had heard before, and not even a whisper from Malachi or Russell or Jeff. Alex bumped her again. She felt his thoughts pushing at her, insistent, but she pushed him away. She knew what he was trying to tell her and she didn't want to hear it.

She took one step back. Nobody seemed to notice. Of course they wouldn't. They didn't need her, not really. Nobody needed her. Not little, invisible Hazel. It didn't matter how good she was or how smart or that her homework was always done or that she was the only one of the four with silver eyes. If she turned and ran, they wouldn't notice. And she wouldn't have to see Jack die or be here in this darkness.

That's right. Go home.

Hazel took one more step away. Then, Alex growled and took her hand in his mouth, his teeth sharp on her skin.

"Alex, what are you doing?"

StayIneedyoutheyneedyoustay.

"Hazel?" Jeff turned around and held out his left hand. Russ already held his right. "Malachi needs us together, as a tetrad. Didn't you hear his mind-talk?"

I told you.

Go home.

"Hazel, we need you," Russell said and held out his hand. She could see the light pulsing between them, the light reaching out for her hands from both of theirs. She shuddered, one foot stepping back, the other forward, led by her hand.

"I'm here," she whispered and stepped forward, Alex rubbing himself against her, and took Jeff's and Russell's hands.

Jack

Jack's chest wound hurt as he walked from the van to the highway patrol car. He could feel a slight, warm wetness beneath the bandages—of course, he was bleeding again. The burns on his back hurt as well, as his shirt rubbed against them. He wanted to tear off his shirt and scratch the hell out of his back. He glanced back at Father Jamey and Ben, holding Malachi, standing by the church van. Hazel, with Alex by her, Jeff, and Russell stood around them, enclosing the two men and the boy in their rope of light. He could see all their auras, bright and moving as if they were the northern lights. A white brilliance shone out from between Malachi and his father: the twelve-pointed star, Jack thought. He looked up for the first time in what felt like a long time, to see a clearing sky. The wind was tearing apart the thick cover of dark clouds, in ragged chunks, as if the sky had been filled with grey cotton candy. Broken swirls and wisps snaked and turned and broke again, vanishing, dissolving. He watched as a grey veil was ripped from a golden orange moon. He could see only a few stars dimly, as the aurora borealis danced behind the thinning clouds.

God, please let this work, let them get to the gate if I do this.

He turned and walked the rest of the way to the patrol cars, the blue lights still flashing. Thomas stood in front of the cars, flanked on both sides by state troopers whose shadowed faces, like the rifles in their hands, seemed to be locked in place, as if they were wearing masks.

"Hello, son. Left your banking job for one with law enforcement?" Jack asked, wondering somewhere in his head just why was he trying to be funny. *Has my son become so powerful he can control men such as these?*

Thomas stood very still, dressed in black: turtleneck, pants, shoes. A five-pointed star hung around his neck, pulsing faintly with a sickly green light. "What do you want now? You know I have won—there is no way that boy will reach that gate—not in the next fifteen minutes. And look—it's right there." He pointed to his right, through the trees, up a low rise, where a faint white light glowed close to the earth.

"Take me instead, like you wanted to before—like you've wanted to for so long. You know what power there is in a parent- or a child-killing. Let Malachi go free and you will still have the power you want when you take my heart," Jack said and took a step forward, then another.

"How can I trust you? And them—they rescued you before," Thomas said as he crossed his arms across his chest. The green light began to spread out from the star on his chest, oozing across his arms, up his neck, his face, and his dead eyes. Behind the troopers Jack could see four or five Fomorii, their red eyes pairs of tiny infernos, the moonlight glinting on their scales. One idly twitched its fire whip and sparks hissed and popped. Behind them the dead faces of what must be would-be witches and warlocks, wolves at their sides.

"They did that; I didn't ask them to. I've never lied to you."

"You miserable, pathetic old man. No, you never lied to me. How could I ever have believed you loved me—not that love itself isn't a lie. There's the fire and the altar. Prepare him."

"No, let me," Jack said and as a frozen-faced woman stepped out of the crowd to pull at his shirt. She looked at Thomas, who nodded. Jack slowly took off his clothes, dropping them one garment at a time to the ground until he stood again naked before everyone. For a brief moment he was cool as the wind that was scouring the sky clean of storm clouds rushed over him. Then, a step, two, three, toward the fire and the altar, he felt the heat close to his skin, the sweat coming to his skin as it had been waiting just below the surface.

He glanced quickly back at the others. He could only see their outlines. Malachi was now standing by his father, and the light from his star was almost blinding.

Jack lay down on the altar, spread-eagled, arms and legs pointed to all four corners. The fire was a few feet away and roared and snarled. The burn on his back hurt like it had never hurt before and the wound on his chest had reopened, the blood painting his skin scarlet. He looked up into the aurora borealis. Surely that meant something, he thought, surely that is a good sign. That and the moon, still golden and large, even though it was high in the sky. He could hear Thomas's people moving closer; they were humming *aaaaaeeeeeiiiiioooooouuuu*. His son chanted in a language he couldn't recognize. Jack raised one hand and reached out for Thomas. The shining knife fell.

Ben

He looked at his watch as Jack lay down: 11:48.

Malachi

The instant Thomas reached his hand into Jack's open chest and lifted out the heart, a red light flashed, seemingly from within the heart itself. The twelve-pointed star on Malachi's chest grew even brighter still, in response to the heart's fire. The star and the heart pulsed in union.

Malachi did not look away. He wanted to, as he knew his father, weeping, was. *This is for you, Uncle Jack.* He held up the star and *pushed*. Jack's heart shone even brighter and Thomas screamed and screamed. The altar fire went out, and the table fell over, and Jack's body suddenly grew incandescent. Jack's heart shone even brighter as Thomas tried to cram as much of the heart into his mouth as he could, blood covering his hands, his arms, his face. Then Thomas screamed, spitting out pieces, pulling the heart out of his mouth, as he kept screaming: "It's burning me—my mouth —tongue—my hands—I'm burning up!" Thomas, his screams beyond words, finally tore the fiery heart out of his hands, as he writhed on the ground. All the others—even the Fomorii—stopped, as if whatever had animated them had left. Malachi *pushed* again with the star and the blue lights on the state police cars exploded and more screams, more falling to the earth in pain. Blue fires consumed the cars. Jack's body still glowed, as if all the fires had come to rest in his flesh, to guard it and keep it safe.

"Dad, Father J, guys, come on—now, let's go. It's time," Malachi said and lowered his arm. The twelve-pointed star's glowing had dulled, until only a pale outline shone around it, against Malachi's chest.

"Jack, oh, Jack," his father whispered, the words between his sobs.

The others came up, slowly, staring at the blue fires, the ones in front of them in pain on the ground. Russell spoke first, softly: "I could have helped you, Malachi. I can make fire, too."

"I know, Russ, but I was barely able to control what I was doing. Let's go. If Uncle Jack hadn't let happen what he did, we would have lost."

Malachi took his father's hand and the others followed him, across the gravel parking lot, into the brambles and briers, their clothes tearing and ripping, skin snagging, onto a narrow, almost invisible path, into the woods. Above them the aurora borealis glowed even brighter, in even more fantastic shimmering colors.

Ben

The Devil's Tramping Ground, at any other time, Ben thought, would look plain and ordinary and even a bit trashed. A circle of packed earth, with beer cans, Styrofoam cups, hamburger wrappers, and other debris at the outer edges, and grass and weeds and rocks in the middle. Tall scraggly pines, oak saplings. But at 11:53—*all that with Jack took only five minutes?*—on Samhain, the circle was no longer plain; rather it glowed and shimmered with an intense white light, as something luminous beneath the earth was coming to a slow boil. The air was charged. Hazel's hair, unbraided, twisted and coiled, like golden brown snakes. Russell's fire-red thatch and Jeff's dark brown sparked and popped. Malachi's curls—no, tendrils, golden snakes—were as bright as the circle. Alex's fur shone like polished silver. And all of their eyes—Ben looked away. He knew his eyes didn't have the same fires.

Five explosions, one after the other, rocked the night, and pine branches and cones and needles rained on them. Ben looked back to see through the trees what had to be the patrol cars burning, their gas tanks blown, and God knows who and what else that had been near by.

Jack died so we could be here. Please let it be worth it.

"Thomas is on his way. Those explosions didn't get him," Father Jamey said from behind Ben. "I have this new vision—just now, as if my eyes just changed, I can see things, through things. Never mind. Thomas can't hurt you anymore—what he tried to do with Jack's heart backfired. But join hands and set foot on the circle. I don't think he can even touch you once you do that."

"Father J, aren't you coming with us?" Jeff asked as he took Russell's hand. Ben took Hazel's hand and waited for the priest's answer, one foot on the circle, the ground pulsing, the other on the still earth. Malachi took his other hand and stepped with both feet onto the Devil's Tramping Ground. Whatever sickness lingering in his body vanished then.

"No, I'm not going. You are all called to go; I'm called to stay. All of you, on the circle, join hands altogether. Nine times, counter-clockwise—go on, it's 11:56."

Ben stepped onto the circle, followed by Hazel, then Russell and Jeff. Immediately he was cut off, surrounded on both sides by diaphanous walls of light. Alex followed Hazel onto the circle and stood as close to her as he could, his fur touching her skin. Ben could see through it dimly, the priest's smiling face, the pine trees, the narrow path, and what must be Thomas.

They began to walk, counter-clockwise, around the circle. Russell kept count: "One. Two. Three—"

Ben could see some of the others who had waited in the road following Thomas, coming through the trees. They were dark shapes through the light barrier around them; he couldn't make out individual faces, hands, arms, jackets, shirts. Their eyes were red. Thomas tried to attack the priest, but Father Jamey easily pushed him away.

"Four," Russell said, his voice high with excitement.

Thomas struggled to his feet, with the bloody knife in his burnt hand. The priest grabbed his arm and took the knife and tossed it away. Then Thomas charged the light barrier and bounced off, screaming again in pain.

"Five. Six. Seven." No one else spoke except for Russell.

"Eight. Nine."

"Okay, keep holding hands. Don't let go," Ben shouted. *Why am I shouting?* Then, he heard, muffled, but louder, Thomas's mob. And inside the circle, in the exact center where there had been grass and weeds and rocks and the ashes of an earlier fire, there was now a singing blue fire. Malachi's star glowed blue in return and it sang back to the fire.

"Your mother said it was also a key. Unlock the door, son. Russell, let go of his hand, but keep your hand on him—don't let go—he can get the star off. I'll keep hold on this side."

As Russell moved his hand from one part of Malachi's body to another, Malachi lifted the star over his head. He held it in both of his hands for a moment and then, gently, swinging the star on its chain, he tossed it into the heart of the blue fire.

For a long moment, nothing happened. They all could see the star, a brighter blue, then a blue-white, then white, then the fire exploded, flames shooting out in spirals and tongues, caroming off the light barrier. The blue fire raced around the circle, around them, through them, and the white where the star had been began to distend, as if it was being pulled into a line. When the line was seven or eight feet tall, it began to expand until a door stood in the middle of the circle, a door of blue and white fire.

"You go first, Mal," Hazel said.

Then, Malachi, holding Russell's left hand, and Russell, holding Jeff's left, and Jeff, holding Hazel's left, and Hazel, holding Ben's left, Alex right beside her, then Ben—one by one—they went through the door.

Father Jamey

When Ben disappeared, the light barrier dropped and the shining ones, who had followed them, began to file or fly or walk or run through the door. Thomas knelt on the ground, groaning, holding his twice-burned hands in his armpits. His mob was unable to move. When the last passed through, the door shimmered, and closed into a thin line, which then shrank down into the dwindling blue fire, and then only glowing blue ashes remained.

"You lost, Thomas," the priest said gently to the man who was at his feet.

"But I took hith hearth—I even ate it—look at my burned mouth, my tongue. Ith have his blood all over me," Thomas said, looking up.

"He was a willing victim, an innocent sacrifice, not like the others you tricked or drugged. You lost Malachi's power when he went through the gate. And his crossing over released all those forces you wanted to control. Now they just are. Watch."

"You're wrong, you goddamn cockthucking priesth—"

"Watch."

The light within the earth, in the circle around the blue ashes and blue coals, began to pulse. The surrounding ground rippled and throbbed and moved, as if it were no longer solid, but water, waves, at the beach. Then, a pause, and like waves before a storm, ripples in a pond from a tossed stone, the light spread out from the circle, riding the moving earth.

"No, no, no, no, NO!" Thomas cried and tried to get up, but it was too late. The light caught him, wrapped around him, and bore him to the ground, writhing and twisting as he burned. Some of the others ran, screaming. Others fell, as Thomas did, caught in the burning light. A few—who looked like Fomorii—exploded. Still others stood transfixed, as the light washed over and around them, taking away their frozen faces as it spread farther and farther out from the circle on the ground. More rings of light following the first burning white ring—different colors, red, orange, yellow, green, blue, indigo, violet—rainbow after rainbow after rainbow.

Finally they stopped and the glow of the circle and the blue ashes and coals began to fade. The ones who had fallen were still; Thomas's body smoked.

"What am I doing here? Where am I?" a woman said, who stood a few feet away from Jamey. Before the circles of light had spread, before Ben had stepped through the gate, she had taken a swing at the priest with a machete. The blade had bounced off his aura and she had frozen then. The wolves with her had all run howling off into the trees.

"What's happened? I want to go home," she said. Now that Jamey could see her face, he saw she wasn't a woman, but a young girl, a teenager, African-American, no more than sixteen or seventeen. She wore a McDonald's uniform and her dark hair fell in beaded braids around her face.

"It's a long story," Jamey said. "Things have changed. Come on, I'll get you home."

She took his hand and they walked out of the woods. In ones and twos and threes, those who had not fallen came behind them.

IX
After
Friday, November 1, 1991

The Rectory, St. Mary's Catholic Church, Garner, North Carolina

Jamey

FOR THE FIRST TIME SINCE HE HAD ARRIVED AT ST. Mary's in Garner, Jamey Applewhite didn't make his Friday morning office hours. He had a good excuse: he didn't get back from southwest Chatham County and the Devil's Tramping Ground until just before dawn. He wasn't sure about the time because his watch had stopped just after midnight, the hands locking in place when the rainbow-colored rings of light had passed through his body. He had talked with Althea, the young black woman who had been standing there, stunned and confused, after the rings of light had passed, for two hours and then he had driven her home, back to her apartment in Chapel Hill, on North Greensboro Street.

"You were seduced, Althea, by darkness, by evil. You aren't the first; you won't be the last," he said, as he pulled the van into the parking lot near her building.

"But I always go to church, Father. I've been going to church all my life, St. Paul AME, over on Merritt Mill Road, I even sing in the choir . . ."

Finally he had told her to go inside and go to bed. Jamey gave her his number and directions to St. Mary's; maybe, he thought, as he headed for 54 East, she would. He doubted she would talk to St. Paul AME's minister.

Why didn't I tell her there is darkness in all of us? That it is an integral part of human nature and if we deny or embrace it, we give it power and we leave ourselves vulnerable to people like Thomas? If she calls me and comes to Garner, I will tell her. I will tell her about my own darknesses. I will tell her about Thomas.

Jamey tried the radio on the way home: WUNC 91.5 FM's all-night jazz wasn't on. He turned the knob as far as it would go in either direction, AM and FM: the radio waves were silent. Maybe it was the continuing aurora borealis, maybe the rainbow rings broke up radio waves, maybe the stations' staffs were just as stunned and confused as Althea. Just as well, he thought, they probably had no idea what to say. Not yet, anyway. He had never known NPR to be at a loss for words before, but there was a first time for everything. He wished he had found the words to say to Althea. He knew he would have parishioners coming with questions—huge, larger-than-life questions—to which he wouldn't have a lot of answers. *The world has changed. Magic has been released. Good fought evil and for now, good has won. No, I don't think your missing wife, husband, son, daughter, friend, whoever, will ever come back.* That might work, he had thought, as he drove east into the dawn.

Now—what time was it, eleven, eleven thirty?—he wasn't so sure if the answers he had come up with on the way back would work. Jamey got out of bed to check the clock on his dresser to be sure the time was right. That clock was an old-fashioned wind-up; it still worked. Yes, he had slept almost all morning and he was still tired, still sleepy. Those answers might work for some—but what about those who had dreams like he had? He glanced into the mirror over the dresser: yes, his ears were still visibly pointed; yes, his blue eyes had a faint silver glow to them. On the top of the dresser, a rosary, St. Anthony and the Christ Child prayer cards, a thin, red-leather-clad book of prayers. A crucifix hung on the wall by the mirror. Two white votive candles sat on the dresser right below the crucifix. Yawning, he glanced about the room—bed, dresser, night-stand and lamp, closet, the two windows. Small bookcase and table in one corner, chair, another smaller lamp. Just like the bedroom of most priests he knew.

Except a changeling lived in it. His aura flared then, an intense white-yellow, and with one slight wave of his hand, he dropped a tiny spiral galaxy of light into the air. Then, he leaned over and blew gently and the galaxy dissolved. His aura dimmed, but didn't altogether fade. It was as if a pale haze surrounded him, the faint echo of fog, of a low, barely glowing cloud.

And yes, Jamey had had an erotic dream about *three* other people: a man, and two women. He had known them—their faces, their eyes, their hands as they had touched him, their bodies. He could still feel their hands on his skin. He had never seen them before or dreamed of them before; he didn't know their names. Even so, Jamey knew them and that they were close, in time, not yet in space. There was only a fine, faint disturbance in the ether of molecules displaced by their approach. *They're looking for me.* They were the rest of his tetrad. He wasn't, if the dream were true, the only changeling who had not been called to cross over.

But I am a priest. I can't marry anybody, let alone three other people. Can I?

But the world had changed.

When would they find him, these three with whom he would make four? He knew he had to stay here, to listen to the questions of his parishioners. Was he air, water, fire, or earth?

But I am a Catholic priest. I have no doubts that this is what I am supposed to be, what I am meant to be.

But the world had changed. How much remained to be seen.

Hallie Bigelow

When the rings of colored light—at that point, bands of light—passed through Hallie, it had been sixteen minutes after midnight. Her wristwatch had exploded when the blue band had touched her, the crystal shattering into fine dust, the green digital face flaring into a quick, green fire. When the violet band passed, only darkness remained. Hallie had lain very still then, waiting, on the cushions she had dragged in her office from the teachers' lounge. She hadn't been the only person to spend the night in the school. There had been a good twenty or thirty waiting for her when she had driven in from Leadmine Road. People from the neighborhood, with their kids, Camille Bondurant and her boyfriend, Caroline and Charlie Perkins, Rob Warner, who taught fourth grade, his partner, Carter. Michael Murphy, the gifted and talented specialist and his partner. They were carrying sleeping bags, deflated air mattresses, pillows, quilts. She had told them to use the mats in the gym; most of them had slept in there.

How long she had lain there, waiting for another colored band, Hallie didn't know. Finally she had slept, only to waken when she heard voices outside her office door. Somebody was up—or somebodies were, Hallie thought. She decided to lay there on the floor awhile longer, wondering what they were talking about, what they saw outside, if the trees and grass and evergreen shrubs and the steps leading down to the street or the street lights and the houses looked any different, if they were still there.

The magnolia by her window was still there. Did it look the same? After staring it, Hallie decided it did and slowly got up, thinking: *just because things look the same doesn't mean they are.*

Off the coast of Tir Mar, out to Sea

It was morning. Where there had been dark ships, a dark, fanged prince, with eyes of glowing fires, a dark, sharp-clawed lieutenant, hungry for a feast of souls, the sea was clear. But, still barely visible on the far horizon, a small and getting smaller dark shape. Eventually the dark shape disappeared.

The White City, on the Carothian Coast, The Northeastern Peninsula of the Continent of Tir Mar, Faerie

Ben

Once the door of blue and white fire closed, it took Ben a long moment to just be able to focus and see what was around him, where he was, where the others were. The sky was different, a darker, deeper blue. The air: sweeter and warmer, and he knew, as he inhaled, the sea was near. Four very ordinary just-like-back-home-on-Earth sea gulls confirmed the sea's nearness. Their plaintive cries, for a moment, made him think it hadn't happened; they had only gotten as far as the beach back in North Carolina. It was a very short moment, as he looked down at the flowers around him: none of these had ever grown in any garden or meadow in North Carolina. But he recognized a few: the tiny, twinkling star-blooms, the spicy fragrance from the violet ones cascading down a rock wall. Valeria had told him and Ben remembered. He looked down again: there, in the grass, burnt, its chain missing, was Valeria's twelve-pointed star. Ben picked it up and dropped it in his pocket; maybe some day Malachi would want it.

They were in Faerie, in a walled garden, with flowers and bushes and small trees, by a small house that seemed to have grown out of the ground, on a street, in a neighborhood, in a city. The house to the left and the right and across the street—all had grown out of the ground. Not all of them were white, but rather soft earth tones: beige, dusty pink, a fine grey, a faded orange. A few, up the street, were ivory, cream, eggshell, and behind them, the city walls were white. Tall, silver-white golden-leafed trees lined the street on both sides. There were no lawns; instead other small walled gardens or what could only be described as tiny meadows, with thick grasses or a thicket of more silver-white trees. The whole effect was an odd mixture of the neat and the untidy.

Ben knew, without doubt, that Valeria had lived in the house, walked in the garden, on the street, in the city. He had brought Valeria's son home to his mother's garden. There was no sign of all the others who followed them to the Devil's Tramping Ground. Much later, Ben was to find out what happened. Everyone who had followed them had also walked on the Straight Road that led between the gate in the human universe to the gate in the fairy universe. There were other gates besides the Devil's Tramping Ground on Earth, all fixed and set in one place. Most of the gates in Faerie were not: they shifted and moved, depositing people in first one place, then another, responding in some way to whom the Straight Road walkers were, where their fairy ancestors had lived.

But his charges were all here in the garden: Malachi, Jeff, Russell, Hazel, and Alexander, the cat.

Now, what was he supposed to do?

The Prime Mover

She saw them before they saw her, standing bewildered in Valeria's garden, by the small house where Valeria had lived when she was Prime Mover, the garden in which she had been when she had gone on that furlough to Earth from which she had not returned. Today, Valeria had returned, in the presence of the human she had loved there, and the son she had born there, and the other three who completed Valeria's son's tetrad. Larissa, who had been Second and had succeeded Valeria as the Prime Mover, had come alone, despite the protests of Roth and Thorfin. Fortunately Tasos had gone back into the ocean or she would have had to argue with the swimmer, as well as the two centaurs. At least Hazel's dragon and winged horse had said they preferred to wait.

"We met the two boys first, when they were dream-visiting," Roth said, shaking his red tail with a hint of anger, his nostrils slightly flared. *If he had a mane, he'd been shaking it at me. Not that his head of hair isn't close to a mane.*

"I know, but—"

"So we should meet them here, now, now they have crossed over," Thorfin interrupted, his black tail twitching as much as Roth's red one. "They will be expected us. Seeing us will make them more at ease, more comfortable, and they can see that there are others like them here."

"And I should get the dragon for the girl? The winged horse? No, you will see them all soon enough. I am the Prime Mover; I took Valeria's place," Larissa said impatiently. "I have to do this alone. Besides, they are still very young—even Russell has only just turned thirteen, I don't think they have even begun to figure out how they are like the two of you."

She sighed. The two centaurs, their hooves loud on the stone of the street, had not been gracious in agreeing, huffing and snorting, swishing their tails. She watched the man and the children and the cat from behind a rhian tree. All five and the cat just stood there, looking—no, they were dazed. Enough. Why should she be nervous anyway?

Larissa stepped out from behind the tree and walked toward them, waving when at last one of the children saw her and called out and ran toward her. Then he stopped, his face frozen. *Malachi. He thought I was his mother.* The cat got to her first, bounding over the garden wall, up the street, to jump on her shoulders and lick her face, *pushing* at her with a jumble of excited thoughts and images.

Can I, will it be okay, would anyone care, are there other cats?

Yes, you can, it will be fine, I don't think anyone would care, but there are acceptable and unacceptable behaviors, here too, and yes, there are other cats like you. Ben, she saw, between pushing Alex down and laughing and wiping her face, trailed behind them, uncertain, although he was smiling. She reminded herself that he was probably the most bewildered of them all. The children had made dream-visits; he had only memories of what Valeria had told him over ten years ago.

Hazel

Hazel missed her grandparents; she wished she had been able to tell them good-bye and why she was doing this, why she was linked to these three boys and how she had changed. She walked just ahead of Ben toward the fairy woman who walked toward them from wherever the street this house and garden were on led to. Not so much a street, really, she thought, but rather a wide path of hard-packed earth. Later, she would find out there wasn't much need for streets as there had been back in Raleigh or Garner—on Earth. Streets were for cars and trucks. Fairies flew.

Hazel wanted to hold Ben's hand. She wanted to ask him if she could go home and visit. She wanted to ask him what would happen if she changed her mind and wanted to go home to stay. Would it be all right to leave Malachi, Jeff, and Russell here without her? Couldn't they find another person to be the fourth, to be earth? She felt that there was nothing that would make any of the three want to go home—home would shift for them to here. Jeff's mother had abandoned him; his father had hurt him, and would hurt him again if he came back. Malachi's father was here; his mother was from here, and here was where she had wanted him to be. And here was where he had to live, more so than any of the others. Russell's parents were like Jeff's; they had just done their abandoning and hurting in different ways. But, what would she be going back to? To a house where, yes, she was safe, but also where she was invisible. Her grandparents' lives wouldn't be disrupted by her absence—she knew she had been the disruption from the day she had arrived.

We have to stay awhile, first, Hazel, and see. Come here.

Okay, I'm coming.

The fairy woman waited for them where Alex had stopped her. He was wrapping himself around and around her, his purring loud and rumbling, as if he had swallowed a huge outboard boat motor. The woman, Hazel thought, was beautiful. Her hair was golden with grey streaks and fell down her back in a long, thick mane; a silver circlet crowned her head. Her dress was long and blue and silver and sprinkled with golden stars.

"Oh, you're here; you're finally here at last. Now, all Faerie will be renewed," the fairy woman said as she let Alex push his big head into her legs so she could pet him, stroke his fur, tell him he was beautiful and amazing. The boys got to her first, and she kissed and hugged each one, Malachi last and the longest; he seemed to press into her, as if he needed this hug more than the other two boys. Hazel waited beside Ben, wishing Alex would come back to her side. "And I'm Larissa, the Prime Mover, the First on the Dodecagon, as Valeria was. I will show you the city; I should have told you that first."

"But what do we do," Ben asked. "Where do we go? Where do we live?"

I won't ever leave you Hazel don't be afraid of this don't leave me.

Alex had pushed his way back to her, and was pressing his head into her, as he had done since he was a very tiny kitten. *But all this scares me and I miss Grandma and Granddad.*

We have to stay awhile, first, Hazel, and see.

"You? You have four children to raise, Ben," Larissa said, "and I imagine we will ask you to serve on the Dodecagon, the Council of Twelve, to represent the changelings. You are one of the few full-blooded humans here. There is a library at the university here, too. As for the rest of you: grow up, learn things, be educated—you didn't think there would be no school here, did you?" she said, giving Russell's red hair a quick tug at his scowl. "And figure out what sort of adults you will be. Now let me show you the White City. You will live in that house back there, where you arrived. That was Valeria's house here in the City. It's yours now, Ben."

Hazel?

Okay, Alex, I'll wait and see.

From the journal of Ben Tyson, the first night in Faerie, Samhain

Our first walk in the White City was a slow one, and not because we were tired, or even because we stopped often to look or because Larissa wanted us to see one thing or another. No, our first walk was a slow one because of all the people who came and talked to us, touched us, laid their hands on our faces—which I know now is a form of greeting—if they were First-born, touched our foreheads with their fingertips if Second, and for the different Thirds, the pans, the centaurs, the mers, the sylvans, it is different, and I can't remember them all. (I am not even sure if I should capitalize all the species' names. I wonder if there is a fairy Chicago Manual of Style.*) They watched us as we walked, Russell and Jeff, Hazel and the cat, Larissa and me and Malachi, from their houses—some of the houses. Two-thirds of the houses, Larissa told me that first morning, are empty.*

The war with the Fomorii was long; it began before Valeria or Larissa was born, and I know how long-lived the First-born are. Victories, defeats, truces made and broken, retreats, advances. The First Island, their Eden (Atlantis?)—they know where it is—was—sank, taking with it the fairest of the cities, and millions of people. The White City, here on the coast of their northern continent, Tir Mar, a coast that looks like Maine, was where they retreated, to regroup, rearm, and fight again. Finally there was victory, but the cost was all these empty houses. That is why they called Malachi and the others back—the changelings taken to the human universe in the very first years of the war, fosterlings they had hoped to retrieve before too many of our years and their years passed. If the changelings had not returned, if Thomas and his black magic and his red-eyed Fomorii had won, then Faerie's victory would have been a pyrrhic one, and two universes would be lost, theirs and ours.

Although Larissa tells me this is mine now, I can't quite say it or write it. I still feel like I am a visitor here, that at some point, I will have to go home, walk the Straight Road again.

The Fomorii have gone back to their universe, another room in the House of Creation. For now.

I thought the fairies would fly to greet us, swooping down like great birds. But, Larissa tells me, it is considered bad manners for adults to fly within a city. In and out of a city is another matter. The children, the few of them left, were told not to fly just yet by their parents. To wait, give us time to settle in. By the time we reached the end of the street where Valeria had lived, they had started to come out of their houses. They came, most of them, in fours: one golden-haired, bronze-eyed; one red-haired and green-eyed; one hair almost black, with blue-green eyes; one brown-haired, silver-eyed. Air, fire, water, earth. The gender combinations don't seem to matter. The children reminded me of collie puppies, everywhere, flashing, a few flying, glowing, making starry trails.

They came and they touched us.

Malachi looked at me when one tetrad swooped down on my four like a flock of crazed crows, shouting and laughing.

Go ahead, I told him.

I watched him take off. Larissa told me children sometimes stay airborne for days, especially after they first learn to levitate, to fly. I asked her if I could learn and she only said she didn't know, but she would try to teach me.

Valeria's street led to another, more houses, and another, then we reached the open-air market and the great city square, a park, a plaza, a fountain.

And I met two centaurs—Roth and Thorfin—who knew Russell and Jeff quite well.

Malachi

"Thanks, Dad," Malachi had said and flew straight up and up and up, until he could see the entire White City below him, enclosed in its shining white wall, its houses like nests of glowing jewels spilled out of a bag, the domes of the temples, the arches and spiraling towers of the schools, the Tower of the Dodecagon, growing out of the city's heart. Just outside the walls, a forest to the south, gardens to the west, and to the east and to the north, rocks, a cliff, and below, white sand, and the sea, the sea, the sea.

He turned and spiraled and flipped and fell back on the warm air and floated and rolled over and over again. It had been so long since he had felt so well. Below him, he could see the others. He could pick out his father's aura, and the other three, auras he knew as well as his own. *Uncle Jack should have been here.* Then he flew straight up, up, up, and up, the city dwindling and shrinking, the sea growing and growing, the sky so close, so blue, so deep and shocking a blue, like no blue he had ever seen on Earth, and the clouds. Oh the clouds, they were almost alive in the sky. And there: yes, a dragon, very far away and red and golden, its wings molten in the sun, flying as he was, for the sheer pleasure of the flight.

Then he dropped, his aura flaming behind him, the tail of a golden comet, a falling stone of light.

From Ben's journal

We stood at the edge of the great plaza and watched. First-born, the Fairies, the Elfin, I suppose all the words we used, the Daoine Sidhe — except they are not little. The Second-Born: Dwarves: stout, hairy, eyes blinking against the light, or shielded by hoods — Larissa whispered they live mostly beneath the ground. The Third-born: people of the wood. Centaurs and pans. Sylvans, the tree people: dryads, wood nymphs. Hamadryads: oak-folk. Birch-men and women. Beeches. Hollies. Willows. Shapeshifters, the wer. Beasts like Alex, whose mind-speech touched me, flickering words, stray thoughts, odd images. All the Threes, she said, are, well, a bit wild. In the sea there are dolphins, and the swimmers, the mers.

There are so many colors here, sharp and clear against the white — here in the plaza, the public buildings, the temples, are all white. The centaurs' horse-bodies are magnificent, not as big as a Percheron or a Clydesdale, but much bigger than any horse I have ever seen back home. Roans, sorrels, chestnuts, bays, palominos, appaloosas, white, black, grey . . . And the dripping, dark green swimmers, a few, hurried, anxious to get back to the sea, others in the fountains. Beasts — Talking Beasts — great bears, large-sized mice, porcupines, wolves, panthers who come up and nudge against Alex . . .

I am just making a list.

It will take me forever to learn all of who they are and what they can and cannot do.

I wonder if I will ever feel at home here. I look at Hazel and wonder the same thing.

And others like my four children, bewildered, excited, dazed changelings. The Fourth-born?

The day we arrived, Samhain, is a holy day, the New Year.

The temple chimes rang and sang in the wind from the sea, a constant melody.

I wish I had a camera—I will have to ask Larissa what they do to record memories—when two of the centaurs made their way through the crowd. Not so much for them—by then I was on sensory overload. No, I wish I could have recorded the looks on Russell's and Jeff's faces. They knew these centaurs; they had told me about them: Roth and Thorfin. Roth a red-golden-chestnut, his beard and hair, golden red, and Thorfin, a glossy black, his beard and hair even blacker.

Jeff

For all Russell's bravado, his bigger size, his quick temper, Jeff knew he was the stronger and the braver. Was it, Jeff had once wondered, the difference in how they had both been hurt? Russell's mother had left him, choosing as far as Russell ever knew, the child she loved best. His father had only taken him in when his grandfather had gotten sick. Then, the succession of stepmothers, with the last one the worst. Russell was her target. Not that he hadn't been his father's for years. Russell had shown Jeff the scars on his back, buttocks, and legs.

Jeff had no visible scars like Russell's to show. The places he had bled had long since healed. Jeff's scars were all interior and were only tangible in darkness. His father's hands hadn't bruised like Larry White's had. But Jeff still knew exactly how and where his father had touched him, each fingerprint on his skin. His mother had left, too. She had fixed him breakfast and sat with him as he had eaten it, just the two of them, his father already gone to work. Jeff remembered everything she had fixed that morning: wheat toast, soft poached eggs so he could wipe the plate with the toast, orange juice, milk. His *Star Wars* lunch box on the counter: apple and pear, sliced cheese cubes, thermos with hot cream of tomato soup, half an egg salad sandwich, a fistful of Oreo's in a baggie. She had dropped him off at school, waved, and he waved back, and he had never seen her again. She refused to talk to him the times she had to call later.

Jeff had told Ben most of what had happened and he had told Ben about Russell's scars and how they got there. Jeff had told no one else but Russell everything that had happened, at night when they had to stay first in Malachi's house, then at Father Jamey's church.

No, there isn't that much different in how we got hurt, not really, Jeff thought. But I didn't let it break me. Why it had finally broken Russell, when the shadow had come for him, Jeff wasn't sure. And he wasn't sure if his shadows had come for him that he wouldn't have broken, too.

Russell froze when they came to the plaza. Jeff didn't know for a few minutes until he turned to say something to Russell, to point out the Tree-people, and their hair, the leaves that kept falling around them. Russell wasn't there. Jeff had to tell the others to go ahead and he went back to where Russell was standing, in front of one of the silver-white trees.

"Russ, it's okay," Jeff said, and took Russell's hand. He felt a quick, electric surge of energy between them, as Malachi had told them would happen now. "I'm scared, too. But we're here; we're together; we're safe."

Russell couldn't look at Jeff, although he didn't let go of Jeff's hand. "But, I was the dark one; I gave in."

"It doesn't matter anymore," Jeff said and hugged Russell quickly. It was, he realized, something he had wanted to do for a long time.

"Promise?" Russell said, finally looking up. Jeff saw Russell was crying.

"Yes."

Jeff gently led Russell into that great, loud throng of so many different peoples, talking, laughing, crying, shouting, moving, touching, colors shifting, shimmering, bright, interwoven with liquid light, wind chimes, and high above it all, sea gulls wheeling and turning.

"Look, our centaurs—there they are," Jeff cried and they were: Roth and Thorfin, cantering through the crowds toward them, Ben and Malachi and Hazel and the cat and Larissa stepping back to let the two great horse-men through, the two of them laughing.

"You're home now," Roth said and took Russell's hand. "You don't have to be afraid anymore."

Thorfin nodded and took Jeff's hand. The centaurs' hands were huge, swallowing the boys' hands, and then they picked each boy up and drew them into an embrace.

From Ben's journal

I wish I had at least some of my books from back—home—with me. Larissa tells me that I will find plenty of books in their university library. What does one study in a fairy university, I wonder? Instead of clothes, I brought some of my journals; I figured we wouldn't have a problem here getting more of the former. The rest of my journals— those on diskettes—I left with Father Jamey, to share, as he said, with those who didn't cross. There is no way I could have used those diskettes here. Fairies know almost nothing of machinery; they are iron-sensitive, for one thing, and why invent the wheel if you can fly? I am writing this on what feels like vellum, with a quill pen, a bottle of black ink beside me.

Poor Hazel. She may not stay—if she can go back. No one has asked that question yet. But the boys—my son, Russell, and Jeff—this is their place, their true home. They are flowers slowly blooming, flowers that had not known how much they needed water.

I forgot Alex. It is not yet natural for me to think of him as sentient, but he is now. The children have no problem with it, of course. Larissa assures me I will get used to it—that said after introducing me to a rather earnest bear while we walked on the plaza that first morning.

Russell

When Roth picked up Russell, with those huge hands and arms, and hugged him against that huge chest, Russell felt as if he had finally come home. Jeff was right: he was safe. He felt another electrical surge between his skin and the centaur's—not like Jeff's, but akin. When the centaur finally put him down beside Jeff, Russell found himself tongue-tied. He could only laugh and shake his head, no matter how much each of the two centaurs teased him, ruffled his hair, tugged at his ear points.

"What's the matter, boy? If I didn't know you are a talker, I would say you are mute," Thorfin asked.

"I—uh—I—can't—the words—I don't know where they are. Not right now," Russell finally said, knowing his face was red enough to match his hair.

"Leave him be, Thorf," Roth said, smiling down at Russell. "He's got some sorting to do. Why don't all of you go up on the wall? You can see the whole city, get a sense of where you are. We'll show you the way."

Russell took Jeff's hand again as they walked with the two centaurs, Malachi and Hazel and Ben and Larissa and Alex coming behind them, talking, and looking. Jeff's hand, Russell thought, feeling a now-familiar electrical surge, weaker than before, more of a reminder, really, was familiar and known. He knew Jeff—or did he? Just in the few hours that had passed since walking through the Gate and on the Straight Road Jeff seemed to have straightened, his face was brighter, as if a shadow had begun to fade. Except for that, Jeff looked as he always did: somewhat shaggy dark brown hair, falling over his eyes, those ears, and the glowing blue-green eyes, small, half-a-head shorter than Russell, slight. Regardless, Jeff looked different. Russell wondered if *he* looked different. And there was something else that *felt* new, but that Russell recognized as old, even though he knew he had never recognized this something as being a part of him before, and Jeff was a part of it—or would be. But he knew he could not name this *something*, not yet.

"Russ? What are you thinking so hard about?" Jeff asked softly, talking below the loud voices of the two centaurs who were, with Larissa, answering questions about this and that.

"Something I'm working out. I'll tell ya later, I promise. C'mon, here are the steps up to the top of the wall."

From Ben's journal

"I see a land more fair than any I ever saw. Its hills are clothed with trees and I see shining rivers between broad meadows, and high places where the wind blows. Beautiful is the rippling of grass on these high places, and the running of the deer there. Very beautiful are the mountains with the light upon them, and the flowering valleys, beautiful white waves upon the shore. Surely there is no music like the music of those waves."

I could just hear the music of those waves from the top of the city wall, the wall facing the sea. It drops straight down, a sheer rock face, to a jumble of boulders at its base, a rocky beach that gradually becomes faintly glowing white sand and there is the sea. These sea gulls—am I imagining that their cries are somehow more melodic than the ones on the North Carolina coast? They look to be exactly the same and Larissa tells me many of the beasts are the same—more or less. Faerie changes those who come, whether on two feet or four or on wing or claw or hoof.

I memorized that quote. I think it is from a book by MacCana, but I'm not sure. Whoever wrote had to have been here some way or another.

The sea, the sea, the sea. Green and blue and silver and white. The smell, the air, the white waves on that white beach.

Faerie is changing me. I don't know how, but it is. Will I be something other than human, the fourth-born, the last-comers? I don't think so, nor would I wish it so. We have our gifts as well. I guess I will have to wait and see what happens.

I brought my son and those to whom he has bonded—his tetrad— here. I saved my son's life; I had to do that or die trying. I kept my promise to Valeria; I kept my promise to Jack. All of us, Here and There, have managed, for a time, to defeat the Dark. I don't imagine for one minute that the victory is permanent. I am tempted to write: and they lived happily ever after, and close this book and not write again, but I know that it wouldn't be true if I did either. Hazel was as happy as the boys were to see the ocean, but she is not yet truly happy to be here. I don't know how she will sort herself out. Russell's shadow has only begun to lift; he has only begun to know who he is and the knowing is going to be painful for him. Jeff has his own shadow, his own ghost, to put to rest. The two of them are going to learn a great deal about themselves and each other as they grow up here. Malachi, of all of them, is the most whole, yet even he has to grow up, sort out his magic. I do not know when I will tell them what Larissa told me as we walked: the juvenile tetrad, formed at puberty, isn't permanent. There will be a second tetrad formation when they become adults, and reformation of the juvenile tetrad is rare. And since the war, some adult tetrads never formed—earth did not find fire, air did not find water. Couples and triads instead. She told me Valeria was the only survivor of her tetrad: fire. If she had lived, would we be looking for two more? Could I have shared her? Third tetrads, Larissa said, are rare and difficult.

So, Valeria wasn't whole, either. Neither am I. No, Alex is the most whole.

Malachi, Hazel, Russell, and Jeff

They stood together, the four of them, set slightly apart from the four adults. Larissa and Ben stood to one side; Roth and Thorfin, to the other. The four children stood in between, leaning into the white lip of the wall of the White City, looking down at the sea. Alex, his front paws on the white lip, stood between the children and the centaurs, but only for a short while. He sat down and began to wash, starting with his paws, so that he could wash his head. A barely visible current passed in and around and through the four of them, crackling in the salt air, like the last kernels to be popped. For a long time, or so it seemed, no one spoke. They all were content to smell the air, feel the sun, listen to the singing of the gulls, and the faint, faraway sound of the waves on the sand, and to watch the sea. Malachi saw the dolphins first, leaping, white-silver flashes above the water. Jeff saw the swimmers, in dark counterpoint to the dolphins' flashes. Russell was sure he recognized the dolphins. And farther out, Hazel saw a dragon, its wings at full-spread, over the water.

No one could tell, later, just whose idea it was, perhaps, it was the idea of all four—something Larissa told them would happen more and more. But it was Malachi who first floated a few feet up from the wall's stones, the others drifting up with him, until they were just above the wall. Then, as if blown by a sudden wind, they dropped, then dove down and out, out, and out, and down again, swooping down the grey rock face that grew into the white walls, and out, over the rocks at the bottom, and out again, over the white sand, over the waves, over the sea.